Guarded Hearts

By

C. L. Hadyn

Also by C.L. Hadyn

Off Track

The Danegeld

Special operators are taught to think outside the box, and sometimes that includes thinking outside the regulations, but Marine Raiders are first, and foremost, Marines, and Marines obey regulations. After 'Don't' Ask, Don't Tell' was repealed, the Marine Corps Commandant issued a policy that gay Marines were not to be treated any differently than any other Marine, or discriminated against in any way in the performance of their duties. I attended the training sessions for the new policy and was impressed by the way the Raiders said "Aye, aye" and drove on, despite any personal reservations they may have had. I'd love to hear what you think of Guarded Hearts. Contact me at caltrop19@aol.com.

Blurb

Wren lifted a single teardrop from his face to study it. He didn't know what made him let the water works loose. *Liar, liar, pants on fire* his inner child chided. His eyes were leaking because he was confused and, okay, he was afraid. He yearned for what he suspected he would never achieve. He wanted a lasting relationship with Geordy. He wanted the idyllic family life Geordy had with the Campbells, and he wanted to be loved for himself, for being Wren and not a Marine Raider, not a mixed martial arts fighter, not a bladed weapons expert, just plain Wren who loved William Shakespeare, cuddles, and a keen wit to return his teases. He cried because he truly didn't believe those things were written in his stars.

Chapter One

Marine Sergeant Wren de Lassy stood in resigned silence as the staff sergeant read out the dorm room assignments. MARSOC Command had denied his request to live off base because he was single, below the rank of staff sergeant, and there were too many vacant dorm rooms.

He waited to be assigned a room with three other Marines. Men who snored and farted and moaned in their sleep. Men who thought nothing of flicking on the overhead light at 3:00 a.m. to undress after a weekend of drinking.

At twenty-six, he was too old for this shit. He grew up with a king-size bed all to himself, and the thought of downgrading to a single bed was not at all appealing, but all Marines learned to suck it up in boot camp, and so he would.

His attention returned to the here and now when a violent expostulation from a Marine standing to his immediate left assaulted his ears.

"No, Staff Sergeant, I won't do that. No way in hell will I room with Sergeant Campbell, and I don't care how many times you quote the regulation to me, I'm not sharing a room with a fag."

Wren turned his attention toward the man singled out by one of the Marines, and discovered a mountain standing at least six feet, four inches tall, and with a torso like an oak trunk.

Sergeant Campbell's lack of reaction to his accuser outing him for being gay surprised him and made him pay closer attention to the Marine. Campbell didn't glare at his accuser. He didn't even have a frown line between his eyes to show a scintilla of emotion, but simply stood at ease and waited for the staff NCO to straighten things out without any input from himself.

Before he could stop himself, Wren called out, "I'll bunk with Sergeant Campbell."

While he had the satisfaction of seeing Campbell's eyebrows lift in surprise, he also saw speculation in the eyes of the rest of the Marines. Now it was his turn to show no emotion as he faced the staff sergeant, whose breath whooshed out in relief at the unexpected volunteer.

"Okay then, listen up, Marines. Rogers, Levitz, Vogler, and Hernandez will take Room 301. Campbell and de Lassy will take Room 304."

He didn't even try to keep the smirk off his face. He and Campbell would share a bedroom large enough to sleep four men, the ideal arrangement if you had to live in the dorm.

The staff sergeant continued to give instructions. "You have the rest of today and this weekend to settle in. Dismissed."

Wren picked up his duffel and headed upstairs to his new room. The heavy thumps on the stairs behind him, told him the mountain followed. He didn't acknowledge Campbell until he stepped over the threshold to room 304. "Are you a left side of the room sleeper or a right?" He turned to find Sergeant Campbell standing in the center of the room with his eyebrows making a solid line above his nose.

"Are you...?"

"Gay?" Wren finished the question. Before Campbell could ask for clarification, he continued, "Does it matter?" If he hadn't been watching closely, he wouldn't have noticed the slight rock back on Campbell's heels.

"No, I guess it doesn't because I don't date Marines. I especially don't date anyone in my battalion, company, or team."

"So good to know I'm safe. I'm Wren de Lassy. And you are?"

"Geordy Campbell, and I'm a right-side sleeper."

His seeming insouciance over Geordy's sexual orientation obviously had his new roommate puzzled, and the devil in him liked it that way.

"Pleased to meet you, Geordy Campbell." He turned away and started to unload his clothes into one of the dressers on the left side of the room. He didn't speak until he carried an armload of books over to the built-in bookcase above one of the desks on his side of the room. He was well aware his new roommate mirrored his actions, but he was curious as to what the man valued in reading material. A quick glance at the number of books in Geordy's bookcase impressed him. The man was obviously a reader; it would make living in the dorm easier to swallow. His illusion shattered when his new roomie squared off with him.

"Just so you know, I sleep in the nude."

Wren couldn't help it—he held his stomach as he doubled over, laughing. "Okay, not a problem. I guess we can both practice averting our eyes when one or the other of us walks buck-ass naked to the head to take a piss in the middle of the night."

He was about to start putting sheets on his bed when another question stopped him.

"Why?"

Time to introduce Geordy Campbell to de Lassy 101. "Why do I sleep nude, or why did I volunteer to be your roommate?"

Geordy tossed him a glare and growled, "The roommate part."

Wren dropped the sheet and turned to face Campbell. "I don't give a flying fuck whether you are gay, hetero, or some interstellar species of weird. What I do care about is not sharing my living/sleeping quarters with three other guys who think drinking until you puke is a fine idea for a weekend. I also dislike sharing a room with a total slob. I pick up after myself, and I hope you do so, too, and not just on Thursday nights before Friday room inspections, but if you don't I'll happily fling your mess back to your side of the room."

With crossed arms and an evil grin evident on his face, Sergeant Campbell replied, "No worries, I'll do the same for any of your junk landing on my side."

Wren wasn't finished emoting. "I'm guessing you would've preferred renting someplace by yourself on the economy, as would I, and I think you're like me in that you're tired of sharing space with people who don't accept or appreciate a need for quiet to read, and a need to put things back where they got them."

Geordy nodded his agreement.

"I think the fact you didn't just empty the entire contents of your duffel bag into one of the drawers and call that unpacking is a sign we'll do okay as roommates."

Geordy surprised him by not answering but moving closer to study the titles of the books in Wren's book space. He surprised him further by switching to fluent Arabic after he picked up his Arabic dictionary.

Without hesitation, he answered Geordy's question in the same tongue. "I do speak Arabic. I spent eight years in Saudi Arabia. You might call it immersion training. My adopted brother speaks it, too. My brother, Ross, told me it's one of those use-or-lose skills, so I try to keep in practice."

Wren moved close enough to read the titles in Geordy's bookcase, and he was impressed. There were Arabic, French, Tagalog, Spanish, and Russian language books, and, curiously, the poems of the Persian poet, Omar Khayyam. There were also books on masonry, wood-working, and history, both modern and Civil War era.

He picked up the volume entitled, *Sherman's March to the Sea.* "Where are you from, Geordy Campbell?"

"I'm from a little town in Cumberland County, Tennessee, called Beltrees. Beltrees is Gaelic for grove." Geordy grinned and added, "Beltrees, Tennessee, was settled by Clan Campbell in the eighteenth century."

Wren gave him a suitably impressed face then changed the subject. "I'm hungry and the chow hall is serving dinner. Care to join me?" The sudden suspicion on his new roommate's face stopped him in his tracks. "Oh for God's sake, that was a friendly offer. I have no ulterior motives. I'm hungry, and I'm walking to the chow hall to eat. You can either accompany me or starve until I return if you don't want to be seen with me. Makes no difference to me. As I said, you aren't much of a threat to me."

He backed off a little when Geordy got right up in his grill.

"And why is that, de Lassy? If you aren't gay, why do you want to hang with me?"

Wren put a little more space between them so he didn't go cross-eyed. "It isn't a matter of wanting to be seen with you so much as a matter of we're Marines who happen to be in the same company, same team, and now the same room. We need to work together, and better to work together as friends and roommates than adversaries." He held out his hand, "Are we going to be friends, Geordy Campbell?"

He maintained the gesture until Geordy's shoulders eased their tight posture and he shook hands.

"Aye, friends it is. Let's grab some dinner. I'm hungry as well."

Chapter Two

No matter how many years he had in the Corps, Monday morning PT came too damn early for his liking. Wren groaned at his new roommate's ability to fling the covers from himself and hop out of bed. Apparently, early birds got to use the bathroom first.

He snickered to himself as the lewd thought entered his mind. And slugabeds got treated to the sight of a very fine, nude male body. Campbell rocked the Marine weight standards. He was anatomically perfect. Wide shoulders, defined pecs, chiseled abs, cut groin, biceps that were firm but not bulging, and narrow, narrow waist. Put all that with Geordy's handsome face and proportionately-sized package, and you had any woman or man's ideal.

But he had higher standards. For him, the brain had to be as beautiful as the body. There had to be intelligence behind those thickly lashed hazel eyes. His personal standards demanded someone who discoursed on something more than football, baseball, or their latest PT score.

As to feminine standards, he liked a woman who dressed well, fashionably, but not provocatively. It was a big turn off for him when a woman used her body's attractiveness as camouflage for a mediocre intellect. But, he had to admit, as an initial attractor, being a step above butt ugly helped.

Ah, shit, contemplating male or female anatomy didn't help soften the morning wood. He dragged himself out of the rack and headed for the sink to brush his teeth and shave while his roomie finished in the bathroom.

He was surprised to receive a "Good morning," from Geordy as he passed him at the sink. He half expected a non-verbal grunt or silence, but the polite greeting was welcome. He returned the greeting and quit the sink to let Geordy shave.

The day started off on a discordant note. First out the door, Wren ran right into a leering Sergeant Vogler. "Hey there. Well, de Lassy, did you get any sleep at all or did your new roomie wear you out?"

Wren didn't respond. He was too busy repeating, "Don't kill the motherfucker" to himself. He ignored Vogler and headed downstairs. Geordy almost plowed into him when he came to a sudden stop. The kissing noises Vogler made echoed loudly in the stairwell. The idiot didn't know who he was insulting. He possessed the ability to kill the man so quickly Vogler's lips would still be in the puckered position when his body hit the floor. But his sensei, and his psychologist, would be very displeased with his lack of discipline if he did so, and thus he permitted Vogler to continue breathing.

Geordy correctly interpreted the anger on his face because he offered an apology.

"I won't hold it against you if you get tired of being hassled and ask for a new room assignment. In my experience, men like Vogler aren't intelligent enough to live and let live."

He startled a laugh from his roommate by replying, "Who says he gets to live?"

Sergeant Levitz's comment surprised both of them as he passed by and stated, "The Uniform Code of Military Justice says so. It frowns upon murder, whether deserved or not."

Geordy grinned at Wren. "Uh-oh, trouble in paradise. It hasn't taken Vogler long to earn his roommates' dislike."

***

8

Captain David Schuyler studied the room assignments for his team. He and his master sergeant, and the Naval corpsman attached to the team, being married men with families, lived on the economy. The rest of the team for Fox Company, 3rd Marine Special Operations Battalion, lived in the dorm.

An involuntary huff escaped him when he came to the names Campbell and de Lassy.

"What? Is there a problem, Captain?"

Schuyler turned to Master Sergeant Durwood McClean, Team name Woody, and grinned. "I see the two geniuses found one another. There must be some sort of gravitational pull involved."

Woody scratched his head. "Geniuses? Are you being sarcastic? This is a bunch of newbies needing to be whipped into shape, hopefully, in time for our deployment to the Philippines at the end of next month."

"No, they actually do qualify as geniuses. Sergeant de Lassy's IQ is 140 and Sergeant Campbell tested out at 145. And neither one of them can be described as nerdy. De Lassy is a former mixed martial arts competitor, who won more than he lost, an edged-weapon specialist, and his Military Occupational Specialty is Explosive Ordinance Disposal. He also speaks Arabic and French with a 4.0 rating. Campbell's credentials are also impressive."

"Ah, about Sergeant Campbell, Captain—"

"If you are about to tell me Sergeant Geordy Campbell is a self-confessed homosexual, I already know. I daresay he raised a few of the psychologists' eyebrows during his psych evals, but his record in Force Recon was outstanding. He earned a Bronze Star with V device, and a Purple Heart for being wounded in combat, and the shrinks were prepared to waive his sexual preference for two reasons: one, the new regulations say homosexual Marines cannot be discriminated against, and two, the man is just too damned smart. He speaks Arabic, Russian, Tagalog, Spanish, and French. He probably also speaks Scots' Erse or Gaelic, since he was raised in a Scottish community in the mountains of Tennessee."

"Hmm, a mountain man. That could come in handy."

The captain, team name Pacer for his love of marathons, had no clue why Woody thought so, but pressed on. "According to his personnel file, Sergeant Campbell was a mason before entering the Marines, so he can lay claim to on-the-job experience for his engineer MOS of constructing base camps and building houses for the third world nations we visit. He's also an Expert with a rifle. Must be from squirrel hunting in the Tennessee hills."

Captain Schuyler tossed the assignment roster on his desk. "Well, Master Sergeant, time to meet the team. Let's see how they gel during this morning's run."

***

Captain Schuyler waited until Woody got everyone formed up then gave them the bad news. "We're going for what I like to call a shakedown run. Don't worry, it will only be fifteen miles instead of the usual twenty-two I like to run."

He waited until the groaning stopped. "Of course, if you'd like to help me practice for the next marathon, I can extend the distance. No takers? Okay, let's move it out, ladies."

Wren turned around to give Vogler the stink eye when he not so *sotto voce* commented there was only one "lady" in the formation this morning. However, Vogler's tasteless remark didn't leave even a tiny dent in Geordy's armor. The man was impervious to insults. It was a good thing the all-knowing man upstairs sicced the homophobe on Geordy because Vogler would run with difficulty for the rest of his life if he ever tried dissing him.

While running fifteen miles at a stretch didn't appeal to him, he did enjoy running. Having long legs and good cardio endurance helped, but having the smarts to not attack the run like a sprinter left him at the back of the formation. Jogging along at a steady, easy pace made fifteen miles more than manageable.

He enjoyed the run until Vogler fell back to jog next to Geordy— as he knew he would. Geordy ignored him, at least he tried, but Vogler stumbled over nothing at all and fell into him. It knocked his roommate completely off-balance, and he took a full-body sprawl on the only stretch of asphalt they'd encountered since they started the run.

Vogler turned back and laughed at Geordy as he sat up and examined the damage to his knees. "Well, there's proof positive swishes can't run like real men."

He did a silent ten count to keep from swiping Vogler's legs out from under him to give him a taste of what landing on asphalt felt like. Maybe it was the expression on his face or a keen sense of self-preservation, but Vogler moved on before he acted on the urge.

Captain Schuyler, loping along several feet behind the team, stopped and waited while Wren hauled Geordy to his feet.

"That's a pretty bad road rash you've got on both knees, Campbell. You want me to send Doc over to check it out?"

"No thanks, sir. I'm good. Compared to being shot, this doesn't even hurt. It looks worse than it is. Guess I need to pay more attention where I place my feet."

Geordy gave his roommate a minute head shake to keep his lip zipped when he started to offer an opinion on the cause of the mishap.

"Yeah, that would save wear and tear on your knees, Sergeant Campbell. But it seems you aren't the only one who needs to pay attention to where he's running." Schuyler moved off before Geordy made any comment.

He, however, didn't feel the need to ignore the elephant accompanying them on this run. "Please tell me you'll let me help you hide Vogler's body where no one will ever find it after you beat the shit out of him."

Geordy took a few long strides to catch up to the rest of the team before answering. "Sorry, beating the shit out of Vogler holds no appeal. I find touching that douchebag totally repugnant."

Wren reminded himself to shut his mouth before he swallowed a horsefly, and just shook his head at Geordy's equanimity. "You are a better man than I, Gunga Din. You are also bleeding into your boots. Are you sure you don't want the corpsman to check out your knees?"

Geordy just shook his head and grinned. Nay, I'm a Scot. It would take more than a wee scrape to make me see a corpsman."

Chapter Three

Drawn by an unusual scent, Geordy wrapped a towel around his waist, and walked back from the bathroom to the common sleeping-study area to find his roommate sitting in the lotus position on his bed, and drinking an cup of something aromatic. "What are you drinking? That doesn't smell like coffee?"

"This is cardamom tea. I got used to drinking it when I lived in Saudi Arabia. I also got used to eating yogurt, dates, olives, and flatbread for breakfast, which I intend to do most mornings. My cammies are getting snug from the greasy chow-hall breakfasts. I prefer lighter breakfasts. Would you like a cup of tea? There's plenty of food to go around, if you'd care to join me."

Geordy grinned at Wren's surprise when he said, "Sure, I'll try anything, once." When de Lassy came out of the lotus position, he shook his head in admiration. "I'm flexible, but not that flexible. Do you do yoga?"

Wren answered as he poured another cup of tea from the electric kettle he'd purchased the last time he was on leave, and assembled a plate for Geordy. "Yeah, I do. It keeps me limber, especially now that I no longer compete in mixed martial arts on a regular basis. One of the guys in Bravo Company told me about a dojo in Jacksonville, so I might check it out this weekend. Now that my sensei, Tomodashi-san, isn't slamming my body to the mat on a regular basis, I'll need to seek another dojo so I won't forget everything it cost a lot of pain to learn." He didn't say anything else until Geordy had a chance to sample the yogurt and dates. "My brother Ross tells me I suffer from a dangerous condition. I'm extremely curious and lack a verbal filter. I'm working on the filter, but my curiosity sometimes, like now, overrides it. Why do you manscape?"

Geordy slowly put the piece of flatbread back on his plate. "Manscape? What in the hell is that?"

"It means you wax your chest and trim your pubic area."

Geordy briefly cursed the Marine Corps for insisting unmarried men live in communal dorm rooms. "Back at you, why do *you* manscape?"

Wren grinned and rubbed his smooth, hairless chest. "I don't mind going first. I got used to manscaping, and I dislike feeling like one of the great apes when I let my fur grow out. Also, like a lot of Marines, I go commando when deployed, and I really hate catching my pubic hair in my zipper. What's your reason?"

Geordy's inability to control a blush made his roommate grin even wider. "I started trimming the pubes in boot camp. My bunk mate caught a case of the crabs and didn't bother to tell me until after he used my towel. Crabs travel. It was less hassle to keep that area shaved after that. I don't like to feel critters running around down there, and some of the places we deployed to in recon didn't make personal hygiene a high priority.

Wren shuddered in remembrance and prompted, "And the waxing?"

Geordy shrugged. "I had a lover who preferred it. It only takes once to learn waxing thick chest hair is pretty painful, so I keep it up rather than having to go through that again." Geordy switched the subject. "This is good. Where did you buy these dates?"

"At a Fresh Market in Wilmington. They sell the Medjool dates and the good Greek yogurt, olives, and flatbread. It also has the cardamom tea. My brother Ross is a gourmet cook and practically lives in that store in the DC area."

"Mind if I tag along the next time you go? I think you're right about the chow hall. Maintaining the weight standard is difficult when you're as large and as solid as I am. This is pretty filling without being high calorie." Geordy choked on a piece of bread when Wren added, "And it will keep you regular."

He picked up the book lying open at the foot of Wren's bed and opened it to the page marked with a piece of paper. It was quantum physics, and the paper had an equation Wren was in the process of solving.

Since Wren started the question-and-answer period, he asked one of his own. "What in the hell are you doing in the Corps, de Lassy? If you're smart enough to work quantum physics problems, you should be working in some giant science lab for more than you'll ever earn as a Marine Raider." He was surprised to find his question wiped the grin right off his roommate's face. He thought about rescinding it, but he really wanted an answer. De Lassy, despite living with him for three days, was still an enigma. He was well-read, personally neat, possessed a keen intelligence, outrageous sense of humor, and, while outwardly an open book, was still very much a private person. Not receiving a reply, Geordy turned away to begin dressing but stopped when Wren began speaking.

"That's a good question, Roomie. The easy answer is, I don't yet know what I want to be when I grow up, so I'm trying different things to eliminate what I don't want to be."

"So, you don't intend to make the Corps a career?"

Wren stood and stretched. "Haven't totally decided yet, but fifteen-mile runs, getting up early for PT on Monday mornings, and not being able to punch out total assholes like Vogler are some of the things I can add to my 'This Isn't Fun' list."

Geordy shook his head. "Since that pretty much defines being a Marine, why are you still here?"

De Lassy's eyes lost focus. "I had what you might call a restricted childhood. I didn't go out much, and my entertainment came in the form of books. When I went to college, I liked the freedom to do what I wanted, when I wanted, but...the freedom to do that made me edgy. I like having a definite routine to my life, and my martial arts training, while intense, gave me a routine in its repetitive exercises, and the Corps does so as well."

Wren pointed to the clock on his desk. "And if we don't finish dressing ASAP, we'll be breaking one of the Corps most sacrosanct routines, being on time for PT."

***

He wanted to turn around and ask Geordy if they fast forwarded a few months to return to February, because he had the distinct impression Ground Hog Day was upon them again, like in the eponymous movie. In a complete replay of yesterday, the first person he ran into in the hall was Vogler. *I either need to not be the first out the door or bestow a knuckle sandwich on the bastard to shut him the fuck up,* crossed his mind as he faced off with Geordy's nemesis.

"Spill de Lassy, does your lover boy wear pink jockey shorts, or does he go commando?"

Geordy's hand come down on his shoulder and squeezed a warning. He was tempted to ignore it, but Hernandez's comment made him laugh instead of risking a stint in the brig by knocking

Vogler's teeth down his throat.

"Hey, *pendejo*, you're much too interested in Geordy's sex life. Maybe you're one of those closet homos."

Levitz, who promptly followed Hernandez down the stairs, added another P-word—putz—as he passed Vogler.

Rogers, who had yet to speak a single word to them since the room assignments, surprised both of them when he gave them a fist bump to the arm as he headed down the stairs.

Fortunately for Vogler's longevity, Captain Schuyler broke them all apart to pursue their specialties for the next two weeks. For himself, that meant perfecting shape charges, constructing booby traps, and learning how to recognize and dismantle IEDs. Although his work was far more dangerous, he was glad it didn't require spending the entire day outside in North Carolina humidity, building things and knocking them back down, as Geordy did.

In between specialty training, MARSOC added extra fun by throwing in night navigation, trips to the shoot house, and his personal fav, the dunk locker. He wanted to kick himself by letting a groan escape when Schuyler announced they were to spend the day learning how long they could hold their breath underwater. Vogler heard him and immediately zeroed in to heckle.

"What's the matter, de Lassy? Can't swim? Maybe your roomie will teach you how to do the breast stroke."

He closed his eyes and counted to ten. Truth of the matter was, he was a decent swimmer but not a natural. Being born in Denver, Colorado and then spending his formative years in water-scarce Saudi Arabia had cheated him of the usual years most kids got living at the local swimming pool every summer until they grew gills. Consequently, he worked damn hard to satisfy the swim requirements of Force Recon.

He tuned out Vogler's digs as he tightened his grip on his rifle and got ready for the abandon ship drill of jumping from an eight-foot tower in cammies, boots, helmet, flak vest, and service rifle. He could do this drill in his sleep, given the times he had to do it in boot camp, and then again in recon training. He didn't hesitate to jump when it was his turn to do so. *Damn, Vogler rushed his jump before he cleared the area beneath the tower.* He didn't panic until it became evident Vogler had no intention of removing himself from his back until he finished using him like an underwater surfboard to cross the bottom of the pool.

His lungs ached from lack of oxygen by the time Vogler got off him, despite trying to twist and remove the guy from his back. He considered dropping his rifle, helmet, and flak vest to the bottom of the pool so he could break free, but Vogler stopped playing piggy back before he had to. He surfaced to find him being dragged to the side of the pool by Geordy. He was too busy hauling oxygen into his lungs to listen in on their whispered but obviously terse conversation.

Damn, he had to jump again since he failed to complete the swim. So, too, did Vogler and Geordy, but this time the water safety officer separated them to ensure things went smoothly. One thing he did notice was Vogler walked alone on their way back to the dorm to change into dry clothes. It was obvious Vogler's roommates were not at all happy with his performance this morning.

His attention was also drawn to his roommate, who seemed to be engaged in a conversation with himself. Geordy didn't bring up the pool incident, but his muttering to himself made him lose his tenuous hold on his temper. "What are you grumbling about? If you want to tell me something, just spit it out."

Geordy stopped walking and didn't speak until the rest of the team squelched their way past. "I'm no' used to apologizing, so I'm trying to come up with the words."

Wren winked at his roommate and offered, "Well, I have tons of experience, so tell me who you need to apologize to, and I'll help you come up with the right words, unless you think you need to apologize to Vogler for some cockamamie reason."

Geordy growled, "Nay, not Vogler, It's you I need to apologize to."

"What the fuck for?"

"For putting you in Vogler's line of fire. I expected him to make my life miserable, but I didn't think he was stupid enough to take you on, too. I'm sorry for the fact you are now targeted for his bullshit because you volunteered to be my roommate, and I'll bet losing my temper with him this morning only strengthened his determination to hound me out of the Raiders and, if he can manage it, you as well."

"I think you might be overly sensitive. He was just eager to jump and didn't see me under the tower."

Geordy stared off down the street as he spoke. "That was no accident this morning. He deliberately rushed his jump to land on you. While I don't think he intended to let you drown, it was still a rotten thing to do to a fellow Marine. As much as I detest him, I would never do anything like that to Vogler. Perhaps you should ask the staff sergeant for a room change."

He didn't answer as he turned around and started walking. He didn't stop until Geordy caught up to him and asked, "What?"

He squared off with Geordy. "No, I don't need an apology from you. Vogler is the one who needs to apologize to me. No, I'm not going to change my room assignment. I like where I'm at, and I don't want to pack my shit up again. And no, I'm not going to stoop to Vogler's level and try to retaliate because, were I to do so, Vogler would be dead, and I don't want to wear an orange jumpsuit for the next ten-to-twenty years. It clashes with my hair."

He had another thought and stopped walking so suddenly, Geordy stumbled into him, and he had a new appreciation for how solid his roommate was. Campbell's grip on his arm kept him from kissing the pavement.

"You asked me why I joined the Corps, and now I'm asking you. Why didn't you keep searching for a career less fraught with societal onus than working with die-hard, homophobic Marines, or do you like getting up in everyone's grill, Geordy Campbell?" He had to quicken his pace to catch up to his roommate, who resumed walking. "Well, what's the story, Campbell?"

"When my father kicked me out of the family after I came roaring out of the closet, I wanted to prove I was as much of a man as he was, so I chose the Marine Corps, but I would serve in the Corps on my terms, which meant not denying who I was to anyone else ever again." Geordy gave de Lassy a wry grin. "And, out of all the services, the Marine Corps Dress Blue uniform is the best, and, all modesty aside, I'm drop dead gorgeous when I wear it."

Geordy's last, outrageous statement started him laughing. He laughed so hard he had to sit down on the curb until his breath returned. When he held a hand up, Campbell dragged him back to his feet and they continued walking.

"Ah, so you *do* understand why I chose to bunk with you." When Geordy came to a sudden standstill, Wren fluttered his eyes at him then punched him on the arm. Hard. "I so admire a man in uniform." He snickered all the way back to their room.

C.L. Hadyn

Chapter Four

Captain Schuyler tore his eyes away from his computer when a fast food bag was placed on his desk. Opening it, he took out a large loaded hamburger, fries, and a chocolate shake. He grinned wryly at his master sergeant. "Either something is going very well or the shit has hit the fan and you're trying to soften the blow. Which is it, Woody? Why are you plying me with a gut bomb and a chocolate shake?"

The master sergeant crossed his arms over his chest and shook his head at Fox Team's commander. "Because a problem reared its ugly head, Captain. Did you get a chance to read the peer reviews? We're into our third week now, and I thought things were starting to gel, but the reviews say different."

"Yep, I read them and agree with the assessment. Vogler and Campbell, and possibly de Lassy, don't enjoy breathing the air in each other's vicinity. Not that I think the fault is with Campbell or de Lassy, but Vogler is determined to shame Campbell into quitting, and I believe de Lassy is on his hit list as a secondary target for not being anti-gay." Schuyler took a huge bite of the burger and washed it down with a swig of the shake before continuing. "I happened to swing by the chow hall before starting on my paperwork, and what I saw made me think the situation will eventually resolve itself."

Woody remained skeptical. "What did your recon turn up? If it was Vogler eating lunch with Campbell and de Lassy, I want photographic evidence." Captain Schuyler offered him some fries, but he declined. "Shit, no, I'm not eating fries. Those things will send me over the weight standards. And I'm not going to tell you what the salt on them can do to your blood pressure."

Captain Schuyler laughed as he retracted his offer and gobbled the fries. "Now, there's the real difference between thirty and forty-something, Master Sergeant."

"I say this with all respect, Captain. Fuck you. Tell me what happened in the chow hall?"

"Campbell, de Lassy, Rogers, Levitz, and Hernandez were sitting at the same table, and they were enjoying themselves, if you went by the joking and horseplay going on."

"And where was Vogler?"

"It took me a while to locate him, Woody. I think he was sitting with someone from Bravo Company, but the sneer on his face said he didn't approve of his roommates consorting with Campbell and de Lassy."

Master Sergeant Durwood McClean rubbed his chin and stared out the office window. "Hmm, Bravo Company, you say? Perhaps Vogler would be a better Marine in Bravo Company."

Captain Schuyler wadded up the burger refuse and tossed it into his trash can. "Working on it, Woody, but I need to let things come to a head." Schuyler rubbed his hands together and pointed to the clock. "Chow time's over. Let's stand back and observe what happens for this next block of instruction. De Lassy's going to be the instructor for a little tactical knife fighting. Rumor has it he can slice and dice with the best of them."

"Are you sure you want to give de Lassy a real knife? He's held his temper around Vogler so far, but I wouldn't put too much temptation in his way. I don't think Vogler is smart enough to tell when it would be prudent to shut his yap. De Lassy's a good Marine, and I wouldn't want to lose him. And I sure as hell don't want to do the paperwork for a"—Woody made quotation marks with his fingers—"safety incident."

"Now whose blood pressure is elevated? At ease, Master Sergeant. It'll be rubber knives for the demonstration and practice, but I asked de Lassy to bring one of his throwing knives for a demonstration. I want his edged weapon abilities to leave a lasting impression on his teammates. Maybe it will instill some caution in Vogler the next time he thinks about heckling him or Campbell."

***

Wren faced his team in boots, cammie pants, and a T-shirt. He held a hard rubber tactical knife in his right hand, and began his instruction with, "There are some instances where having a knife beats having a gun." His opening statement got an immediate response from Vogler.

"Not if I'm the one with the gun, it doesn't."

He grinned at his heckler. "Let's test that, shall we?" He nodded at the master sergeant, and Woody ejected the clip and retracted the chamber as a safety measure, before handing the unloaded weapon and a holster to Vogler. Wren continued the lesson. "I'm going to put on a tactical vest and sheath the knife where we carry it while Vogler straps up. Who can gauge the distance between me and the gunslinger known as Vogler?"

Rogers surprised everyone by calling out, "Fifteen feet, give or take."

Noticing Vogler was ready to go, he went into the knife fighting stance as taught by the Israeli Defense Force and stood equally

25

balanced between his front and rear legs, with the heel of his back leg raised off the ground. "Vogler, I'm going to ask someone to say 'Go,' and then you draw your weapon and I'll draw mine."

It was Captain Schuyler who barked, "Go."

The barrel of the .45 pistol never cleared the holster before he swiped the blade of his rubber knife across Vogler's throat. After a moment of stunned silence, a general babble of, "Shit, de Lassy moves like a blur. Damn, Vogler was fast, but de Lassy had him killed before he could aim his weapon," erupted from the team.

Wren stepped back and faced the class and resumed the instruction with, "In the Middle East, knives are a part of their culture. If you find yourself in close quarters with the enemy, you can be certain he'll have a knife on him." He pointed at Geordy, the tallest man on the team, and asked him to serve as his opponent. "The knife is a great equalizer. It doesn't care how big your opponent is because if you know how to use it, he won't get the chance to overpower you."

Geordy stepped forward and faced the group as Wren used the point of his knife to draw an imaginary square on his torso.

"Let me explain the pyramid to you. There are eight slash points." Wren demonstrated by dividing the square into eight triangles. "And nine stab points." He, once again, lightly poked the tip of his knife on the triangular areas on the square that were made by the slashes. The ninth stab was directly in the center of Geordy's chest.

Geordy stood still while Wren demonstrated the slash and stab motions.

"Always follow a slash with a stab. Why? Because with the adrenaline pumping through your opponent's body, he won't feel the first slash. He will feel the stab. Okay, everyone find a partner and practice holding the knife in a regular grip first. Once you get the hang of that, we can go into the reverse grip."

"Hey, look, I'm the Jewish Errol Flynn," Levitz called to Wren as he lunged at Hernandez.

Wren called everyone to attention. "To advance, push up on your rear leg and take a step to close the gap. Spring step, not a lunge. The legs move an equal distance when advancing, so no lunges. A lunge leaves you open for counterattack because you can't change directions if you are committed to a lunge, and your enemy has time to slash your hand to make you drop your weapon, or he can stab you in the throat, hook out, and slash you across the chest. Now listen up, the only time the enemy won't drop his weapon if his fingers are cut is if he is hopped up on drugs or alcohol, so don't assume you can disarm someone with just that initial slash."

Maybe it was bouncing from pair to pair to critique footwork or correct grips, but he thought the time went by in a blur until Captain Schuyler called for a halt.

"At ease. I asked Sergeant de Lassy to bring one of his throwing knives to demonstrate another type of knife fighting." He turned to Vogler to add, "A throwing knife is the equivalent of your long gun, Sergeant Vogler. Think of it as a standoff weapon, like your sniper rifle, but one that doesn't require a silencer. Sergeants Hernandez and Levitz, take the target silhouette from the master sergeant and tape it to that tree."

When the silhouette was attached to the tree, Captain Schuyler motioned for de Lassy to approach. He was surprised to find him wearing his uniform blouse with no throwing knife in evidence.

"Are you ready to begin the demonstration, Sergeant?"

Wren grinned at the captain and spun around to face the target. A soft thunk followed, and everyone, the captain included, let out a whoosh of surprise to find the handle-less blade quivering from the bull's-eye on the man-shaped target. He rolled back the sleeve of his left arm to display the leather sheath strapped to his forearm.

Everyone cracked up when Levitz said, "Fuck me, I'm never getting on your bad side, Blade."

***

Geordy joined in on the friendly heckling on the way back to the dorm. Wren had a team name, now, and he wondered how soon his teammates would forget he had any other name but Blade. However, when his roommate agreed to continue the knife training in the common area outside the dorm, Geordy begged off. He needed to move, to engage in a different form of exercise, and so he headed to the gym for some bag work. Boxing was his stress relief, and he needed to punch something until he couldn't lift his arms. He was honest enough with himself to admit he wasn't venting his frustration on the heavy bag over Vogler, but Wren.

Something about the way he moved when he was demonstrating how to kill your enemy in nine stabs triggered an ache he thought he buried a long time ago. De Lassy moved with the fluidity of a panther. An extremely handsome, fluid, panther.

It took an hour of mindlessly hitting the bag over and over again, until his arms ached, and he soaked his T-shirt and gym shorts, before Geordy calmed down enough to head for the showers. Until he drew Wren for a roommate, no other Marine had ever jarred his equanimity. A voice from behind stopped him before he could enter the locker room.

"What's the matter, Campbell? No stomach for knife fighting?"

Geordy gritted his teeth. He had enough strength left in his right arm to lay Vogler out flat, but that would be exactly what the homophobic son of a bitch wanted. He ignored the pest and kept walking into the locker room, but Vogler was so intent on harassing him, he followed. He lucked out, the locker room and shower stations were empty. Geordy seized the moment, turned to face Vogler, and began undressing.

"Is this what you wanted Vogler? Did you follow me in here hoping to get a peek at my junk? If so, take your time and get an eyeful, because you aren't going to get a second chance. You seem a little slow on the uptake, so I'll say it again, you aren't my type. I prefer men with brains."

Geordy dropped his gym shorts and stepped out of them. He didn't back off until Vogler started to splutter, and then he headed for a shower. Vogler was nowhere in sight when he dried off and got dressed and, silently thanking the big man upstairs for a small reprieve, Geordy found his roommate gone when he returned to their room.

**

Captain Schuyler capped the third week of training with a night land-navigation course. Since most of his team were former Force Recon Marines, he didn't think any of his team would get lost enough for him to turn out the entire company to locate a lost Marine.

Sergeant Campbell cracked him up when he crossed the finish line ahead of everyone else.

"Guess all that coon hunting in the mountains of Tennessee paid off, Captain."

What did surprise him was Blade de Lassy coming in second. Once again, he had to laugh when, after congratulating Blade on his excellent time, Blade pointed at Sergeant Campbell and said, "I'm good with a compass, and it was a clear night with lots of stars to navigate by, but what made it easy is Mountain leaves a size 14 track a visually impaired person could follow."

Schuyler had to agree with Blade, Mountain was a pretty good name for Campbell. If the sergeant planted his feet, not many men possessed strength enough to shift him, if he didn't want to be moved.

As he waited for the rest of the team to complete the course, Schuyler began to think his team was finally beginning to gel. Team names were being used. Campbell had just been christened Mountain, de Lassy was Blade, Levitz, the coms guy, had been awarded the name Byte for his speed on the computer keyboard. Hernandez, the team logistician, claimed Mexican descent, and so was named Tecate in honor of his favorite beer. The nickname awarded to Rogers, the team coxswain, was Mercury after the Mercury engines attached to the Zodiacs they used in training. Of course, the corpsman, Petty Officer Ferri, was the standard Doc. The only team member still lacking a team name was Vogler. He overheard several of the team direct a few names at the man, but they were said more in insult than affection. And none of the insults directed at Vogler had been from Sergeant Campbell. The Mountain, it seemed, could not be moved to anger.

Chapter Five

As Wren knew he would, he surprised the hell out of Geordy by reaching down and dragging off his covers. Lucky for him, his roomie didn't follow the sheet up with a punch to his face but, still, the sight of Mountain levitating from the bed in a single motion was impressive.

"What the fuck are you doing, Blade?"

"Burning daylight waiting for you to stop making those snarly, gargly sounds and wake the fuck up. Since the Mountain won't come to Mohammed, Mohammed took matters into his own hands. Rise and shine, Sleeping Beauty."

Geordy glanced over Wren's shoulder and immediately pointed at the wall clock to snarl, "Seven fucking o'clock in the morning? Didn't you get the memo? We're allowed to sleep in on weekends."

He put himself between Geordy and his bed when he turned to climb back in. "No can do, roomie. I promised to take you with me the next time I went to Fresh Market, and today's the day."

Geordy didn't answer, but spread his stance and crossed his arms over his chest and glared at him. He bit his lip and kept his thought from spilling into the silence. As far as nude poses went, this one was a killer.

"I'll bet the damn store doesn't open until nine, so what's your hurry, Blade? If you don't move away from my bed, I will be happy to carry you back to yours, but you won't like the landing."

Oh you're wrong, Mountain, I would love the landing, especially if you follow me down. He shook the second prurient thought right out of his head. "We need an early start because I plan on checking out the dojo in Jacksonville before we head to Wilmington."

The last was said while dangling in the air. Geordy had picked him up and swung him away from his bed.

"Fine, you go to the dojo and swing by here when you're finished. I should be awake by ten o'clock."

"Nice try, Mountain, but no. I need you to accompany me because, if the sensei decides to test my ability, you'll need to scrape me off the mat and pour me back into my truck. Don't worry, I'll still be able to go to Wilmington after, if you put me in the child's seat of the shopping cart and wheel me around in Fresh Market."

As he'd hoped it would, that word picture started Geordy snickering. He laughed all the way to the bathroom. As he waited for his roommate to make himself presentable, Wren took out his favorite book, *The Complete Works of Shakespeare*, closed his eyes, and stuck his finger on the page when the book fell open. "*Taming of the Shrew* it is, then."

He just managed to stifle the yip of surprise when Geordy nudged the side of his bed with his foot.

"Did you change your mind about going to the dojo? I'm going to be pissed if you woke me up early just to sit there and read."

He closed the book with a loud clap. He had no idea how long his roommate stood staring down at him, but the devil in him took over and he began to quote, "No shame but mine: I must, forsooth, be forced to give my hand, opposed against my heart, unto a mad-brain rudesby, full of spleen; who wooed in haste, and means to wed at leisure."

"Yeah, yeah, *Taming of the Shrew*. In case you missed it, my name is not Katharina, and there's no chance in hell of me wooing or wedding in haste or leisure today, so shift that Norman ass off the bed and let's ride."

Geordy's recognition of the quote shocked him so much he almost forgot his gear bag and turned back for it, only to come chest-to-chest with the Mountain, who'd been trying to exit the room. Sheesh, the man was truly made of granite.

Wren studied the adult class as they ran through their katas while standing in front of the Jade Dragon Dojo's plate glass window, but he wasn't sure which man was the sensei. Tomodashi-san was always easy to spot because he was five feet tall and moved like Jackie Chan. Whoever the Jade Dragon's sensei was, he ran a tight dojo; the students were performing their exercises with great dedication. There was no horsing around.

He hoisted his gear bag and nodded at Geordy. "Guess I need to introduce myself before they start individual sparring. There are seats along the wall for you to watch. One thing, take your shoes off when we enter. No street shoes allowed."

When a tall man separated himself from the group and walked toward them, he gave Geordy wide eyes. The sensei was not your usual, short Asian, and not a hundred percent Japanese or Chinese. The word Eurasian popped into his head. He had the Oriental hair and slanted eyes, but his eyes were as green as his own.

"May I help you?"

"Yes, Sensei. My name is Wren de Lassy, and I would like to sign up for one of your advanced classes. I train with Sensei Tomodashi in the DC area, and I compete in MMA. Er, I used to compete until I joined the Marine Corps, but I want to keep in shape."

"Would that be Sato Tomodashi?"

"Yes, Sensei."

"He is a hard taskmaster."

"Very much so, Sensei. He also trained my brother, Ross."

The sensei offered his hand for a shake. "My name is Dai Waleska. Yes, I'm aware my looks don't match my name. I can offer you training in taekwondo, karate, and judo. What dan are you?"

Wren bowed. "I am third dan, Sensei."

Dai grinned and pointed to the gym bag. "Did you bring your protective gear with you?"

"Yes, Sensei."

"Excellent, go suit up. This will be a real treat for my class. I'll spar with you and assess your skill. This is an intermediate class, and it will demonstrate what they can aspire to if they apply themselves."

He crossed to the side of the room where Geordy was seated to retrieve his gear, and whispered, "Oh, this is so going to hurt. The sensei is wearing a red-and-white belt, which means he's maxed out the black belt levels. And, he's a giant. The length of his arms and legs puts me at a disadvantage. I thought I was making a joke about you having to wheel me around in Fresh Market, but I think the joke's on me."

Geordy held out his hand. "Give me the keys to your truck. I'll need it to return to base after the sensei breaks every bone in your body."

"You're all heart, Mountain."

"Mountain? Why do you keep calling me Mountain?"

"Yeah, about that, Captain Schuyler heard me call you that and it stuck. He's already broadcast it to the rest of the team, so you are forevermore to be called Mountain."

"I'm going to enjoy watching Sensei Waleska wipe the mat with you for sticking me with that moniker, Blade."

"I'll try to make my demise entertaining, Mountain." Wren grabbed his bag and headed for the locker room. Having the room all to himself, he mentally prepared himself as he would for an actual MMA bout. He didn't think the sensei would pull too many of his punches or kicks.

After bowing to his new sensei, Wren blocked the opening spinning back kick and countered with one of his own, and the rest of the hour flew by. He barely managed a final, respectful bow to Sensei Waleska at the end of the lesson without doing a faceplant on the mat.

He withdrew to the locker room to shower and dress, and ruefully thought that his utility as a sparring partner fell in the range of what not to do. Tomodashi-san was good, but Dai Waleska was frighteningly better. The man was a blur when spinning or punching, and he was very aware the sensei hadn't unleashed his full power, probably so he didn't need to clean blood from the mats.

As he tested the water before entering the shower, he grimaced at the thought that popped into his head. *Note to self, never, ever piss off Sensei Waleska.*

The dojo was empty by the time he came out of the locker room, except for Geordy and the sensei, who were seated side-by-side and talking like old friends.

"Ah, Sergeant de Lassy, come sit, and we'll discuss your needs. You have talent, and it is more than evident Tomodashi-san did an excellent job of training you, but I can make you better. I studied Shaolin Kung Fu in China, so my level of training is more extensive than Tomodashi-san's. Do you want a class setting or one-on-one instruction?"

"If the Sensei can spare the time, I would like one-on-one."

"I teach an advanced class on Thursday evenings. You can attend that class, and I'll work one-on-one with you for an hour after."

"That would be excellent, Sensei, but I might not be able to attend all of the sessions. I'm in Marine Special Operations, and we do deploy, frequently."

"Yes, yes, many of my students are Marines, so I know there will be times when you cannot attend. That means you will work harder when you return. Since you are third dan, I know you will apply yourself. Are we agreed, then?"

Wren stood and bowed to his new sensei. "Yes, Sensei. Agreed."

***

Geordy hardly dared to breathe as he watched Wren spar with the sensei. From the sensei's opening move until he called time, his roommate acquitted himself well. Not to say he won the bout, but he was still standing at the end of it.

He was honestly impressed with Wren's speed and ability to take a hit and power through it, but he kept his comments to himself until Blade switched off the engine in the parking lot of Fresh Market.

"You really are a weapon, aren't you? Your team name of Blade doesn't do you justice, because you are more lethal than a knife. What drives you, de Lassy?" Are you some kind of violence or danger junky, or are you a masochistic sonovabitch who likes having the shit beat out of him? He waited for his answer, which Wren didn't give him until he wrapped his arms around the steering wheel and laid his head atop them.

"You can eliminate the 'likes having the shit beat out of him' part. As to loving violence, can't say I enjoy that, either. My brother Ross labeled it as directed violence. Directed away from hurting myself or anyone else. Yeah, I do have some anger issues, but this is the way I direct the anger. My targets are sanctioned ones, you might say." He sat up and turned to give Geordy direct eye contact. "And before you begin to worry you might someday make the target list, you can stop. My brother got me counseling when I needed it, and I know the cause of my anger, and that one day I'll grow up enough not to be angry anymore, but for now, I'm doing it this way, and the only person who suffers any dings is me."

Geordy grinned over the hood of the truck when Blade groaned as his got out. "I can bring a cart out to the truck and wheel you into the store, if you can't walk."

"Wise ass. And if you say one word about the way I hold onto the cart to shop, I'll readjust my target list. First item I'm purchasing is a giant-sized tin of herbal balm. I'll need it if I want to walk erect tomorrow."

His roommate caught up to him in the cereal aisle and they compared purchases. Wren had the expected yogurt, flatbread, olives, and dates, and a conspicuously large tin of balm. He held up a package of cardamom tea bags and the balm. "I wonder if I stir a spoonful of balm into the tea it will act faster. The sensei didn't leave any area of my body untouched."

Geordy pursed his lips and deadpanned his response. "You could try it, but I guarantee your intestinal tract and colon will not thank you."

"I'll bow to your medical expertise." Wren picked up a package from Geordy's cart and snorted. "Steel cut oats? Let me guess, the breakfast of Scottish champions."

"Aye, we Scots do like our porridge."

"I don't see any milk in your cart, and you already passed the dairy section."

"Only sissies and Sassenachs pour milk on good porridge. I prefer agave syrup and dried cranberries and black walnuts. And since this is the instant version, all I'll need to add is hot water. I bought a large enough box of it to share. We can switch between the Middle East and Scotland for our breakfasts."

Geordy aimed his cart for the checkout counter, but stopped to grin over his shoulder when Blade exclaimed, "Hey, did you just call me a sissy?"

"No, I said sissies and Sassenachs, but you're nay a sissy, and Sassenachs are English. As you say, de Lassy is a Norman-French name so you're nay a Sassenach.

Mollified, Wren offered, "Since your insult was directed at the English and not me, let's go to the Italian restaurant across the parking lot from here. I ate there the last time I came up here and they serve great food. I could use a few carbs right now. Come on, my treat for letting me drag you out of bed so early this morning."

Geordy accepted, but if he knew his roommate had intended to repeat his annoying rise with the dawn routine again the next morning, he wouldn't have passed up dessert.

"There had better be a life or death reason why you are waking me up early again." He reared back when a tin of pungent balm was held under his nose.

"I need some assistance, Mountain. I woke up with everything, including my nerve endings, hurting. Can you spread some of this ointment on the areas I can't reach?"

The "shiiit," escaped him when Blade turned his back to him. He was sporting some extreme bruises on his torso. "I thought you wore protection when you sparred with the sensei."

"I did. Can you imagine the damage if I fought without it?"

"Right now, the only thing I'm imagining is how long it would take a bruise of that size to fade after death."

"Funny, Mountain. Don't make me laugh, I don't need any more hurt. Please smear some of this stuff on me, and be gentle."

Blade stood in stoic silence while he gently worked the ointment into the bruised areas on his back. It was no small relief to say, "There you go," and for his roommate to walk back to his bed to lie on his stomach. It gave him the opportunity to pull the sheet over himself and turn into the wall to hide the erection he was sporting. Only when Wren's breathing deepened in sleep did he jump from the bed like a scalded cat and head for a shower, a long, cold shower.

His roommate was messing with his head. He was attracted to him but why? Yeah, he was handsome, but he worked with handsome men every day in the Corps. Yeah, de Lassy had brains, but so did a lot of fellow Marines. That left the dangerous aspect. Was he attracted to Wren's leashed wild child? Marines were taught to fight and kill, so being on the lethal side didn't make him stand out from other Marines.

Geordy banged his head on the tiled wall of the shower when the revelation hit him. His—roommate possessed all of these attributes in one mouth-watering package, and was totally clueless of the effect he had on him. For the first time since he'd joined the Corps, Geordy regretted his vow to abstain from romantic involvement with a fellow Marine.

A shiver stopped his internal dialogue, and Geordy turned the water off. He glanced down at his shriveled dick and shook his head. "Well, one mischief managed."

He called himself a coward for refusing to let his eyes feast on Blade, lying face down and nude on top of his bed, as he picked up his bag gloves. Time for relieving some stress by knocking the heavy bag around at the gym. Hopefully, his roommate would be dressed or at least fully covered by the time he returned.

Chapter Six

After his first full session with Sensei Dai, Wren thought the confidence course would be a breeze. Captain Schuyler surprised them this morning by canceling the morning PT in favor of seeing how well they could problem solve as a team, but the captain and first sergeant weren't going to be the ones judging them. There would be impartial monitors observing each station.

Things went smoothly until the wall, a twelve-foot wooden barricade that had to be scaled before anyone could continue on in the course. The team agreed the wall was too tall to take a headlong run and jump high enough to reach the top to pull yourself up and over. After a brief discussion, the team went with Levitz's suggestion they form a pyramid at the base and Mountain would be the first up, followed by Mercury, as they had the longest reaches. Mountain and Mercury would then pull the team, one-by-one, over the wall when they neared the top. Blade would go last because, with his martial arts training, he could leap higher than the rest of them, so wouldn't need the pyramid to jump within reach of Mountain and Mercury.

Everyone scaled the wall until only Vogler and he remained. He put his back against the wall so Vogler could climb on his shoulders to grasp Mercury's and Mountain's outstretched hands. Vogler made no attempt to be polite as he climbed up his body, and went out of his way to dig his boots into his shoulders as he pushed off, but Vogler's parting words made him want to grab the ass of his utilities and haul him back down so he could stomp the son of a bitch into unrecognizable goo.

"I'll bet you can't wait to leap into the arms of your lover, de Lassy. Why else would you volunteer to room with a homo?"

In fact, he started to reach up to snatch the bigot back to the ground, but Vogler made connection with Mercury and Mountain to pull him the rest of the way up, so he backed off to wait his turn, and thus had a clear view of Vogler refusing Mercury's hand to hang with both of his hands wrapped around Geordy's outstretched arm. He was very aware Vogler deliberately hung like a dead weight so the top of the wall dug into Geordy's midsection. He gave a small grunt of encouragement as Mercury overextended himself to grab Vogler's T-shirt to help Geordy haul him up and over. Once again, Vogler made no attempt to assist his teammates, but remained a dead weight the whole time.

Still simmering from Vogler's homophobic remark, he backed up and took a flying leap for the wall. He wanted to catch up to Vogler and truly make a dead weight of him, but the man had already moved on to the next station, and he was distracted by Mercury's comment to Geordy.

"I hope Vogler goes head first into the mudhole when we reach it. The bastard batted my hand away so he could put all of his weight on you."

Wren waited for Geordy to comment, but all Mountain did was put his hands to the small of his back to stretch out the kinked muscles and roll his shoulders. Holding a 155-pound body using only your arms and shoulders had, indeed, put a strain on the muscles of his back.

As Geordy moved off, he shook his head. He wondered what would make the Scot lose his temper. He also wondered if there would be anyone still standing when he did.

The mudhole was no one's favorite obstacle. The objective was deceptively simple, cross a narrow beam that traversed a wide, deep pit of liquid goo. In reality, the wooden beam bounced like a spring, and if you lost your balance, you ended up covered in slimy mud for the rest of the course. And to add insult to injury, you couldn't advance until you successfully walked across the beam, but dripping slippery mud with every step made that wickedly difficult.

As he waited his turn, he didn't worry about crossing the mudhole. He had excellent balance and quick reflexes and usually made up course time by running full out across the beam.

Geordy elected to go first and climbed up and stepped out onto the narrow board. Mountain didn't hesitate but crossed the beam like he strolled on a sidewalk, and not a skinny piece of wood six feet over a sucking swamp.

Tecate made the team laugh by attributing Geordy's excellent balance to Tennessee ridge running.

Up next, he started across the beam, but the vibration of another person coming onto the plank made him wobble. In previous crossings, only one man at a time walked the plank. He held out his arms like a tightrope walker and recovered his balance, and continued on, until he was bumped from behind and went sailing straight for the mud. The bastard Vogler didn't even slow down to laugh or to say sorry.

Mercury offered his hand to pull him out of the viscous goo. Damn, now he needed to run the beam again, and spend the rest of the course trailing droplets of mud while being chafed in tender places by his mud-stiffened cammies.

Wren completed the remainder of the course under Geordy's

watchful eye. He knew his roommate intended to intervene to keep him from spending the night in the brig if, instead of merely muttering "don't kill the motherfucker," he did go for Vogler.

***

Uh-oh, this was not going to be a good start to Friday morning, Captain David Schuyler thought when Woody entered their shared office carrying an offering of coffee and a sheaf of papers and closed the door. Master Sergeant Durwood McClean never closed the door. A stone-deaf person could hear the master sergeant's version of a whisper, so closing the door indicated a need for privacy rather than mere politeness.

"The confidence course evals from the monitors, and the team peer reviews are in, Captain."

"Ah, that explains the closed door." Pacer took a swig of coffee and scrambled to put Woody's mug back on the desk. "Shit! I grabbed the wrong mug. Master Sergeant, your mug should be confiscated by the Center for Disease Control. I'm sure, if they swabbed the bottom, they'd find an as yet unidentified plague. Don't you ever wash the fucking thing?"

Woody feigned mock horror. "Wash my mug? Not when it took three years to reach this state of perfection. Why a cup of coffee from my mug will put hair on your chest, Captain."

"Hair? The perpetual sludge you keep on the bottom of your mug would grow fur. Maybe we should change your team name from Woody to Wolverine."

Pacer spat into his waste can and changed the subject. "Enlighten me on what the monitors had to say concerning the Confidence

Course, Master Sergeant."

"Do you want the good news first or the bad?"

Captain Schuyler winced. "Um, this being Friday, I want to start my weekend off on a positive note so give me the good news first."

"The monitors say the team plans well together, and they are in good physical shape. Their times on most of the obstacles were excellent."

"But? Please enlighten me, Woody, as to why there is a large red *but* flashing on your forehead."

"But, not everyone on the team has learned to work together for the good of all."

Captain Schuyler made sure he had his own mug before taking another sip of coffee. "Let me guess, either Vogler, Campbell, or de Lassy needs to learn there is no 'I' in team. My vote goes to Vogler."

"Yeah, the homophobe refused Rogers' hand on the wall to put all of his weight on Campbell. Hauling up Vogler's 155-pounds, while impressive, put a real strain on Campbell. He also made de Lassy fall off the beam into the mud by crossing at the same time and rushing him. Our team eval took a real ding on those two obstacles."

Pacer rubbed his temples. The caffeine was not working fast enough to avert a headache. "And what did the peer evals say?"

"They're pretty consistent. Vogler is a bigoted prick, or putz, which I know is Byte's favorite adjective for him. They praise Mountain as being a real team player who helps out any member of the team who runs out of steam and might need to be carried for a while.

"Blade they praised as leading by example and keeping team spirit up with his irreverent humor. What I find curious is the Mountain had nothing negative to say about Vogler. If you take his eval at face value, Vogler doesn't bother him in the least, which is pretty strange, when Vogler makes it a point to be up in his face at every opportunity."

Pacer's eyebrows shot up. "Hmm, condemnation by silence. He said nothing bad, but he also had nothing good to say. What about Blade? I don't expect Blade took the high road after Vogler dropped him into the bog of everlasting stench."

His question started Master Sergeant McClean laughing.

"I guess being a genius gives you a way with words, Captain. Here, I'll let you read de Lassy's comments on Vogler."

He should never have taken a sip of coffee before reading Blade's peer eval of Vogler. He choked, and the coffee went up his nose, only to be snorted all over his desk and the paper he was holding.

"Damn, Woody, Blade does demonstrate a certain facility with the English language. He praises Vogler's prowess in completing a difficult obstacle course while having his homophobic head stuck up his ass."

Woody waited until the captain finished wiping his face and desk to ask, "What are we going to do about Vogler, Captain? He's become a real millstone around this team's neck. You said you were working on a possible solution, did you come up with one?"

"Yes, Master Sergeant, I did, but first I think I need to speak one-on-one with Vogler. If my clear logic fails to penetrate his thick skull, we'll go to Plan B. Go find Vogler and tell him to hustle his ass into the office. Stick close, because I might need you to fetch Campbell to initiate Plan B."

Captain Schuyler motioned for Vogler to enter when he stuck his head in the door.

"The master sergeant said you wanted to talk to me, Captain?"

"Yeah, I did. Take a seat, Sergeant. The evaluations for the obstacle course and the peer reviews are in, and you figure largely in both, but not in a good way. Care to explain why you feel the need to harass Sergeant Campbell?"

Pacer's eyebrows headed north at the instantaneous outburst from Vogler.

"Because he's a raging homosexual who is an abomination to all upstanding Christians, and he doesn't belong in the Corps. I still don't understand how he passed the psych evals."

Captain Schuyler chose to ignore Vogler's anti-gay rhetoric for the moment to ask another question. "How did you first discover Sergeant Campbell was gay? I'm told you outed him at the room assignments. I know you two served in the same Force Recon company. Did Sergeant Campbell try anything there with you?"

Vogler stood and began to pace. "If he had, he wouldn't be part of MARSOC but planted in a cemetery.

"Then what's your beef with him, Vogler? The rest of the team said nothing but good about him. The same cannot be said for their remarks about you. I believe one of them dubbed you the gay basher in his peer review."

"Let me guess, that was de Lassy's comment."

"No, we are not naming names. The team evals only function well if everything remains anonymous. But I would like to know the basis of your beef with Mountain. Did Campbell ever hit on you here in MARSOC? Did he make any sexual comments that made you uncomfortable? Did you ever see him engaging in any homosexual activity in the dorm or anywhere else on base?"

Vogler started to turn his back on him, but corrected the rude move and faced front.

"No, Captain, but before I knew what he was, I invited him to grab a few beers with me and my girlfriend, and her friend. He embarrassed the hell out of me when my girlfriend's friend asked if he wanted to go somewhere private, and he came out and told her he was gay. She told my girlfriend, and my girlfriend got up in my grill. She didn't think bringing a gay guy along for a weekend of two separate hotel rooms for the four of us was very funny."

"Okay. Did Sergeant Campbell know you were setting him up with a date before he accepted your invitation?"

Vogler stared down at the floor before answering. "Uh, no, I just said my girlfriend was going to join us. I didn't know she was bringing her friend along until we got there. But hey, if Campbell was a normal man, he would've enjoyed himself. The girl was hot and, if she didn't lie about extending the invitation to go somewhere else. She was willing to spend the weekend shacked up with Campbell."

"And what did Sergeant Campbell do after announcing he was gay?"

"He paid for everyone's drinks because he and the girl had gone to the bar to buy the next round, and then he said good night, and since he met us at the bar, he drove himself back to base."

Captain Schuyler came out from behind his desk to give himself some pacing room. "Unless Sergeant Campbell is very good at hiding things, I am unaware of any retaliation against you for singling him out for physical and verbal attacks. And before you deny the physical part of that, the monitor's statement is pretty specific about the way you put all of your weight on Campbell at the wall. I also saw the way you tripped him on the run."

"Yes, sir, I did. Sergeant Campbell doesn't belong in the Marines. We're real men, not gays, and he's too stupid to understand he doesn't belong here. He needs stronger persuasion to take his fag self back to Tennessee so he can continue screwing mountain boys.

"Captain, I don't want to find myself in a situation where Sergeant Campbell, or anyone else that swings like him, is on my six. I don't want that worry in combat."

Schuyler shook his head at the realization Vogler was too entrenched in his prejudices to ever meld with any team containing Geordy Campbell. For himself, he didn't really give a damn about Campbell's sexual preferences as long as he kept them to himself and cooperated to move the team toward its objectives, which Mountain already proved he could do.

"All right, Vogler, I hear your objections loud and clear. Wait one."

Schuyler yelled for the master sergeant. When he entered, he pointed to Campbell's nemesis. "You are dismissed, Sergeant. Please rejoin the team in the team room."

"Close the door, Woody, and listen up. I want you to take Sergeants Vogler and Campbell to the empty field they've prepped for construction behind this building. Oh, and find Doc as well. I'll meet you there in a minute."

Master Sergeant Woody McClean grinned at the captain. "Ah, time for Plan B. I'm guessing your plan involves some one-on-one PT, but why do you want Doc Ferri?"

Pacer grinned at the NCO. "This is Mountain we're talking about, Woody. Vogler might need a Band-Aid for a large boo-boo when PT is over."

Woody widened his stance and crossed his arms over his chest before he asked another question. "Yeah, Mountain is aptly named, and everyone knows Vogler's hatred for homosexuals, so how are you going to keep them from killing each other?"

"Not a problem. I'll tell them I'm going to leave them alone to resolve their differences with fisticuffs, but what they won't know is we'll be observing from the corner of the building. If either one of them becomes so consumed with blood rage they continue inflicting blows after the man is down, I'll stop the fight."

After the master sergeant went to round up Campbell, Vogler, and Ferri, Pacer opened the bottom drawer of his desk and removed two pairs of bag gloves and headed to the empty field to await the pugilists.

***

He didn't need a crystal ball to know something was up. The sneer on Vogler's face after returning from the captain's office told him so. The master sergeant herding him, Vogler, and Doc Ferri to the empty field behind the company was another clue.

Geordy kept quiet as they walked to where Captain Schuyler stood waiting for them, and the captain didn't keep them in suspense for long.

"Sergeants Campbell and Vogler, recent evaluations by the team and outside observers tell me this team will never become a functioning unit until one or the other of you finds a new home. I considered arbitrarily picking a name out of a hat to determine who to send away, but that doesn't strike me as fair. What does appear to be an equitable solution is to let you two decide your own fate."

Geordy didn't comment, but accepted the pair of bag gloves Captain Schuyler handed him.

"Doc, the master sergeant, and I are going to leave you two alone to decide who wants to be on the team more. I'll return with the Doc in a half hour or so, and whomever I find still standing stays with the team. The man on the ground will be given a new home in Bravo Company." The captain glanced from Vogler to Campbell and sighed. "I'm sorry I couldn't come up with a less physical solution, but I hope I don't need to caution either one of you that you are both Marines, MARSOC Marines, and though you are taught to fight to kill, you absolutely will not do so in this instance. This is a grudge match, not mortal combat, but if either of you objects to settling your differences this way, speak now, and I'll pull that name out of the hat. No one? Okay, Master Sergeant, Doc, we're out of here."

Geordy finished putting on the gloves and didn't say a word as the captain, followed by the master sergeant, and a silent and solemn Doc, left the field. He barely had time to bring his arms up before Vogler attempted to swipe his legs out from under him. He countered by grabbing Vogler's upraised knee and flipping him to the ground.

Geordy backed away and made come on motions with his gloved hands. He wouldn't waste his breath by trying to reason with Vogler. The man's homophobia made that a useless endeavor, but someone should've told Vogler taunting your opponent was as counter-productive as blowing on a forest fire to snuff it.

"The team may call you Mountain, but I'll bet the Mountain runs from a real fight. Let's see if you cry when my fist smashes into your nose. You'll probably faint at the sight of all that blood, like the fairy you are. I'll bet your closet back in the hills of Tennessee is loaded with frilly dresses in your size, and lace panties to match. Do you wear baby doll pajamas when you cuddle up with de Lassy?"

Geordy remained silent through Vogler's insults, and wondered if Vogler was a devotee of Mohammed Ali, because while he floated around like a butterfly, and tried to sting him like a bee with short jabs that mostly landed on his ribs and gut, he forgot to watch how close he drew to his right hand.

He ended the fight, mid-insult, with a powerful right cross to the sweet spot between Vogler's cheek and jaw. He stepped back to avoid the Marine's flailing legs as he went down, but remained ready to repeat the action. He sincerely hoped he didn't need to hit the man again, because there was something wrong with Vogler's face. The lower portion of Vogler's jaw had receded like the tide from the upper half.

***

"Jeezus! What a haymaker. The way Vogler went down you would have thought Mountain swung a sledge hammer at him instead of his fist."

"Yeah, Woody, I agree, but now I think Doc's services are needed. Vogler is only sitting up because Campbell helped him to. Let's hustle Doc, I think Sergeant Vogler may need something stronger than a Band-Aid."

After one glance at his patient, Doc Ferri didn't mince words. We need to call an ambulance. I don't want to move Vogler around too much. He's either got a dislocated or a broken jaw, Captain."

"I'm on it, Captain." Woody ran back to the office to make the call.

Captain Schuyler turned to study Sergeant Campbell, who remained quietly off to the side watching Doc take Vogler's vitals, and wipe away the drool coming from his patient's mouth. A mouth that wouldn't be closing until someone in the ER realigned, wired, or taped it shut.

"Sergeant Campbell, when the ambulance gets here and the medics ask what happened, I'm going to say a hand-to-hand training accident. What are you going to say?"

Geordy's response came in the form of a question. "The same, sir?"

"Excellent, Sergeant Campbell." Schuyler then knelt and put himself eye-to-eye with the injured Marine. "And you, Sergeant Vogler? Are you going to, when you *can* speak, say this was an accident, or are you going to immortalize Mountain here by saying he felled you with but a single punch in an unauthorized fight? And if you are thinking of saying a punch, let me remind you that your new teammates in Bravo Company won't hold an accident against you but might find your glass jaw hysterically funny. Now hold up one finger for accident and two for fight."

Vogler glared at Geordy but held up one finger.

***

"Paperwork, is the bane of every Marine's existence, Master Sergeant. Now that Sergeant Vogler is tucked into a hospital bed for the night, you can start on the accident report, and I'll finagle getting Vogler's replacement to appear on the Joint Manning Document from G-1."

"Aye aye, sir. I'm impressed at Sergeant Campbell's calm under fire. He didn't show much reaction to shutting up Vogler."

"Then you didn't study him as closely as I did, Master Sergeant. The man was vibrating like a tuning fork. I attribute the shakes to adrenaline burn off, but the expression on his face can no way be described as jubilant when Vogler was loaded into the ambulance. I didn't want to send him back to the team logistical planning for the Philippine deployment, but I didn't want to make him stand out by his absence. I think he's a mature enough man to keep this whole incident under wraps."

Captain Schuyler pulled his gaze away from his computer at the master sergeant's guffaw of amusement. "What?"

"While we may be macho Marine Special Operators, we gossip worse than women. What Campbell did to Vogler already made the rounds of his team. Who, before you ask, are fine with the outcome and won't broadcast it beyond the team."

"Your ability to resolve a crisis is amazing, Master Sergeant."

Sergeant Woodrow McClean's rejoinder to the captain's compliment got stifled by the ringing of the phone on his desk. When he finished with the MARSOC-approved greeting to gender unknown callers, he shut up and listened to whatever the person on the other end of the phone had to say and then hung up.

"Uh, Captain, there's another situation involving Sergeant Campbell."

"What now, Woody? Did Vogler use sign language to rat Campbell out for unauthorized fighting?"

"No, sir, I wish that was the problem, because what the Family Readiness Officer told me is worse. Sergeant Campbell's mother suffered a fatal stroke this morning. He said the Red Cross sent the official notice. He also said there was some sort of family problem with the burial arrangements, and his uncle would be calling him here at this number because of the MARSOC policy prohibiting cell phones anywhere except in the dorms."

Captain Schuyler's response was succinct. "Fuck! The big man upstairs picked today to test Mountain. Go fetch him, Woody. We'll vacate the office and let him take the call with some semblance of privacy."

***

Being called back to the captain's office for the second time in one day didn't give Geordy a warm and fuzzy feeling. Shit, what now? Was his unvoiced reaction to being summoned once again by the master sergeant, who wouldn't tell him why the captain wanted to speak with him.

"Ah, Mountain, take a load off." Captain Schuyler gestured to the chair in front of his desk.

Geordy's stomach dropped at the serious expression on Pacer's face. Was he going to be court martialed for breaking Vogler's jaw?

"What, Captain? I can tell by the expression on your face you didn't call me back here to shoot the shit. I prefer bad news be delivered quickly."

"As you wish, Sergeant. Please take a seat, and that's an order." When Campbell reluctantly pulled the chair farther away from the desk to accommodate his long legs and took a seat, Captain Schuyler continued, "I just received a call from the Family Readiness Officer, and I have the sad duty to inform you that your mother passed away this morning due to a massive stroke."

Pacer gave himself a virtual pat on the back for making Mountain sit before delivering the news, because he doubted both he and Woody combined could lift Mountain back into the chair if he did a faceplant on the floor. He waited until Campbell took his head out of his hands to speak again.

"Your uncle is going to call here on the master sergeant's line to talk to you. The FRO mentioned something about burial arrangements. I am very sorry for your loss, Sergeant. Let me know what you need and I'll make sure you get it."

Geordy faced the master sergeant's desk as the phone rang and heard him parrot the standard MARSOC phone greeting, and sat stoically while the master sergeant offered his condolences before waving him over to take the phone. He didn't speak until the master sergeant and Captain Schuyler left the office to give him privacy, and then steeled himself to ask, "Uncle Aillig? Is it true?"

"Aye, lad. Your mother passed without noticeable pain. One minute she was talking to your aunt Euna, and the next she was slumped over the kitchen table. I'm so sorry to be delivering this news to you, nephew, but your father doesn't want you to attend the funeral, and he put the onus on me to deliver such distasteful news."

For the first time in his life, he had to work to keep his temper from breaking free. He viewed Captain Schuyler's office through a red haze. In a voice made tight with his effort at restraint, Geordy hissed, "Uncle, you tell the man who used to be my father I will be attending my mother's funeral, and he can't stop me. You can also tell whichever of my cousins is presently living in my house to clean up their mess and clear out. I will be coming home, and I don't want company. I'll be there as soon as my leave papers are signed."

Geordy hung up before his uncle had a chance to reply. The rage broke free before he could step away from the master sergeant's desk and, with a great roar, the Mountain erupted. Geordy blindly swiped his arm across the master sergeant's desk and swept off everything but the computer monitor. The cacophony of paper and pencils and wooden inboxes hitting the deck made the captain and the master sergeant come flying into the room.

Rather than receiving the dressing down he expected, the master sergeant merely picked up his coffee cup and cradled his most prized possession in his hands.

"Well, here's a small blessing for this craptastic day. I'm royally pissed at the way you rearranged my desk, Sergeant, but given the circumstances, and the fact you didn't destroy a mug that took me three years to season, I'm prepared to forgive your outburst."

"I'm sorry, Master Sergeant. I'll clean up the mess." With shaking hands, Geordy started to retrieve the scattered paper and pencils until Captain Schuyler intervened.

"Belay that, Sergeant Campbell. I'll help the master sergeant put his desk back in order. I signed off on leave for you starting tomorrow morning at 06:00. I don't want you driving tonight in the state you're in. Once again, Mountain, the master sergeant and I offer our condolences on the loss of your mother. You are dismissed to return to your room."

After Geordy left, Pacer turned to the master sergeant and ordered, "Find de Lassy. I want him to go with Mountain and keep him from killing whoever in his family made him lose his temper like that. I can't afford for Campbell to miss the deployment because he's incarcerated in some Tennessee jail, awaiting trial for homicide."

Chapter Seven

Wren couldn't tell if it was a good thing or bad, the room he shared with Geordy remained as quiet as if no one was in there. He stood in the hallway, hesitating to enter because he had no experience with comforting someone who mourned the passing of a loved one.

Oh, he lost his parents when he was eleven, but the circumstances of their deaths engendered more anger than grief. He had firsthand experience with being abandoned as a direct result of poor life choices. Abandonment didn't cause grief, abandonment engendered rage in the one left behind. But he liked Geordy, and had enough empathy buried deeply within himself to want to ease things for his roomie.

He made a production of inserting the key in the door so Geordy, if crying, would have enough time to dry his eyes. If he was in Geordy's place, he would be embarrassed to be caught crying.

He stood quietly in the doorway as Geordy rose from his bunk and turned his back on him to swipe his face with the back of his arm. That simple action told him how low the Mountain had been brought, and he moved up behind Geordy and wrapped him in a hug. He gave the back of Geordy's head an incredulous stare when Geordy didn't immediately break away.

"I'm sorry for your loss, Geordy. Anything you need just ask."

Geordy's voice was husky as he replied. "Short of possessing powers of resurrection, there's no' much you can do, but I thank you for the offer."

Wren let go of Mountain to go to his locker and pull out his duffel. Geordy had already finished packing his own.

"Well, Mountain, there is something I can do. I can have your six."

Geordy stopped him by barring the way to his bed. "What are you doing? Are you going somewhere?"

"Yeah, I am. I'm going with you. Captain Schuyler ordered me to make sure you don't commit patricide when you return for your mother's funeral. I guess you were a little loud when you told your uncle you were attending your mom's funeral despite your dad's wishes."

He did one of his lightning conversation switches before Geordy had a chance to protest. "I hope there's enough room for me to stay with you wherever we're going in Tennessee, or a hotel near enough I can rent a room. I see you're taking your Dress Blues, so I'll take mine." Wren continued to pack as Geordy just stood there with his head tipped to the side like he'd misplaced his mind.

Before Geordy could voice his objection, a knock sounded on the door, and Wren dropped the highly polished dress shoe he'd been covering with one of his socks so the shine wouldn't be marred. "I'll get it."

He opened the door to find Byte, Mercury, and Tecate standing in the hallway. He stood aside as Levitz led the way inside.

"Hey, Mountain, the master sergeant told us of your loss, and we're here to offer our condolences." Byte gave Geordy a man hug, which mainly consisted of a brief squeeze and a few pats on the back. He was followed by Mercury, who muttered, "I'm sorry, Mountain," and followed up with his own brief hug.

Tecate was the last to step up, but he thrust a pizza box at Wren before hugging Geordy. "We thought you might not be up to going out for dinner, so we got you a pizza and a six-pack of root beer to wash it down."

Geordy widened his eyes before he spoke to keep his tears from falling.

"Thank you, your thoughtfulness means a lot. Will you help me eat it?"

Byte gave Geordy a fist bump to the arm. "Thank you, but no. You created a welcome vacancy in our room, and we're on our way to J-ville to celebrate not having to listen to Vogler's twisted rhetoric ever again."

After the team left, Wren turned to Geordy and handed him a slice of pizza. "You should eat while it's still hot."

"I'm not hungry."

"True that, but you burned a lot of stress calories today, and the rest of the week promises to be even more stressful, so not eating won't help you keep your Scots' temper leashed when we get to Tennessee. Besides, if I work my magic on you, you won't be awake to eat it later."

Geordy gawked at his roommate like he was speaking some unknown language. "What the fuck are you talking about, Blade? Do what right? If you're thinking of slipping a tranquilizer into the root beer, I'll rearrange your jaw like I did Vogler's when I recover."

Wren's grin disappeared, and he spoke softly, but with conviction. "Drugging you is not on the agenda. I don't use, give to, or approve of anyone using drugs needlessly, but here's a wee tidbit you can stow away for future reference. Should you try to rearrange my jaw you'll find yourself sharing a hospital room with Vogler." Before Geordy could work up to thinking smacking him upside the head was still a good idea, he continued, "I was referring to the way you're walking like the anthropological specimen that falls between homo erectus and homo sapiens. In other words, you aren't walking fully erect. I'm betting Vogler's little stunt on the wall pulled a few major muscle groups."

Geordy nodded and rubbed the small of his back.

"Finish your pizza, Campbell, and I'll use what Tomodashi taught me to unkink your back. I guarantee you'll be walking much better tomorrow."

When Geordy tossed the last piece of crust back in the box then crushed the empty can of root beer before adding it to the empty box, Wren ordered, "Strip and climb onto your bed." Rather than explain his directions, he chose to out wait the suspicious Scot. After a terse, silent three-count, Geordy grabbed the back of his T-shirt and jerked it over his head then dropped the sweatpants and boxer briefs he wore, and threw back the covers of his bed.

Wren retrieved his tin of herbal balm, climbed up on Geordy's bed, and straddled his legs. When Mountain tensed, he leaned down and whispered in his ear. "Relax, Mountain, I'm not going to molest you. I prefer my sexual partners to be willing."

As he suspected, Geordy was a mass of knots and kinks. He started at Mountain's neck and worked his way down. His hands ached from the continual kneading, but there were no more knots to unravel as he reached the small of Geordy's back. Other than an initial grunt of pain when he started, Geordy remained silent, but now he distinctly heard the deep breathing of a man sound asleep. Grinning to himself, he withdrew from the bed and covered Geordy with the sheet and went to wash his hands.

He turned out the room lights at ten o'clock. Geordy was still asleep, and he still lacked an answer his own question. Did wanting a man when he was down and hurting make him a sick sonovabitch? He gave himself points for not acting on his desires, but added a few demerits for wishing Geordy had given him the least little sign of returning his feelings. He was beginning to regret not taking the Mountain up on his many offers to change room assignments.

Special operators were trained to fall asleep at will, but Blade took longer than usual to calm himself enough to sleep. He shouldn't have bothered. He was awakened sometime after midnight. Geordy tried to muffle the sound of his crying, but the sound carried in the quiet room. He sat up and asked, "Do you want to talk?"

When he didn't say anything, Wren tried again. "Why don't you tell me about your mother. You must have had a great relationship? I envy that. My mother checked out before we could reconcile our differences, so I can't say I have any experience with losing someone you're close to."

Geordy's, voice, raspy from crying, came out of the dark. "My mother and I were close. She knew I was gay, I think even before I did, and after I came out, she stood alone against my father and brothers when I was kicked out of the house and treated as if I never existed."

There was a long moment of silence before Geordy continued. "And now the vindictive bastard, backed up no doubt by my homophobic brothers, has sent the message through my uncle I'm not to attend her funeral. They don't want to be embarrassed by my presence there. Last time I checked, I didn't have a scarlet G proclaiming my gayness tattooed on my forehead."

He heard the bitterness in his roommate's voice and the strangled sound of a sob being cut off, and hopped out of his bed and gathered Geordy into his arms before he had a chance to reason his roommate might not appreciate the gesture. When no protest broke the quiet, he nudged Geordy until he moved over in the bed, and then spooned his body into his.

"Cry all you want, Mountain, I'll pull guard. You may not believe me, but you aren't as unloved and alone as you think you are."

"Oh yeah, and you're such an expert on the topic?"

"Yeah, I am. I have heaps of personal experience. I had the same sense of despair as you do now from the time I was eleven years old until I turned eighteen, but not because I lost someone I loved, but because I felt I was the one who was lost. Fortunately, a man compassionate enough to offer me comfort, just comfort, appeared in my life at that exact moment I needed him, so now I'd like to repay his kindness in the same manner."

Geordy must've accepted his reasoning, for the tight rein he held on his emotions broke and Wren held on as sobs racked him, and discovered what his occasional girlfriends swore on crossed pinkie fingers was true, crying could be cathartic. He fell asleep shortly after Geordy did.

The lightening of the room woke him up, and he glanced at the clock, 04:30, time to get up and shower since Geordy wanted to be on the road by six. He stepped out of the shower and discovered Geordy standing at the sink washing his face after shaving. Without thinking, he used his index finger to wipe a blob of shaving cream from behind Geordy's ear. "You missed a spot."

Every muscle in his body went rigid with stunned surprise when Geordy turned around and took both his hands in his, and used them to slowly run them down his pecs, ripped abs, and then lower to make the towel drop from around his waist.

Always curious, he remained still and silent to see where Geordy intended to take this. He only began to breathe again when his hands were urged to cup Geordy's package after being guided there, and then, oh hell yes, the gesture was reciprocated on his own dick and balls. He awarded Geordy's gentle squeeze with a murmur of pleasure, but Geordy's caress was disappointingly brief, and his hands, under the direction of the Mountain, moved once again to traverse Geordy's chest and then cup his freshly shaven face.

Geordy never broke eye contact as he asked, "Do you want me?"

The soft burr in Geordy's voice sent a shiver down his body. Bunking with the man for several weeks clued him in that Geordy's Scottish roots came to the fore when he was stressed or angry, and this morning he lay the blame on stress, because the soft way Geordy's hands cupped his own cheeks did not say angry.

Wren moved chest-to-chest to respond. "Yes, I want you," and he began to place soft kisses on Geordy's eyes and lips. He broke off when Geordy faced the mirror and noted their reflections before snugging his body into his.

He guessed some sort of Scottish requirement of fair play made his roommate ask a final question.

"Do you ken what you are about?"

In answer, Wren ran his hands down the front of Geordy, from his pecs to his cock, and gave a slow stroke.

"I ken very well what I'm about." He won a small smile from Mountain when he pronounced the last word "aboot." He rued the fact his tongue engaged before his brain and asked a question before he could stifle it.

"Are you asking because your grief made you relax your prohibition on dating Marines? I don't want to confuse the issue here. I don't want this to come back as I took advantage of you when you weren't thinking clearly."

His mouth went dry when Geordy leaned back into his arms and lowered his eyes in sleepy invitation.

"Nay, grief plays no part in this. This is me wanting the experience of making love to you for just this once."

He squelched down hard on the matter of limitations, but he needed a verbal green light. "Are you sure?"

"Aye, I am. Take me, de Lassy."

That was as all Geordy said before opening his shaving kit and handing him a condom and a tube of lubricant.

He wouldn't make Geordy ask a second time. He sheathed himself but deliberately took his time applying the lube. He had every intention of making his one chance a memorable experience for Geordy, but he made the mistake of peering into the mirror and seeing Geordy's face. It rocked him.

Geordy didn't even try to hide his expression of wanting this closeness, the need, or the vulnerability he was deliberating opening himself to. He had never seen such an expression on any of his other sexual partners, and he suddenly wanted to give Geordy everything he desired.

Wren used every sexual trick he ever learned to bring Geordy pleasure in ways unknown to someone not trained to do so. Geordy's soft sigh of "My bonnie de Lassy" as he came made his own orgasm hit him like a thunderclap, and the reverberations of such passion left an indelible imprint on his heart.

Making love to Geordy marked him and scared the bejesus out of him because he didn't do serious. He did casual, playful, no harm, no foul sex, but Geordy, it appeared, played by different rules. Which he confirmed when, as he disengaged, Geordy whipped around and captured his lips in a searing kiss, leaving him standing spent and confused as Mountain disappear behind the shower curtain.

He started to turn toward the mirror but stopped himself. He was afraid he'd see the same need and vulnerability in his own eyes.

Chapter Eight

Geordy had compartmentalization down like a sonovabitch by the time he picked up his duffel and headed for the door. What his libido told him would be nothing more than scratching an itch turned into losing a vital piece of himself. He never experienced anything close to what de Lassy did to his body as they made love. Always before, intercourse meant getting his rocks off and being polite enough to wait for his partner to do so well, but not this morning. Wren took the act into a whole other realm, and he felt the difference in the very marrow of his bones. For the first time, he experienced love without an agenda or an ounce of selfishness on his lover's part, and now he bore a mark on his soul he didn't know how to handle with his emotions in shreds over his mother's death.

He began to breathe easier when his roommate didn't say a damned thing, just followed him out the door.

"What say you to stopping at McDuck's for ham, egg, and cheese biscuits, and large coffees to go on our way out of town?"

Wren patted his flat stomach. "Sounds good to me," and pointed at Geordy's truck. "That model is a good fit for you, a super-size truck for a super-size person."

Geordy shrugged. "I wanted a truck with a large bed because I haul a lot of rocks. Once a mason, always a mason. I do odd jobs for friends whenever I'm home."

Eating breakfast on the go gave him time to calm down and begin to believe his roommate wouldn't question his gigantic lapse in judgement this morning. Not that he blamed Wren for his tossing his

'I don't date Marines' rule out the window. He couldn't fault him for taking what he so freely offered, but he could fault himself for thinking he could be strong enough to not yearn for more.

He tried giving his assigned escort surreptitious glances out of the corner of his eye, but the only thing he gleaned was his roomie enjoyed his breakfast. Wren spoke for the first time when he sat his coffee cup in the center console and picked up Interstate 40 West.

"If I'm going to have your six, you need to tell me how to separate the good guys from the bad. Tell me about your family. Are we staying at one of their homes, or are we staying in a motel?"

If anyone but de Lassy asked him to describe his family, he would've said dysfunctional, and left it at that, but he didn't know how his father or his brothers would react to his defiance of the order to stay away from his mother's funeral, and truth be told, he wouldn't bet a penny on his ability to keep his own temper leashed. His father's harsh edict marked the last time he intended to turn the other cheek as a response to their ill treatment of him. He owed Blade an explanation since Pacer ordered him to serve as his battle buddy.

Geordy used a lame joke to stall for time to gather his thoughts. "Are you sure you want to know? Describing them might curdle your breakfast."

"My brother Ross says I have a cast iron stomach, so fire when ready, Gridley."

Geordy snickered at the historical reference and began. "My birth certificate reads Geordy Daniel MacEwen. My father, uh, the man who sired me, is Evin MacEwen. My mother's name is, uh, was Kirsten MacEwen nee Campbell. My former brothers are Ramsey and Robert or Robbie."

When he hesitated, Blade asked another question, a hard one.

"You told me you were kicked out of the family for admitting you were gay, but what made you do so? Sounds like you didn't anticipate your father's reaction."

Geordy watched his knuckles turn white as he gripped the steering wheel and loosened his hold before answering.

"Aye, a major miscalculation on my part. Oh, I thought my declaration would surprise him, but I also thought he loved me enough to at least take time to allow his reason to overrule his emotions. You know, I can still recall the entire scene like someone captured it on video so I can replay it at will. We were eating dinner and my brother Robbie, who'd graduated high school a year before me, kept teasing me about asking someone to the school prom. He suggested I ask this girl or that, and I tried to fend him off by saying his choices for my date sucked. Then my brother Ramsey jumped in and said no girl would go to the prom with me if I continued to act so shy and backward in their presence. Maybe I can lay the blame for my abysmal timing on being overly tired from helping my dad lay the foundation for a large fireplace after school that day, but I suddenly had all the teasing I could stand and blurted the only one I was interested in taking to the prom was the cute guy in my English class."

"Shit, I bet that went over well."

Geordy let a sigh escape. "Even my brothers couldn't come up with a smart ass reply to that. My da, however, leveled a glare on me I will remember until my dying day, and said, 'We don't joke about such things at the dinner table.' But when I cast my eyes to my mother, he saw the truth and came roaring out of his chair to ask her if she knew about my sexual preference. At her nod, my father drew himself up to his full five feet, eleven inches, pointed a finger at me like a biblical patriarch, and cast me out."

Wren started to snicker and bit his lip to silence himself when Geordy scowled at him. "Sorry, I know laughing is inappropriate, but your confession just struck me as an error of biblical proportions after your description of your father's reaction. Forgive my insensitivity and continue, please."

Geordy gave a disgruntled huff. "When my mother started to protest, my da cut her off and told me I had fifteen minutes to throw some clothes into a bag, grab the keys to the truck I bought by working after school, and leave his house. He refused to allow such an abomination to contaminate his family for longer than that. But my brother Robbie saying he felt sick to learn he'd been sleeping all these years in the same bedroom with a homo hurt me the most."

Wren turned around in his seat so he could put his back against the door, the better to see Geordy. "Where did you go after you left the house?"

"My mother helped me pack a suitcase and told me to head for my Uncle Aillig's house. Unlike me, she knew what my father's reaction would be because she'd discussed it on the QT with my uncle, and he told her if it ever came to it, I could stay at his place. She told me not to worry, my father would see reason, once he calmed down. I'm still waiting for that to happen."

"Man, awkward in the extreme to show up at the relatives asking for a place to stay because you just outed yourself."

Geordy waited to answer his roommate's comment until he passed a car doing forty in a seventy zone. "Her brother, my Uncle Aillig Campbell, is married to Euna, and they have three boys: Aengus, Caillin, and Conall. And God bless them, for they took me in immediately, and never made me feel like a lesser part of their family.

When I drove up to their house, my uncle told me my mother had called ahead, and then he asked if I had a dollar on me. When I got one out of my wallet and handed it over, he told me I had just purchased my first house, the very same one-room log cabin my great, great grandparents built when they first claimed the land. They moved to the house my uncle lives in now when the children started arriving and the little cabin would no longer hold them."

"Well at least you had some privacy to lick your emotional wounds rather than having to share a bedroom with one of your cousins."

Geordy laughed. "I wouldn't be able to live in the cabin until my uncle and cousins helped me fix it up, but by the time I finished high school the little cabin was in decent shape, and so was I. And that's where you and I will be staying. Don't worry, that old cabin is no longer just one room with a sleeping loft over the kitchen fireplace. You'll have your own bedroom and bath. My cousins take turns living there while I'm deployed to keep an eye on the property, but clear out when I'm home on leave. My aunt and uncle like the arrangement as well, because having at least one of my cousins out of the house keeps their own home from feeling overwhelmed by three grown kids who have yet to leave the nest."

Wren's next question surprised him with its prescience.

"Did your brothers make it difficult to go back to school after you came out? You said Beltrees is a small town, so I'd imagine being kicked out of your family became known fairly soon."

"You're right about Beltrees being a small town. I created quite a stir when I got to school on Monday and, as you can imagine, not in a good way. The football team damn near mutinied, thanks to Robbie telling all of his former football pals. The coach, God bless him, told the team anyone who cared to leave the team could do so, except for his best fullback and the quarterback, who happened to be my cousin Caillin. He had no intention of ruining our chances of going to State finals."

"You played fullback?"

"Yeah, I had the height and speed. My cousin did his fair share of banging team heads until they realized I presented no threat to them. But they never quite got used to showering with me after a game. A small hurt, one of many I suffered that year, but the coach, Mr. MacArthur, never treated me any different from the rest of the team, and once he learned my father kicked me out and wouldn't be paying for my college, he hooked me up with the guidance counselor, and they finagled a scholarship for me at the University of Tennessee. An academic scholarship. Even though we did go all the way to take the State championship, I had my fill of football by then."

Wren bumped Geordy on the arm and asked, "And did you take the cute boy in your English class to the prom?" He guffawed when Geordy instantly turned red.

Geordy squashed his embarrassment enough to wink at his battle buddy. "Yes, I did. And we did what the hetero couples did that night, we helped each other bust our cherries, and promptly lost interest in each other. His parents moved to California, and he got into UCLA." Geordy glanced down at the gas gauge and turned to Blade. "I'm going to gas up at the next exit, and we can grab lunch."

"Sounds like a plan. My bladder thinks that's a stellar idea since you ordered us the gallon-sized cup of coffee with breakfast."

Geordy chuckled. "No one said you had to finish it."

"But the challenge was implied." Wren squirmed and pointed to the road sign. "I hope I can keep my legs crossed for one more mile, but don't count on me pumping the gas. I'll be making a beeline for the head."

With gas tank filled and bladder emptied, Geordy joined his roommate in the line to order lunch. He pointed to the salad option on the overhead menu. "You might want to order something light. When my Aunt Euna sees you, she's going to try and stuff you full of good country cooking. She does not approve of the Marine Corps weight standards."

Wren resumed his questioning over their broiled chicken salads.

"So, how did Geordy MacEwen become Geordy Campbell?"

Geordy put his fork down and wiped his mouth. "I guess, like my mother, I always hoped my dad would...I don't know, maybe not accept my sexuality whole-heartedly, but miss me enough to soften his views enough to allow me to return home, but that hadn't happened by the time I turned eighteen and headed to college. He didn't attend my graduation from either high school or university, and he still hasn't spoken a word to me."

Wren reached across the table and gave his arm a fist bump in commiseration.

"What about your brothers, Ramsey and Robbie? Did they come around?"

Geordy sighed and shrugged his shoulders. "I wish my brothers would follow his example in the silence category. They go out of their way to taunt me. My brothers are the reason Vogler couldn't get my goat. After Ramsey and Robbie, he couldn't possibly come up with an original insult or dirty trick to beat the ones Ramsey and Robbie played on me. So, to answer your question about the name change, when I reached legal age, I went to the courthouse and filed for a legal name change. If my father no longer claimed me as a MacEwen, the

Campbells did. I asked my uncle for permission to take his name, and it speaks to his excellent character that he got all emotional and said it made him happy to have another good man in his family." Geordy stared at nothing over his roommate's shoulder and then added, "Of course, my mother was sad we now had different names, but she understood why I gave up on being returned to the MacEwen fold."

Wren began gathering his trash and held Geordy's gaze. "Well, piss on them, they didn't deserve you. The MacEwen loss turned into a win for the Campbells. Moving on, what did you major in in college?"

"Damn, de Lassy, you should switch your MOS from EOD to Interrogator." He continued filling in the history of the MacEwens and Campbells until he pulled into Beltrees and began to take the back road to his house. After a twelve-hour drive, he wanted to get the hell out of the truck. Blade now knew more about his life and feelings than the man who donated the sperm to create him.

Chapter Nine

Geordy's strong hands gripping the steering wheel captured Wren's attention during what Geordy laughingly called his interrogation, and he wiped his own palms down the length of his jeans to stop the tingly itch.

His posture stiffened when he realized his palms were itchy because he denied them contact with Geordy. To give Campbell a break from his steady questioning, he put his ear buds in, not so much to listen to the French language tape on his phone, but to analyze this new phenomenon.

As a tactile person, he enjoyed touching and being touched. Of course, in the Marines the touches came in the form of hand-to-hand combat practice, fist bumps, or the occasional brief man hug, and, therefore, were more painful than pleasant, and not of any duration to register as arousing.

This morning's interaction with his roommate stirred up his longing for sensual, skin-to-skin contact. Yes, there had been sensual contact this morning when he made love to Geordy, but the physical act had been one-sided, and he felt...what? The word bereft popped into his mind. His palms tingled with the desire to touch Geordy's body again, to stir enough desire in the Scot to return his touches in the same way. But with Geordy's self-imposed limitation on the act, he doubted that would ever happen.

The corner of his mouth quirked at the thought this trip to Tennessee might turn out to be a sexually frustrating one of short-tempered Scots with overwrought emotions engendered by grief. It made him question Captain Schuyler's choosing him to serve as Geordy's cooler.

He jerked the earbuds out to hear what Geordy said. "What? Sorry, I'm listening to a language tape." Yeah, right. I didn't hear one word on the tape because I'm imagining the two of us in bed wrapped head-to-foot around each other like a mythical ouroboros.

"I said, this is Beltrees. We'll reach my house in a minute or two."

He stowed his phone and began to pay attention to Geordy's hometown. If he had to pick a primary color for Beltrees, he'd choose green, bright green. Grove aptly described the place, because you couldn't spit without hitting a tree. And they were still in the mountains because he could feel the truck begin to climb as they passed through the town's main street.

He liked the way the trees became a green tunnel over the two-lane road, and he liked the low bridge over a wide, fast-moving stream even more. His rubber-necking came to a halt when the truck stopped after crossing the bridge and Geordy shut the engine off. He was stunned to find a log cabin amidst, no surprise, more trees, and the breath whooshed out of him.

"*That's* your one room cabin?"

Geordy ducked his head in a shy grin. "Aye. My cousins and I improved it a wee bit."

Wren hopped out of the truck and walked up to the cabin. The restoration left him speechless. The modern tin roof was a deep-forest green, and wrapped over a porch that, from what he could see, encompassed the front and sides of the cabin. The cabin was one-story, with a large Palladian window at the front. The logs were chinked with white and stained to a deep, rich brown. He couldn't claim to be an architect, but the logs appeared to be hand-hewn.

Geordy stopped his admiration of the exterior by walking past and dumping his duffel at his feet before he climbed the porch steps and unlocked the front door. Wren didn't wait to be invited inside, just stuck to his roommate's six as he entered his home.

"Wow! This is fantastic. Did you buy the plans for this, or is this your own design?" Not waiting for a reply, he did a slow revolution and took in the sleeping loft over a modern island kitchen with stainless steel appliances, an open floor plan with a separate dining alcove, and a great room with a fireplace large enough to roast an ox. The unusual design of the fireplace drew him farther into the room.

Wren ran his hand over the smooth river rocks swirling up to the fifteen-foot ceiling. "This is absolutely beautiful."

"Thank you. This design took me two summers to finish. One summer to pry the stones from the stream we crossed, and one to place them in the pattern I visualized."

He reluctantly tore his eyes away from the fireplace and took in the large leather sofas, the leather armchair, and the carved oak coffee and end tables, and chuckled in amusement. "My brother, Ross, would approve of your decorating style. He loves the comfortable Danish modern style as well. His town house in Alexandria, Virginia, is decorated with similarly-styled clean lines, leather, and stainless steel. This decorating style must come embedded in the Viking genes."

Geordy pointed to the right. "The master bedroom is there, and...." He stopped speaking because Wren already stood inside the room.

Geordy's bedroom confirmed his roomie had a sensual side. Sensual, not sissy. The bedroom housed a king-size bed; the walls were timbered halfway and whitewashed on top. He admired the corner fireplace, French doors leading to a back porch running the length of the house, and the view of a green wooded valley.

He ran his hand along the black mink bedspread with its matching shams, and observed, "Since this house is situated east-west, I'm guessing the sunsets from the porch are magnificent."

He barely heard Geordy's reply because he stopped dead in front of the picture hanging on the wall at the foot of the bed. Anyone lying in bed would have an excellent view of the drawing. Wren jumped when Geordy's hand clamped down on his shoulder.

"I see you discovered my one major art purchase. The artist is Nels Kirkegaard."

He had to force air past his constricted throat to speak. "What...what made you buy this particular drawing?"

Geordy laughed. "I don't know why I bought it, maybe because I couldn't get it out of my head after I saw it. I decided to go sightseeing in Washington, DC, before I went on my second deployment to the sandbox, because, sad to say, I had never visited our nation's capital before. After hitting the major tourist sights, I wandered around Georgetown and happened upon a gallery featuring Kirkegaard's work. The gallery had a large canvas of a forest that reminded me of home, but even though I could never afford such a magnificent painting, something in the artist's style and sense of color attracted me enough to continue through the exhibit. This painting, or I should say pen and ink with touches of watercolor, I saw before leaving the gallery, and I couldn't get it out of my mind." Geordy stepped closer to the drawing and pointed. "At first, I thought Kirkegaard's drawing featured a woman sitting with her back turned and with her face half in profile looking down at a book on the floor, but as I walked the streets of Georgetown, something bothered me about the proportions."

He cleared his throat, but the huskiness remained when he asked, "How so?"

Geordy delicately ran his finger down the glass covering the subject's hair. "Yes, this glorious mane of wavy, red-gold hair is long enough to be a woman's, but the shape of the shoulders said masculine to me, as did the one foot you can see. The enigma compelled me to return to the gallery for another visit."

Wren turned away from the painting. "Yes, Kirkegaard's drawings have hidden depth."

Geordy straightened the frame. "I sold my truck rather than store it for a long deployment, because I knew my combat pay would more than cover the down payment for another one when I got back. Maybe that wad of cash influenced my decision, but I bought the painting and had the gallery ship it here."

Geordy considered Blade's words as he studied the watercolor. "You know, I never get tired of studying it. Each time, I discover something new, like the way the light is shining through that metal screen to send small beams of light all around the central figure. And the way the woman or man, if my guess is right, is contemplating the book with a half-smile on her face, you wonder what she or he is reading." Geordy laughed sheepishly, "Come along, then, enough of my art critique. I'll show you your room."

As they left Geordy's bedroom, Wren glanced back and stared at the drawing. He knew exactly what the boy had been reading, *The Complete Works of Shakespeare*, his favorite book, and the only thing he took with him as a remembrance of that episode of his life.

He returned from his exploration of the guest room and bathroom to watch as Geordy filled two stainless steel feeding bowls with dry food.

"Do you have dogs?"

Geordy hefted the filled dishes and grinned. "Maybe a dog, and a free-loading critter. My cousin Conall left me a note before he cleared out this morning. He's been feeding a stray coon hound who hasn't yet decided if he wants to stay."

"Coon hound? I'm not familiar with that breed."

Geordy responded with typical Scots' brevity. Think bloodhound, only black and tan."

"Do coon hounds eat a lot? Those are pretty large bowls of food." Wren nodded toward the dishes in Geordy's hands.

"No more than other dogs of their size. The other bowl is for Rob Roy. Follow me out to the back porch and bring that bottle of bourbon and the two glasses I put out. We can watch the sun set."

Curious to meet Rob Roy, and always up for a glass of bourbon, he readily hefted the bottle and glasses. He set them on the small table between two cushioned grape vine chairs, and took a seat as Geordy placed the dishes at each end of the porch.

Rob Roy didn't keep him waiting to make his acquaintance. Not five minutes after Geordy placed the food on the porch and took his own seat, a large raccoon waddled up to the porch and headed for him. He wanted to laugh, but kept quiet as Geordy addressed the coon.

"Good evening, Robbie. Conall tells me you got into a tussle last night with an interloper who tried to share your dinner. Well, you needn't worry. There are now two bowls."

He had to admit the damned raccoon rocked cute by sitting up and clasping its hands while listening to Geordy. He appeared to understand every word, for the moment Geordy stopped speaking the coon headed for his dish and began chowing down.

"Aren't you afraid he might be rabid?" he asked, as Rob Roy enjoyed his evening meal.

"Not at all. I scatter peanuts treated with the vaccine each year for Rob Roy, and any other coon in the area, to ingest.

"Hsst, no sudden moves now. Here comes the hound. Conall believes some bastard abandoned him because he's gun-shy. Loud noise sends him running."

Wren sat still as the hound advanced slowly, sniffing the air as he did so. His and Geordy's scent didn't scare him off, for he edged to the end of the porch and turned his body so he could both eat and keep an eye on them.

The display of dominance from Rob Roy made him bite down hard to keep a laugh inside. The coon marched across the porch and, when the dog backed off from his feeding dish, grabbed a handful of the kibble and returned to his own bowl.

He glanced at Geordy to find him shaking with silent mirth.

"Well," Geordy whispered, "Rob Roy just told the hound whose territory this is, but I'm impressed with his kindness in allowing the dog to eat. The poor bugger is verra thin. I think he's been on his own for quite some time."

Geordy turned his attention to uncorking the bottle of bourbon and pouring it into two man-sized cut-crystal glasses.

As he accepted the glass offered, Geordy asked, "I want to propose a toast, if I may?" He followed his roommate's lead and stood gazing out over the valley as green leavers turned to gold in the setting sun.

"To Kirsten Campbell MacEwen, may God keep you in his love, and I thank you for all the love you gave me."

He didn't say anything, but raised his glass and nodded as he followed Geordy's example by taking a sip of bourbon, and what a sip. He never tasted anything so smooth, or seen any other bourbon so deeply colored. The bourbon intrigued his palate with a hint of something he couldn't identify. When Geordy resumed his seat, he turned and picked up the bottle to see the brand. He found no label at all.

"Who makes this? This is the best bourbon I ever tasted."

Geordy sat back in his chair and held his glass up to the light to study the deep-brown liquor. "I think Campbell Dhu would be a good name for this bourbon."

"Dew, like in the morning mist, or dew like that strangely fluorescent-green soft drink?"

"Nay, not D-E-W, Dhu as in D-H-U, for black. I made this the summer before I left for university, and salted ten bottles away for a special occasion. I guess my presence here today qualifies as special, although I wish I could have waited for a happier one."

"Well, I'm honored to share this magnificent bourbon with you, happy occasion or not."

Geordy took another sip and continued. "The summer I turned seventeen I moved into the cabin. I wanted my independence badly enough to put up with the inconvenience of stepping over and around construction materials. One morning I decided to poke around in the barn's loft."

"I don't know if you noticed the barn when we drove in, but the cantilever design was a popular model when my mother's great, great grandfather built it in 1870. We passed by it too quickly for you to notice the wide loft overhanging the open, bottom portion. The loft stored grains and hay, and the large open bottom contains log cribs and stalls for livestock, with enough area left over to store farm machinery. Some of the logs used to face my cabin came from the ones stored there."

"Yeah, you're right, I only caught a quick glance as we drove in. I've never seen a barn shaped like that."

"The barn backs up to a hillside, and, like the watercolor in my bedroom, something about the loft's proportions bugged me. I discovered what after tapping on the back wall. I found a false wall, and once I figured out how to pry the thing open, I discovered the back wall of the loft opened into a natural cave."

He leaned forward in his chair and laughed. "This is beginning to sound like a Hardy Boys adventure novel."

Geordy sported an ear-splitting grin as he nodded his head. "Yeah, very much so, with me just turned seventeen, on my own, and now the discoverer of a secret room. Naturally, I ran and got a flashlight, and played Lord Carnarvon walking into King Tut's tomb for the first time."

"Please, tell me you found treasure. I'll be disappointed if you didn't find anything but moldering hay."

"I found my great, great, great maternal grandfather's Pennsylvania long rifle, hidden just inside the entrance. As I walked farther into the cave, I found a large room with nothing but empty barrels and cork-stoppered glass bottles. After more thorough exploration, I also found a number of ledgers with my great, great granddad's notes on how to make whiskey, the original cost of the grain, and the cost per bottle, and his customer list. The copper still sat in the farthest room, and vented to the outside through a natural gap in the cave ceiling."

Wren rubbed his hands together with enthusiasm. "What a great find."

"As you'd expect, I couldn't help myself after that. I had to try and duplicate the process. I mean, I had the major parts already in the cave, the barrels, the still, the recipe. I needed grain, and being summer corn, barley, and rye were in plentiful supply. I made enough to fill two barrels, and I let them age in the cave after I filled ten of the bottles to take to the house." Geordy chuckled. "I had the same sensation of wanting to keep a weather eye out for the revenue man like old moonshiners did. The law still frowns on distilling hard spirits without a license, but I absolved myself of any wrongdoing with this science experiment by not selling or producing another batch. And I have to say, aging made this bourbon a damned fine sipping whiskey.

He held his glass out when Geordy offered another pour. "What did your uncle have to say about your foray into distilling?"

"He doesn't know. This has been a secret until now, but one of these days, I'm going to use that ledger to write a book. My great, great, great grandda passed the skill down to his son, and his son, et cetera, and the Campbells stopped their whiskey business sometime before World War II, but before that happened, the Campbell men kept their families fed by using the liquor to bring in cash money, and to trade for food during the Depression. There is even a note in there from one of the customers, a United States Senator, who swore President Hoover found Campbell bourbon to be the best he ever tasted. And that letter is a rare historical gem, since the date puts it in the middle of the Prohibition era."

They sat in companionable silence, sipping the Campbell Dhu until Geordy glanced at his watch. "Come on, the chicken and green beans should be warm enough by now."

"Chicken? You were never out of my sight, so when did you cook?"

"I didn't, my Aunt Euna made the chicken last night and had Conall leave it in the fridge. She also made potato salad, green beans with bacon, and cornbread to go with."

"I'm suddenly drooling with hunger. Let's eat."

Wren groaned and rubbed his distended stomach when he left the table. "God, my brother Ross is a gourmet cook, but he's got nothing on your aunt Euna. That fried chicken could win a blue ribbon at the state fair, and cornbread is something I wouldn't normally order, but I polished off three huge pieces."

After helping Geordy clean up the kitchen, he returned to the back porch and stretched out in the hammock hanging between two of the porch pillars. The faint gleam of light from two glowing eyes, made him think Rob Roy kept him company, but, no, the coon hound had returned.

When Geordy opened the back door, he whispered, "Guess what, you have a dog. The hound decided to stay."

After Mountain eased his bulk into a chair near him, he pointed to the dog and asked, what are you going to call him?"

Geordy rubbed his chin in thought and began to run through Scottish names. He disagreed with his choice of names. "Hey, I didn't major in history, or animal husbandry, but I don't think coon hounds are Scottish. Why don't you give him an American name? How about Davy Crockett or Daniel Boone?"

Geordy tilted his head to consider the suggestion, and his teeth flashed white in the darkness when he smiled. "Aye, Davy Crockett is a good choice. He served as a US Congressman representing Tennessee."

Wren fixed his attention on the hound and called, "Hey, Crockett." He almost fell out of the hammock when the dog sat up and bayed. "Well there you go; the hound chooses Crockett."

His attention was caught by mysterious, flickering lights, and he flew out of the hammock. "Lightning bugs. I forgot these things existed. Wow, there must be a gazillion of them. Gotta catch one." He stopped his pursuit, briefly, when Geordy ribbed him.

"Maybe we should change your team name from Blade to Peter Pan."

"Peter Pan? Why Peter Pan?"

"Because I don't think you ever grew up."

"Oh come on, you stodgy Scot, join me. Don't worry, I won't pull their bottoms off to use them for chemlights, but you gotta admit, they're fun to catch and release."

Geordy took the dare and danced around the yard with him to pursue the glowing insects, who offered brief illumination as they swirled around them. Crockett chose to remain on the porch, safe from wayward feet.

Chapter Ten

It was hard saying goodnight to Wren and turn off the lights after he headed to the guest room. Now something else was hard—and he didn't mean difficult, he meant rigid. The faint moonlight coming through his bedroom window illuminated the tent he made of the sheet. It was going to be a long night of tossing and turning, wishing he could toss his self-imposed code of conduct out the window to fly away like the lightning bugs.

He didn't drop off to sleep until sometime after 3:00 a.m., the last glowing numerals he remembered seeing from the clock on his nightstand. His eyes pinged open at 5:30 a.m., and he rolled out of the sack. No sense just lying there.

Recalling his roommate's rousting him out of bed on a weekend for a trip to the dojo, and then again the next morning to apply balm to his sensei-inflicted bruises, Geordy thought waking Blade up to accompany him on a run only fair. He pulled on a pair of running shorts and sneakers and headed for the guest room.

Feeling like a voyeur, but unable to stop the urge, Geordy eased open the guest room door and got the reward he hoped for. Wren lay on his back with the sheet covering his torso from the waist down. At rest the man was a veritable feast for someone who made a practice of denying himself. From his straight, aquiline nose, to his high cheekbones and lips neither too narrow nor full, he was hard to ignore. Maybe the man upstairs heard him when he recited his perfect mate requirements and fashioned one Wren de Lassy to go.

Blade stirred, and Geordy rushed into action before his guest awakened and found him drooling in the doorway.

Advancing, Geordy grabbed the corner of the sheet, ripped it off, and got the surprise of his life. A yelp was startled from him when his roommate used some sort of martial arts move to bring him down on the bed and straddled him. He blinked up at his less than happy battle buddy.

"Uh, I was coming to wake you for a run."

Wren glanced at the clock, now showing 5:45 a.m., and shook his head. "Not only no, hell no. I'm not getting out of this bed, especially when I have such a warm, firm mattress to lie on."

He stretched full-length over Geordy and nuzzled his neck.

Geordy's mind was still assessing the unexpected outcome. The fact his guest was completely nude and lying on top of him, bare chest to bare chest, caused more than a few blown circuits. In the absence of rationality, he went with pure reaction and ran his hands from the nape of Wren's neck to cup his buttocks and press him into his rampant erection. Wren echoed his groan, and Geordy flipped him over so he was on top. He pressed the advantage and kissed the sleep from Wren's eyes. And, at that precise moment, his cousin Aengus spoiled paradise.

"What the fuck is that?" Wren escaped Geordy's embrace and sat up.

Geordy joined him at the side of the bed and answered. "That would be my cousin Aengus proving the notes of a bagpipe can be heard three miles away. He's been playing the pipes since he was ten and plays each morning at 6:00 a.m. People in Beltrees don't bother setting their alarm clocks because they know the pipes will wake them promptly at six."

Wren grinned. "I would think a rooster would be kinder on the ears."

Geordy returned his wry grin. "I wish Aengus *was* a rooster because wringing his neck sounds like a marvelous idea. Come on, pull a pair of shorts on, and come running with me."

"And what am I supposed to do with this?" Wren stood and blatantly stroked his erection.

Rules be damned, go for it, just go for it, his libido urged. Geordy moved close and kissed Wren's temple as he reached down and cupped his package. "You do what I'm going to do, ignore it. Go get your sneakers on, I'll meet you on the porch."

The instant response of, "You're a cruel, cruel man, Geordy Campbell," had him chuckling all the way through the house.

As they ran along the stream, Crockett burst from the woods and circled them, wagging his long tail like he'd waited months for someone to run with.

Blade pointed and laughed when the dog put his nose to the ground and began following the scent of something in an erratic, jagged pattern.

"I think whatever creature Crockett is following must've been drunk to leave that trail."

Geordy snorted at the observation. "I better call him off before he trees whatever it is. Coon hounds have excellent cold noses."

"Not to sound like a wise ass, but don't all dogs have cold noses?"

"By cold nose I mean they can follow a scent trail that's gone cold. Not all dogs can do it." Geordy whistled, and Crockett bounded over, the trail forgotten in favor of loping along in front of them, and lifting his leg to mark the occasional tree, blade of grass, rock, twig, and any other stationary object that would hold his scent to proclaim his ownership of the territory.

Geordy gave Blade a fist bump and declared, "Now for the best part of the run," and took the two-lane road that led to his uncle's house. It was a steady slog uphill, and they both saved their breath until they reached the clearing around his uncle's place.

"My aching calves! Tell me, is there any level ground at all in Tennessee? We've been running uphill for the last hour," Wren complained as he bent over to relieve the stitch in his side."

Geordy considered the question. "Aye, there might be some, but none on this property." He turned around and started back down the steep road. "We're eating dinner at my uncle's this evening, so I'll wait until then to introduce you to my aunt, but you'll meet my uncle and cousins when we have lunch at the pub."

Since he'd yet to get his wind back, his question came out in a series of puffs. "What do your uncle and cousins do for a living?"

Geordy, used to the steep terrain, answered with no noticeable shortness of breath, and he shot him the finger by way of comment on his aerobic superiority.

"My uncle and cousins run the local watering hole. I guess you could call them publicans. But my cousins also have moneymaking hobbies on the side. Aengus is a piper and plays at weddings, funerals, and anywhere else a piper is needed. He's also a master woodworker. Most of the furniture in my place, and my uncle's, was made by Aengus.

"Caillin is a potter and weaver, and he's won awards in both. He does a brisk business on the Internet. He made the dinnerware we used last night. My cousin Conall is a farrier. He has a real way with the horses. I don't believe he's ever been kicked while shoeing one."

Geordy pointed to Crockett, who was lounging on the porch with his tongue lolling. "Ah, the hound beat us back. Let's clean up, and I'll make breakfast."

***

The shower in the guest bath was a work of art. Multiple jets and large enough to fit two grown men quite nicely. He surmised the stall's fieldstone slab lining was Geordy's handiwork as well.

Just thinking his name made him imagine the two of them soaping each other's backs, and he tilted his head down to find his dick onboard with the idea. *Down, boy. Let's show some restraint here*. He finished off his shower with a cold rinse.

The smell of frying bacon and coffee led him directly to the kitchen, and he pulled out one of the barstools and remained quiet as Geordy slung cast iron skillets around like a pro.

"Who taught you to cook? These fried eggs are done just the way I like them."

Geordy handed him a basket of fresh-baked scones and pulled out another stool to sit next to him on the island.

"My mother and my aunt taught me. After I got kicked out, it was either learn to cook or starve to death if I wanted to live on my own."

He took a large bite of the scone after slathering it with butter and a dollop of the black jam Geordy put out. "Mmmm, these scones are good. What kind of jam is this?"

Geordy picked up the canning jar and twirled it around in front of him. "Elderberry. My mother put it up last year from the bushes growing at the back of my property."

He added another dab of jam to the remains of his second scone and moved it around in his mouth as he considered. "I'm guessing this is what you flavored your bourbon with."

He saw the surprise and confirmation of his guess in Geordy's eyes.

"You have a verra good palate. Not many people would've been able to name it. Yes, the summer I did my little science experiment, there was a bumper crop of elderberries, and I mashed them up and let the juice soak into the insides of the barrels and dry before charring them. In the course of my research, I read some distillers used barrels that previously held Spanish sherry to flavor the whiskey, but I didn't have any of those, so I used the humble elderberry. I think it's the elderberry juice that makes the bourbon such a dark color."

"An excellent choice to season your barrels. Your Campbell Dhu would sell well once people sampled it." He left off praising Geordy when he noticed the blush creeping up his neck. He changed the subject. "What's on the agenda for this morning?"

Geordy glanced at the wall clock. "Are you up for some fishing? The stream has a few deep pools that may or may not contain some trout. Let's delay lunch so the pub is less crowded when we get there."

"Fishing sounds great. My brother's friend, Troll, er, Colonel Trollinger, if you aren't privileged to call him by his team name, has a cabin in the Pennsylvania mountains where we hunt deer and fish when he invites us. So what kind of fish do you catch around here?"

"There's brown trout and some bass in the stream. Let me fetch the poles."

When Geordy returned he had two poles, a creel and net, and a .45 strapped to his waist, and he couldn't resist it. He pointed at Geordy's sidearm. "Are the fish in Tennessee that hard to land?"

"Verra funny, Blade. The pistol is for the black bears. Berries are plentiful this time of year, but a bear is an omnivore that might think fighting you for a fat brown trout beats berry picking."

Three hours and four decent-sized brown trout later, Geordy accepted the last filleted fish from Blade and added it to the creel. "We'll have these for dinner tomorrow, but now we need to clean up and head into town. The lunch crowd should be thinning, so my uncle and cousins will have more time to visit."

***

He was impressed. The bar or pub as Geordy called it, actually had a wooden sign hanging from an ornate wrought iron support proclaiming it to be the Scammered Scot. The inside was designed to be welcoming and cozy, just like he imagined a true English or Scottish pub would be. He immediately recognized Aengus's handiwork in the Celtic design carved in the front of the long bar and the backs of the chairs.

They had taken but one step past the threshold when a cry of "Cousin Geordy," went up and they were surrounded by three extremely tall men. He had to back off and crane his neck to see the men's eyes. He stepped away and observed the three cousins give Geordy bear hugs and whisper their condolences into his ears. Geordy spoke the truth when he said the Campbells treated him as a true part of the family.

When the private moment was over, he took in the impressively tall black-haired Scots and nudged Geordy. "You could've warned me the Campbells were related to Rubeus Hagrid." His remark made the tallest cousin roar with laughter and thwack him on the back, sending him belly first into the bar.

"A Harry Potter reference. I like it. Who's your friend, Geordy?"

Geordy made the introductions. "Blade, uh, Wren de Lassy, this is my Cousin Aengus, and to his right is my Cousin Caillin, and to his left is my Cousin Conall."

He was developing a crick in his neck, but he gauged their heights to be 6'8" for Aengus, 6'7" for Caillin, and judging by the way Conall topped Geordy by at least two inches, 6'6" for Conall.

Before he could think of the potential consequence, he offered his hand. Thank God he was used to pain, because right now he wanted to roll on the floor holding his mangled hand after three exuberant handshakes from the powerfully built cousins.

"Are you a Marine like Geordy?" Conall's question earned him a brotherly shove from Caillin.

"Of course he is, ya wee daftie. Do you not see his haircut? No one else but a Marine wears it that short."

Aengus inserted himself between his brothers and averted further physical contact. "Come along to the family table and have some lunch. I see the Marine Corps is still starving you. Cousin, you've lost ten pounds since last I saw you. We've Ma's shepherd's pie on the menu. Shall I fetch it?"

Geordy turned to him, "My Aunt Euna makes an excellent shepherd's pie. You'll like it."

Before he could do more than nod, Blade found himself seated at a large table with a Reserved sign on it, and staring down at a piping hot plate of pie and a large mug of ale. Mountain didn't lie—the pie was excellent and brimming with fresh vegetables and a rich, creamy sauce. Even ale tasted better than he remembered.

His and Geordy's enjoyment of the meal came to an end when a guttural curse disturbed the peace.

"What the fuck are you doing here? I told Aillig to keep you away.

You dishonor your mother by your presence, and I'll not stand for it."

Blade slowly put his fork down and waited to see what Mountain would do. He stood when his roommate pushed himself away from the table.

Once again Aengus took charge. "Now, Uncle Evin, keep your temper behind your teeth. This is a public place, and such language is not permitted."

Aengus turned to Geordy. "I'm sorry, Cuz. I thought your da had left. He and Da were in the office arranging for the wake to be held here on Thursday."

Geordy shook his head and gave a motion with his hand to say it didn't matter.

Evin MacEwen, however, wasn't about to be brushed off. "You are an abomination, and the reason your mother is lying cold as a stone in the funeral home. You don't belong here."

Geordy turned ashen and rocked back at the hateful accusation, and then drew himself up to his full height to glare down at the shorter man. "I will pay my respects to my mother, old man. You gave up the right to command me when you cast me out of the family."

Evin MacEwen was a barrel-chested, faded-ginger-haired man, who, Blade noted, appeared more than capable of slinging large slabs of stone around without much of a problem, but he went on alert when the man's face suffused with anger, and his large workworn hands curled into fists at the Mountain's come back.

"And I'm glad I did. I won't have the MacEwen name soiled by your deviant ways."

His martial arts training gave him the advantage of recognizing the beginning of an attack, and he caught and held Geordy back when he charged. "Remember you are a Marine Raider, Mountain," he urged in a low voice as he tightened his grip when Geordy started to fight off his hold.

Geordy went still when Aengus, Caillin, and Conall added their bodies to the scrum, and a deep voice spoke with clear authority.

"Enough, Evin. I'll forgive you the language this time because you had a few too many drinks to assuage your grief over losing your wife. Now, take yourself off, and I don't want to see you back here until you can be civil. But know this, I did convey your wishes to Geordy, but I agree with him. He has the right to pay his respects to his mother. I would hope you and your sons do not turn my sister's funeral into a public family feud, but you'll get one if you continue to publicly condemn my nephew."

After Evin MacEwen slammed out of the pub, Aillig Campbell eased his white-faced nephew back into his seat and turned to Wren with outstretched hand.

"So, you're Geordy's friend. Welcome to Beltrees and my pub. I'm sorry you had to witness that, but grieving family members aren't always mindful of their words."

Aillig turned to Caillin and ordered, "Bring the bourbon, Son. I think we can all use a dram to take the sour taste from our mouths."

He went easy on the bourbon in case his services were needed as a driver because he hadn't missed the way Geordy's hand shook as he lifted his glass and downed the generous shot of whiskey. But Mountain surprised him by limiting himself to just two drinks, and he said so as they headed back to Geordy's house after promising to show up for dinner that evening.

As he turned on the road leading to the cabin, he turned his head to where his roomie was slumped against the door. "You know, Mountain, your ability to control your temper is downright scary at times. I thought an entire Raider team was going to be needed to hold you after what your father said to you."

Geordy straightened and shook his head, ruefully. "So did I. His tirade about having a gay son is nothing new, but that comment about me being the cause of my mother's death hit me hard and I started to lose it. Thanks for having my back, Blade. I wouldn't be able to attend the funeral if I was locked up for giving the bastard what he so richly deserves."

Geordy stared out the windshield and asked a rhetorical question. "Why is it only a parent knows how to deliver a mortal wound to their child with mere words?"

Wren flashed back to his last conversation with his mother, and understood the awful, absolute truth of what Geordy referred to. "I don't know, Mountain, but they can and do."

Always able to think on his feet, he asked as soon as he stopped the truck in front of Geordy's cabin, "Hey, show me the barn. I want to see the still and the barrels."

Geordy, who'd fallen silent after his last question, merely shrugged and headed to the barn.

He didn't want a tour so much as a way of keeping his teammate from brooding, so he listened and asked questions about the distilling process. It impressed him how the original Campbell moonshiner used a false wall and the mountain's natural foliage to camouflage his illegal distilling.

As they left the barn, he spotted the logs in the crib below the cantilevered loft and suggested, "If you want, I'll help you split and stack some of those logs for next winter's fires."

Damn, Geordy thought that was a wonderful idea, and both of them were hefting axes and splitting logs before he could think of a less strenuous way to keep his hurt, grieving friend occupied.

He wanted to shout "hallelujah" when Geordy glanced at his wristwatch, an eternity of forced labor later, and declared it was time to feed the critters, catch the sunset, and enjoy a wee nip. Wren fervently hoped the fire in the bourbon would have a backfire effect and kill the fire in his loins at the sight of a shirtless, sweat-dewed Geordy standing with hip cocked and an axe resting lightly in his hands. *Gah, macho fantasy much?*

Fresh from a shower, and having no idea what the appropriate dress for dining at the Campbell's would be, he knocked on Geordy's bedroom door, and re-tucked the towel around his waist when it started to slip. Geordy appeared at his bedroom door similarly attired, and his Adam's apple bobbed when he swallowed hard. He rushed into speech. "Are we dressing for dinner? I brought some khaki pants and a polo shirt, but that's as fancy as I packed, except for my Dress Blues."

Geordy didn't answer right away. Instead, his eyes roamed from the top of his head, to the towel around his waist, and hung there a moment before answering his question.

"Nay, your jeans and T-shirt will be fine. My uncle and cousins will be coming straight from work, so they won't have time to change into something dressier."

"Got it." He turned around to head back to his room, but was pulled into Geordy's arms. He tilted his head back for easier access when Geordy's lips grazed his neck.

"You're a good friend, Blade. I know you kept me from brooding this afternoon, and you probably have the blisters to prove it."

He kept his body loose in Geordy's embrace when all he wanted to do was spin around and confront his teammate. He ground out,

"No problem," rather than yelling, "Fuck friend, I want to be your lover, Geordy, confusing-the- hell-out-of-me-with-mixed-signals, Campbell."

He was still so wound up, he almost snapped the shoelace on his sneaker as he finished dressing and went to find Geordy. Geordy handed him two bottles of Campbell Dhu when he found him in the great room.

"Here, take these. I'm going to fess up to moonshining. I want to drink another toast to my mother and see what my uncle thinks of my distilling attempt."

He tried to hang back when they entered the Campbell residence and stepped aside to let Geordy greet his aunt, but quickly found himself wrapped in a hug and praised for being a good enough friend to stand by Geordy at such a sad time.

Totally flustered to find himself being fussed over, he fended Geordy's aunt off with a compliment. "You have a lovely house, ma'am. I see Aengus's talent in the furniture, and I'm guessing the brightly woven fabrics and outstanding pottery is Caillin's work."

Euna relieved him of the whiskey and shooed them out to the barn. "Speaking of work, Geordy, you can take that bag of apples on the counter out to Conall and help him feed the wee beasties while I finish preparing dinner."

The aforementioned barn was huge. It made Geordy's seem like a lean-to. He followed Geordy past open stalls until they found Conall in the last one, measuring grain into a feeder. Conall grinned at them and started to talk smack.

"Good timing as always, Cuz. I just finished mucking out the stalls and putting in the feed."

When Geordy grinned and held up the bag of apples, Conall

handed a tin can full of dried corn kernels to Wren.

"Since this is your first time to see them, you get the honor of calling the beasties to dinner. Go to the end of the barn and stand to the side of the opening and shake the can. Make sure you aren't standing in the opening because they don't let anyone stand between them and their food."

The grins on the Campbell faces clued him in to this being some sort of test, but he was game. He marched to the door and rattled the can.

"Ach, put some arm into it," Conall urged."

He complied with vigor, and froze as the ground began to shake. "Oh my God," was the only thing he had time to yell before plastering himself to the side of the barn as four, four-legged, furry behemoths came charging his way.

Hugging the wall, Wren waited as the overly large blue roan draft horses headed for their stalls and began to munch on what was in their feeders. *Wee fucking beasties, indeed*, was the only coherent thought in his head at the moment.

"What are they? They aren't Clydesdales."

Geordy spoke up. "They're Belgian Percherons. Percherons are taller than Clydesdales, and these particular ones are tall for Percherons. Here, why don't you give the baby an apple?"

Blade could only shake his head in amazement at the four enormous heads hanging out of the stalls with ears twitching in curiosity. "Uh, which one of these earth movers is the baby?"

Conall pointed to the stall nearest to his cousin. "That would be the one who will steal the whole bag of apples from Geordy if he moves just an inch closer."

Wren peered at the tiny apple Geordy handed him and then at

the large muzzle of the Percheron and then back at Geordy. He didn't bother getting upset when Geordy laughed, because he could tell the fear of having his entire arm swallowed was writ large on his face. It was Conall who reassured him by reaching into the sack and feeding one to the horse in front of him.

"These beasties are verra gentle. They don't bite, but make sure to flatten the palm of your hand so they don't accidentally pinch you."

He did as Conall bade and laughed when the apple disappeared in a flash. He was knocked back several paces when Baby nuzzled him for another.

"They are amazing. What do you use them for, plowing?"

"They are draft horses, but they are also good for jumping. We use them as war horses, the original purpose for which they were bred. Each year the Campbells attend clan gatherings in the spring, and Ren faires in the summer. My brothers and I, and Geordy, when he's able, participate in the jousting. These horses also pull the wagon we use to carry our equipment and goods we've made to sell."

Geordy added, "And hay wagons at Halloween, sleigh rides at Christmas, the 4th of July parade float. The Campbell Percherons are well-known in Beltrees. This four-in-hand team gives the Budweiser Clydesdales some real competition."

A hollow thud reverberated in the stable and Conall laughed and pointed to the last stall on the right. "Uh-oh, Cuz, you made Baron angry by paying too much attention to Bruce. Go give him some sugar before he kicks down his stall."

Wren had seen the size of the hooves as the horses thundered past him and recalled Geordy telling him Conall was a farrier. He couldn't imagine being kicked by a horse with a hoof big enough to wear a shoe the size of a garbage can lid, and said so as the three of them walked back to the house.

"Ah, the Percherons have verra sweet dispositions. They can be playful but are seldom ornery." Conall nudged Wren and winked. "And I have verra quick reflexes."

An honest-to-gosh dinner bell sounded, and Conall rubbed his hands together. I'm about as hungry as one of the horses. Come on. Let's go in and grab a chair before my brothers clean the table like a swarm of locusts."

He found himself seated between Mountain and Conall on one side of the long oak table, and facing Aengus and Caillin, while Aillig claimed the head and Aunt Euna the foot. As he studied the Campbells, it struck him that at six feet he was one of the smallest people in the room. Even Geordy's Aunt Euna stood eye-to-eye with him. There had to be something in the Beltrees water to grow such large people. He forgot to engage his filter for he blurted, "I feel like the lone aspen in a forest of giant oaks."

Damn, the dinner conversation came to a screeching halt, and six pairs of eyes landed on him to assess his statement. Aunt Euna saved him from terminal mortification. Or he thought she had as she began to tell him of a trip to Colorado.

"You know, Aillig and I took a vacation out to Colorado just last fall, and the mountains were beautiful. The aspens had just changed into glorious gold and fairly shimmered when you saw their leaves rippling in the breeze.

"You're a handsome lad, Wren. You make a bonnie aspen."

His face began to flame at the compliment. He had no experience with being part of a large family and fussed over by a mother. The interaction between the sons and parents was also foreign to him. He never, as Caillin and Aengus did with their parents, served his parents before himself. He eased up on the guilt a little when he remembered his mother never cooked anything that didn't come in a microwavable aluminum tray, and his dad never came to the table to eat if there was a good sporting even on TV. The Campbells were his idea of a model family, and, for a brief moment, he regretted never having had the experience of one.

Euna's compliment returned him to the present and made a blush warm his cheeks. It turned to flaming red when Caillin stopped eating long enough to lean forward and study him closely. His comment of, "Oh look, Ma, your bonnie aspen just changed color," made Geordy laugh and squeeze his thigh under the table.

Geordy did warn him about his aunt's penchant for feeding Marines a proper portion, but he failed to tell him how damned good the food would be. The barbecue ribs, fresh corn on the cob, homemade coleslaw, and biscuits just kept coming, and he had no idea where he was storing it all. To give the fork-to-mouth action a rest, he asked a question.

"I see you wear kilts to work in. Aren't you afraid of flashing the customers if you have to bend over?"

Aengus fielded the question and stood to demonstrate. "These are not real kilts, these are the modern urban version more suitable to being washed frequently. And we're not worried about flashing because a true Scot only flashes if there's a strong breeze, and we work inside. Also, Ma makes us wear black spandex boxer briefs so we won't get arrested for decent exposure. It's shocking how many of our female customers try to lift our kilts for a wee peek."

"Don't you mean indecent exposure?"

Aengus winked at Wren. "Nay. When the Good Lord was handing out cocks and balls, the Campbells got their fair share of both, so anyone lifting our kilts gets a verra decent exposure."

Geordy chimed in. "Too bad you were at the back of the line when he was handing out brains."

Everyone, including Aengus, roared at their cousin's jibe.

After dinner, Aillig and Euna retired to the back, screened-in porch, and he pitched in to help the cousins clear the table and load the dishwasher. Geordy washed and oiled the cast iron skillets and set them in the warm oven to season, and he made a note to self to tell Ross how to do it.

After drying his hands, Geordy picked up the two bottles of whiskey and motioned to Aengus to bring glasses. "I want to propose a toast to my mother, and I want you to tell me what you think of this bourbon.

When Geordy finished pouring the bourbon, he raised his glass and said, "To Kirsten Campbell MacEwen. A loving mother, a good sister, and a loyal wife. May God keep her in his eternal embrace."

Wren echoed the response of "To Kirsten," and waited as the Campbells sampled Geordy's bourbon. Their response was instantaneous and positive.

Aillig picked up one of the bottles and gave Geordy a questioning look when he didn't find a label. "What brand of bourbon is this? I need to stock it in the pub."

He held out his glass for another sample, and then held it up to study the color. "I don't think I've ever seen a bourbon this dark."

Aengus also held his glass out, and his cousin refilled it and the rest of the glasses as well. "I know you didn't buy it in Beltrees, because there'd be a run on the ABC store."

"Nay, I didn't buy it at all, I made it."

Blade grinned at how quiet the back porch became, and waited for the questions to start.

Aillig drew closer to his nephew. "What do you mean you made it?"

Geordy turned to him for help, but he grinned and said, "You're on your own, Mountain. Time to fess up."

And so Mountain told the entire story to a rapt audience of Campbells, and finished with, "I named it Campbell Dhu for its dark color."

Caillin asked, "How much did you make, and when do you plan to make more?"

Euna entered the fray. "Caillin, moonshining is illegal. You need a license to distill liquor. There will be no more Campbell Dhu once the two barrels Geordy made are gone, and those will be consumed privately by this family."

Aillig, the publican, started to protest, but thought better of it when Euna leveled a speaking look at him. Instead, he turned to his nephew and said, "If you ever decide to quit being a Marine, you have a real calling for bourbon making. I know your recipe would become Beltrees' preferred drink."

Aillig tilted his head to Euna, who nodded back, and he crossed to a side table and retrieved a bulky envelope. "Geordy, I want to give this to you before you head home. This letter is from your mother. She left it in my care because she didn't think Evin would give it to you."

When Geordy accepted it, Aillig continued. "I don't know what's in it, but I think my sister wrote it as a sort of contingency. And now I want to discuss the timetable for saying our goodbyes. The viewing will be on Wednesday from six to eight at the funeral home. I arranged for you to visit at five. I hope you don't think I'm ashamed of you being here, but I would like to send my sister off in a dignified manner, and I don't believe Evin MacEwen and his sons remember the definition of the word dignified. I know you want to pay your respects, so this was the easiest and least confrontational way to do so that I could come up with. I hope you aren't offended."

"Nay, Uncle. I thank you for your consideration in the matter. What of the funeral? Do you think my attendance will cause a disruption?"

"The funeral will be at ten o'clock on Thursday. Disruption or not, you have every right to attend, but it saddens me to say I couldn't get your father to let you be one of the pallbearers. You will stand with us at the graveside, and if Evin thinks about making a scene, he'll find himself gagged and bound until the priest has said the last blessing over your mother. You are a Campbell, and I demand you be treated with the respect due the Campbells."

And with that, Geordy said his goodbyes. Wren tried to stand off to the side, but Caillin grabbed him, and he was hugged and kissed like a card-carrying member of the family. Apparently, Campbells, once they decided to like you, weren't afraid to demonstrate it.

Once home, he sensed Mountain's quietness was a sign he wanted to be alone to read his mother's letter, so he excused himself on the pretext of wanting to read until he digested the massive amount of food he consumed this evening.

"Good night, Geordy. I think your family is awesome. Sometimes choosing the family you want, rather than the family you were born with, can turn out well. What you have with your aunt, uncle, and cousins makes me envious."

"I agree, sometimes your second choice is the better one. Not a day goes by that I don't thank God for the Campbells standing by me.

Good night, Blade."

Chapter Eleven

Geordy's hands shook as he ran them along the length of the legal-sized envelope. This would be the last time he ever received a letter from his mother, and for that reason he didn't want to open it. The thought, if he never read it, it wouldn't be the last made him grimace at the skewed logic, and he took a sip of the drink he poured himself and inserted his thumb under the flap to reveal the letter inside. It was dated the previous year.

My Dear Geordy,

I'm writing this letter in the strange hope you never need to read it. I would like to say this in person, but after a trip to the hospital because of a stroke, I reconsidered. Keep your Scots' temper down, Son, for I asked my brother not to tell you of it because you are deployed to someplace far away, and I don't want you to worry about me. The work you do can be dangerous, and I won't have you distracted worrying about me. But the wee stroke reminded of my mortality, so I'm leaving this in case God doesn't grant me the time to express my feelings to you, face to face.

I'm sorry for many things, Geordy. I'm sorry your father is so intransigent in his beliefs as to lose the love of a good son. I'm sorry to say, as of this writing, his belief in the rightness of his actions remains unchanged, but I don't intend to stop trying to change his thinking. I'm sorry for the way your brothers so easily forgot all of the wonderful times they had with you, and all the beautifully kind things you did for this family. I'm sorry Beltrees is such a small town because of the way you had to endure the whispers and shunning by people I thought were friends.

Most of all, I'm sorry for not realizing how difficult it would be for you after declaring your feelings. Admitting to your sexuality took courage, but I'm sorry I couldn't make your path a little smoother. The way you maintained your dignity throughout all the condemnation your father and brothers hurled at you made me very proud to call you son. You turned into a strong man, a kind man, despite the injustices served you, and you made your mother very happy to call you her son.

I will leave you with a piece of advice my mother gave me. I hope you heed it better than I did. Never fall in love with a man who lacks music or poetry in his soul. Your father is one such. Oh, don't get me wrong, I love your father, but he possesses no softness, no dream of anything other than to provide for his family. But, in his defense, he at least remembers to tell me he loves me from time to time. And lest you think he somehow duped me into an unsuitable match, I was aware of your father's failings before I married him. He was my choice, even though he lacks the poetry to express the softer emotions.

I think that is why you always got along better with the Campbells than the MacEwens. The Campbells do possess music in their souls. Your cousins produce art and music, and your aunt Euna confided to me that my brother wrote beautiful poetry in his love letters to her while they were courting. My brother chose Euna as a wife because she, too, shows the same spark.

Geordy, although you were forced to guard your heart against those who would wound it with their prejudices and lack of understanding, it is my hope you will one day discover a man who makes your soul sing in harmony with his, and, if you do, don't be so foolish as to let him go.

I close with a request. Geordy, sing me to sleep one last time. Send me on my way to meet my maker with the sweet sound of your voice singing my favorite song.

And here is my final blessing for my lovely son who does possess both music and poetry in his soul:

May the God who made you welcome you home,

But may he grant you a companion to sweeten your life before he does.

All my love,

Ma

P.S. The few worldly goods I want to leave you are packed into my cedar chest. Your father will give it to you, because I made sure to put it in my will. However, I'm enclosing my great grandmother's claddagh ring in this envelope. As your great-great grandma had large strong farmwoman's hands, I'm hoping it will fit your companion when you find him.

Geordy upended the envelope, and the gold ring fell into the palm of his hand. As he caressed the smooth gold, the wall he erected around his emotions to read his mother's letter cracked wide and crumpled as easily as the paper did in his clenched fist.

Blind to everything, he began rocking back and forth sobbing. While he couldn't form words through his sobs, he hoped his mother would hear his thoughts from Heaven.

I'm sorry, Ma, oh Christ I'm so sorry. I left without thinking how difficult it would be for you to stay behind. Forgive me, please forgive me. I found my poet, Ma, but I can't keep him. I can't be the Marine I want to be if I keep him, and I don't think I'm strong enough to make the choice.

Geordy covered his face in embarrassment when Wren, sat down next to him on the sofa, but he didn't resist when he pulled him down to his shoulder and continued to rock him. He needed the comfort of Blade's arms too badly to pull away. He clung to him and cried until he had no more tears left. He started to apologize when his roommate began to disengage, but Wren stopped him.

"Shhh, you have every right to mourn the loss of your mother. Let me take you to bed. You don't need to be alone tonight."

Geordy stood like a zombie and watched Wren drop the jeans he must've pulled on to leave his room. He made no protest when he undressed him and led him to his bed, and he made no demur when he began to stroke him from the nape of his neck to the small of his back and back again, but after several moments he was compelled to ask, "How do you do that?"

"Do what?"

"How can you make your touch so comforting and not at all sexual? I can feel the difference. You are soothing me with no sexual overtones and I.... If I was stroking you like that...."

He stopped touching Geordy to consider his question, and then resumed the stroking as he answered it. "A long time ago, I was taught to give what was truly desired. You don't desire sex tonight, you want comfort, and I am happy to give it to you.

"Who...?"

He lengthened his stroke to curve over Geordy's right buttock. "Relax and concentrate on my touch. Your body doesn't want explanations tonight, it wants soothing. It wants to release all the tight knots and tenseness accrued from holding your grief inside. Be at ease, Geordy. Enjoy my gift of comfort."

Geordy was sound asleep in fifteen minutes.

***

He studied Geordy's face by the moonlight streaming through the window. Mountain appeared relaxed and momentarily worry free, but the handsomeness of the Scot made him groan inwardly and roll face down to keep his erection to himself.

He awoke to bright sunlight, the cat screech of a bagpipe and a heavy weight on his chest and across his thighs. It took him a few moments to assess the strange feeling.

Recalling his rescue of Geordy the night before, he moved enough to see the top of Mountain's head. The man had snuggled close, and it was his head on his chest, and his leg thrown over his thighs that kept him pinned to the mattress, but, thanks to a full bladder, he needed to vacate the bed, now.

Hoping Geordy was too tired to wake when he moved, he wriggled away from him, and eased over the side of the bed. He froze when Geordy gave a murmur of discontent, but breathed easier when the man simply rolled over and cuddled the edge of his pillow.

Blade grabbed his jeans off the floor and headed back to his own bedroom to use the bathroom and cover his bare ass. Now that his bladder was no longer clamoring for relief, and his teeth were brushed, he headed to the kitchen to make a pot of coffee. If he needed a cup, Geordy would need one more. As he plugged in the old-fashioned percolator, the sight of mist rising from the warming ground drew him out the front door to stand on the porch.

Wren leaned against a pillar and studied the phenomenon. It was something he hadn't witnessed since leaving the mountains of Colorado a long time and another lifetime ago. He stood perfectly still to absorb the total calm and solace the mountains exuded.

He lifted a single teardrop from his face to study it. He didn't know what made him let the water works loose. *Liar, liar, pants on fire* his inner child chided. His eyes were leaking because he was confused and, okay, he was afraid. He yearned for what he suspected he would never achieve. He wanted a lasting relationship with Geordy. He wanted the idyllic family life Geordy had with the Campbells, and he wanted to be loved for himself, for being Wren and not a Marine Raider, not a mixed martial arts fighter, not a bladed weapons expert, just plain fucking Wren who loved William Shakespeare, cuddles, and a keen wit to return his teases. He cried because he truly didn't believe those things were written in his stars.

It had taken months of intense psychotherapy to realize, more than anything else, he was afraid of being abandoned yet again. It had happened to him too many times, and he didn't think he possessed the courage to survive if he declared his true feelings and Geordy didn't reciprocate. And the chance he wouldn't was more of a sure bet than a chance. Geordy's opinion on dating fellow Marines had been stated often enough.

He was so into the moment, he jumped when arms surrounded him. He forgot about the tears coursing down his cheeks until Geordy's thumbs wiped them away.

He snuggled into Geordy's chest and wrapped his arms around Geordy's. Being nothing if not quick witted, he offered a plausible excuse for the emotional display. "I forgot what mountains feel like. I grew up in Denver, and my family would go camping in an alpine meadow during the summer, and waiting for the sun to burn off the morning mist made me think I'd awakened in a whole new, fresh world. Until this very moment, I didn't realize how much I missed the mountains."

***

Geordy released Wren from his embrace and took a seat on one of the porch rockers. "Morning is my favorite time of day here as well."

When Blade turned to him, he caught his breath. He'd only fastened the bottom two buttons of his jeans, and the gap at the top showed the smooth expanse of skin between navel and an area he wanted to explore more than anything else this morning, but he owed him a thank you.

"I want to thank you for last night and the night before that. I'm not the easiest person to be around right now, so much so, I'm impressed by the restraint you show in not drop-kicking me across the room for my gloominess."

"That's okay, Geordy, you don't need...." Blade stopped when he waved him off.

"No, I need to say different. You are a good friend, Blade. Despite telling you how I feel about getting close to another Marine, you are compassionate enough to offer comfort without expecting anything in return, and I'm grateful. That being said, I want to be honest with you. I wanted to say this in my bedroom, but you were gone before I woke up."

"What did you want to tell me?"

Geordy reached out and snagged the waistband of Wren's jeans to tug him closer. "I wanted to say, I want you, de Lassy. I want to make love to you. I can't deny it any longer. Sleeping in your arms was the closest to heaven I've been in a verra long time."

Geordy spread the opening of Wren's jeans wider, and put his lips to the smooth flesh and sucked. Wren trembled, and his breath whooshed out when he used the flat of his tongue to lick upward and encircle his navel.

"I want you. Give me permission."

Wren had to clear his throat before speaking, "I want to be wanted very much, but only after you kiss me like that again."

Geordy smiled up at Blade with a Cheshire cat grin. "Like that, do you? Your wish is my command." And he took his time and kissed him thoroughly, only to startle a laugh from him when he stood and threw him over his shoulder in a fireman's carry.

As he carried Blade back to his bedroom and dropped his briefs to join him on the bed, Geordy asked, "Tell me what you like. I want to learn how you like to make love."

Geordy removed Wren's jeans and moved between his legs and sucked on the same spot that had unexpectedly set him off. It was only when he groaned and gave a total body shudder that he backed off and grinned at his handiwork—a quarter-sized love bite graced the area of flesh that had first aroused him this morning. He didn't think Blade would complain about being marked because boxer briefs and jeans would cover the secret.

"Um, that's a good start." He took Geordy's hands and brought them up to his chest. "I like my nipples pinched when you are inside me, I like long, slow strokes, and having your hands anywhere on my dick is a surefire way to please me."

Geordy covered himself with a condom and began to anoint Wren with lubricant but took time to ask, "And what displeases you?"

Wren gave a small huff. "I am not a wham, bam, kind of guy. I give as good as I get, but I resent a selfish lover. I like to cuddle after, and I like to be, um...well, petted is as close as I can describe it. I like feeling your hand running over my body."

Geordy was not a selfish lover, so he listened to his partner's cues, and pinched as hard as he was told to. He tried to be cautious, but Wren lit up like a Roman candle when he gave him what he was asking for, and so he continued.

He discovered making love to Blade never followed a formula, there would be no routine patterns involving rote body thrustings. This morning, the way he writhed beneath him, an image of himself as a cobra tamer made him snicker. He was beginning to think the man was double-jointed, and had the stomach muscles of a belly-dancer, but then he couldn't think another coherent thought for Wren gave a great shout of his name and he echoed it with Wren's.

Remembering Blade's caution about cuddling, Geordy used his last reserve of strength to give him a slow stroke, starting at the nape of his neck and ending around one tight butt cheek, before spooning him. His eyes slammed shut and he hopped a bullet train to oblivion. The aroma of coffee being wafted under his nose brought him back to the station.

Geordy sat up in bed and accepted the mug offered to him. His lips curled into a smile to match Wren's, and then he had to be careful not to spill hot coffee on his bare chest at his outrageous comment.

"Oh. My. God. Geordy Campbell has the moves of a top-notch porn star." Wren leaned down and kissed the bloom of embarrassment off Geordy's cheeks. "Don't worry, it will be our little secret. I meant it as a compliment, Geordy. You are a fantastic, considerate, inventive lover, in case no one ever told you so."

Geordy wanted to rip out his tongue when his question dimmed the celebration. "Wren, are you gay or are you bi? I can't get a read on you."

Geordy put his coffee mug on the nightstand and exited the bed in a rush when his roommate didn't answer, just left the bedroom. Geordy caught up to him right before he entered the guest bathroom. "What did I say? Is that a sensitive subject?"

Wren stared past his shoulder and focused on nothing at all.

"No, not sensitive, but I can't give you an answer because I've never stayed with a man or a woman long enough for them to capture my heart. A long time ago, like your decision to not date fellow Marines in pursuit of a career, I made the decision to keep from falling in love too deeply. As you know, that's an easy decision to make after you get hurt one time too many."

Geordy stood frozen in place as Blade shook his head before reaching out to caress his cheek.

"I'm not lacking in intelligence, Mountain. This is an exception to both our rules. You're vulnerable and, although I restrained myself not to capitalize on your vulnerability, I am very aware we aren't within fifty miles of the flagpole. This is a perfect example of what happens in Tennessee stays in Tennessee. And I'm fine with that because, like you, I'm not eager to deep six my career. I want a few more years in the Corps, and we're both up for E-6 in the next couple of months, and we both want that promotion. Also, I'm not stupid enough to risk my heart to someone as conflicted as me."

For the first time, having his own thoughts and words flung back at him hurt. Geordy could do nothing else but shake his head in silent agreement. In keeping with his mercurial sense of humor, Wren grinned and pinched his cheek.

"Well then, let's make the most of Tennessee, shall we?"

As soon as his roommate verbalized his thought, a horrified expression appeared on his face.

"Oh God, Geordy, I take back what I said about not lacking intelligence. I forgot the sad event that brought us here. Please, please let me take my foot out of my mouth and say, I'm sorry. I can be a selfishly sybaritic bastard at times."

Wren shut up and came into his arms when he opened them, and returned the hug he gave him. Geordy laughed at the sheepish blush on Blade's face when he answered his question of what was on the agenda for today. "Since we've spent the morning riding each other, why don't we spend the afternoon riding the wee beasties. I already know you're a verra fine rider, Wren de Lassy."

***

Wren studied the small saddle perched on the broad back of Bruce with a great deal of trepidation. To stall for time, he asked, "How much does Bruce weigh?"

Geordy, who thought nothing of crossing under Bruce's very tall head to get from one side to the other, answered, "Just a little over 2,000 pounds."

His voice squeaked as he exclaimed, "Why that's a ton of horseflesh. Conall says they can jump, but I can't see how they can do more than walk."

"Oh Percherons are verra strong. They can cover thirty-seven miles in one day at a steady trot." Geordy finished saddling Bruce and let the reins trail on the floor of the stable as he went to fetch another horse to saddle. When he came back leading Baron, the sight of his roommate trying to fend off Bruce made him snicker.

"Uh, Mountain, tell Bruce to behave. He keeps nipping at my pockets, and he actually grabbed the sleeve of my T-shirt and pulled me back when I tried to walk away."

"He'll behave once you give him the apple you put in your pocket. Horses have verra good noses, and they do like their treats."

It was a relief to see an actual mounting block when Geordy led the horses out of the barn. He'd wondered how he was going to reach the stirrups on a horse whose back was even with the top of his head.

Now that Bruce had his treat, he didn't even shrug when he swung his leg over and gathered up the reins. He knew how to ride because Ross insisted he learn when he told him he was going to try out for Marine Special Operations. Ross had learned when he served in the Green Berets. However, he was skeptical how much authority he could command over a fur covered Bradley tank with only thin leather reins to guide it.

But he didn't ponder the thought long, because Geordy mounted Baron and dug his heels in, and gave a great whoop as Baron broke into a gallop, and Bruce followed suit. Fortunately, the two-lane road was wide enough to accommodate the horses who, being paired side-by-side to pull the wagon, insisted on continuing in that vein. God help any car wanting to pass them was Wren's wry thought.

He had to admit it was fun pacing through the woodland scenery, up one hill and down another until Geordy put an end to his idyllic reverie.

"We'd better return and clean the beasties up. We need to eat dinner early since my uncle scheduled me to be at the viewing by five."

Wren's hand rubbed his stomach when he realized they'd skipped lunch. Aunt Euna's dinner had been more than enough calories to carry him until now. However, wiping down, curry-combing, mucking out stalls, and carrying water and grain to feed each of the four horses made him forget last evening's feast. His belly was growling by the time they returned home, and Geordy handed him two food bowls and pointed to the back porch.

"It won't take me long to pan fry the trout we caught yesterday, so we can enjoy a few minutes on the porch. Ah, Rob Roy and Crockett are waiting for us."

"Are you sure they're waiting for us or their food?" Wren took the food bowls and placed them on opposite ends of the porch. Both animals were face down in their respective bowls before either he or Mountain had a chance to sit down. The coon versus hound truce was obviously still in effect.

Since showing up for a viewing smelling like horse would be an affront to the mourners, both he and Geordy hit the showers after cleaning up the kitchen. Wren, wearing khaki pants and a black polo shirt, found Geordy at the kitchen island wrapping a white ribbon around a small spray of flowers.

"What's that for?"

"I'm making it for my mother. She took a cutting from her garden and planted a heather bush out back when I moved in, so I'm adding it to a wee bit of the rosemary from the cooking herbs I grow. Rosemary for remembrance. I'll put it in her casket since I didn't send her any flowers, and I want to...." Geordy's voice faltered.

He snatched Geordy's keys from the counter. "Why don't I drive this evening?" No surprise, the drive to the funeral parlor was a quiet one.

He said several mental thank yous after discovering the viewing room could be made private by closing the sliding doors. He ushered Geordy inside and then closed the doors and stood in front of them. He hoped Mountain's father didn't get wind of this visit, because he didn't think MARSOC condoned brawling in a funeral home, but Evin MacEwen would not disturb his roommate until he finished his goodbye to his mother.

It gave him weird flutters in his belly, but he mentally thanked Geordy's mother for the excellent job she did raising him. He must've zoned out after that because he was a little slow on the uptake when a voice, with an echo, asked, "Who are you?"

The resemblance of the two men to Evin MacEwen clued him in he was being confronted by Geordy's brothers. He didn't think it would work, but he remembered Pacer's order to keep Geordy, and by extension himself, out of jail, so he called up his manners.

"My name's Wren de Lassy."

"Well, de Lassy, move out of the way. We're here to see our mother."

"I'm sorry, the room is presently occupied. You may enter when the room is free."

"And who the hell gave you the authority to determine that? You don't work here."

He guessed it was Ramsey who spoke, but it didn't matter if it was Ramsey or Robbie, they weren't going to interrupt Geordy.

"I'm sorry to make you wait, but it shouldn't be much longer. The room will be free at six, which is the scheduled time of visitation."

The brother who had yet to speak nudged Ramsey. "Don't you remember Da telling us? He's Geordy's catamite."

Catamite? Read a dictionary much? A catamite is a young boy kept by a pederast. I no longer qualify. Wren broadened his stance and prepared himself for whatever these lack brains decided to do. As he focused his attention on the brothers, he realized Geordy didn't bear much of a family resemblance. They were under six feet and had lighter hair with a lot of reddish tones. They were stocky, not overly attractive, and lacked the refinement he saw in Geordy and the rest of the Campbells. It was a good bet Geordy took after his mother.

His concentration on the brothers shifted to Geordy when he came out of the viewing room.

"Ramsey, Robbie, you may go in now."

"You are a nasty piece of work, Geordy. Da told Uncle Aillig to tell you to stay away and yet you still came. Haven't you embarrassed this family enough? You wrecked Da and Ma's marriage, and now you're wrecking her funeral by bringing along one of your boyfriends."

Blade glanced Geordy's way and wanted to tell him if he didn't stop grinding his teeth like that, he'd need a dental appointment when they got back to MARSOC. Geordy's low growl made him focus on the MacEwens once again.

"Your grief has overridden your common sense, Ramsey, so I won't give you want you want. There will be no fighting tonight. However, after the funeral, I'll gladly show you how finished I am with listening to your filthy mouth. And you can consider yourself included in that offer, Robbie."

Wren relaxed when the arrival of Aillig and his sons made the brothers back off. Aengus, Caillin, and Conall flanked Geordy and stared down at the shorter MacEwens.

Geordy and he ran into Aunt Euna on the way out, and, once

again, he got a hug and kiss along with Geordy. All too aware his presence would cause comment among the mourners, Geordy headed straight for his truck.

Like the ride to the funeral home, the ride back was equally quiet, and Wren was at a loss. He lacked previous experience with viewings or funerals. When a teammate was lost in combat, there'd been no casket, only the boots, rifle, and helmet set on display for the team to contemplate and say their private goodbyes. He didn't know what to do or how to treat Geordy. Should he try and cheer him up, sit quietly with him, stick his nose in a book and give him space? Who the fuck knew.

Geordy solved the conundrum for him by handing him a generous glass of bourbon, as he sat on the sofa and patted it in invitation.

"Grab a seat. Now that I've told you about my family, I would like you to tell me about yours. Talk to me. I need the distraction."

Ah shit! What to say? He didn't want to lie to Geordy, but if he actually did tell him about his life and his family, he doubted Geordy would continue to think so highly of him.

He settled for what he imagined every good spy knew. Tell a lie as close to the truth as you can make it.

"I already told you I was born in Denver, Colorado. After I lost my parents, I spent seven years living in Saudi Arabia. Eventually, Ross de Lassy became my legal guardian. At eighteen, I was too old to think of him as a father figure, but brother worked. He brought me back to Alexandria, Virginia, to live with him and his partner." Wren twisted around to face Geordy and grinned. "You might recognize his partner's name, Nels Kirkegaard." The cachet of Nels' name worked. Geordy was instantly distracted from his life story.

"So, how did your brother Ross meet Nels Kirkegaard?"

He set his glass of bourbon on the coffee table and stretched out with his head in Geordy's lap. "My brother took an early retirement from Army Special Forces and opened an inquiry business."

"Inquiry? What exactly is that?"

Blade took a moment to savor Geordy running his hand through his hair before answering. "Ross is very, very good at finding things, people, and secrets. If you want to find someone, find out what someone is up to, or where something was lost, you hire Ross. He was finishing up a case and encountered Nels. He ran into him again the same night at a local Irish pub that is a favorite of his old team's when they are in the DC area. Nels and he hit it off, and he hired Nels to help him remodel his townhomes when he told Ross he was very good at woodworking. I think your cousin Aengus and Nels would get along famously."

"But I searched him on the Internet, and it said Nels is Danish. And what's such a great artist doing handling power tools?"

Wren picked up Geordy's hand and placed it back on his head. He wanted Geordy to continue running his hands through his hair.

"Nels *was* Danish, now he's a naturalized US citizen. And when he worked for Ross, he didn't paint full time. In fact, he never showed his paintings in public at that point. But once he and Ross were married, Ross encouraged him to paint full time."

Geordy's shock at his reference to marriage registered through the stiffening of his posture. "Wait, wait. Ross and Nels are...are...?"

"Gay? Yep. They make a cute couple. The dark-haired Norman and the blond Viking."

"Ah, so I was right."

He craned his head at an awkward angle to see Geordy's face.

"Right about what?"

"The model in the picture I bought isn't a woman but a man."

"Ouch! Why'd you pull my hair?"

"That's for not telling me you knew Nels Kirkegaard. Did he tell you the name of his model?"

Ah fuck, the very thing he wanted to avoid since he encountered the watercolor in Geordy's bedroom. Hoping Geordy and Nels never got the chance for a tête-à-tête, he replied, "Uh, I think that particular drawing was done before Nels and Ross hooked up and he came to live in the DC area."

Well, bless all guardian angels who are placed in charge of miscreants such as himself, Geordy accepted the explanation. He had a few more moments of having his hair stroked before Geordy spoke again.

"Blade, can I ask a favor of you?"

"Sure, ask away, Mountain."

"In my mother's letter, she asked if I would sing her favorite song at the graveside. I want to do it, but I don't think I'm strong enough to get through it without breaking down. Would you...would you stand where I can see you? If I focus on you, I think I'll be able to sing without embarrassing myself."

He sat up to give Geordy his complete attention. "I'd be honored to do that for you. Just point to where you want me to stand, and I'll hold the position until you finish the song."

Geordy reached out and ran his thumb over Wren's prominent cheekbone. "I'm going to be selfish and ask for another favor. Sleep with me tonight? I really don't want to be alone."

For answer, he stood and offered Geordy his hand. "You needn't call it a favor. I want to sleep with you tonight." *And every other night until we take the final sleep, but you won't ask it of me, will you, Mountain?*

Chapter Twelve

Geordy sat on the front porch and did some deep breathing exercises to calm himself as the sun rose. He woke with his mind whirling like one of those fidget spinners because, just like not wanting to read his mother's letter, he didn't want to go to her funeral this morning to put an official end to Kirsten MacEwen. But that was the curse of being a fully grown man—go he must, and go he would.

His mind skittered away from funerals to contemplate the fact that a gorgeous, warm body still graced his bed. Wren de Lassy defied description. Last night, the man loved him so well, he couldn't come up with any descriptive adjectives. Soft, tender, exquisite were close, and yet they weren't exactly right.

Wren was hard to define. He fooled the eyes. There was so much more...the word iceberg popped into his mind. Yes, de Lassy was an iceberg. What you saw on the surface in no way told you what was buried beneath the water.

Geordy scrubbed his face to rid it of emotion when the door opened.

"I'm really beginning to dislike your cousin Aengus. This tune is different from the kind he usually plays."

"Aye, this one's a lament. Aengus is playing for my mother since today is the funeral." Wren stunned him by climbing into his lap and hugging him.

"Are you okay, Mountain? Anything I can do?"

Geordy wrapped his arms around Blade and hugged him back. "Just you being here with me is all I need. Had I come alone, my visit would be spent in a jail cell, and not at my mother's funeral. I love this place, but sometimes I harbor such anger toward my family I just want to...to...."

Wren supplied the words. "Go berserk? I think that feeling comes embedded with the Danish Modern furniture in your Viking DNA." He laughed. "And it doesn't help that the Marine Corps has taught you how to do it with maximum effect. Come on, Mountain. Instead of contemplating mayhem, think of what you want for breakfast. As incredible as this may sound after the way your aunt stuffed me this week, I'm hungry."

He mimicked Geordy's Scottish burr, "And a man must keep up his strength with a bowl or two of guid Scots porridge if he wants to keep a cock stand long enough to impress."

***

Wren checked himself out in his bedroom mirror. Yep, everything was in its correct place on his Dress Blues. He picked up his uniform hat, called a cover by Marines, and headed to the great room to wait for Geordy.

"You are very handsome in your Dress Blues, Blade."

Wren spun around at the compliment and, for once in his life, words failed him. Geordy spoke the truth when he said he was dropdead gorgeous when he wore the Blues. To cover his pregnant pause, he resorted to his wise-ass persona.

"Dibs. I found you first, everyone else can just eat their hearts out."

Geordy grinned and tossed his white gloves into his cover and headed for the door.

The Catholic church was made of good Tennessee limestone and sandstone, and Wren asked if Geordy or his father and brothers did the work.

"Yes, and Aengus carved the pews, and Caillin wove the fabric covering the kneelers and the altar cloth. Both Campbells and MacEwens are well-represented in this parish, and that's why the church is packed. Most everyone liked and admired my mother, and she was a member of the altar society."

He followed Geordy into the last pew and took a seat. He didn't know if people were giving them big eyes as they went past because their uniforms stood out from everyone's version of funeral attire, or because they knew of the MacEwens' objection to their gay son/brother's presence. He followed Mountain's lead and sat with a stoic face until the MacEwens and Campbells entered the church. All the men wore the traditional dress kilt, and even Aunt Euna had the Campbell arisaid folded across her shoulder. It was to be a true Scottish funeral.

He was about to remark on Aengus's absence when the drone of a bagpipe came from the vestibule, and everyone stood as the Campbell piper paced in to "Amazing Grace."

Wren had to admit, the service was impressive in its simplicity and sincerity. Kirsten MacEwen would be missed by her many friends. He gave Geordy quick glances out of the corner of his eye to gauge his emotional state, and the Mountain appeared to be holding his own. At least until his uncle and cousins joined his brothers to carry the casket to the waiting hearse for interment in the cemetery. The hair on the back of his neck rose to vigilance as Geordy's white-gloved hands gripped the wooden pew in front of him until the casket passed by, and then cursed under his breath, "Damn you Evin

MacEwen for denying me this last honor." He relaxed when Geordy gave no indication he would do anything violent.

To his way of thinking, the graveside resembled a Hatfield-McCoy burial. The MacEwens on one side, the Campbells on the other, and the clueless townsfolk scattered in between. He returned from his mental musing when the priest murmured the final "Amen," and Geordy signaled him.

"I need you to do that favor for me. Stand somewhere at the foot of the casket and make sure I can see you."

People started to leave, but Geordy raised his voice and stopped them. "My mother had a last request of me. She wanted to hear her favorite song one last time." He nodded to his cousin Aengus who began the opening notes of "Danny Boy."

Geordy's clear tenor froze everyone in place. Even his brothers and father didn't move, but Wren thought it might've been because Aillig and his sons clamped large hands over their shoulders to keep them in place.

Mountain's voice was wondrous, and the sad song too apropos for anyone to remain unaffected. Blade stood at attention and never lost eye contact with his teammate, despite the tears running down his own cheeks. No one who wasn't made of granite or completely deaf could remain dry-eyed. Except for the MacEwens, their imperviousness to Geordy's angelic voice was based on hatred. His father and brothers wore grim, tight-lipped expressions, and made it evident by the black scowls cast Geordy's way they didn't approve of his tribute to his mother.

Wren swallowed several times to squelch the sob rising in his throat when Geordy sang the last two lines about sleeping in peace until they met again. He remained in place as Geordy put his arms around his mother's coffin and whispered his parting words. However, when Geordy straightened with sightless eyes and staggered as he took a step away from the casket, he rushed to his side and put his arm around his waist to lead him back to the truck.

"What now, Geordy?" he asked as he put the truck in gear.

"We're supposed to go to the pub for the wake, but I need to go home first. I need out of this uniform. This collar is strangling me. I can't breathe."

"Home it is, then." He didn't comment when Geordy leapt from the truck before it stopped rolling, just followed him into the house at a much slower pace. The Mountain needed some alone time.

Geordy surprised him by changing clothes in record time. He came into his bedroom wearing jeans and an untucked white dress shirt as he was hanging up his uniform. Geordy rocked sexy, but he kept that opinion to himself as Geordy handed him a glass of bourbon.

"Here's to the first of many. I plan on getting shit-faced, so you are the designated driver. Don't worry, if you overindulge as well—my aunt Euna drives a mean truck. Let's go. One last hurdle to jump and then we can put Beltrees and the fucking MacEwens in the rearview mirror."

He finished tying his sneakers and followed Geordy out to his truck.

The pub was packed, and it took him a while to find a parking spot. He suggested Mountain hop out and go ahead, but the suggestion was nixed.

"No, I'm not entering without my wing man. I'm certain my father needed some liquid courage to not disgrace himself by breaking down at the funeral. He's probably pretty lubricated by now, and Evin MacEwen is a belligerent drunk, so I'm going to wimp out and let you run interference. My uncle Aillig got him to agree to an orderly funeral, but knowing my father and brothers, that agreement does not extend to the wake."

And, as Wren discovered, no truer words were spoken for the MacEwens, father and sons, confronted Geordy as soon as he walked through the door. Blade stood balanced on the balls of his feet because Geordy was spot on about Evin not being cheerful when he had a snootful.

Evin shook his fist under Geordy's nose. "Leave. You're not welcome here. I won't stand for you contaminating this room. It was bad enough you came back to Beltrees, but bringing along another deviant is beyond the pale. Did you enjoy sucking his dick before coming to your mother's wake?"

Evin's voice was slurred, but it carried well in the total silence of the pub. Everyone stood frozen in place at the coarseness of Evin's accusation.

Wren was reluctant to look at Geordy because he didn't want to see murder in his eyes. Surprisingly, the great animal roar freezing everyone in place did not come from Mountain. It was Aillig who crossed the room in three strides and picked Evin up by the scruff of his neck.

"I will reimburse you every fucking penny you spent on this wake, Evin MacEwen, but you and your sons need to leave. *Now.*"

Evin started to protest, and Aillig shook him. "Leave on your own two legs or leave on a stretcher. Your choice. Some might think too much whiskey made you say such a vile thing, but I know better. No amount of whiskey can make a man say that to his own son. You're a hateful, vengeful man, Evin MacEwen, and as God is my witness, I'm glad my sister left you for the peace of Heaven. I don't want to see you or your sons in my pub until you apologize to Geordy and his fellow Marine."

Although Evin MacEwen stood a foot shorter than Aillig Campbell, he was a Scot, and Scots seldom backed down, whether in the right or wrong. Flanked by Ramsey and Robbie, Evin poked a finger into Aillig's chest and declared, "It will be a cold day in hell before I apologize to anyone who gives shelter to a homosexual. You Campbells let an abomination before God soil your home, and I'm telling you I only kept my peace with you at my wife's urging. Well, she's gone now, and I no longer need to be civil to you or your family."

Evin stared Aillig squarely in the eye, spat on the floor, and left.

It was the local sheriff who defused the situation by going up to Geordy and wrapping him in a bear hug. "Geordy Campbell, welcome back to Beltrees. I'm sorry such a sad occasion brought you back. Who's your friend?"

Wren wanted to hug the cop for starting a reception line of sorts. There were too many people who shook his hand and thanked him and Geordy for their service to remember names, but at least everyone was talking again, and the food and drinks were being consumed like a major horror show event had never taken place.

He kept a close eye on Geordy who eschewed solid food for liquid forgetfulness. He couldn't blame him. His own parents were never good role models, but at least they never shamed him in front of an entire town.

"Can I buy you a drink, Sergeant?"

Wren turned around to find the sheriff holding two glasses of whiskey. "Sure, uh, Sheriff MacAlister."

"Most folks around here just call me Jimmy Mac." The sheriff pointed to Geordy surrounded by a group of his mother's friends. "You know, I was on the same football team with Geordy and his cousin Caillin. We went all the way and won the state championship, and I swear Beltrees High hasn't ever had another quarterback or fullback to match the Campbells."

Jimmy Mac took a sip of his whiskey and nodded at Geordy as he said, "I'm ashamed to say we were hard on him when he came out, but Geordy's steady calm in the face of our taunts won us over. He was a good football player, and I'll bet he's a good Marine. You don't need to worry if Geordy has your back in combat because he's more of a Campbell than a MacEwen, and every Campbell I've ever known is a worthy man."

Aunt Euna cut off Geordy's bender. "Aengus, Caillin, help Wren walk your cousin to his truck." Euna turned to Wren. "Can you handle him? Once the night air hits him, he'll regret having drunk so much."

"Yes, ma'am. I can handle Geordy. The Marine Corps teaches a course on handling drunken teammates." He grinned at the bald lie, and Euna returned it.

Euna gave him a kiss on his cheek and whispered, "I've always thought it a shame he had the misfortune to be born to a man who couldn't recognize the golden son from the two made of clay, but at least Geordy found a golden friend in you. I'll see you and my hungover nephew tomorrow night for dinner. Tell him not to worry, I won't make anything spicy."

***

Geordy took a seat on the front porch as the sun cleared the horizon. Aware of the consequences for overindulging in spirits, he came prepared. He slid his sunglasses down over his sensitive eyes as the first ray of sunshine reached the porch and the first note of Aengus's pipes wafted through the air.

Geordy left Wren asleep in his bed and came outside to try and master his mortification. Having a teammate help him worship the porcelain god by keeping his head above water and out of the vomit was a new and, please God, one-time experience.

He didn't make overindulgence a habit, but last night Evin MacEwen finally got to him. Frequent exposure to his father's usual litany of "my son the homosexual, deviant abomination," made little dent in the thick skin he developed, but the coarse, crude words he leveled at Blade last night pierced right into his heart. He heard the death knell over the deafening silence of the shocked mourners. His ties to the MacEwens were severed.

Bless Uncle Aillig for interceding because a little voice in the primitive part of his brain told him if he raised his hand to his father, he would not stop until the man never spoke again.

"Well, that's a different fashion statement for you, Mountain. Sunglasses and boxer briefs. Are we sunbathing this morning? If so, I came dressed for the occasion." Wearing nothing but boxer briefs, Wren slid into the chair beside Geordy's.

Geordy turned to Blade and slid the glasses up on his head, winced, and slid them back over his eyes. "I owe you an apology and a thank you."

"I'm assuming the thank you is for me keeping you from drowning in the toilet last night, but what's the apology for?"

"I want to apologize for the horrible things my fa— No, I'll never refer to Evin MacEwen as my father again. I'm sorry about what that nasty sonovabitch said about you and me in front of the entire population of Beltrees."

Wren stretched his long legs out in front of him. "Ah yes, the sucking my dick statement. No worries, Mountain. I just chalked it up to penis envy on his part."

Geordy lifted his sunglasses to gawk at Blade for the outrageous comment. His impish grin started a giggle in his stomach that rose in crescendo to a full-blown belly laugh. "You're a real piece of work, de Lassy."

"Oh I am, Mountain, I truly am. I'm a genuine masterpiece."

"Well, come inside, masterpiece. I can't hang you on my wall, but I will feed you a bowl of porridge and a cup of coffee." He didn't know how to interpret Wren's strange expression, but he did follow him into the kitchen so he forgot about it as he began measuring out the oats and plugging in the coffee pot.

What started out as a sunny day dimmed to overcast, and Geordy considered whether or not to take umbrellas with them on the walk Wren suggested. Both he and Blade peered out the window when they heard the sound of a truck driving across the bridge to his property.

"Oh, what fresh hell is this?" he muttered when he identified Ramsey's truck.

"Have your cousins come to call?" Blade wanted to know.

"No, not my cousins, but my brothers, and they probably think they're going to deliver a long-delayed beatdown for me coming here and them having to leave the wake last night. If it comes to it, and I sort of hope it does, watch Robbie's left hook. He's been very successful with it, but that's the extent of his boxing ability. You are cleared to kill the bastard and call it self-defense."

"And what about Ramsey? What's his talent?"

"Ram's a grappler. He likes to squeeze the air out of you and then stomp you. But my arms and legs are longer, and I'm quite a bit faster. He'll try to blindside me, but that's not happening today."

Wren shook his head and didn't comment until the MacEwen brothers climbed out of the truck. "Having had the displeasure of meeting your former brothers, I'm soooo glad I'm an only child." He huffed out a snort of laughter at Geordy's comeback.

"If we do this right, I'll be one, too. Come on, time for a little hand-to-hand combat practice."

Geordy, followed by his roommate, stepped onto the porch, and Mountain allowed his brothers to reach halfway between their truck and his front porch before calling out. "I didn't invite you here, so state your business and then remove your ugly asses from my property."

His brothers were flummoxed by his unaccustomed rudeness, but Ramsey found his tongue when Blade stepped up beside him. "Oh, what's the matter, fag? Did Robbie and I interrupt your fun with your pretty boy?"

Wren parked one hip on the porch rail and lifted a sardonic eyebrow toward Geordy to ask, "Is Beltrees in some kind of time warp, or is it just your brothers who talk like hillbillies?"

"Just these two troglodytes, I'm afraid." When Ramsey started to advance, Geordy pointed, "Not another step unless you like swallowing your own blood. I'm not going to take any more of your insults, and if you insult a fellow Marine and a guest in my house this morning, you'll do so at your own risk."

"Guest? Is that what you're calling him? Why don't you call him what he really is, your butt boy?"

Blade stopped Mountain before he could clear the porch. "Oh do let me." He jumped over the railing and moved to stand chest-to-chest with Ramsey, grinning when the man backed off in a hurry. Never taking his eyes off Ram, he asked, "Am I still cleared hot?"

Geordy spoke loud enough for everyone to hear. "You are. My brothers haven't had the stupid knocked out of them for quite some time, and they are overdue for the forcible insertion of some intelligence."

He didn't move a muscle as Blade placed himself between his two brothers. There'd be no blindsiding his fellow Marine, but he did wonder if he was armed. He hoped not. It might be hard to explain a slit throat to Jimmy Mac as just a friendly disagreement.

***

Wren grinned broadly at the two brothers who seemed less confident now he stood so close to them. "I never discuss my sex life with strangers, but I am compelled to correct your mislabeling of me. The hair on my balls says I'm no longer a boy. Sorry to disappoint, but I'm not playing show and tell so you can verify I speak the truth. Neither one of you is close to being my type."

Wren won the bet he made with himself. He'd bet his smart mouth would make Ramsey charge him. He sidestepped easily and his rigid-hand strike went straight into Ramsey's solar plexus.

He remained relaxed but alert as Robbie stared down at his brother and back at him, obviously confused by what had just happened. His takedown of Ramsey had been so fast and unexpected, the younger brother could only give his gasping, gargling brother a confused stare rather than a hand up.

Blade saw the moment Robbie realized he stood close enough to try for a left hook to his face, and he prepared to defend against it, but Robbie never got beyond cocking his fist back before his lights went out.

Geordy shook his hand to take the sting away. "Damn, Robbie has a head harder than granite." Before he could comment, Geordy turned his attention back to Ramsey, who'd stopped gasping and managed to pull himself into a sitting position. "I guess the little lesson you and Robbie planned to teach me this morning backfired."

Ramsey spit at Geordy's feet. "We came over to deliver Ma's cedar chest. Da wanted it out of the house because he's done with you and with all the Campbells, and he didn't want a single thing left in the house that belonged to you."

Geordy didn't say a word, just motioned to Wren to help him, and went to the truck and lowered the tailgate. Wren got the other end when he slid the chest out of the truck bed, and they carried it up on the porch.

Blade bit his lip to stifle comment when Geordy ignored Ram's protest as he picked the unconscious Robbie up like a Marine duffel bag and dumped him in the truck bed. He didn't bother turning around to see what the MacEwens were doing as he helped Geordy carry the cedar chest inside, but he did mimic Mountain's wide grin when the rain that had been threatening all morning came down in buckets.

"Well that should revive your brothers. So what else can we do for fun today?"

He was surprised by the sudden gleam of mischief in Mountain's eyes.

"We can climb up to the loft and listen to the rain on the tin roof."

He followed Geordy up the ladder, but didn't think it sounded particularly like fun until his head came above the floor of the loft and spotted the double bed placed strategically between the eaves.

They helped each other undress, and Wren didn't speak until both of them were in the bed. "Do you know what an ouroboros is?"

Geordy gave him a considering stare before answering. "Aye, the pictures depict it as a snake or a dragon swallowing its own tail."

For such a large well-built man, Geordy's blush was sweet when he finally got it.

Of course being Wren, he couldn't resist a visual hint. He licked his lips and gave his erection a long, slow stroke before rolling over on top of Geordy to take him into his mouth. He was delighted to find essence of Mountain right up there with Campbell Dhu.

A sizzling crack of lightning illuminated the loft, and a deep rumble of thunder imitating the tympani section of a Philharmonic orchestra shook the entire cabin and levitated him off the mattress with a loud, "Jesus!"

Geordy snuggled closer and chuckled. "And that's why there are no atheists in foxholes. Mother Nature has one hell of a wakeup call. If we both shake a leg, there's enough time to clean up and pack before going to my uncle's for dinner."

Chapter Thirteen

Aillig rubbed his hands together in delight as Geordy carried in five more bottles of Campbell Dhu as a going away present. But as Geordy poured everyone a drink but himself, Aillig teased him.

"I see you inherited the Campbell head for whiskey, Nephew."

"If you mean having enough smarts not to push it, then, yes, I have. I had enough yesterday to last me quite a while.

Euna Campbell called them in to dinner, and Wren was the first to seat himself. "Whatever we are having for dinner, ma'am, is making me drool. I didn't think I had any room left to eat anything, but the aroma is making my stomach growl."

Conall sat next to him and gave him a nudge that sent him careening into Geordy, who'd seated himself on the other side.

"That's Ma's pot roast, so tender it'll melt in your mouth."

The meal ended with a chorus of oohs, as Euna passed around heaping bowls of strawberry shortcake.

Wren leaned in to Geordy to whisper, "On the count of three, loosen your belt two notches and I'll do the same. Monday PT is going to suck."

After helping with the cleanup, Geordy didn't linger but sought out his aunt and uncle to say goodbye. He followed along to say his own.

As Geordy leaned down to kiss his aunt's cheek, Euna stopped him.

"Geordy, your mother had a beautiful tradition with you, and it would be an honor to continue it. Will you let me give you the blessing?"

Geordy hugged his aunt, and his voice was raspy as he gave his consent. "Thank you verra much for continuing it, Auntie." He went down on one knee in front of his aunt, and the rest of the Campbells drew close.

Wren found himself being nudged to stand next to Geordy, and Caillin whispered, "You too, Wren, take a knee."

Euna placed one hand on Geordy's shoulder and the other on Wren's and began the Campbell blessing:

"Be true to yourself.

"Be true to the Marines you serve with.

"And may God grant you safe return to the family who keeps you in their hearts while you are away."

Euna made the sign of the cross on Geordy's and Wren's foreheads and hugged them both. She laughed at Wren's stunned expression.

"Catholic or not, a blessing never hurt anyone, and in the short time you've been in Beltrees, we've adopted you as part of this family, so we'll include you in our prayers."

"Thank you, ma'am. Such a beautiful tradition should be continued, and I'm honored to be included."

Aillig draped an arm around Wren as Geordy traded farewell arm bumps with his cousins and steered him off to the side.

"It eases a man's mind when his sons make good, trustworthy friends. Although Geordy was born my nephew, I consider him a son. I'm happy Geordy has you for a friend. You'll watch each other's back and keep an eye out for each other in dangerous situations. And I hope the insult you received from the MacEwens, won't dissuade you from coming back to Beltrees."

"Thank you, sir, I'd like that. I'll watch out for Geordy. Geordy's team name is Mountain because he's strong both mentally and physically, so I don't think watching over him will be much trouble."

***

Geordy had started to pull away from his uncle's house when Caillin hailed them to wait up. He went around to Wren's door and motioned for him to wind the window down.

"I almost forgot to give you this."

He took the tiny pottery bird from Caillin's hand. It was a wren and glazed in the same color brown as the real bird.

"Thanks, Caillin. your talent as a potter is amazing. When did you do this?"

Oh, I was finishing up a vase and had leftover clay, so when learned your name I knocked it out and fired it up with the vase."

Wren turned the bird this way and that, and commented, "A very pretty little bird I'm named after, but not a very manly name like Aengus, Caillin, Conall, or Geordy."

Caillin disagreed. "Are you not familiar with Celtic mythology, then?"

"Just a few random facts. Why, is a wren significant?"

Geordy fielded the question. "A wren is the messenger of the gods and thus a sacred bird. He's called the Drui-en or Druid bird by the Irish, and Dryw in Welsh. The wren makes his nest in the Druid's house, and his nest is protected by lightning. A wren symbolizes wisdom and divinity, and auguries were made depending on the direction from which his calls came. In Scotland, killing a wren brings verra bad luck. A wren was sacred to the Celtic Thunder god, Taranis, who lived in an oak tree. Taranis called lightning for his weapon. And, finally, the poet William Blake summed it all up.

"He who shall hurt the little wren

Shall never be belov'd by men."

Wren held the bird up and studied it with a greater appreciation. "Wow, thank you very much, Caillin. I'll take good care of it."

Once home, Geordy headed for the couch while Wren opted to change out of his jeans for sweatpants, declaring it was good they were leaving before he had to buy larger-sized jeans.

Geordy closed his eyes and laid his head on the back of the cushions. He had to admit he was tired. This last week tested his mental and emotional endurance, and the verdict was still out whether he won or lost. On the emotional side, it was a large loss. He cried more in the last week than he had in his previous twenty-five years. He was relieved Wren had a deep core of empathy, or the number of times he gave vent to his grief would shame him.

On the visceral side, he was stronger and curiously liberated. He thought raising his hands against his brothers would bother him, but knocking the shit out of Robbie broke any familial ties he had left, and he suffered not a smidgen of guilt. This visit amply proved his brothers were more MacEwen than he. Aside from taking the name Campbell, Geordy believed he was a Campbell in his very soul.

There was only one unresolved item on this trip, and it was a doozy. The sofa cushion moved as Wren sat down next to him, and he called himself a coward for not having to wrestle with that conundrum this evening.

He turned toward his roommate. "Are you tired?"

"It depends."

Geordy opened his eyes and asked, "On what?"

"On where I'm sleeping tonight. If you say the guest room then, no, I'm not tired, I think I'll read for a while."

"And if I say in my room?" Geordy didn't resist when Blade reached for his hand and held it to slowly run his thumb over the back of it.

"Then, yes, I'm tired, and sated with both food and sex. I want to sleep just wrapped around you, Geordy."

He stood and pulled Wren up as well. "Come along to my room, then. We've an early start tomorrow, and neither one of us has had much sleep this trip."

His resolve to honor Blade's cuddle request lasted until the moonlight streaming through his open window faded and was replaced by the dark grey presaging sunrise. One last time, just this last time, he temporized with himself, as he began kissing Wren so gently he thought he wouldn't wake him, but as his passion rose, so, too, did the urgency of the kisses he placed on his body. Blade woke when he put his mouth over his nipple and sucked *hard*.

"Ah, my bonnie de Lassy, you are a wondrous lover," Geordy gasped when Wren slithered down his body and took him in his mouth. "But let's make this last," and Geordy flipped him over and covered him with his body to capture his mouth and stroke his tongue with his own.

In hindsight, he should never have used the word "last" in any connotation. Wren flipped him on his back like he weighed no more than a sack of flour and sprang from the bed.

"Oh fuck no, Geordy. I understand what you're trying to do. You're saying goodbye, and I won't stand for it. A long time ago, I made up my mind no one was ever going to say goodbye to me again, unless it was on my terms. You're trying to put me back in the, 'I don't date Marines box,' and I'm telling you you don't need to try. What we did here was just a...a compassionate interlude. I showed you compassion at a time when you needed it."

Stung by Wren's choice of wording, Geordy snorted. "Compassionate interlude? You do have a way with words." He watched, speechless, as Blade's incandescent anger ignited.

"I'm very aware we aren't a couple, aren't dating. There is no need to say goodbye to me as if you think I didn't get your message. So you can go back to being the "I don't date Marines," person you are, and I will go back to being the, 'I don't give a fuck who you date,' Marine that I am, and we can both continue to be roommates, teammates, and Special Operations Marines who need to work together to prepare for a training deployment to the Philippines. Now hustle your ass out of bed and get dressed. I want to reach MARSOC before midnight.

***

Wren waited in the truck as Geordy locked the front door to his house. He didn't miss the buttoned-up expression on Mountain's face as he walked toward him. *Two can play this game, Geordy Campbell. I'm a Jedi Master at compartmentalization. People have abandoned me so many times in my life I can compartmentalize my dreams. You are just one more person to add to my box.*

He could tell by the tentative peek Geordy cast his way as he started the truck, he was wondering if he was going to be angry or pout the entire way back to North Carolina. Little did Mountain know, pouting had been beaten out of him in Saudi Arabia, and he'd lost that penchant for good.

He turned to Geordy, and asked in his normal, upbeat voice, "Is there any fast food restaurant on the way out of here that offers salad on their breakfast menu?"

He wanted to laugh at the instant relief appearing on Geordy's face to think he went peacefully back into Geordy's little box of Marines he didn't date. If his roomie bothered to open his box, he wouldn't find him there, because he was in the box he fashioned for himself. But he needed to add more padding to his. The head-to-toe abrasions he incurred from Geordy stung like a son of a bitch.

Chapter Fourteen

The door to dorm room 304 was ajar, and Geordy gave Blade a "what the fuck?" look as he pushed his way inside, certain he locked the door before they left for Beltrees last week.

He stopped just past the threshold when a Marine sitting at the desk got up to confront him.

"Isn't it customary to knock before entering someone's room?"

Geordy squared off with the unknown squatter. "It is, unless it happens to be your room. Who the fuck are you, and what are you doing in our room?" Geordy crossed his arms and waited for an answer.

Wren simply bypassed him, tossed his bag on his bunk, and waited for the stranger to make the next move.

"Ah, you must be either Mountain or Blade. I'm betting Mountain, given your build. My name is Leonid Vladimir Tolstoy. You can call me what everyone else on the team does, Vlad."

Geordy studied the tall, lanky, blond-haired, blue-eyed Russian. It didn't take much deductive reasoning to peg him as Russian due to the name and the heavy accent that made him sound like Bela Lugosi playing Dracula.

"Thanks for the intro, Vlad, but you failed to answer the 'what the fuck are you doing in our room' part of the question."

Vlad extended his hand and grinned. "I'm your new roommate. I had a choice of bunking with Levitz, Rogers, and Hernandez, but I prefer to be the third man in the room and not the fourth. I didn't touch any of your stuff because he is a bad thief who steals from his neighbor."

As he shook Geordy's hand, Vlad switched to Russian. "*Vy tot, kto govorit po-russki?*"

Geordy fired back, "*YA govoryu po-russki.*"

Wren shook his head and began unpacking. "I'm assuming Vlad asked if you speak Russian and you said you do. Gee, Vlad, you just turned this room into a mini United Nations. I speak Arabic and French, Geordy speaks Arabic, French, Spanish, Tagalog, and Russian, and of course we all speak English...more or less."

Vlad laughed. "United Nations, I like that. That means, as the Russian delegate, I have veto power."

For Geordy, the verdict was still out on whether or not Vlad would work as a roommate. "Uh, Vlad, did anyone in Room 301 mention I'm gay? That you would be rooming with a gay Marine?"

"*Da.* It's no problem. I'm a sniper. I won't have to be close to kill you, but Levitz, Rogers, and Hernandez vouched for you. They told me what their former roommate said about you, and I say to you slander, like coal, will either dirty your hand or burn it. They tell me Vogler got burned with one punch, Mountain."

Wren crossed in front of Geordy on the way to his closet to stow his dress uniform and added, "No worries, then. Geordy doesn't date Marines." Knowing that came out sounding bitchy, he took some of the sting away by adding, "But both of us sleep in the nude."

The tension in the room eased when Vlad shrugged his shoulders. "Is there any other way to sleep? MARSOC didn't issue pajamas or bathrobes."

Geordy tossed Wren a "can you believe this guy?" grimace and started unpacking. When he finished, he asked, "Anyone up for chow?"

He got a "Bring on the salad" from Blade, and a "Perhaps," from Vlad.

Mountain cocked his head at the vague answer. "Well, which is it? Are you coming with us or not?"

Vlad grinned and clapped Geordy on the back. "Never mind, perhaps I'll go with you."

Geordy stopped dead and stared at the Russian. "You know, after a rough week and a twelve-hour drive, my patience is non-existent. Either come with us or find your own way to the chow hall."

Vlad winked at Blade, who was leaning against the desk with an amused expression on his face. "Ah, I see you do not yet understand Russians. We have three strong principles: perhaps, somehow, and never mind."

Geordy snorted and walked out of the room. He didn't bother turning around. He didn't care whether Wren or Vlad followed him to the chow hall or not, the last week left him too exhausted to give a shit.

Blade stared at Vlad's heaping tray of food and then back at the Russian. "Are you going to eat all that?"

Vlad noted the solitary, small salads on his new roommates' trays and countered with, "Are you going to eat only that? I have a good Russian appetite, which my mother describes as a hollow tunnel leading to an abyss. I'm never too full to eat, and I never gain weight."

As Vlad dug into enough food to feed four Marines, four starving Marines, Wren began to probe their new roomie. "Where are you from, Vlad?"

"New York by way of Moscow."

"Were you born in the United States?" Geordy wanted to know.

"*Nyet*. I was born in Moscow and came to New York when I was ten. My father was a very important man in the Russian mob, and he was sent to New York to set up business."

Taking the last bite, Vlad patted his belly and sat back. "There is a long history of being thieves in my family. We are part of the *Russkaya Mafiya*, Russian Mafia to you, and card-carrying members of the *Vorovskoy Mir* or Thieves World. Both my father and my uncle ended up in prison. My father died there, but my uncle is still in a Russian gulag. My brother, Kiril, is upholding the family tradition by working his way up to Brigadier to the *Pakhan* or Boss."

Geordy blinked several times. "Are you saying you were in the Russian mob before joining the Marines?"

"*Nyet*. My *babushka*, my grandmother, a very determined, devout woman saved me. She didn't approve of her sons being criminals. The day I graduated high school, she walked me down the block, under the pretext of showing me what she wanted to buy me for a graduation present, and pushed me right into a Marine recruiting station."

Blade asked, "What did your brother Kiril have to say about that?"

Vlad grinned. "I don't know, I never went back. I already had my green card, and once I completed my three years of honorable military service, I kept reenlisting. I've stayed completely free of the mob." Vlad stood, removed his T-shirt, and turned around. "No Russian *mafiya* tattoos mar the perfection of my body. After I graduated first in my class at sniper school, I sent a picture to Kiril of me holding my sniper rifle, along with the message he'd never see the bullet that comes for him if he tries to bring me back."

"Okaay," was all Wren said before Geordy asked the next

question.

"What team were you on before coming here, and why did you leave it?"

For the first time, the brash Russian avoided direct eye contact with his new roommates. "I was in Bravo Company, and I asked to leave. There was an unfortunate occurrence with the wife of one of my teammates. While I did not commit adultery with, or covet my teammate's wife, I did purchase a lap dance from her."

Vlad nonchalantly clapped Mountain on the back when he choked on his iced tea, and continued the explanation for his transfer to Fox Company and his new team.

"I went clubbing with a few of the guys to that topless bar along Route 17 on the way to Jacksonville, you know the one, The Bar None. My birthday coincided with payday so I decided to treat myself to a lap dance. All I can say was, the woman who performed it was outstanding. She had moves like a Turkish belly dancer. I was telling the rest of the guys of her talent when I mentioned the interesting tattoo she had of a winking eye on her left breast. I told my friends to ask for the Korean girl with the winking eye tattoo, and in the next instant, I was lying flat on my back with the imprint of a fist on my cheek."

"Oops, sounds like you poached on someone's territory," Blade offered.

"Yes, but not deliberately. My teammate thought his wife was just serving drinks at the bar for extra money to cover their household expenses. He was ignorant of the fact she performed lap dances as well. I apologized to him when I found out she was his wife, and he apologized to me for losing his temper, but I could tell he got angry every time I walked into the room, so I asked for a transfer, and this team had a sudden vacancy due to a… training accident."

Someone called his name, and Blade turned around to find Byte, Mercury, and Tecate headed their way. The rest of meal was spent catching up on the planning for the deployment.

***

Captain Schuyler staggered down the rickety gangplank of the local ferry to step on the beach of a remote island somewhere in the farthest reaches of the Philippine archipelago, and restrained himself from kissing the sand as a sign of relief. His team clapped him, none too gently, on the back as they passed by, and made snide comments about a Marine marathoner's lack of tolerance for high winds and heavy seas.

He kept his lip zipped because he'd weathered enough Pacific typhoons on aircraft carriers to make the old *Victory at Sea* movies seem tame, but the dangerously overcrowded passenger ferries were not designed to do anything but wallow and bob like corks even in the calmest of seas. As he picked up his gear and plodded after the team, Pacer bitched to himself that after two months of intensive planning, feeling like he was going to hurl didn't come close to being a reward for all that hard work.

Vlad cracked him up as he squeezed his shoulder as he passed and murmured another one of the Russian proverbs he was rapidly becoming notorious for.

"Who has not known the sea has not known sorrow."

As he walked up to the team compound, the long faces on his team told him something was amiss. Mountain clued him in.

"Captain, our 'Hearts and Minds' brethren didn't do much to

make the compound livable. I think they just tossed sleeping bags on the floor. There are bars on the windows, and one or two electrical outlets in the secure room, but not much else. The showers are one step above Lister bags."

Pacer snickered at the reference to the US Army Green Berets, the original builders of the team house. This training site rotated between Army, Marines, and Navy, and it was obvious their Army brothers didn't feel the need to construct anything approaching comfort, probably thinking, and rightly so, their Marine brethren were used to austerity.

Schuyler swallowed his nausea and started issuing orders. "Mountain, unpack the power tools and make this more of a Hilton than a hovel. Blade, start a thorough inventory of all things that go bang. Byte, I want to be connected to Tecate in the embassy. I'm sure he'll be happy to learn he's sitting in air-conditioned comfort back in Manila, drinking Philippine beer while we sweat buckets to make this place livable. You can also tell him he may need to push more construction supplies our way, ASAP.

"Doc, scout out a good site for sick calls and treating the villagers. Vlad, count the weapons and ammo and spare parts and safety gear. And, Mercury, start getting the Zodiacs ready to go. I'll help anyone who needs helping."

Geordy stepped forward with a hammer and a box of nails. "That would be me, Captain. You can help assemble simple sleeping platforms. They won't be cushy, but at least they'll be off the ground. The critters will have to climb to mess with us."

Several hours later, everyone stopped what they were doing when Doc Ferri called out, "Hey, Captain, take a gander at this." Doc opened the door of the lone refrigerator to display a 24-pack of cola.

"I was checking out the fridge, in my capacity as Food Safety Officer, and discovered this welcome gift. I say we give a grudging toast to the Green Beanies since the fridge is clean, plague free, and the soda cold."

Within twenty-four hours the camp was livable to Marine standards, and their efforts attracted a sizeable crowd of village children, who found the giant men in boots and shorts very amusing. Mountain became their instant favorite when he constructed a bean-bag toss using some spare lumber and a few squares of canvas stitched together and filled with beach sand. As a side effect, it kept the kids out from under their feet.

Courtesy of hard work the day before, Captain Schuyler now had a desk fashioned from their packing containers and a couple of boards, and he and Byte had 5x5 connectivity to Tecate in Manila and Woody at MARSOC. Blade found, thank God, nothing missing in his inventory of explosives, Vlad was happily filling magazines with bullets, and Mercury was filling outboard motors with gasoline.

Since the local cook failed to poison them with last night's dinner, things were improving, except for the latest intel report. The terrorist group, Abu Sayyaf, was active again, this time deliberately targeting Americans, and the island they presently occupied was smack in Abu Sayyaf territory. Pacer reviewed the exfiltration plans one more time and left his desk to call for Blade.

When Blade stuck his head in the secure room, Pacer said, "Grab a machete and follow that trail that starts behind this building and find out where it ends. Don't draw attention to yourself, but I want you to recon the area for a possible evac site. Take Mountain with you. He can use a break from sawing and hammering."

"Aye aye, Captain." He sought Geordy out and explained the

mission as he handed him a machete. "If we encounter any of the villagers, we'll just say we're out for a little stroll."

***

It was weird and uncomfortable walking through the jungle alone with Mountain. Their return from Beltrees to find Vlad sharing their room marked the end of their private time, and, he realized it was also damned depressing to discover he was as relieved as he was not to have to face each other in the silence of the evenings with only themselves in the room.

Oh, he was aware they were back in their respective boxes, and had dragged the boxes back to neutral corners, but it didn't keep him from caring about Mountain, and his opening question showed it.

"How are you doing?" He expected him to say, "I'm fine," but that was not what he got.

"I miss you, Blade. I miss the camaraderie. I understand the need for distance between us, but I still miss the ease with which we got along. The fact this separation is my own damn fault makes it worse."

Knowing it was a risky move on so many levels, but helpless to stop himself, Wren checked both ways down the trail they were on, and stepped into Geordy's arms for a hug. "I miss you, too, Geordy. I understand your reasons, believe me, I do. I'll try not to be so distant."

He broke the hug and pointed up into the canopy. "Unless we want to be baptized in urine by that very long-tailed monkey staring down at us, I suggest we move along."

Their recon ended at the sea. The trail traversed part of the island, and there was enough vegetation growing close to the narrow beach to hide a Zodiac. Blade reported their observations to Captain Schuyler who seemed happy with their findings.

***

As a Mobile Training Team, they were supposed to teach certain subjects to fit the group assigned. The present group disembarking on the island was a Muslim Special Action police unit from Mindanao. With the Moros long history of rebellion against the United States and the Philippine government in particular, the all Moro Special Action team had never been permitted side arms, but now the Special Action Force was being armed because Mindanao was under martial law due to the killing of two unarmed Moro police officers by Abu Sayyaf and a splinter Islamist group calling themselves Maute. The subjects the police most needed were marksmanship, crowd control, command and control, Explosive Ordnance Detection, and maritime operations. The Marine Raiders from Fox Company were prepared to teach what they needed to know, but it soon became obvious not all the police officers valued instruction from United States Marines.

Captain Schuyler hid his anger behind a grin when he introduced himself to the ranking officer, who frowned at him and didn't stop to shake the hand he offered. A Lieutenant Ali Shani Mambuay offered excuses as he grabbed his hand and pumped it enthusiastically.

"Many pardons, Captain. My Commander, Captain Hamza, harbors a long-standing distrust of Americans. His great grandfather fought against your General John J. Pershing when the Americans took over governance of the Philippines in the 1900s. Whatever you need tell him, I will serve as your conduit."

Lieutenant Mambuay barked something in rapid Malay and two

NCOs double-timed it to his side. "This is Sergeant Ariraya and Sergeant Dori. We all speak English, some better than others, so your men may convey orders to our enlisted men through them."

As a chain of command, Pacer could live with it. Previous experience taught him most Filipino officers didn't concern themselves with mundane affairs. The grunt work was carried out by the enlisted, with little or no input from their officers, unless they screwed up, and then they could expect verbal and even physical abuse to rain down on their heads. What took him aback was the general air of distrust verging on hostility toward his men. Most Filipinos were cheerful and outgoing, but it soon became obvious the only Moro who smiled or willingly talked to any of his Marines was Lieutenant Mambuay. Pacer sighed to himself. This was going to be a very long five weeks.

***

John Adams took a moment to savor his first sip of coffee for the day and gazed around his office. Being selected to head the Middle Eastern desk at CIA Headquarters in Virginia was a reward for all his hard work as the CIA rep in the American Embassy in Riyadh, Saudi Arabia.

Jack, as he preferred to be called, thought it was also a reward for his wife who had to put up with the restricted life of a Western woman living in Saudi Arabia. He grinned to himself when he recalled asking where she wanted to take their first stateside vacation, and she'd replied, "Anywhere that doesn't have one effing grain of sand."

His reminiscing ended at the sight of his second-in-command,

Anthony, the Ant, Tonelli, entering his office with a clearly marked Top Secret folder and his own cup of coffee.

"Whatcha got there, Ant?"

"Something to start your Monday off with a bang. This is about the incident with Jabir Elmoudowi."

Jack wondered what the Ant found funny enough in the first statement to make him snigger over the word *bang* until he mentioned Elmoudowi. Jack winced at the name. Elmoudowi was Hizballah and Hamas's choice for all things involving C-4 or Semtex. Reputedly Lebanese by birth, Jabir was the go-to merchant of death for anyone who wanted something vaporized and had enough money to pay for his expertise.

The incident Ant referred to was the CIA's attempt to put the bomb maker on the permanently retired list via a Marine directed drone strike in Afghanistan. All they had was a name, a partial, useless fingerprint, and a reputation. Elmoudowi was a *nom de guerre,* and Lebanon the rumored birthplace for the man, but Uncle Sam wanted him bad enough to hit the Afghan safe house on a less than solid piece of intel. No joy though, Elmoudowi must have been tipped off before the strike, because they were unable to match a body to his fingerprint in the building the drone hit. Jack still had some hope that maybe they didn't find any trace of Elmoudowi because he truly had been vaporized. There were documents and artifacts collected from the rubble pointing to his presence in the building, but so far, they lacked physical confirmation.

"Sorry to burst your bubble, Jack, but the recent bombing in Kabul that killed twenty Afghan military is confirmed as having Elmoudowi's signature all over it."

Jack sighed. "So we didn't kill him with the drone strike."

Ant took a slug of coffee and put his mug down before answering. "Nope, and he's pissed. He's blaming the Marines, and he's issued a Marine-specific threat. Time and place of payback to be determined by him." Ant handed the message traffic over to Jack.

"Do we have any leads as to where he might be holed up?"

"No, he's gone dark again. We do know that he can choose a new identity from several aliases he purchased. As soon as one of them pops up, I'll let you know."

Ant flipped through the folder and extracted a photograph and a photo-copied document. "And I think we now know why the bastard is taking the drone strike so personally. Read the translation of the letter and then check out the picture."

"Please tell me that's a shot of Elmoudowi."

"We should be so lucky, but no." Ant sat back in his chair and pushed the letter toward Jack and waited for a reaction.

Jack started to read then jerked his head up to stare at Ant with his mouth gaping. "This is a love letter from Elmoudowi!"

"Yes, it is." Jack tapped his finger on the glossy, 8x10. "And the man in the photo is who it's addressed to. We found it in a secret compartment of a wallet we collected after the drone strike. The owner of the wallet is, or I should say was, Dawud Afif. Afif was the son of a wealthy Saudi lawyer. He was in Afghanistan to fight at the side of his lover. From what we've pieced together of his legend, Elmoudowi had twenty years on Afif, but, hey, according to this letter, the age difference didn't matter.

"Not that Elmoudowi is saying the real reason behind him declaring open season on all Marines anywhere in the world, but he is vowing to honor his comrades-in-arms who lost their lives in the drone strike via some sort of spectacular payback of his time and choosing, and at his own expense. And of course, every fucking Jihadi website, newspaper, blog, or chat room is encouraging him to make it count. Some have even offered to martyr themselves so his plan will succeed."

Jack picked up the photo to study it, and had his second shock of the morning. He'd met this face. For the first time, he believed everyone in the world did have a doppelganger. The first time he encountered this face was in Saudi Arabia when Ross de Lassy rescued his kidnapped friend, Nels Kirkegaard, from a sexual predator closely related to the Saudi royal family. Ross also rescued a teenager purchased by the predator as a young boy and kept captive in his private harem for seven years.

Jack used his Agency connections to fudge the paperwork to fly the boy, now named Wren de Lassy, out of Saudi Arabia and back to the States so as not to embarrass the Saudi royal family.

Despite Dawud Afif being a brunet and Wren de Lassy being a strawberry blond, they shared the same face. A spark of excitement burned away Ant's bad news as a plan began to gel, but until they managed to learn Elmoudowi's new name and location, he would keep the doppelganger's existence under wraps.

Chapter Fifteen

Captain Hamza handed Lieutenant Mambuay the vial. "Give this to Sergeant Dori. He's to take it to the village headmaster's son who cooks for the Americans. Have him tell the cook to pour this into whatever he makes for dinner for the American Marines the day after tomorrow. And while he's at the headmaster's house, he's to remind the headmaster of what will happen to his family and his village if he alerts the Americans. And be sure to remind Sergeant Dori not to be seen leaving or coming back from his errand."

Lieutenant Mambuay put the sleeping draft capable of putting all the Marines into a sound, dreamless sleep, into his pocket. "I'll convey your orders to Sergeant Dori, sir, but I think we should soften our attitude toward the Americans just a little. We've kept to ourselves a little too well, and I think the Marines are beginning to wonder at our resistance to their overtures of friendship. Perhaps we should give the appearance of warming to them to lure them into thinking they've made headway into winning us over to their godless side. It will make what we do to them the day after tomorrow even sweeter."

Captain Hamza studied his second-in-command and considered the suggestion. He didn't think Lieutenant Mambuay was losing his nerve, for Ali Shani Mambuay was the one who kept the compromising of the police unit secret by killing the two policemen in their unit who resisted joining Maute. It enabled the newly formed Maute unit to keep the training engagement with the United States Marine Special Operations unit with no one the wiser.

He would take his subordinate's suggestion, for killing the Marines and taking their weapons to return to Mindanao as a heavily armed Maute force would be a very sweet coup. He would enjoy reading the newspaper articles about the massive damage to Philippine National Police prestige this attack would cause, and the sensational headlines would attract even more followers to their cause.

"A sound observation, Lieutenant. We must watch for an opportunity to engage more with the American dogs without seeming like we are up to something. Now go and give Sergeant Dori his orders."

He accepted Lieutenant Mambuay's salute and returned it with a soft, "*Allahu akbar.*"

***

With morning PT over and showers taken, Pacer met his team at the table for breakfast. He was discouraged. This was going on week three and still no feeling of appreciation or cooperation from the team they were sent to teach, despite giving them the necessary interruptions of training to say their required prayers.

Physical training was a slog. The Filipino officers didn't participate at all, and the NCOs barely encouraged the enlisted to meet even the most minimum standards of physical fitness. Part of the reason for the general malaise might be their diet of starchy food and meager portions, but his team had experience with other units who, while they might not like the Marine version of exercise, at least made an effort. Pacer hoped the ingrained Moro reserve was the cause, rather than something his Marines had done to offend them.

So far, the only activity this police team seemed to like was marksmanship. Pacer called the breakfast meeting to order with, "All right, I'm out of ideas for getting this unit to loosen up. Can anyone offer any suggestions for how we can get them to accept training without having to pour it down their throats like a water-boarding session?"

Pacer cast his gaze around the table and the silence was deafening. "Right, don't all speak up at once. Let's go around the table. Vlad, you're up."

"Vlad started out with, "Perhaps," and grinned back at Mountain and Blade who made rude noises as they recalled the three Russian principles he taught them. "Perhaps I'm not the one to start. Divine assistance made my job easier."

Byte wanted clarification. "Divine assistance? How so?"

"Being Russian, I know when fools shoot, God directs the bullet. At least now they all shoot in the same direction. That first day was fucking scary when they shot whenever and wherever the hell they wanted. They are at least listening to our range and safety commands now, but their side arms are so old I swear those Model 1911s Manila supplied are the same ones we used in the Spanish-American War."

Byte went next. "Sergeant Ariraya is making some progress on radio procedures, but, like the pistols, his equipment is so old it keeps breaking. Maybe this unit isn't resisting us, maybe they're just depressed over the shit they were issued."

Mercury broke in. "You can't use that theory on our Zodiacs. You would think that people who live on islands would be eager to practice maritime procedures, but it's like pulling nails to get them to get in and out of a moving boat."

Mountain started laughing and drew everyone's focus. "I think I know the reason for that. The last time we did that drill, Sergeant Dori pointed at a banded krait keeping pace with his boat. Granted, sea snakes aren't aggressive, but you still need a pair of large cojones to willingly jump in and swim with them. We know the bite of a sea snake can't pierce a wetsuit, but jumping into the water in T-shirts and shorts is another matter."

Blade spoke up, "I don't know why a snake would scare them. They could just pull out their handy-dandy *balisongs*, and we'd all be dining on snake sushi that evening. Which reminds me, Captain, thanks a heap for asking if anyone had a knife at my first knife fighting class."

The table erupted in laughter at his reminder. Pacer's innocent query filled the air with the distinctive click-clack of butterfly knives opening. As the team soon discovered, everyone in the police unit carried one. The display of knives banned in most states certainly caught their attention. Fan knives were banned because, even though they were folded pocket knives, they could be brought to bear very quickly with just one hand.

Pacer's eyebrows rose when Blade informed the team North Carolina was one of the few states permitting the carry of the lethal pocket knife, but he reasoned, if anyone would know, their bladed weapons expert would be the one.

Doc Ferri's observation brought everyone back to the issue at hand. "You know, maybe it's just me, but the locals seem to be mimicking the same air of reserve as the police. Ever since the cops got here, the locals are keeping their distance from us. I moved my treatment site much closer to the village, and they still seem reluctant to even seek first aid unless severe pain and/or bleeding is an issue. Even the kids don't show much interest in what we do any more, and we were practically tripping over them when we first got here. I get that this police unit is Muslim, but we aren't Muslims, so I don't understand why the villagers are being so standoffish."

The lightbulb going off in his head made Pacer sit up. Maybe the villagers weren't unhappy with the Marines so much as distrustful of the Moros. Philippine politics were every bit as convoluted as the Syrian, Iraqi, or Afghani, but that was a four-star problem. Fox team's job was more in line with what Lord Alfred Tennyson said in The Charge of the Light Brigade. "Theirs not to reason why, theirs but to do and..." His mind shied away from finishing the quote.

Aware he was no closer to figuring out the reason for the police attitude toward them, Pacer shut up and let everyone finish their breakfast in peace.

***

For the afternoon session, Doc Ferri was doing his best to teach emergency first aid with the pitifully inadequate contents of the police medical kits when Blade spotted Captain Hamza leaning up against a tree, smoking a cigarette, and giving only minimal attention to learning how to save the life of one of his men.

He had the cynical thought Captain Hamza might pay closer attention if he ever considered the possibility he would be the one needing the emergency care. A movement above the captain's head drew his attention. *Whoa.* A bright-green snake with a yellow belly had just raised its head off the branch above Captain Hamza. He could swear the snake licked its lips right before slithering toward its unsuspecting target.

He didn't hesitate. In a fluid motion he withdrew his throwing knife from the wrist sheath and flung it at the snake. His aim was spot on, and the snake, pinned to the tree, writhed and struggled to free itself as all hell broke out among the Moros, who thought their commander was under attack.

Lieutenant Mambuay got things calmed down by pointing to the dead snake dangling above Captain Hamza's head. Blade was gratified to find his fellow Marines screened him from the wrath of the Moros. Mountain, Vlad, and Mercury stood between him and the agitated police.

Attitudes changed dramatically when Captain Hamza picked himself up from the defensive position he'd taken when he saw the Marine fling a knife at him, and walked toward his rescuer with his hand extended.

"Thank you very much for saving my life, Sergeant."

As he took the proffered hand, Blade asked, "So the snake was poisonous? I couldn't tell from where I stood, but I didn't think you'd appreciate having a snake drop on you, so I opted for removing the snake."

Sergeant Dori handed Blade his throwing knife and held up the limp snake. "Yes, very poisonous. This is a Philippine pit viper. They usually hunt at night, but Captain Hamza standing right under the tree presented an easy target."

And that was the perfect segue for Doc to cover emergency first aid for snake bites. After the class, Captain Hamza invited Captain Schuyler and the rest of the team to share dinner with them, and given the Filipino love of singing, a karaoke sing off.

In a change from their previous coldness, the Moro unit was surprisingly gracious in their role of hosts. The meal of chicken and rice was quite good, in Pacer's opinion, and he began to relax at the friendly ribbing between his team and the police unit. His attention was drawn to two men carrying long lengths of freshly cut bamboo. He leaned in to Captain Hamza to ask its purpose.

"Ah, you Marines use calisthenics or running for aerobic exercise, but we use *tinikling*. *Tinikling* is good aerobic exercise and develops hand coordination, foot speed, and rhythm. These poles are twelve feet long, and the two clappers will keep the beat starting with two taps while the poles are held apart, and then one clap when they are together. The tempo will increase as the dance progresses."

Captain Hamza hailed one of his men. "Corporal Said is our best *tinikling* dancer. Allow him to demonstrate, and then see if any of your men can best him."

After watching Corporal Said's bare feet move faster and faster as he danced in and out of the clashing poles, the Marines gained new respect for the Filipino version of PT, but when challenged by the rest of the Moros to try and best the corporal's performance, only Blade was game.

As he removed his boots, he whispered to Mountain, "My ankles are already starting to complain about the abuse they are about to receive. The cops are saying this is a dance or an exercise, but I can see its potential use as an interrogation technique. Make a man dance while getting his ankles struck repeatedly is a good inducement for him to tell everything he knows just to stop the punishment."

Blade addressed the two clackers before he attempted putting his foot between the poles, "Be gentle with me." Their hoot of laughter didn't reassure him.

He thanked his martial arts training for lasting as long as he did, but his effort was pretty poor compared to Lieutenant Mambuay's. Even Captain Hamza showed him up.

Mountain, who'd gone along with Private Nazir to hook up the ancient karaoke machine the Moros brought with them, rescued him from further injury when he foolishly volunteered for a second attempt.

"Hey, Blade, stop hopping around like a grasshopper on speed. Let's see how good the police are at line dancing."

Mountain started singing "Boot Scoot Boogie," and the Marines, led by Pacer who was from the Lone Star state, formed into a line and began dancing. Marine issue shorts and rough suede boots replaced fancy Tony Lama boots and jeans, and the dancing Marines immediately captured the enthusiasm of the cops, who lined up behind them to mimic the steps.

When that song finished, Geordy introduced the next song, saying, "Here's to the great state of Tennessee," and launched into "Walking in Memphis."

Captain Hamza followed him with the old Kingston Trio hit of "Scotch and Soda," and his smoky voice was perfect for the song, but hysterically funny for a Muslim to be singing about alcohol.

Everyone took a turn singing, even those, like Levitz, who couldn't carry a tune even if you strapped it to a caribou. Wren hoped his lack of participation wouldn't be noticed, but no such luck. He protested, uselessly, he didn't need to sing since he volunteered twice for the ankle bashing. Mercury made him laugh when he suggested the monkeys in the treetops might serve as backup if he was really bad.

Shamed into participating by the hoots and jeers of his teammates and the police, Blade took his time selecting a song and then began to sing Michael Bublés' "Home."

He winked at Geordy, who stood off to the side with his mouth agape, amazed by his clear tenor.

***

Hearing Wren sing, about being surrounded by a million people and still feeling alone, made Geordy shiver inside as he identified too closely with the lyrics. He flashed back to his mother's letter and knew, without a doubt, his adherence to his dating rule cost him, as his mother described it, a man with music and poetry in his soul, and a companion to cure his feeling of living separate from everyone else.

He didn't need to be hit over the head to realize Wren de Lassy completed him, but when he got scared at the sudden intensity of his feelings in Beltrees, and spouted off his protective mantra about not dating Marines, his teammate took him at his word and shut down.

The brief hug Blade gave him on the trail was just that, brief, and more one of concern than sexual interest. The fact he lacked the balls to say or demonstrate his true feelings depressed him all to hell. He cringed as he recalled his fabrication about missing the camaraderie. Fuck camaraderie, he wanted de Lassy in his life, and in his bed, but he hesitated too long on that jungle trail and, once again, Blade moved on.

Wrapping up the festivities and returning to his bunk brought his over-wound nerves some relief, until Blade climbed into the bunk next to his. His conscience zinged him with, *too bad you're such a craven coward, but at least you have all night to lie here and remember sleeping with your arms wrapped around Wren.*

Chapter Sixteen

Geordy yawned and stretched after helping Doc set up the folding table and chairs. Today was village sick call, and, since he spoke the best Tagalog, he served as interpreter for the villagers with medical complaints.

"What's the matter, Mountain, didn't you sleep well? You're usually the most chipper one among us in the mornings," Doc observed as he opened his medical kit in preparation for receiving patients.

Geordy worked the kinks out of his neck and shoulders as he answered. "Guess I'm just missing an actual mattress instead of a sleeping bag thrown over a wooden platform." No way in hell would he admit to staying awake listening to Wren breathe while fantasizing being alone with him on a deserted island.

"Heads up, Doc, here come your first patients."

Doc Ferri noted only three women carrying babies or small children, and sighed. "Maybe now the police aren't so standoffish in their interaction with us, the villagers will feel free to mingle with us again. I bet some of them have medical issues I could assist with, if only they would tell me about them."

Doc had to raise his voice over the crying baby being carried by the old woman who was last in line.

Geordy kind of felt sorry for Doc this morning because none of the villager complaints required anything beyond the most basic treatment. A child with an ear infection: antibiotics dispensed, done. A second-degree burn from getting too close to a cooking fire.

Analgesic ointment dispensed, and done. However, the third woman, the one with the crying baby, turned the day upside down and sideways.

As she passed the squalling baby to Doc, the woman turned to Geordy. "There's nothing wrong with my grandson. I pinch him to make him cry. Tell the doctor to examine him as if there is."

Geordy focused on the woman and saw fear and something more in her eyes. He saw determination. He quietly passed her message on to Doc, who didn't blink an eye as he did as she requested and unwrapped the baby's diaper to begin a complete checkup.

"Is there something you wanted to tell us, something that doesn't involve the health of your grandson?" Geordy he picked up one of the baby's hands and shook it just a little to gain his attention enough to make him stop crying.

"The headmaster sent me to warn you. He can't tell you himself because he and his family are being watched. He chose me because my father fought with the American guerrillas in World War II, and, like my father who wouldn't bow to the Japanese invaders, I won't bow to these Muslims."

Geordy scanned their perimeter to ensure no one else was interested in this conversation before asking, "Who is watching the headmaster, and what does he want to warn us about?"

"The men you are training are Maute. They kept themselves hidden in Mindanao, but their entire unit secretly joined Maute. Tomorrow, the headmaster's son, the one who cooks for you, will put something they gave him in the food he will serve you for dinner or they will kill his family. He was told this will not poison you, only make you sleep. He doesn't want to do this, but he wants his parents and his wife to live."

Before Geordy could stop the woman, she reached down and surreptitiously pinched her grandson, starting another bout of outraged crying. He felt a little better seeing the regret in the woman's eyes as she turned to face him again.

"I hope my grandson will forgive me, but making him appear to be in pain was the only thing I could think of to explain my visit. These bad men threatened us by saying Maute will return to our village and kill us all if we warn you."

Geordy handed Doc a sterile package of ear swabs, and, Doc, who'd picked up enough of the dialogue to run with the fake exam, opened them and began cleaning out the infant's ears.

"Why do the police want to put us to sleep?"

Even Doc faltered in his ministrations to the infant at the woman's answer.

"Once you are asleep, they will come into your rooms and cut off your heads. They will leave them on bamboo poles to send a message to America that Maute is a force to be reckoned with. They want your weapons and your boats. They will use the boats to escape and the weapons to kill many Americans once they return to Mindanao. Now I must go, but you must believe me if you don't want to lose your heads."

Doc handed the woman a tube of ointment. "Your grandson is quite healthy except for diaper rash. This ointment will help." When the woman took the medicine and left, Doc turned to Mountain. "I got about a third of that conversation, but from the little I did understand, the shit is about to hit the fan, or am I wrong?"

"You're not wrong at all. Now you know why the police didn't warm up to us and why the villagers kept their distance. The Maute terrorists intend to put our heads on pikes and steal our weapons so they can kill more Americans. God bless that woman and the headmaster who put his entire village in jeopardy by sending her to warn us."

Geordy glanced at his watch. "Great, lunchtime, we need to tell Pacer about this over lunch and come up with a plan. The old woman said our cook plans to spike our dinner tomorrow night, so that doesn't leave us much time to figure out a course of action."

"Yeah, and while you are talking to the team, I'm going to get chummy with the cook. I want to watch as he prepares our lunch. I did understand the woman when she said he doesn't want to put those knockout drops in our food, but maybe I can persuade him to substitute plain water, so if anyone is spying on him, they'll see him add a liquid to our food. How the rest of this plays out will be up to Pacer."

***

"Damn, Mountain, you could've waited until my mouth was empty before dropping that bomb," Pacer wheezed as he finished coughing up a lung. "Your comment about putting our heads on pikes made me swallow a forkful of rice the wrong way."

Pacer slid his glance to the police dining area and noted no one there was paying them the slightest attention, but still leaned in to mimic Mountain's whisper. "So, H-Hour is sometime after dinner tomorrow. Until Manila gives us some rudder steer, act like everything is copacetic. Byte, you and I will be talking to Tecate and Woody as soon as lunch is over. The rest of you will continue with your scheduled classes. I don't think I need say to wear your poker faces."

Pacer turned his attention to Vlad when he muttered, "*Bozhi Moi.*"

"What's the problem, Vlad?"

"I finally teach them to hit what they're aiming at, and the next thing they'll be aiming at is us. And the scheduled training for the rest of this afternoon is marksmanship."

Mercury snickered. "Let them shoot as much as they want. There will be less ammunition for them to steal the day after tomorrow."

Pacer sported a huge grin as he informed his team, "I just came up with a scathingly brilliant idea. If we end up having to do a hasty exfil, Blade, I want you to wire the safe room. We'll put whatever we can't take with us in the safe room, and you can give whoever tries to get in there a very loud surprise. There are thirty of them to seven of us, so our heads may end up on bamboo stakes, but at least they won't be able to use United States Marine-issue weapons and ammunition to continue killing Americans. We'll revisit that after I talk to Manila and MARSOC."

Blade rubbed his hands in anticipation. "No problem, Captain. I packed everything I need to make opening that door a very unpleasant experience."

Doc Ferri came back to the table and motioned for Mercury to make a hole so he could sit next to Pacer. "I just spoke with the cook and he confirmed what the old woman told us. He even showed me the vial containing something too viscous to be water. I haven't a clue what Maute gave him, but the fear on his face is real enough. He let me replace what's in the bottle with plain water, and tomorrow he'll add it to whatever he cooks, just in case anyone from the police unit is watching him. He suggested we make a production of eating the evening meal and then retiring early as if we're tired."

"That's a good plan, thanks, Doc." Pacer continued to give his team instructions. "Now, Byte, you're with me. I need to speak to Manila before we go final with our plans. Remember, Raiders, business as usual. I'll let you know what Manila says this evening after dinner. We'll meet in the safe room, and I'll be sure to tell Lieutenant Mambuay we're conducting a planning huddle for the field exercise scheduled for the day after tomorrow. The planning huddle is posted in the schedule, and since the field exercise is a graded event, I don't think he'll question us being out of their sight for a while to do planning."

***

Mountain and Blade were the last in to dinner that evening. Mountain because he was responsible for constructing the mockup of a Philippine house for the hostage rescue exercise, and Blade because he had to measure doors and windows for constructing the charges used to storm the building.

Constructing a building was hot work in the tropics, but Mountain found doing so this time particularly frustrating since, if the Maute attack went off when planned, his sweat and sunburned skin would be all for naught.

Geordy began to fantasize about an ice-cold beer as he pounded in the last nail, but fantasize was all he could do. MARSOC regs said no drinking on deployments, but no worries—he'd have to be an idiot to drink when the Muslim unit they'd been sent to teach wanted to lop off their heads. Blade echoed his thoughts for his ears only as he finished his measuring.

"I sure would like to play mouse at the keyhole to learn what

Manila comes up with for extricating us from this colossal clusterfuck. Can you say intel screw-up? I'll bet there are a few tight sphincters in the G-2 section this afternoon. I sure as hell wouldn't want to be the one to inform whoever runs the Philippine Police one of their units went rogue right under their nose."

Geordy's lips twisted in a sardonic grin. "I'll bet heads are going to roll, but hopefully not ours. I'm done here, so let's go get some chow and catch up on what Manila had to say."

***

They returned in time to overhear Pacer tell Lieutenant Mambuay they were invited to an American-style barbecue after the hostage rescue exercise.

Blade lost his appetite when the lieutenant accepted the invitation with a laugh and a wink. "It will be our pleasure to share dinner with you."

The Maute bastard knew, if their plan succeeded, the American Marines would never be eating that or any other meal ever again.

He must've hesitated or given some small sign the lieutenant's response hadn't pleased him, for Mountain's hand clamped down on his shoulder and encouraged him to keep walking. He felt better when Geordy muttered, "Yeah, and we'll be serving barbecued crow."

Vlad slid over so Mountain could take a seat next to Byte when they joined the team for dinner. Glancing around the table, Blade could tell everyone wanted to question Pacer about what higher headquarters wanted them to do about the situation, but their dining area was in plain sight of the one the police used, and no one wanted to risk letting that cat out of the bag.

Pacer had everyone's attention as he began the brief in a low voice after everyone crowded into the secure room. "Listen up Raiders. Manila wants us to exfil tomorrow night a few hours before the planned attack. We'll use the beach at the end of the trail Blade and Mountain did the recon on. Which means, Mercury, you need to invent some plausible reason for taking one of the Zodiacs to that side of the island tomorrow."

Mercury pulled himself away from the wall he leaned on and gave Pacer his full attention. "I'm ahead of you, Captain. I think I can disable the Zodiacs without tipping off the police if you give me an order when either Captain Hamza or Lieutenant Mambuay is near enough to hear it."

"Sure, Mercury, what do you want me to order you to do?"

"You say something like, 'Mercury, we'll be using the boats for the exercise, so I want you to do a complete engine check and top off all the gas tanks.' That will give me a plausible reason for inspecting and fiddling with the engines. I plan on filling the gas tanks with seawater and topping them off with a very small amount of gasoline, so whoever checks the tanks will see the gas floating on top and think they are full. They'll get a big surprise when they start those engines up and only get a couple of feet away from the beach before they conk out."

Byte clapped the coxswain on the shoulder. "I never would've guessed you were so devious, Mercury."

"I can also fiddle with one of the engines to make it stutter, and then I'll ask for permission to do a shakedown ride to see what the problem is. I'll head to the exfil site and stash it and walk back. I'll be sure to claim, within hearing of the terrorists, the engine failed, and we'll get it towed back after the exercise."

Pacer shook his head in approval. "Excellent, Mercury. Sounds like a solid plan. And for the rest of you, tomorrow will be training as usual, but we'll end instruction early under the pretext of allowing the police to do their final planning.

"During dinner tomorrow, I want everyone to sort of whoop it up. You know, the usual trash talk between teammates. Blade and Mountain, you are to hang back and not eat until the rest of us are almost finished eating. If we stagger the times when we eat, the police will need to wait longer to begin the attack to ensure we're all asleep.

"Uh, Doc, make sure there's nothing but water in that vial before our cook seasons our dinner. If you can, find out what the headmaster's plans are to protect his village. I recommend they find a hiding spot somewhere on this island until this issue is resolved."

"Aye, sir, I'll speak to the cook."

"Blade, after you eat dinner tomorrow, I want you to slip inside and begin wiring the safe room. Mountain, you'll go with him to make sure we leave nothing of use in any of the other rooms, by which I mean any gear Maute might find useful."

Mercury broke into the conversation. "Captain, what are we supposed to do once we're all on the beach? The next closest island is a mile away, and we haven't done a recon, so we don't know what kind of reception we'll get if we try to land there. And seven of us in one Zodiac is not optimal for a long-range trip. Is Manila sending someone to pick us up?"

Pacer grinned at the team coxswain. "I'm hoping we won't need to do a reprise of a Viking raid on that island. They're sending a chopper from the carrier group, and Blade and Mountain already verified that beach is wide enough for a quick landing.

"We'll need to be at the beach by midnight, but we'll start the exfil at full dark. I wish Doc had been able to ID the liquid in the bottle, then we might know how soon we needed to appear asleep enough for the police to make their move, so for lack of hard data, let's say they'll hit the team house at midnight, which means lights out at eleven."

Vlad asked the question everyone wanted to know the answer to. "What are the rules of engagement? Are we cleared to shoot back if they fire first?"

"That's a definite, yes, but I hope we can break away from here without being spotted, and I hope the chopper picks us up before they know we've bugged out of our quarters. Since all of us might need to squeeze into the Zodiac, I'm making the command decision to forego full protective gear. It'll be tactical vests and helmets with the NVG mounts. However, I want to go on record as saying going without our armor closes my sphincter tighter than a clam."

Blade spoke up, "Well if the cops break into the safe room, there won't be any of our gear intact for them to use after we leave."

Pacer counted on his finger for emphasis. "Here's the order of egress: Mercury goes first to get the boat in the water and ready to go, just in case we need to exfil by water. Vlad, you'll go with Mercury to find a good shooting spot to cover the rest of us on that beach. I'll follow with Byte to maintain contact with Manila and whoever they patch in from the carrier group. Doc, you'll come with Byte and me. That leaves Mountain and Blade. I don't want the secure room armed until right before your scheduled exfil time. Mountain you'll cover Blade as he works, and then the two of you haul ass to join us on the beach."

Geordy punched Wren on the shoulder. "I'll supervise nimble fingers here so he doesn't have a premature detonation."

After the snickers died down, Pacer added, "Work fast Blade, because only Maute knows when the actual attack will occur after all lights go out at 23:00. Keep your fingers crossed they took note Mountain and Blade ate later than the rest of us, and so will need to wait an hour or two after that make sure we're all in the Land of Nod."

Vlad summed up everyone's mood before they ended the meeting. "Well, if they do attack before we vacate this building, they'll find that not everyone who snores is sleeping."

Chapter Seventeen

Pacer didn't have to roust anyone out of bed the next morning. Everyone was up and alert on what might be the last day of their lives. Blade cracked everyone up at breakfast and eased some of the tension with an observation.

"Does anyone but me find today's training schedule ironic?" When he got blank looks, he continued. "No one finds it even slightly fucked up to be teaching our erstwhile terrorists how to construct or disarm explosive devices in the morning, and hand-to-hand combat in the afternoon?"

Blade chuckled at the wide eyes and open mouths he saw around the table. It broke the tension and everyone dissolved into laughter.

Glancing at his watch, he stood and announced, "Onward into the breach to teach, um, breaching."

Pacer followed and nodded to Mercury to do the same. When they drew close to the assembled police, Pacer couldn't prevent the onset of heartburn to find their usually reluctant students bright-eyed and eager to absorb everything Blade would teach. He deliberately called a good morning to Captain Hamza and Lieutenant Mambuay to get their attention before turning to address Mercury.

"Hey, Mercury, I want you to give the Zodiacs a good going over. We're using them in the exercise tomorrow, and I want you to make sure they're running smoothly. Oh, and be sure all the tanks are topped off. We don't want to run out of gas in the middle of the exercise."

Mercury responded with, "Aye aye, Captain," and moved toward the beach to begin his inspections.

Pacer was damned proud of his team. Blade taught his class with his usual combination of expertise and humor. Mercury was plainly seen giving every Zodiac a thorough once over. Vlad loaded magazines with blank ammunition for the coming exercise in plain sight of the police. Mountain helped Doc inventory his medical supplies, and Byte worked with Sergeant Ariraya to breathe some life into the antiquated coms gear.

The idea the terrorists would have functioning coms made him a little goosey until Byte shot him a surreptitious wink that said no way in hell would the police radio be running by this evening.

An outboard engine's sputtering on and off, and Mercury's voluble swearing interrupted his thoughts. He turned to face his coxswain when Mercury called out from the beach.

"Hey, Captain. Something's wrong with this engine. I need to take it for a spin to see what the problem is."

Pacer didn't miss the fact that both Captain Hamza and Lieutenant Mambuay turned his way, very interested in his reply. "Sure, do what you need to do to have that engine running smoothly by tomorrow."

Captain Schuyler itched to go inside to begin sorting what would go into the safe room to be destroyed, but continued to play his part by circulating among the police and offering assistance and/or encouragement to some of the lower enlisted who were a little intimidated by Mountain's size for the hand-to-hand block of instruction.

Right before they broke for dinner, Mercury made quite a display of approaching him. Wringing wet and sunburned, Mercury gave a good impression of being thoroughly pissed off with his attempt to fix the engine. Pacer noted Sergeant Dori sidled closer to overhear Mercury's report.

"I took that Zodiac for a test drive and got halfway around the island when the motor conked out and wouldn't restart. I think the problem is in the fuel line, or maybe a gasket, but I won't know until I disassemble the engine. I had to swim to shore and beach the boat."

Mercury turned to Pacer. "Captain, will having one less boat cause a problem for the exercise?"

Pacer appeared to consider Mercury's question and replied. "Nah, the observers can walk to the exercise area and observe from the beach. If Captain Hamza wouldn't mind, he can have one of the boats tow the broken one back tomorrow after the exercise is finished."

Captain Hamza, who now stood next to Mercury, nodded his agreement, and Pacer announced the end of training for the day.

"Captain Hamza, we're breaking early to allow you to do your final planning. The exercise, as agreed, will start with a beach landing near the hostage sight at 0600. We are now strictly hands-off as trainers and are now your official observers. Good luck tomorrow."

Dinner was a rather raucous affair with the Raiders ribbing each other as they openly consumed the ubiquitous chicken and rice prepared by the cook. At least Doc gave them all the nod before forks were lifted to signal the food was free of ketamine, Rohypnol, or whatever other drug would render them senseless long enough to separate their heads from their bodies.

As previously planned, Blade and Mountain came to the table just as everyone else was getting up. Pacer kept them company as they ate. He kept his voice low as he asked, "Are we set? Is everything we aren't taking with us stowed inside the safe room?"

At Mountain's nod, Pacer asked, "What kind of surprise can Captain Hamza, or whoever opens the door to the security room, expect?"

Blade grinned and kept his voice low to answer. "Well, I was going to go with something sophisticated until I remembered the Keep It Simple Stupid rule. Since the safe room is the last room in the hallway, I anticipate the police will open each door before that one to determine if we're hiding in any of the other rooms."

Pacer nodded his agreement of Blade's reasoning.

"Once they've eliminated all the rooms, the only one left is the safe room. Let's just say, whoever opens that door, and whoever happens to be standing in the corridor outside, will gain instant martyrdom. I doubt the building will remain standing once that door is opened." As he knew he would, Pacer started to question the timing, so Blade eased his worries. "Nothing will be connected until Mountain and I are the only two left in the building.

Mountain smacked Pacer, none-to-gently, on the arm. "Tell Vlad not to shoot at anyone until he's sure he doesn't have Blade or me lined up in his reticle."

Pacer nodded and then deliberately pantomimed a huge yawn. He raised his voice to add, "I'm turning in early. We need to be at the top of our game tomorrow, so make sure you two hit the sack by midnight."

After Pacer left, Wren leaned in to Geordy and whispered as he took his last forkful of rice. "You know, Corporal Said has been watching us since we sat down to eat?"

Mountain put his fork down and stood. "Excellent. Now he can report to Captain Hamza that he'll have to allow extra time to make sure you and I are asleep. C'mon, Blade, since our room is the closest to the path, you can help me remove the wooden bars from the window. And we'd better hustle because full dark is only an hour away."

Blade removed the last bar from the window and turned around to find Vlad standing right behind him. "Shit, Vlad, I'm going to tie a bell on you. Damn, sniper, your creeping around is going to scare me to death, and then I'm going to have to come back as a ghost to kill you."

Vlad's teeth shone in the moonlight as he grinned and recited another proverb. "Don't worry, Blade, you can't die before your death."

Blade gritted his teeth over Vlad's cockamamie proverbs, but Mercury entered the room and he forgot about retaliating.

Mercury flipped his NVGs down and stated the obvious. "Time to head to the beach," and swung his leg over the window sill but hesitated at Geordy's caution.

"Keep an eye out for the police. Corporal Said was a little too interested in watching us eat this evening."

Pacer entered the dark bedroom. "No watchers so far. I just visited the head and didn't spot anyone. I guess the police really are doing some planning, probably on how to kill us, but I didn't see anyone lounging around outside." Pacer pointed, "Mercury and Vlad, head on out. I'll give you fifteen minutes and then Byte, Doc, and I will follow. Last I heard from Manila, things are still a go on their end. Now all we need is for Captain Hamza to have enough patience to wait until sometime after midnight to attack."

Vlad got a chorus of muffled snorts from everyone when he asked, "Did someone think to remind Captain Hamza that patience is a virtue?"

Pacer went along with the levity. "Mountain, don't forget to switch off the rest of the lights at eleven. Oh, and, Blade, make sure you remember to let the cat out." And with that witticism, Pacer swung his NVGs down and climbed out the window, followed by Byte and Doc.

***

Sitting in the dark beside Wren, waiting for eleven o'clock, which his watch told him was ten minutes away, made his stomach flutter, but not with fear. There were things he wanted to say, but was now a good time? Would there ever be a good time?

Geordy closed his eyes and called himself a coward and wondered why Wren de Lassy could bring out the very best and the very worst in him. He thankfully stopped his mental self-flagellation when Blade nudged him with his shoulder and stood.

"Time to go leave a note on the safe room door to remind whoever is still standing after they open the door to let the cat out. I only need a couple of minutes to get everything connected, and I'll meet you back here after you put all lights out."

As he walked through the dark hallway to return to their room, Geordy's NVGs picked up Blade standing in front of the window waiting for him. With the room blacker than the inside of a terrorist's heart, Geordy gave himself permission and flipped his night-vision goggles away from his face to grab him, spin him around, and deliver a kiss to cock up his toes. Wren's moan of pleasure rewarded his daring.

"Your timing sucks, Geordy Campbell, but if we die tonight, I'll go with a smile on my face," Wren tossed over his shoulder as he pulled his NVGs over his eyes and climbed out the window.

They were halfway to the beach when Captain Hamza, accompanied by Murphy, blew their timetable all to hell. The sudden explosion made the leaves tremble around them, and both he and Blade checked their watches, 11:45, and verified Captain Hamza did not possess the virtue of patience.

Murphy showed up in the form of Sergeant Manara Dori, who stepped from his place of concealment and leveled his weapon at Wren. Geordy, thanks to his NVGs making everything totally green and without much depth, couldn't tell who acted first, but Blade flung out his hand to toss his knife at the sergeant, and the report of Dori's weapon broke the night's silence once again, and both men fell.

Geordy doubled-timed it back and tossed Sergeant Dori's body off Blade like the man weighed nothing more than a coconut. He began to breathe again when his teammate spoke.

"Damn, that was a nasty surprise. Guess we don't need to tiptoe through the jungle, anymore. Let me collect my knife, and then let's get the fuck out of here. Guess my little surprise didn't kill everyone because I don't think that's a herd of monkeys coming down this path. Hope Vlad can tell the difference between friend and foe."

Geordy grinned savagely as he offered Blade a hand up. "I'll be easy to spot. No one else is as tall as me. You, maybe not so much."

Wren wheezed out, "Don't be so cock sure. He'll have to shoot through you to hit me because I'll be on your six like a burr on wool sock. Damn, got a stitch in my side. Where the hell is that beach?"

His question was answered by the report of Vlad's long gun and the scream of his target going down.

Vlad managed to scare Blade a second time in one night by appearing on the path right behind him. The sniper wisely chose not to tease him because this time he was armed.

Vlad pointed toward the beach. "You up for a swim? Mercury launched the Zodiac when the explosion went off earlier than planned. C'mon, Raiders, pick up the pace, I don't think losing one of their own to my long gun has deterred them."

After being hauled into the boat by his teammates Mountain asked, "How much time before that chopper gets here, and where's it going to land? I think we've just blown the beach landing."

Pacer answered. "The bird is on the way. I called and stepped up the pickup as soon as I heard Blade's surprise. As to the landing site, we'll have to let the pilot choose whether or not he wants to land somewhere farther along on the beach, or head for another island. For now, all we need to do is keep out of firing range of those police guns."

Byte reached over and gave Mercury a nudge. "Hey, Mercury, I just remembered the stuttering sound this engine made yesterday. You didn't pour sand in the engine, did you?"

Pacer shushed the general ribbing of Mercury to listen to something coming over the coms. "Guys, keep your eyes peeled for the chopper. He's coming in dark and low. And fast, very fast."

They all ducked in reflex as the bird flew over them. They also grabbed the sides of the Zodiac to keep from spilling out when the chopper descended to hover just above the water.

Pacer gave Mercury a quizzical head tilt, and Mercury shrugged. They'd both seen the chopper's wheels sink beneath the water's surface and the loading ramp being lowered. "Uh, Sergeant Rogers, what do you think? We've never practiced loading a Zodiac into a hovering chopper before."

"Piece of cake, Captain. I watched the video."

Pacer stared at his coxswain for a second. "You did? How many times?"

"Just once, sir. The only tricky part is the timing. I'll need to shut the motor off and pull the prop up before it hits the deck of the chopper. The water in the cargo area and our forward momentum should carry us the rest of the way inside."

"Okay, then, let's see how closely you paid attention to the video, Sergeant. Crank this mother up."

Mercury gave a quick, "Aye aye, Captain," and lined the Zodiac up with the back end of the chopper and increased speed. "Hang on," was the only other thing the taciturn coxswain said before he nailed the entry in one try.

The Raider's remained silently in the raft as the ramp closed, and the chopper began to climb. No one spoke until Byte said, "If this is flying first class, I want my money back."

After the laughter quit, Doc asked, "Everyone okay?"

He got five yesses and a, "Uh, Doc, I think I've sprung a leak." His and everyone else's gazes turned toward Blade.

Doc ordered, "Make a hole," as he moved from the back of the Zodiac to the forward area to check on Blade.

"Where are you hit?"

"Not sure this qualifies as a hit, Doc, maybe just a scrape." Blade began unfastening his tactical vest, and inhaled quickly when he found his T-shirt soaked through with blood. Adrenaline was a good painkiller...until it wore off. He tried to twist to see the wound, but that made him suck in a painful breath, so he stopped squirming and just let Doc do his thing. He turned his eyes in Mountain's direction and found his eyebrows formed a solid line. *Why the fuck is he mad at me? I didn't volunteer to get shot.* Doc turned his attention away from puzzling out Geordy's unexpected reaction.

"Well, you have indeed sprung a leak. What happened to whoever shot you?"

"Ah, that would be Sergeant Dori, and he won't be bragging about bagging a Marine. I evened the score with my throwing knife."

"You lucked out, Blade. This is just a flesh wound, but you're going to need some stitches. I'll slap a bandage on you until the carrier's medical staff can stitch you up.

Vlad earned jeers and some jostling from his team when he offered, "The bullet is a fool; it only hits where there is a hole."

Pacer's team spent the rest of the flight going over their individual experiences. They knew there'd be numerous debriefings aboard ship in Manila and back at MARSOC before they could stand down from this mission. They also knew whatever happened to the surviving Maute terrorists stranded on that island would be up to the Philippine government.

Chapter Eighteen

Jack Adams stopped reading the classified file when a knock came at his office door and he waved Anthony Tonelli in. "I'm guessing something must have happened, Ant. I can't recall the last time you had such a strange expression on your face. I can't decide if you're happy or pissed."

"I can't either. We got a lead on Elmoudowi. One of his aliases just popped up. We also got another one-over-the-world Internet blast from Elmoudowi saying the time, place, and martyrs for paying back the Marines have been chosen. Big bang to follow."

Jack sat back in his chair and motioned the Ant into the chair in front of his desk. "Shit. There's goes my hope Elmoudowi would drop the whole revenge thing. Where in the world is Waldo's evil twin now?"

"This particular Waldo is going by the name of Stavros Andino, and if our source is to be believed, he's painting Monaco red."

Jack sat back in his chair and had to rein in his temper. "Monaco? What in the hell is he doing in Monaco? Please tell me we have a picture of this Stavros Andino."

"No joy yet again. The alias pinged our system when a high-priced rental agency ran a credit check on Stavros Andino. Not finding any negative credit information on the name, they rented a mini-villa to someone by that name. Elmoudowi used an intermediary, so we don't have any photos of Andino aka Elmoudowi. You want me to arrange for someone to go to Monaco and snap a photo of the man? According to the rental agreement, he doesn't take possession of the rental property until next month."

Jack steepled his fingers and thought about the Ant's suggestion for a moment. Making up his mind, he nodded his head. "Yeah, have one of our agents set up surveillance of that mansion. If we're lucky, we'll snag the bastard's photo for our wanted list. I want a likeness to put a big X through when we take him out. In the meantime, I think there might be a way to cozy up to Elmoudowi to uncover how he intends to pay back the Marines, so keep your fingers crossed the person I have in mind for the job can be persuaded to take the mission."

The Ant stood and grinned down at Jack Adams. "Fingers crossed and toes as well. Let me know if you need my help in persuading him. I'll rob my kids' piggy banks if you can't meet his financial demands."

Jack chuckled. "Thanks, but I don't think offering money will work with this guy. I'll need to come up with another hook. Now, get the hell out of here and let me work."

After Ant closed the door, Jack sat back and took a little mental journey back to the operation that freed the famous painter, Nels Kirkegaard, from sexual slavery. The rescue had been effected by an Army Special Ops team led by then Captain Trollinger. Damn, what was the man's first name? He didn't recall. Most of the Spec Ops teams used team nicknames. Trollinger was Troll, and, oh yes, they called Ross de Lassy Lassie or Dawg.

He knew de Lassy was retired, but Trollinger might still be in the service. Jack buzzed his secretary. "Maggie, work your magic and find me an Army Spec Ops guy with the last name of Trollinger." He spelled it for his secretary. "And yesterday wouldn't be soon enough to locate the guy."

Maggie, God bless her, had his answer in five minutes.

"Mr. Adams, there is an Army Special Operations Colonel by the name of Christian Trollinger. He's newly assigned to Joint Special Operations Command at Fort Bragg. His phone number is...."

Jack began dialing the number as soon as Maggie recited the last digit. He suffered through the formal military greeting and said, "This is Jack Adams calling from Langley for Colonel Trollinger. Is he available?"

Dropping the word "Langley" gave his call priority. Troll answered a moment later.

"Is this the Jack Adams I knew from a place with a lot of sand?"

Jack laughed. "Yeah, the very same Jack who used to break out in a rash whenever we met." He was surprised when there was a moment of hesitation before Troll spoke again.

"Uh, if this is about pay back, I need to say this line is not secure, Mr. Adams."

Jack hastened to assure Troll. "No need, I'm just calling to congratulate you on your new assignment. You've been promoted a couple of times since last we met. You had such a good team, I'm sure you must miss them."

Troll laughed, and Jack relaxed his tight shoulders and kept to his plan.

"I don't miss the fuckers at all, I brought them with me. Speaking of new assignments, have you been promoted from playing in the sandbox to bird watching in Virginia?"

"Bird watching? I like that, Troll. You must have attended charm school since you left the sandbox. Are you asking me if they put me out to pasture? The answer is no, I just graze in greener ones now."

Jack changed the subject and got on with his schmoozing. "Hey, you still friends with de Lassy? What's he up to these days?" Troll took the bait.

"Yeah, Ross and I are still buds. He came hunting with me last fall at my parents' cabin in Pennsylvania. We each bagged four-point bucks. There's lots of venison in my freezer...at least until this weekend. My crew's coming over for venison burgers and beer.

Jack, not a fan of gamey meat, shuddered and kept the ball rolling. "What ever happened to the kid I sent home with Ross?"

"You mean Wren? He turned out well. Graduated with a degree in mathematics from George Mason and developed quite a following when he was on the MMA circuit."

Jack moved the phone away from his ear so he could give it a disbelieving gawk. This was getting better and better. He replaced the receiver. "So, what's he up to now? Is he teaching math someplace?"

He had to back away from the receiver again when Troll guffawed into the phone.

"Would you believe he joined the Marines? He served in Force Recon and then made the MARSOC selection, probably in no small part due to Ross teaching him his knife fighting techniques. The kid took to edged weapons like a duck to water."

Jack began to breathe easier for the first time since Troll picked up the phone, but there was a very important thing he needed clarified, and no time like the present to ask.

"Uh, MARSOC? I thought he was...." He let the sentence go unfinished, and Troll didn't disappoint.

"If you are asking if he's gay, I'm not going to answer that. Wren is Wren, and he has a different viewpoint from ours. Whatever his sexual persuasion, MARSOC didn't cut him from selection. And a word of advice, should you ever meet him again, the kid is too good with his hands, feet, and knives to risk pissing him off by asking him that question."

Oh, thank my lucky stars and my previously MIA guardian angel. Possessing the intel he needed to proceed with his plan, Jack ended the call by again congratulating Troll on his new command assignment.

As soon as he hung up, he punched his intercom and bellowed, "Maggie, find out which unit Wren de Lassy is assigned to at MARSOC, and don't add my request to your to-do-later list. This is a hot target. Oh, and see if you can find a recent picture of him, preferably out of uniform."

"Will do Mr. Adams. You will be late for your budget meeting in the director's office if you don't leave now."

With a murmured "Shiiiit," Jack took a nanosecond to eyeball his desk and make sure he didn't leave any classified material out or on an open screen. Finding nothing, he grabbed the figures he needed and flew by his grinning secretary, who was on the phone, hopefully, to MARSOC.

***

With Pacer's team back on base, the work load was grueling. Debriefings, followed by briefings, followed by filling out missing gear statements, Limited Technical Inspections of their NVGs and service weapons, and whatever else the powers at MARSOC deemed necessary to do bring their status back to ready for another deployment.

Everyone cheered the arrival of Friday, with its promise of two days of sleeping in, but no more so than Wren. The little ding he'd received from Sergeant Dori felt, at first, like someone was prodding him with a hot poker. Now the damned thing just itched. He considered putting Tecate in a headlock when the logistician crowed about not having anything to count, inspect, or store since Blade blew it all up.

When Captain Schuyler announced everything was finished to his satisfaction and they could all escape from MARSOC for a week's leave, his good humor resurrected itself. The cold beer and pizza the team shared that evening on one of the picnic tables outside the dorm helped finish mellowing him out, until Byte wanted to know where everyone was going to spend their leave.

He didn't have an answer for Byte. Neither it seemed did Geordy, for he just shrugged and said he needed to consider his options.

Vlad garnered hoots and comments when he said he was going to spend his leave in the neighboring town of Richlands learning to ride horses from a girl he met before their Philippine deployment.

"She's going to teach me to ride horses then I'll teach her how to ride a Russian bull." Vlad's pelvic thrust spoke volumes.

Full dark and killer mosquitos drove them back to their rooms, and he started to ask Geordy if he wanted to come to Alexandria, Virginia, with him to meet Ross and Nels, but he left the question unasked when Geordy's cell phone rang and he stretched out on his bed to answer the call.

Vlad began packing for his horseback adventure, and he grabbed a physics book and sat at his desk to work one of the problems. Neither Geordy nor Vlad believed him when he said he found doing so relaxing, but burying his head in a book was also a way to give Geordy some privacy while he was on the phone.

The sudden change in Geordy's tone of voice made him switch to eavesdrop mode. The Mountain had never flirted with him in quite that manner, so he listened, unabashedly, to the conversation as he moved his pencil over the paper in an attempt to solve a problem he was no longer interested in.

"Sure, I remember that bar in North Myrtle Beach, but I remember what we did after that more. Yeah, time does fly, but I, uh, travel a lot for my job." Geordy stretched and then put his arm behind his head and laughed. "Hey, I just got a week's leave. How about we meet at that restaurant that serves those primo grouper sandwiches? Fantastic. What hotel are you staying in? Wow, beachfront no less. Okay, I'll be there tomorrow, and we'll catch up over lunch."

After Geordy hung up, he closed his math book and got his suitcase out. He didn't stop packing to answer Geordy's question as to where he would go until he crossed to his dresser and grabbed a week's worth of boxer briefs to add to the jeans in the suitcase.

"I'm heading home. I haven't seen Ross and Nels for quite some time, so I'm going to turn in. I want to hit the road early enough to get to Alexandria by dinner."

He was so focused on avoiding eye contact with Geordy he narrowly missed being struck on the butt by Vlad's towel as he came back into the room from taking a shower.

He confronted the sniper. "Tell me, Vlad, is there a Russian proverb that says how short snipers' lives are?"

Vlad appeared to consider the question then grinned evilly. "I suppose you could substitute sniper for soldier in the one that goes: 'When a soldier dies, he's too bad for Heaven; and he drinks so much the devils won't take him to Hell.'"

Wren closed his eyes and shook his head. He admitted defeat by pulling back his covers and falling into bed, and turning into the wall so he wouldn't have to watch Geordy pack. His desired departure time of six in the morning was too damned far away for his liking, but with any luck he could be up and away before either Vlad or Geordy woke.

Two hours of tossing later, he cursed himself for not just hopping into his truck and heading home as soon as he finished packing. Every time he closed his eyes, the damned box appeared. Not just any box, but the unpadded one Geordy wanted to put him in.

His head hurt from trying to interpret Mountain's mixed signals. What the fuck was the deal with him, anyway? First a hug in the jungle, then a kiss worthy of a Hollywood love scene before they blew their supplies to smithereens, and now he was supposed to crawl back in the "I don't date Marines" box and be happy while Geordy reengaged with an old flame? Oh hell to the fuck, no.

He threw off the covers, got out of bed, and imitated Vlad's sniper moves as he made the bed, grabbed his clothes and shaving kit, and headed to the bathroom for a quick shower and shave. He nearly had a heart attack when he opened the bathroom door and ran straight into Vlad. As he disengaged himself from the sniper's arms, he started to curse, but remembered Geordy was still asleep so he kept his voice low.

"You've just had your last surprise. I'm buying you a cat collar with a bell. You're damned lucky you didn't come at me from behind or you'd be going on sick call instead of leave," he warned Vlad.

Vlad surprised the hell out of him by actually giving him a man hug.

"I just wanted to say goodbye and enjoy your time with your family. I sometimes wish I could do the same, but I enjoy living more. Kiril would make my life short and miserable if I ever returned."

As he cleared the doorway, Vlad added, "Remember, Blade, if you don't crack the shell, you can't eat the nut."

And that little cryptic proverb kept him company all the way to Virginia.

***

Ross de Lassy kissed Nels's shoulder very lightly so he wouldn't wake him. He had a new client showing up at the ungodly hour of eight o'clock, because the man wanted to fill Ross in on his problem before he headed into work, and Ross, considering the hefty sum the man was willing to pay, accommodated him.

Ross moved quietly through his study and into the kitchen. He needed coffee to jump-start his brain so he wouldn't give his new client the impression he was a lackwit.

He stopped in surprise to find the light on the percolator glowed green. Wren must be up, and, as Nels would quip, something was fishy in Denmark. Wren enjoyed sleeping in whenever the Marine Corps authorized him to do so, and especially when he'd partied till the wee hours these last two days.

Ross poured himself a cup of black coffee and went in search of his former ward. He found him in the great room wearing a pair of Marine Corps sweat pants and staring out the window at the row houses across the street. He almost dropped his mug of coffee when he turned around.

"Whoa, what the fuck is that?" Ross pointed at the healing wound.

Wren wore a decidedly sheepish countenance as he answered.

"This? This is nothing but a scratch."

Ross moved closer and bent down to study the "scratch." He traced his fingers over the dots made by stitches, and called him on it. "Bullshit, that's a flesh wound, not a scratch. Been there, done that, and know one when I see one. Why didn't you call us?"

Wren took a sip from his own coffee mug before answering. "I didn't want to worry either you or Nels, because this didn't rate getting the both of you worried enough to drive down to MARSOC. The worst thing I had to deal with was the itching until the stitches came out."

Ross stared into Wren's eyes, and there was something there he was wrestling with, and he didn't think getting wounded was what was bothering him. Well, he might think he successfully changed the subject, but his, "I didn't want to worry you," wouldn't dissuade him from digging deeper.

Ross glanced at the wall clock and saw he had a little less than an hour to winkle it out of him, so he dove right in. "A plausible explanation, but now I want the real reason you think Nels and I don't want to hear what's going on with you. You don't call us when you're wounded for real, and then you show up here with a bigger, invisible wound, and we're just supposed to ignore the gaping hole in your psyche? Trust me, those kinds of wounds don't heal by themselves." He was amazed Wren caved so easily.

"What do you do when you like someone who is even more conflicted than you?"

Ross followed Wren to the sofa and sat down facing him. "By like do you mean like as in friend or like as in love interest?" He didn't miss the wince on Wren's face as he leaned forward to clasp his knees.

"I guess you could say love interest when he lets me, and he only lets me when there is no danger of anyone discovering the fact that he and I are...."

He groaned and put his face in his hands. "We're both Marine Raiders, and we both want to advance in our careers, and we're both smart enough to realize that's not going to happen if we come out of the duffel bag, so to speak."

Ross threw an arm over Wren's shoulders. "Tell me about him."

He gave Ross Geordy's biography and concluded with, "As soon as we return to MARSOC, Geordy puts me back in the 'I don't date Marines' box, and, though I don't think he notices, he hurts me more every time he does so. I was going to ask him if he wanted to meet you and Nels, but he got a call from an old boyfriend, and he's spending the week with him at the beach, and all I can do is feel jealous. I didn't think I had a jealous bone in my body until I met Geordy Campbell."

He stared out the window and grimaced. "I'm seriously considering using a rusty spoon to scoop my brain out, just so I can stop thinking of him."

Ross mulled Wren's information over for a few minutes. "Have you told Geordy anything about your life? I mean other than about Nels and me?"

Wren shook his head. "No, what good would that do except send him screaming to the staff sergeant for a new room assignment? I think Geordy has enough baggage to carry without adding mine to his load."

Ross squeezed Wren's shoulder. "The easy solution is to chalk this up to life experience and move on, but you're a de Lassy, and de Lassys never choose easy."

"True that, Ross. I spent this leave trying to move on, but"—he waved a hand over his crotch—"some parts of me haven't gone along with the plan."

Ross didn't say anything, just grabbed Wren and wrestled him to the floor, and the game was on. Wren surprised him by breaking the hold and locking him up so tight he couldn't move.

Nels strolled into the room and announced, "Someone is going to be late for their meeting if he doesn't hop into the shower, ASAP."

Ross headed to the bathroom, with Wren expressing a desire for pancakes and half a hog for breakfast, and Nels telling him they could accommodate his wishes at the corner diner.

***

Sunday night, leave over, thank the *fuck*, Geordy thought as he parked his truck in the MARSOC parking lot. He was so ready to put this past week behind him. All he had to show for his time at the beach was a tan and a desire to wait at least a year before consuming any kind of seafood.

As he grabbed his suitcase and headed toward the dorm, he continued the same conversation with himself he'd started when he reached Myrtle Beach, South Carolina. A monologue that went something along the lines of, "Ye'r a right stupid bastard, Geordy. How could you even think substituting anyone for Wren was a good idea?"

Geordy was furious with himself. He thought he'd outgrown the idiocy of giving his little head the majority vote, but the pleasure center between his legs pulled off a successful coup by refusing to go along with his plans for a much-needed vacation. So, instead of coming home mellowed out from a week of sexual release, he was wound tighter than a drum head, and his mood verged somewhere between churlish and rabid.

He wanted to punch himself in the head for not shaking Stefan's hand and turning right around and heading back to the base. He knew as soon as he saw him his previous attraction for the man had died. Hell, he couldn't find the slightest spark of interest in the man, and his dick seconded the motion.

As he climbed the stairs to the third floor, Geordy thought for what he hoped would be the final time of Stefan. The man was handsome in a trendy, metrosexual kind of way, but one glimpse and Geordy's heart told him this vacation would be a bust. Granted, Stefan could hold his own in a conversation, he was a community college professor, but Geordy resented the fact he couldn't share the majority of his life with him. Having to say, "Sorry, can't talk about it, it's classified. No I can't tell you where I'm going, or when I'll be back, or when I'll leave, because that's classified," didn't lead to a long-term, stable relationship, and that's exactly what he wanted, a long-term, stable relationship, but with someone who understood what he did for a living, and certainly someone who didn't cringe every time the word gun was mentioned.

Ironically, it was Stefan who hammered the last nail into the coffin of their association. If he *had* been into the man, their conversation in the diner would have devastated him, but instead, the relief had been instantaneous.

They met at the seafood restaurant as planned, and he ordered a grouper sandwich then had to gag it down because he didn't want to be at the beach at all, and he sure as hell didn't want to spend a week solely in the company of Stefan. For God's sake, the man was wearing a tie and suitcoat at the beach. If he was trying to dress to impress, Geordy would have preferred he wear short tennis shorts and a tight T-shirt, not swaddle himself in yards of fabric. Funny, he was usually the one who didn't meet dress standards, preferring jeans or cargo shorts, T-shirt, and flip-flops, unless there were generals in attendance, but here at the beach he fit right in.

If he had to pick a word to describe their conversation, after not seeing each other for a year, he would have chosen desultory, or maybe lethargic. Strained was a close third. The ice breaker was a simple question. He asked Stefan about his life since last they met, and the man almost came apart at the table.

Stefan couldn't meet his eyes as he dropped the small bomb about meeting the love of his life. That prompted another question, which he took time to put into polite words when he really wanted to ask, "then why the fuck did you invite me to spend a week at the beach with you?"

Stefan had wanted to be sure, and, after seeing Geordy walk in, he was, absolutely, positively sure that whatever he and Geordy had a year ago was dead and buried. Geordy could understand that, he echoed the feeling.

He ended up spending a week at the beach by himself. The water was great, the sand not at all annoying because he didn't have to low-crawling through it, or run on it in full gear, and he had a savage tan. Too bad he couldn't stop his brain from thinking of Wren while he sunbathed, although cold beer helped.

Geordy reached for the doorknob to his room and the happy spark of anticipation that Wren might be inside pissed him off. With a snarl on his face, he entered the room and felt supremely foolish when he found no one inside. What the hell was wrong with him? Instead of being relieved he wouldn't have to act like he'd spent the week getting his rocks off with Stefan, he was disappointed, and a little sad not to find Wren sitting in the lotus position on his bed working a math problem.

Geordy stowed his clothes and hit the shower. Thanks to the little brain coming back from wherever the hell it went for vacation, the shower would be a cold one.

Chapter Nineteen

Never more so than this moment did Wren admire the Marine Corps' ability to work you so hard you had no time to think of anything else but how good it was going to feel to fall into your bunk and go comatose for eight hours, instead of torturing yourself by wondering what or who Geordy had done at the beach. The taciturn Scot didn't feel the need to share, and he vowed to cut out his own tongue with his tactical knife before he asked.

Schyuler's team was given a "hey you" assignment because one of the African teams bowed out due to personnel losses. One of their Marines broke a leg in a water-skiing accident, another came up for a school he needed to attend to make rank, and another had a family emergency. Since Pacer's team returned early, they were selected to fill in.

Wren didn't mind at all, he could use his French, and there might even be time at the end of the mission to take a safari.

He walked into the morning planning meeting only to get called into Pacer's office. Funny how getting called into the COs office always made you review your previous actions to explain why your commander requested your presence so he could tap dance on your liver. Nope, nothing he could think of. Like a good boy, he kept his hands, feet, and pecker to himself on the last leave.

"Is there something you need, sir?"

Pacer waved Blade in. "I just got a call from the Command Deck. You're to report to the SCIF immediately."

He wrinkled his forehead in puzzlement. "The SCIF? Why?

What's this about, sir?"

"No clue, but the word ASAP was stressed. Shake a leg, Blade."

He double-timed it to MARSOC headquarters and buzzed for entrance into the Secure Compartmented Intelligence Facility, all the while asking himself why Sergeant Wren de Lassy was an item of interest at headquarters. He couldn't think of a single thing his team left out on the Philippine op debriefings, or anything in any other category to necessitate his presence in the SCIF, so the only thing to do was shut his mouth until someone enlightened him.

Once inside, he was shown into a bare-bones conference room and told to wait. His enlightenment came when Jack Adams walked into the room.

"Good morning, Wren. Do you remember me?"

He rose from his chair and shook the man's offered hand. "Yes, sir, I do but, no insult intended, I can't say seeing you again brings happy memories. What's all this about, Mr. Adams?"

Jack pushed a paper across the table. "Read this and then sign it. I can't tell you anything until you do."

Wren speed read the paper. "So, if I even talk in my sleep after I sign this, I'll be doing a permanent tour of Leavenworth, right?"

"That about sums it up, but I don't think I need worry about you having loose lips. Your guardian, Ross, probably already told you what happens to special operators with verbal diarrhea."

He signed the paper with his usual flourish, passed the document back, and waited for Jack Adams, who he remembered was a high-ranking member of a three-letter government agency, to explain the reason for his visit.

Jack began with a question. "Did you catch the news about the bombing in Kabul two months ago?"

He nodded. "Yeah, it took out twenty Afghan military and three Marines from Camp Pendleton."

Well, the man responsible for making that explosive device is Jabir Elmoudowi. Your MOS is EOD so you understand that bomb makers have signatures. The Kabul bomb had Elmoudowi's all over it.

He sat back in his chair and stared into Jack Adams' face. "Okay, so what part do I play in that?

"Let's save that for later. We've been after Elmoudowi for at least a year at this moment, but he's heavily protected by some powerful hitters, mainly because he's very good at tailoring his explosives to fit the mission."

Wren nodded. "The best are masters at it."

"Half a year ago we had intel, I'm not going to lie to you and say it was reliable intel, but we learned Elmoudowi was going to be in a certain Afghan village, in a particular Afghan hut, for a meeting with one of his clients. We were so excited to get a location on the man we sent in a drone strike. It leveled the hut, but no joy. We found traces of the man's presence in the hut, but no body parts or DNA to confirm a kill. What we did learn shortly after the strike was that Elmoudowi was supremely pissed. He went on the Internet to declare war on United States Marines. It was a Marine drone that took out his friends."

His gut started to cramp. Jack Adams wanted him for something, but he wasn't a Tier One operative, so he didn't think it was to join the hunt for Elmoudowi, so why the fuck was he here? Impatient to know, he asked, "And what part do you want me to play in this? I'm not part of black ops."

"No, you're not, but your face gives you an in." Jack pushed the photo of Dawud Afif across the table."

"You want me to impersonate Elmoudowi?"

Jack shook he head. "No, I don't. Not that I think you couldn't build a bomb, but the man in that photo isn't him. That's Dawud Afif, Elmoudowi's lover."

Wren sat back in his chair and shook his head. The clandestine elephant had just wedged itself into the SCIF conference room. He stared over the table at Adams and the CIA agent met his eyes. Jack wasn't blinking, just waiting for him to make the next move.

"You want me to impersonate Elmoudowi's lover?"

Adams nodded but didn't speak.

"Aside from both of us having had relations with the same sex, I'm not sure our bodies will be an exact match. The man might not be circumcised, and I am. I don't think gluing a foreskin on me will be convincing." *Gah, did I just say foreskin? Yeah, I did, but, shit, you don't drop a bomb like this on someone and expect him to keep his cool. Also, what happens if Dawud shows up while I'm making the beast with two backs with Elmoudowi?*

His blunt statement made Jack laugh until tears came into his eyes. "You are still the Wren I remember. It appears Nels wasn't one 100 percent successful in teaching you to filter your words."

"Not totally, no, but the Corps continues where he left off. Bottom line, Mr. Adams, what do you expect from me?"

"Dawud Afif won't show up to ruin your play. The reason Elmoudowi declared a personal jihad against Marines is because Dawud was killed in that drone strike. We were unaware Elmoudowi swung that way until our onsite forensics unit opened a secret compartment in Dawud's wallet and found a love letter from Elmoudowi. Your mission is to insert yourself into the bomb maker's presence intimately enough to find out his timetable and location for his plan to kill Marines. At present we don't know whether he intends to hit Marines in Afghanistan, the States, or some embassy anywhere in the world. And we don't have the exact date for his attack, either."

Wren tapped Dawud's picture. "Why don't you just blow the motherfucker up?"

"We tried, remember? Also, there's the little glitch in not knowing what the motherfucker looks like. That's where you come in. We just learned an alias he recently purchased will surface in Monaco at the end of next month. We want you to go to Monaco, hang out at the clubs frequented by gays, the casinos, the yacht club...anywhere a gay, wealthy bomb maker with tons of money might go for fun in Monaco. One sight of you, and I don't think Elmoudowi will be able to stay away. He'll find you, and you'll strike up a, um, close, personal friendship and subtlety pump him for the time and place he intends to hit Marines."

Despite the cold sweat of anxiety running down his back, he was furious. He didn't even try to filter his next words. "So, do you enjoy the pimp business, Mr. Adams?"

It was a fair hit, and Jack took it. "You're my first client. If you expect me to be embarrassed to ask you to do this, you're going to be disappointed. The lives of innocent Marines, and perhaps collateral civilian lives will be lost because Elmoudowi is a sick, twisted bastard who gets his jollies killing people for money. I would use my own son, if it would save lives and end Elmoudowi's."

De Lassy gave him cause for hope by asking a very direct question.

"Will I have backup or is this a suicide mission?"

"Your cover story still needs to be fleshed out, but you will be accompanied by an agent acting as your executive assistant or as security for a wealthy client such as yourself."

"Is this agent gay? Does he speak French or Arabic?"

Jack tilted his head in puzzlement. "I'm sure we could find one who speaks French and/or Arabic, but gay? Does he need to be gay to serve as your backup?"

Wren drummed his fingers on the table a few seconds before answering. "Yeah, I think he does. It's been my experience that truly heterosexual, abundantly testosterone-rich men, to include government agents, don't function well around gays. If, and this is a big if, if he sees me interacting in a sexual manner with Elmoudowi, he might just be a little slow on the trigger when the time comes. My life may not mean a rat's ass to you, Mr. Adams, but I kind of like it. So, I'm going to offer you a deal breaker. If I can persuade a certain Marine to act as my backup, I'll accept this mission."

"Whoa, hold on there." Jack made pushing motions with his hands. "You are the only one cleared to hear the details of this operation. I don't like the idea of bringing in an unknown entity who doesn't work for the Agency, and who may opt out after hearing my plan."

"I'm not lacking in intelligence, Mr. Adams, but I did say this was a deal breaker. I think I can persuade the man to serve as my backup without mentioning Elmoudowi's name or Dawud Afif's. He's as loyal, if not more so, to the Corps as I am, so I think he would accept the mission. However, if he doesn't, you'll need to come up with another plan. I'm not offering to prostitute myself for Uncle Sam, no matter how many references you use to loyalty, apple pie, or the American way of life, unless I can trust with absolute certainty the man on my six."

"I can't afford to wait too long for this Marine to make up his mind."

Wren sat back and crossed his arms over his chest. "As soon as you tell the powers that be outside this conference room that Sergeant Geordy Campbell needs to report to the SCIF, you'll have his answer. The only thing I ask is that you let me show him Afif's photo, and you give us some privacy while I make my pitch. Don't worry, I won't mention Afif's name, but a picture is worth a thousand words in this case."

He sat alone in the conference room while Jack Adams had Geordy paged. Since Adams didn't return, he guessed Geordy was on his way. With nothing to do but wait, he began to study the room. No visible cameras mounted on the walls. Good, what he had to say to Geordy didn't need to be a matter of MARSOC record. And he was pretty sure the room had no recording devices, because Jack Adams wouldn't want a record of this briefing getting out and messing up his plans.

Geordy entered with the same puzzled expression he'd worn on his face, and he began to doubt Mountain would serve as his backup with what little he could tell him, but he had to at least try.

"What's going on, Blade? Why are we here?

"Take a seat, Geordy. I will have to leave some large gaps in what I can tell you, but should you accept the mission, they will be filled in. The nearest example that comes to mind is, you're being asked to buy a pig in a poke. A pig you won't be allowed to see until you pay for it. A particular agency wants me for a highly classified mission, and I want you to serve as my backup."

"You need to be a wee bit more specific if you want me to consider it."

"One of the three-letter government agencies." His lips twisted to match Geordy's grimace.

"Why you? You're a Raider, but not Tier One." Geordy sat back and crossed his arms over his chest.

Wren passed Dawud Afif's picture across the table.

"Wow, you found your twin. Let me guess, you're supposed to impersonate this man."

He crossed his own arms over his chest and stretched his legs out under the table. "Not exactly, no. And before you ask, I can't tell you anything else about the op unless you agree to serve as my backup."

Geordy picked up Afif's picture and studied it again. "Will you be in any danger, or is this just going to be a bodyguard gig for appearance only?"

He gave Mountain direct eyes as he answered. "The potential for danger is quite real."

"Why me? Why are you asking for me instead of Vlad? He's deadly with a gun."

Mountain's question made him sit up straight and slide his hand, palm down, across the table. He stopped very close to where Geordy rested his own hand.

"Two reasons: one, because you speak French and Arabic, and two, because I need for the man on my six to hold some affection for me. I didn't ask for this assignment, I don't want this assignment, but it's important enough to at least attempt it, but not without you at my back.

"Time to fess up, Geordy Campbell, do you still have a smidgen of affection for me buried inside you, and is it enough to put your own life on the line? Listen, if you say no, I'll understand. No harm, no foul if you open that door and run like hell."

Geordy stared down at the hand a scant inch from his, and sat up straighter to ask another question. "If I do run, will you still take the assignment?"

He filled his cheeks with air and blew it out in a long stream. "Yeah, I probably will. I said I wouldn't if you didn't back me, but, yeah, it's important enough that I need to do it."

He held his breath until he felt Geordy's hand cover his and squeeze.

"Aye, then, I'll do it. I'll cover your six."

Wren grasped Geordy's hand in both of his, and called out, "Going once, going twice, sold. You just bought yourself a pig, Geordy Campbell, and now let me show you how ugly it is."

He crossed the room and stuck his head out of the door to call Jack Adams back inside.

***

When Jack met Geordy Campbell, he realized, despite Wren's lack of a verbal filter, somewhere along the line he'd acquired good self-preservation instincts. Campbell was huge and impressed him by appearing as intelligent as he was dangerous. Maybe his cockamamie plan would work.

After shaking Geordy's hand and introducing himself, Jack launched into the brief, this time, filling in the blank spots since de Lassy had agreed to serve as bait.

"This is the way this is going to work. You are now on relaxed grooming standards. Grow out the high and tight haircuts. Facial hair is optional except for de Lassy. I don't want Elmoudowi to have to filter out a beard or mustache before he recognizes your likeness to Afif."

"Gee, and I so wanted to try out a ZZ Top, wild mountain man beard."

Jack just shook his head at Wren's skewed sense of humor. "You are to go back to your rooms and pack because you're leaving with me."

"Wait, our team is about to go on another training mission. How do you plan to explain our disappearance?" Geordy asked.

"Your CO will be told you've been picked up for a special mission, and that's all he'll be told. I'm whisking the both of you out of here before people start asking questions you can't answer."

"Where are we going?" Geordy continued the questions.

"There will be accommodations for you at Langley while we bring you up to speed for this operation. Each of you will go through specialized training, and solid backgrounds will be invented for both of you, including new wardrobes to reflect them."

Wren turned to Geordy. "Don't worry, we won't be going under cover as drag queens. You're a handsome man, Mountain, but not in a dress." Both Jack and Mountain snorted their disbelief he'd dared to voice such an observation.

"I don't think I need to say no communication with family is permitted, but consider it said. Your CO or master sergeant will tell anyone who calls you're part of a deployed training mission and you'll call them when you return."

Geordy jumped into the lull when Jack took a breath. "We *are* coming back to MARSOC, aren't we? I signed up for this one mission, not to be on permanent retainer to your agency."

"Yes, this is a one-shot affair. I won't insult either of you by offering anything as crass as money, but the way it usually works with any military seconded to the Agency is you will go to the head of the list for your next promotion. You'll be promoted outside the zone."

Blade quipped, "Great, we just jumped the line for staff sergeant."

Jack grinned like a canary who'd bamboozled a cat. "It will be for Gunnery Sergeant. When I cleared this with MARSOC's Commanding General, he told me you, and I also saw your name on the list, Geordy, would sew on the staff sergeant stripe today. The announcement was to be made by your CO this afternoon. Congratulations, Staff Sergeants. Not that either one of your will be wearing a Marine uniform for a while. Oh, one last formality." Jack shoved a paper at Geordy. "Sign on the dotted line."

When Geordy did so and returned the pen, Jack stood and rubbed his hands together. "Just call me Mephistopheles. I now own two Marine souls. Hot damn, the mission to bag Elmoudowi is on!"

Blade muttered as he and Mountain followed Jack out of the SCIF. "I never would've guessed Mephistopheles favored Brooks Brothers' suits."

Jack dropped his newly recruited agents off at their dorm with a final reminder to keep their lips zipped while they packed, and informed them they wouldn't need much except casual clothes and shaving kits. All else would be supplied by the Agency.

Even though he'd expected Geordy to press him for more details, the manner in which the Scot did so took him by surprise.

As soon as the door to their room closed behind them, Geordy swung toward him and herded him until his back was against the wall, and he was caged in by two very strong arms.

He went rigid, but not from surprise, when Geordy put his lips next to his ear and whispered, "How did you meet Jack Adams? I get the feeling you and he have met before. He isn't as shocked as he should be that you are gay. Did you tell him I'm gay as well?"

He couldn't help himself—well, yeah, he could, but he didn't want to—and he put his cheek next to Geordy's to answer. "I told you I lived in Saudi Arabia for a while. What I didn't mention was I had a Saudi lover."

Geordy jerked back a step in surprise.

"I lived with him until he...um, died, and then Ross became my legal guardian and I went to live with him in Alexandria, Virginia. Jack Adams was working at the American embassy and handled all the paperwork to renew my passport because I, um, let it lapse." Wren frantically prayed, *Please, please, please don't ask for closer details on how that transition went.*

"Why didn't...?"

He rushed into speech again before Geordy could ask another question. "I didn't come right out and tell Jack you were gay, but I sort of implied it when I said you wouldn't be freaked to work with a gay, and you spoke French and Arabic, which I thought might come in handy for this op." He made no move to leave Geordy's embrace, just waited for him to make the next move, as his story had enough gaps to drive an up-armored Humvee through.

Geordy cupped his cheeks and gave him direct eye contact as he whispered, "I told you I'll cover your six, but one day I hope you'll trust me enough to tell me the whole story of your time in Saudi Arabia. You must've loved the man very much by the amount of sadness filling your eyes whenever you mention that country."

His stomach plummeted to his feet with Geordy's observation, and, for an insane nanosecond, he wanted to confess everything about the vilest experience of his life. Thank God sanity returned before he could open his mouth, but he needed to say something to cover his pregnant pause.

"If I ever tell anyone about that time of my life, it will be you, Geordy Campbell, but now is not the time. I'm not ready, and neither one of us needs the distraction, but I do want to say thank you for backing me up. If the situation was reversed, you wouldn't need to ask more than once for me to cover your six."

Geordy crowded Wren with his body. "Prove it. You said you needed to be sure the man at your back held some affection for you, so show me you have the same for me."

Wren stared at Geordy and watched his eyelids drop slowly over those hazel eyes right before he claimed Geordy's mouth with his. He rubbed his stiff cock against Geordy's, and the friction nearly made him come in his uniform pants.

He gave a frustrated growl when Geordy broke away with the announcement they needed to gather up what they wanted to take with them.

As he turned away to pack, he wondered if Geordy had forced his response because he was unsure if he cared for him or as punishment for drawing him into a strange and dangerous situation. Fuck it, he didn't have the time or the inclination to work that advanced math problem.

Chapter Twenty

Two weeks later, both Geordy and he had their covers down pat. Geordy's cover was as his personal security. Hired through a London Security Agency by one Colin Daniel MacAulay, Mr. Geordy MacEwen would serve as his personal bodyguard. Mountain transformed himself by growing out his Marine haircut and adding a full beard. The beard bugged him in a sort of déjà vu way until he recalled seeing a picture of King George V and his look-alike cousin, Tsar Nicholas II, on the Internet. Geordy had also disguised his voice by giving free rein to his Scottish burr.

His own cover was more, as he thought of it, tongue-in-cheek. He got to be a physicist who worked for a government agency he didn't care to name. However, if someone did run his background, it would say he worked for NASA and had several scientific patents under his name. It would also reveal, for a single man in his late twenties, Colin Daniel MacAulay made a decent enough salary to pay for his lavish vacations. Anyone questioning his need for personal security would be told about a disastrous vacation in France the previous year, where he was severely beaten by a couple of homophobic thugs, and would never again travel without protection.

Wren accepted the slip of paper Jack Adams handed him and Geordy as he drove them to the airport to begin their hunt for Elmoudowi.

"Memorize that number and then give the paper back to me."

"Who does this number belong to?"

Jack took his eyes off traffic for a moment to give Wren a serious response. "That's the number Geordy or you will call to report anything of interest you winkle out of Elmoudowi, or I should say Stavros Andino. It's also the number you call if the whole operation goes south and you need to be extracted ASAP."

Geordy jumped in before Wren could ask another question. "Once we find out what you need to know, what becomes of Elmoudowi?"

Jack caught Geordy's eyes in the rearview mirror. "You call that number and, after giving a plausible excuse for leaving, you walk away. The Agency will handle things from there."

Wren turned around in his seat to verify Geordy got the unspoken message. By the tone of Jack's voice, they had no worries about ever encountering Jabir Elmoudowi anywhere else in this world.

***

Geordy grinned wryly at the thought of how far a Tennessee boy had come. His long legs appreciated the first-class seating as the plane carried them across the big pond to London's Heathrow Airport.

The plane began its descent, and he nudged Blade into wakefulness. "Return your seat to its upright position, Mr. MacAuley. We're soon to land in London, the home of James Bond, Saville Row, the Beatles, and bangers and mash."

Wren rolled his neck to relieve the kinks then lifted the window shade to stare out at what he could see of London. "I wonder if we'll have any time to play tourist. I'd really like to see Shakespeare's Globe Theater."

Geordy shook his head. "Sorry, playing tourist isn't in the schedule. We've just enough time to pick up the wardrobes designed for us, and the, uh, accoutrements for my security job, and catch the ferry for the channel crossing."

"Ooh, you're using French. Accoutrements, sounds so sexy." He winked at Geordy's splutter. He was well aware Mountain's use of the word referred to the pistol and paperwork needed for his security cover.

Several hours later, Geordy had cause to admire Wren's facility with switching personas. Since they boarded the ferry to take them into France, he hadn't uttered a single word in English. They conversed totally in French, and Colin MacAulay had yet to slip and call him anything other than Daniel MacEwen.

It was excellent practice, and it rubbed the rust off his French vocabulary. He also admired Wren's accent. He sounded like a native speaker.

The long flight and the push to Calais wiped both of them out. Geordy stood back and affected a somber air, one appropriate for his new role as security for an effervescent American, as Wren checked them into the hotel the Agency suggested. He was more than a little stunned to find their accommodation was a suite. It surprised him the Agency didn't try to save some of the taxpayers' money by booking two single rooms, but, apparently, Wren's, er, Colin's cover as a wealthy American was very much in play.

Too wiped out to do more than give a nod to Colin, as he would think of him from this moment on, Geordy slung his suitcase into his room and was asleep five minutes after shucking his clothes and hitting the mattress.

Geordy awoke to the aroma of coffee being wafted under his

nose.

"Wakey, wakey, Mr. MacEwen. Once you've completed your three Ss, you may join me in the living room for breakfast. I took the liberty of ordering omelets and croissants, and, of course more coffee."

Blade dangled a set of car keys in front of him. "Room service also delivered these, the keys to our chariot for the ride to Monaco. And what do you know, the key fob says Mercedes Benz. I wonder which model? I hope it's not a granny wagon. It will be hard to maintain my playboy image in a station wagon."

Geordy reached for the cup Wren offered and was slightly flummoxed when he climbed into bed to sit next to him, propping the pillow behind his back before making an outrageous offer.

"I can help you fix that. It would be my pleasure."

As he followed the direction of Wren's gaze, Geordy realized he was nude, not covered by a sheet, and still sporting morning wood. The fact the present company wore nothing but boxer briefs made his cock think the offer an excellent idea. He wanted to yell, "Tease," when Wren bounded out of bed, laughing.

"If you aren't finished in the bathroom in ten minutes, I'm eating your breakfast as well. I'm starving."

Geordy performed his morning ablutions with Marine efficiency and, as he combed his hair, he asked his reflection how they could squeeze the information they needed out of Elmoudowi in the fastest way. Starting this op with a raging case of blue balls was a good incentive to end it quickly.

***

Master Sergeant Stanley Richardson, team name Otter, stuck his head into Colonel Christian Trollinger's office. "Intel brief in five minutes, Troll."

Troll saved the program he was in and backed out of it. "Be right there. Save me a seat, Otter."

Accepting the Styrofoam cup of coffee Otter handed him, Troll took his seat and turned his attention to Major Szabo, the G-2 briefer this morning. He didn't have to wait long before Major Szabo launched into the classified brief by clicking on the first slide.

Troll studied the bearded Afghani face on the screen and listened closely to the details.

"This is Amin Alizai, local warlord and a verified miss for our side. As most of you in this room are aware, the Marines tried to take out Alizai and Emoudowi, the bomb maker he was meeting with, by leveling the meeting site with a drone strike. Everyone thought the strike had been a success until two months ago a bomb with Elmoudowi's signature all over it took out 20 Afghan soldiers and three United States Marines. It seems the drone strike really pissed him off. He's declared open season on Marines and says he'll pay back our strike with interest. The CIA's been monitoring the Internet and the dark net and says he is bragging that the time, place, and martyrs have already been chosen for the hit. And this morning I have the further unpleasant duty to inform you that Alizai recently surfaced and is operating, once again, near the Pakistani border."

Major Szabo stopped his brief when someone around the table called out, "Then who in the hell did we take out with that drone strike? Did we at least bag some bad guys or are we going to be blamed for killing innocent civilians?"

The G-2 briefer used his remote to click rapidly through several slides before stopping on another photo of a bearded Afghan. "No one meeting in that house could, in any way, be labeled an innocent. This is a photo of Mohammad Orakzai, Amin Alizai's second-in-command. Forensic evidence verified he was killed in that strike."

Major Szabo advanced the slide. "And this is Dawud Afif. His DNA was collected along with Orakzai's."

When Afif's photo hit the screen, Troll sucked in his breath. That face was a friend of his. The last time he saw it was at his parent's hunting lodge. And the truth hit him between the headlights. Jack Adams had played him to get to Wren. Troll muttered under his breath, "Calling to congratulate me on my promotion, my ass. Whatever you're up to you sonovabitch, you needed to find Wren."

Troll left the brief knowing that Amin Alizai had been moved to the head of JSOC's hit list, and he had no problem with hunting and eliminating such a despicable piece of shit, but he also couldn't help but feel guilty over locating Wren de Lassy for the CIA. He was also aware that whatever Jack Adams wanted with Wren, he didn't have a need to know, and so he might never know. The strong, black coffee Otter gave him at the briefing turned to acid in his stomach.

Otter, who'd been sitting next to him when Afif's picture flashed up, rounded on him as soon as they got back to his office.

"I'm getting a funny feeling about this, Troll. That Dawud Afif bears a hell of a resemblance to Wren de Lassy. Please tell me it was just a coincidence Jack Adams called here not so very long ago."

Troll snorted at the word *coincidence*. "You know, Adams always said the team gave him a rash whenever we came to call at the embassy in Riyadh. Now I'm thinking his not so casual call was pay back. Do me a favor. Call down to MARSOC and see if Wren is there. If he is, we'll both breathe easier."

Otter was back in ten minutes. "I had a nice chat with Master Sergeant McClean. I introduced myself as an old friend of Wren's and said I wanted to invite him to a barbecue this weekend. The master sergeant told me not to count on him making the barbecue. He's on a deployment."

Troll didn't bother asking Wren's location, because operation security specified no one outside the special operator's chain of command was ever told the destination or the time of return.

"Shit, if anything happens to him, I'm going to rip that CIA stuffed shirt's head off and drink his blood for duping me into giving up his location."

Otter left his office with a succinct, "I'll bring the straw."

Even through the initial planning for hunting down, capturing, and/or killing Amin Alizai, Troll continued to stew over being used to put the touch on Wren. Now that the CIA had their hooks into him, it was very likely they would continue to use him, and as a lowly staff sergeant, he didn't have near enough rank to tell them to go piss up a rope.

Troll almost laughed when the realization hit him that JSOC had the rank. If he brought Wren under his command, the CIA would have to go through him to use Wren, and only after they tangoed with some heavy-hitting four stars.

Troll stuck his head out of his office and yelled, "Otter, find Gunner. I want both your asses in my office, ASAP."

Fifteen minutes later, Troll spotted Otter out of the corner of his eye and turned away from his computer. "Where's Gunner?" He jumped when a voice responded from the corner of his office.

"I'm here."

"Fuck, Gunner, how long have you been standing there?"

"A couple of minutes. You were busy, and I didn't want to disturb you."

Troll just shook his head. More times than he wanted to count, the sniper scared the shit out of him with his ability to move without making a sound.

"Did Otter brief you on Wren's situation?"

At Gunner's nod, Troll continued. "Here's what we're going to do. We haven't had a bladed weapon expert for over a year now. Not since Sergeant Amos went back to 1st Group in Washington state due to health issues with his son. What say we—and by 'we' I mean one of you—suggest Wren for the job."

Troll turned to Otter. "After you left to track down Gunner, I got G-2 to pull what we had on the incident the Raiders had with that Maute group in the Philippines. Seems like Wren used one of his throwing knives to take out a terrorist during their exfil, and we've all worked with Ross de Lassy who taught Wren everything he needed to know about knives. The next team meeting to discuss our new target is tomorrow. It would be a good time to suggest inviting him to join us."

Gunner stepped forward. "I'll do it. It was Ross who saved my ass when that Indonesian op went tits up, so I owe him one. Besides, anyone who watched Wren practice with his throwing knives on our hunting trips would vouch for him. The kid rarely misses what he's aiming at, and since he learned knife fighting from Ross, I don't doubt his skill with any other kind of knife. To add the icing to this cake, his MOS is EOD, and we can use a younger set of eyes and nimble fingers, now that Otter's grown crusty with age."

Gunner grinned when he heard the expected "fuck you" from Otter.

Troll rubbed his hands together. "Done. Now if the CIA wants to put the touch on him ever again, they'll have to go through us."

Chapter Twenty-One

Wren handed the key fob to the valet and slapped Geordy on the back when a gunmetal-gray E-300 Mercedes sedan pulled up and stopped in front of them.

"Oh, I am so digging working for our uncle," he whispered to Geordy before he tipped the valet and got into the driver's seat.

"Wow, can you believe this dashboard? You could fly a small plane after learning what everything does in this car. Why don't you find out how to punch in our destination on GPS? Go for the fastest route. The sooner we reach Monte Carlo, the sooner we can finish this."

And thanks to German engineering, and the punctilious recommendations of the anonymous navigator, they made it to Monte Carlo in fourteen hours as opposed to seventeen.

When the bellman unlocked the door to their suite in the Hotel de Paris-Monte Carlo, Blade, for once, was speechless at the opulent appointments.

He opened the French door to the small balcony featuring an ocean view, and came back inside to call dibs on the white-and-gold bedroom. He peeked into Geordy's room to discover it was decorated in blue and silver, and he started to snicker.

"What are you laughing at?"

"I'm thinking we got this suite by mistake."

Geordy stretched the kink out of his back before asking, "How so?"

"I think the receptionist saw the regal beard you're sporting and thought you were a member of England's royal family. With that beard you do bear a striking resemblance to His Majesty King George the V. I hope they never discover we're just two Marine Raiders attempting to pull the wool over their eyes. It would be mortifying in the extreme to be bounced out of here for our plebian roots."

Geordy shrugged his shoulders and deftly uncorked the complimentary bottle of champagne and poured two glasses.

As he clinked his glass with Wren's, Geordy said, "Here's to wool pulling, may it never unravel."

***

By mutual accord, they ordered room service. Tomorrow morning would be soon enough to explore the rest of the hotel and walk through the city playing tourist.

He finished showering before Blade, so he let the waiter into the room and stood back while the man fussed about setting out plates and cutlery. Geordy slipped him a healthy tip and then knocked on the bathroom door to give Wren a head's up.

"Dinner's here. Stop playing with your rubber ducky and join me at the table before it gets cold."

Wren came out of the bathroom, also wearing one of the hotel's thick terrycloth robes. "God I'm so hungry I could eat whatever's under that cloche and the cloche itself."

Geordy studied the metal domes covering their plates. "I always wondered what these things were called. Here, pour the wine and I'll unveil dinner."

It didn't take two hungry Marines long to dispatch the haute cuisine, and Geordy refilled their wine glasses and sat back in his chair. He observed without comment as Wren pushed a few peas around on his plate.

"I think people should say pea instead of cheese when they're supposed to smile for the camera."

A, "huh," left his lips before he could think of a clever retort to the left field response. He withheld comment as Wren elaborated.

"When you say, 'cheese,' you show a lot of teeth, like the Big Bad Wolf's first sighting of Little Red Riding Hood. But I think it's sexier if you use French and say, 'Petit Pois.'"

The sexy pout on Wren's lips mesmerized him, and he squirmed around in his chair until he adjusted his bathrobe to give himself more coverage in the lap area.

The impish grin, and wicked glint in Wren's eyes, told him he was having fun at his expense.

Geordy stood and set the half-empty bottle of wine and the two glasses aside then wheeled the serving cart from the room. He joined Wren where he stood in the small opening with an ornate wrought-iron rail that passed for a balcony.

"From a security standpoint, I don't think you need worry about someone coming in through the balcony, if you want to sleep with it open. It would take a lot of rope to rappel down from the roof of this hotel."

Geordy's comment made him sigh instead of come back with a joke. "So, we're now in character? I was...."

Geordy prompted him when he didn't finish the sentence. "You were what?"

He shrugged and fiddled with the sash on his robe. "I was kind of enjoying the moment. The two of us eating dinner in a lavish hotel suite in a foreign country, seemed like a date. We've never been on a date, so I was just fantasizing we were on one. Tomorrow, we have to be in character, but tonight I thought we could...."

Before he could put enough air back in his lungs to reply, Wren turned and headed into his room, calling "Good night," over his shoulder.

Geordy tossed and turned and couldn't find one fucking comfortable spot on the entire king-size bed. He tried every position, and covered every inch of the mattress, and still couldn't fall asleep. What finally launched him out of bed was a vision of his mother's disappointment at his hard-headedness.

He opened Wren's door and called his name softly."

"What?"

He entered the room just as Wren turned on the lamp next to his bed. "I, uh...."

"What, Geordy, is something wrong?"

The sight of him sitting up in bed with the sheet pooling low on his belly didn't make saying what he wanted to say any easier. Shit, facing hostile Taliban forces suddenly seemed easier. Geordy found his backbone and began again. "It felt like a date to me, too. He rushed the next words before he lost his nerve. "And I want to do what would have come after a date with you." He didn't give Wren a chance to speak. He just dropped his robe and climbed into bed and held him tightly when he rolled into his arms.

"Oh God, Geordy, have you missed me as much as I missed you?"

Geordy didn't reply, just flipped Wren over onto his back and kissed him on the one spot guaranteed to keep him docile enough to have his way.

Geordy grinned up at Wren when he sucked on the spot below his belly button and got a "Nuungh" by way of comment. Taking that as permission to go lower, he cupped Wren's balls and swallowed his dick to the root. Wren's hands fisted in his hair, and he felt the urgent tug.

"Geordy, stop, stop. I'm not going to last at all if you keep doing that."

He gave an amused murmur then returned to eating him a piece at a time, until his sac drew taut. He disengaged and stretched over the side of the bed to snag his robe. When Blade began to question his actions, he passed him the tube of lubricant. "Make love to me. I thought of nothing but your body covering mine since we left Tennessee. He grinned with delight when Blade squeezed a dollop into his hand and ordered, "You cover me, and I'll cover you."

Blade touched his hips and he went eagerly to his knees and lost his mind shortly thereafter. Neither one of them lasted long, proving that, while abstinence might be good for the soul, it was hell on the libido.

He woke to bright sun and Blade's body curled around him. The pleasure of it was so right his throat constricted and his heart sped up. The man he held was so beautiful, and, in so many ways, Geordy couldn't count them all, but one attribute popped into his mind. Wren was mercurial, and like mercury he was hard to keep contained, and possibly very toxic to his desire to stay in the Marines. He, by comparison, was more like tin. Resistant to corrosion, non-combustible, durable, low maintenance, and as any medieval alchemist knew, tin in combination with mercury and copper could form gold. Wren woke when he rubbed a strand of his coppery red-gold hair between his fingers. He kissed him and brought him to full wakefulness with, "There's a better word than pea for taking pictures."

Wren gave Geordy owl eyes and asked, "Okaay, what's better than petit pois?"

Geordy nuzzled his ear and whispered, "Porridge." He held on as Blade laughed both of them right out of bed.

Colin didn't ignore him like hired help, but he chose to stay in the background and scan the area around him while Wren, aka Colin MacAulay, shopped or took pictures of the yacht club, the outside of the casino, various fountains and statues. It was a welcome relief to join him at an outdoor café to grab a late lunch.

Wren leaned toward him under the pretext of showing him the lightweight cashmere sweater purchased in one of the chichi shops. It was the same shade of green as his eyes, and both of them knew heads would turn when he wore it.

"So, no one paying any attention to me? No lovestruck stalker?"

"Nope. No one who's paid the slightest attention to you." Geordy feigned interest in the menu. Wild horses wouldn't drag it out of him that Wren did turn heads, both male and female, as they walked Monte Carlo's streets. But none of them were interested enough to follow them.

"Good, that's good. Why don't we return to the hotel and check out the pool for some exercise and then zonk out for a few hours? I thought we'd dine in the hotel's five-star restaurant around ten and then hit the casino. Jack said our buddy Stavros has been known to gamble."

"Since you brought up gambling, try not to lose your allowance in one night."

Wren made a disparaging sound of disdain at Geordy's remonstrance. "You needn't worry. I'm very good with numbers, and no, I don't count cards. I just play the percentages. Jack didn't say anything about whether or not we can keep our winnings."

"Winnings? You do have a large amount of confidence, Mr. MacAulay. I imagine Jack wouldn't have much to say if you returned what he staked you, but I'm pretty sure our mutual uncle has come up with a regulation or two to make you cough them up."

The hotel pool was large and beautiful and surprisingly empty. Both of them were able to enjoy a fairly decent workout. Geordy also ducked his head into the exercise room and gave a low whistle of approval. There was enough equipment in it to keep them in Marine Corps shape.

He found himself slowing down as he returned to the room. Blade had gone ahead, and now he was dawdling, and he couldn't come up with a reason for doing so. Well, yeah, he could, but he didn't want to admit to himself he wanted to run back to their suite, sling his bathing suit across the room and jump his roommate's bones until they both fell sound asleep from sexual excess.

Geordy shook his head at the unusual, prurient thought. De Lassy was the only person who had ever made him lose control. And a tiny voice in his head kept saying, *You like losing control. Admit it, you do.*

Geordy entered the suite and found the living room empty, so he stuck his head into Wren's room and surprised the hell out of him.

Wren gave a little yip and bobbled a small glass jar that came to rest at his feet. Geordy retrieved the jar and found no labeling, whatsoever. "What's this, lip balm?"

"Uh, no, not lip balm."

Geordy twisted the lid and studied the emulsion inside. He sniffed it, but there wasn't any identifiable scent so he started to dip a finger in, but Wren snatched it away.

"You'll want to be very careful with this."

Blade's serious demeanor was starting to arouse his curiosity. "Why? What's in the jar?" He didn't suspect drugs, because he knew of Wren's stance on the use of illegal substances, but the man's reluctance to maintain eye contact puzzled him, and he repeated the question.

"This is what will enable me to perform, should I need to, with Stavros. I'm a good actor when I need to be, but I'm not good enough to become aroused when I have absolutely no sexual interest in the man." *Unless serious pain or dire threats are used as inducements.*

Geordy picked up the jar from the dresser top where Wren had put it. "You're saying this is like some sort of Spanish fly? Does it work?"

Wren massaged his temple to ward off a headache. "I don't have any experience with Spanish flies, but a certain beetle, when ground up and added to other ingredients, can give you an instantaneous erection, and one that won't wilt for a while. And before you ask how I came by that information, let's just say I had a misspent youth, and my partner was twenty years older than me. I asked the Agency for a little assistance, in case I got, um, stage fright, and they gave me this jar."

Geordy uncapped the jar again and stared at its contents. His question made Wren goggle. "Can I try it?" *Yep, the voice in his head spoke the truth. He did like losing control.*

"You can't be serious. I'm not going to sugar-coat this, Geordy. Getting hard as a rock and staying that way until it wears off isn't as exciting as you may think. Even the Viagra commercials warn about the seriousness of prolonged erections."

"Are you saying I'm going to be hard for four hours?"

"No, not if you use it sparingly."

Geordy dropped his swim trunks and untied the sash on Wren's hotel robe. "Then, show me how much I should use."

He waited as Blade put a minuscule amount on his fingertip and then rubbed the cream down his shaft. "How long will this take to...? Oh, Christ!" Blade didn't bother saying, "I told you so," just handed him the lube and climbed into bed.

***

Moonlight reflecting off one of the crystal facets of the chandelier in the living room dazzled his eyes as he woke up, sprawled over Geordy, and uncomfortably aware there was carpet, not a mattress, under them.

He took a moment to piece together the mystery of how they came to be in the living room and not still in his bed. As his eyes adjusted to the ambient light, he studied his fellow Raider and grinned at the smile still gracing the man's face. A small movement drew his attention down the length of Geordy's body, and he whispered, "Stay down, boy, you've had enough fun for one day."

"Who are you talking to?"

He removed his head from Geordy's chest and sat up on one elbow, the better to see him. "I was speaking to your dick."

Geordy groaned and rolled over to face him.

"Please, tell me it's shriveled up and fallen off, because the idea of being a eunuch for the rest of my life sounds pretty damn good."

Wren rolled to his back and chortled at the ceiling. "Whoever said Scots were staid, must never have enjoyed monkey sex with one."

"Monkey sex? What the devil are you talking about?"

He straddled Geordy's body and grinned down at him. "I'm talking of doing the bump and grind in every room of this suite, to include your rather startling suggestion of including this chandelier in the game, you sexy, wild Scot."

When Geordy tried to hide his mortification behind his hands, he lifted them away and leaned down to whisper, "I love your wild child, Geordy Campbell. Tell him he can come out to play again sometime, but without the artificial stimulant."

Wren sprang to his feet and offered Geordy a hand up. "Getcha nekked ass off the carpet, monkey boy. It's time to dress for dinner and go play with Uncle's money in the casino."

Forty minutes later, he walked from his bedroom to find Geordy in front of the large mirror in the living room tying his bowtie like a pro.

He cocked his head and extended the one dangling from his fingers. "Where did you learn how to do that? I spent the last ten minutes wrestling with this thing."

Geordy gave his tie a last flick to straighten it and took the tie from him.

"Isn't it amazing what you can learn to do via a YouTube video? I am now a Jedi Master in bow tying."

Geordy spun him around and lifted the starched tuxedo collar and began to tie his tie, but not before torturing him by blowing in his ear.

"There, that's got it. Now for the rest of my accoutrements."

"Ooh, there's that sexy word again, but I'd have to be a satyr to be able to get another erection this evening, thanks to a certain Scot. Wow, maybe I should call you Bond, Commander James Bond."

Geordy tucked his 9mm pistol in the shoulder holster, and

adjusted his custom-made tuxedo jacket to disguise the bulge then thickened his Scot's brogue, knowing it would make him laugh until he wheezed.

"Thank you, Moneypenny. Shall we go see if M is in the dining room?"

Chapter Twenty-Two

Jabir Elmoudowi didn't know why he came here this evening. Games of chance held no appeal to his broken heart. The last time he visited this casino, he stood over Dawud's shoulder and watched him lose a considerable sum of money at baccarat. Of course, he lost as well. It would be bad form to bet on the bank against his lover. But then winning or losing meant nothing, as long as he and his lover returned to their room and their bed.

A hand resting briefly on his shoulder startled Jabir back to awareness, and someone behind him said, "*Excusez-moi.*"

He moved aside to let the man claim a seat at the baccarat table. He moved again when another man made him shift to the left and took up a position behind the newcomer at the table.

Jabir studied the back of the late arrival's head. He had hair the color of spun sunlight. Curious to see more of the man, he moved an inch to the side to discover a slender man wearing a well-cut tuxedo. There were no rings on his hands, and his wristwatch glinted gold. Studying the man's long, tapered fingers, Jabir recognized the first blush of manhood. Dawud had had similar hands, and this similarity made him feel very alone, and for the first time old.

He closed his eyes, the better to recite his standard curse upon the heads of any Marines still drawing breath. He would send a large portion of them to hell, and very, very soon.

The young man with hair the color of sunset laughed and turned to glance over his shoulder at the man standing behind him when he won the hand, and Jabir's heart stopped. He didn't have a superstitious bone in his body, but only a ghost walking across his grave would give him such a chill. The newcomer wore Dawud's face.

His rational mind called it a coincidence, but his bereft heart wanted to believe his delight had come back to him. Somehow, his beautiful lover found of way to forgive him for leaving him behind in that accursed mud hovel in Afghanistan. But his para-military training made him cautious, and he studied the man standing behind Dawud's twin.

His first impression of the bearded slim man screamed security. The man's eyes moved constantly around the baccarat table, then swung in a broader arc to include the area around the table, and finally to every exit that could be reached in a minimum of time.

His second impression made him as a professional. He didn't fidget. He didn't adjust his coat or his tie. He just stood there with his hands clasped loosely in front of him.

Jabir would bet all the euros in his wallet the man could easily identify every person within a five-foot radius of the table to the police, if an incident were to occur, and anyone who approached his charge with malicious intent would never reach their target.

Elmoudowi stood rooted to the spot until the manifestation of his departed lover picked up his considerable winnings and vacated his seat to another player. Unable to help himself, he followed the couple to the bar. He had to repress a total body shudder when the man ordered a bourbon for himself and a club soda for his friend in flawless French.

He congratulated himself on his ability to guess the man's profession, and his own experience with security personnel didn't require a guess as to whether or not the man carried a weapon. All on-duty security men did.

Jabir spent the rest of the evening shadowing the couple. He needed to learn more about Dawud's twin, namely where he was staying, and if he was married or single. He crossed his fingers for luck. It would be too cruel if the man turned down the offer he intended to make once he knew more about him. The dark-haired man hadn't once dropped his guard, so he would have to be the soul of circumspection.

He hastily placed his untasted drink on a small shelf between two slot machines as the two men headed for the casino's entrance. He noted the time on the paper-thin Omega on his wrist and discovered it to be two in the morning. Maybe they would return to their hotel. He hoped it would be a short distance away, because he wouldn't have time to fetch his car to tail them if they took a taxi or other means of transportation.

***

By mutual agreement, he and Blade eschewed a cab and walked back to the hotel. He gave a small "oof" as the persona of Colin MacAulay dug him in the ribs to crow about his winnings for the evening.

Geordy leaned closer to whisper, "Don't look now, Mr. MacAulay, but we're being tailed."

Blade kept up his joking patter, but got in a question under his breath. "Do you recognize him?"

Geordy nodded once. "Yeah, he's the one you squeezed by on your way to the baccarat table. He's been shadowing you ever since. Do we want to lead him back to our hotel?"

Wren stopped under a street light and, with his back to the street, winked at Geordy and whispered, "Play along."

Geordy gave a slight nod.

Colin MacAulay raised his voice enough to be heard by anyone passing by. "Mr. MacEwen, Daniel, what say you we take in that club I told you about?"

Geordy made a pretense of checking the time. "If you mean Club Bacchanal, there isn't enough time. Colin, people are heading home to sleep, not play. Besides, you should probably put your winnings in the hotel safe before you go anywhere else."

Colin stepped back from Geordy and cocked his head. "You aren't trying to back out of going to Bacchanal, are you? I gave full disclosure about who I am and where I wanted to go, and your agency said you wouldn't balk at accompanying a gay man to a gay club. If your agency misled me, say so, and I'll go by myself."

Geordy straightened his posture and shook his head. "I am not refusing to accompany you to that club, sir. I just thought you might want to go tomorrow, er...I guess that would be tonight, when you're rested and can spend as long as you want at the club." He leaned toward his charge. "You will most definitely not go to that club unaccompanied. From what you told my employers about what happened to you in Paris after you visited a similar club, you shouldn't even consider going to this one without security."

Colin backed off and gave Geordy a small bow. "My apologies for doubting you, Mr. MacEwen. I guess I do need some sleep. I'm starting to sound like a petulant child who's had his favorite toy taken away. You are right, tonight is soon enough to visit Club Bacchanal."

As they reached the hotel's entrance, Blade asked, "Are we still being tailed?"

Geordy grinned at his roommate. "Nope, he left as soon as you agreed to go to the club this evening."

***

A leisurely breakfast, a stroll along the marina to admire the yachts, a cocktail at *La Rescasse*, followed by a seafood dinner at a tiny restaurant they encountered in their wanderings, and sooner than either one of them wanted, Geordy tapped his watch as a signal to return to the hotel and dress for a possible face-to-face encounter with the terrorist, Elmoudowi.

Inside the suite, they discussed several scenarios, none of them perfect, until Blade shrugged his shoulders and said, "Fuck it, I'm just going to be me. If the dirt bag is interested, he'll make the first move. Since it will take me longer to, um, get my groove on, you can shower first."

Finished with his ablutions, Geordy stared at the contents of his closet and snickered. What did a supposedly straight security agent wear to a gay club? He chose dress jeans, a navy-blue silk T-shirt, and matching denim sports jacket. For this evening, his gun would be worn at the small of his back. Not that he expected to be dancing with anyone, but he did wink at his reflection in the mirror. He cleaned up pretty well, even if he had to say so himself.

He parked himself in the living room to read the history novel he'd purchased at the airport, but stopped when Wren's bedroom door opened. One sight of his roommate, and Geordy closed the book and considered canceling any plans for the evening that didn't include undressing Wren and making love until the sun rose.

This was the first time he saw him dressed for clubbing, and reality hit him as swiftly as a heart attack. If he'd ever previously seen him dressed that way, his intention to pursue a military career would have gone up in flames. Wren had dressed his hair with gel or mousse and wore it slicked back from his forehead in a casual, windblown way. He wore black dress slacks with a white silk T-shirt underneath a deconstructed black sports coat. Black, Italian, tasseled loafers without socks, and a slim silver belt accentuating his narrow waist completed the ensemble.

As Blade walked toward him, several things caught his attention. First of all, his eyes were mesmerizing. He'd done something to enhance his large beautiful green eyes. Something that made him not want to see anything but those eyes, but he forced himself to continue his perusal. His silk T-shirt, where it clung to his chest, captured his attention next, and it showcased an extremely nice set of washboard abs. But his walk held him frozen in his chair. Wren didn't walk, he glided like a very large feline animal. Geordy's groin tightened at the way he stalked toward him.

As Blade drew nearer, the scent of his cologne roused his libido. He didn't know who made it, but the thought of finding a large tree to sharpen his claws as he yowled at the moon appealed to him. Thank God he had never worn that particular scent anywhere around MARSOC. He didn't realize the book had fallen from his lap, until Blade retrieved it and handed it to him.

"I want to ask for a kiss for luck, but, um, I don't think that's wise. I can't meet Elmoudowi if we never leave this room."

Geordy's amative urges kicked into alpha overdrive, and he surged from the chair to pull the man into his arms and kiss the shit out of him. With Scottish burr front and center, Geordy stared into kohl-rimmed, crystal-green eyes and whispered, "My God, you're a walking wet dream. Maybe I should leave my gun behind because if that fucker so much as smiles at you, I won't be responsible for my actions this evening."

Wren cuddled in closer and nipped Geordy's ear lobe. "Shooting the motherfucker sounds like a great idea, but our uncle would not be pleased, and there are Marine lives at stake, so let's boogie."

Geordy laughed as his teammate did an over-the-top disco move all the way to the door.

***

The amount of people packed into Bacchanal worried him. Wren began to doubt the target would be able to find him, let alone approach him in the press of gyrating couples. However, when the DJ stopped the music in the middle of a song and announced it was time to spin the wheel, he found a way to gain the bomb maker's attention.

As he and Geordy were soon enlightened, the Bacchanal had a karaoke tradition between the hours of ten and midnight. The DJ stopped the music and pointed to a very attractive blond guy to come up to the stage and spin a large wheel and, once he'd done so, announced, "Ladies and Gentlemen, tonight we sing the 60s. You can choose French, Italian, or English songs from the playlist now being distributed. Anyone who wants to sing, please pick a number from the jar this beautiful hunk of deliciousness has graciously agreed to pass around."

Without waiting to consult Geordy, Colin crossed the dance floor and chose a number. Staying in character, he returned the wink of the blond-haired man who dressed and walked like a fashion model.

"What are you going to sing?" Geordy asked, when he returned.

Colin pointed to one of the selections on the list and smiled back at him when he broke into a wide grin. "Yeah, I know, this is the perfect song."

He didn't hear his number called until almost midnight, and he began to worry Jabir wouldn't take the bait. Although he danced with a variety of partners, starting with the gorgeous blond, who verified his Italian fashion model guess, no slender dark-haired man with silver at his temples, Geordy's description of the man trailing them after the casino, asked him to dance.

Colin handed the DJ his number and waited for his selection to be cued into the karaoke machine. When the lyrics appeared, he picked up the mic and channeled Bobby Darrin as he sang "Dream Lover."

***

Jabir followed the reincarnation of Dawud around the crowded room from a discreet distance. He watched as he danced with other men, and he couldn't seem to take his eyes off the man's pelvis. His target moved like liquid sex when he danced.

He jerked his mind back to reality when the music stopped. One part of his brain recognized the unhealthiness of fantasizing over killing everyone the man danced with, until he alone remained to partner the object of his desire, but the other part fought hard to squelch rationalization for pure, animal instinct. However, both right and left parts wanted to show the object of his fixation how to dance...horizontally. He also suspected the man already knew the steps.

His lust hadn't made him forget to pay close attention to the dark-haired man who shadowed the mystery man, and he now believed he possessed no romantic affection for Dawud's twin, for he never interfered with the man's choice of partners, or joined him when he chose to sit at someone's table, and he didn't show anger or jealousy when his charge flirted with or caressed other men. He just kept him in sight and continued to scan the area for any sign of trouble. Jabir wrote him off as hired help.

He'd made sure to do his homework before coming to Bacchanal, and discovered Dawud's twin to be one Colin MacAulay. His search found where he worked, how much he got paid, and, most importantly for his purposes, he claimed no spouse.

A quick call to a London security agency uncovered the fact that Daniel MacEwen had been hired to serve as Colin's bodyguard. He went so far as to fabricate a story about a friend recommending Daniel and, when he requested his services, the agency told him Mr. MacEwen was currently on assignment. The only thing his computer search failed to uncover was why Colin MacAulay needed a bodyguard.

He was aware Colin's job entailed some level of classified information, but physicists didn't usually need a bodyguard to accompany them on vacation. He suspected it had something to do with the incident in Paris MacEwen had referenced when they were arguing over visiting the club last night. Perhaps Colin had a stalker.

His breath left his body as a dry rasp when Colin mounted the stage and began to sing. *"Dream Lover"? Oh Dawud, is this a sign? Allah is showing mercy on my pain by resurrecting you in such a similar form.* Jabir Elmoudowi wasn't about to turn down such a supernatural gift by being timid. When Colin finished the song, he stepped in front of him as he crossed the dance floor. "May I claim the next dance?"

***

Wren hesitated a moment to study the man in front of him. It was indeed the target, but Geordy understated Elmoudowi's handsomeness. The man mistook his scrutiny for hesitation and rushed into speech.

"You sing beautifully. I thought you were French, but now I'm thinking you're an American."

Wren winked at the man. "As American as apple pie. I only speak halfway decent French because I had a hot French professor in college. I wanted him to be aware of my presence in his class, so I studied extra hard."

He moved into the man's arms when the DJ spun another record, and laughed aloud at his choice; the Everly Brothers were crooning "All I Have To Do Is Dream."

He made Elmoudowi laugh when he opined, "There seems to be a theme here. My name's Colin, what's yours?"

"Oh forgive me, I meant to introduce myself. My name is Stavros. Stavros Andino."

"You are Greek, then?"

"Yes, on my father's side. My mother was Lebanese."

"Do you live in Greece, Stavros?"

"I own several homes scattered about the world. My favorite is indeed in Greece. Have you ever been to Mikonos?"

"Several homes? Sounds like you like to travel, and speak more languages than my solitary French. My associate, Daniel, speaks passable French, but sometimes it's hard to understand his Scottish English. But to answer your question, no, Greece remains on my list of places to visit, but I'm starting to work my way in that direction. For each vacation, I choose another location. I started out in the British Isles and worked my way through France. Italy is next. I'll eventually explore Greece."

"So, what do you do for a living, Colin?"

"I'm a mathematician, a physicist, and please don't ask what I'm working on because it would bore you to death. What do you do to afford all those homes, Stavros?"

"I'm Greek and Lebanese, so I have a natural urge to follow the sea. I run an export-import business that relies heavily on international shipping."

Wren backed away to study Elmoudowi's face. "You aren't related to Aristotle Onassis in any way, are you?" He fluttered his eyelids to show he joked.

Elmoudowi grinned back at his partner. "Sadly, no. My income is far more modest." The song ended, and Jabir didn't want to let Colin leave. "May I buy you a drink?" He relaxed a little when Colin nodded.

"Sure, why don't you come to my table. It's just over there."

He followed the direction Colin pointed, and saw the bodyguard seated alone at a table, nursing water or club soda. He needed to be certain of Colin's affections, so apologized, "I'm sorry. I didn't realize you came with someone."

Colin caressed his cheek before answering, and he couldn't help himself and leaned into it. "That's my, uh, business associate. Come, let me introduce you. One thing, though, Daniel's tolerant of my lifestyle, but he doesn't swing that way, but we're a packaged deal. Daniel goes where I go, except for bed, and even then, I don't crawl beneath the covers until he's checked to make sure there are no monsters under it."

"So, Daniel is your bodyguard?"

"Yes, yes he is. If you are uncomfortable having him around, I understand. Your decision, Stavros. Come, meet Daniel and enjoy a drink with us, or find another partner to dance with you."

Jabir used his thumb to stroke Colin's prominent cheekbone. "I have no problem at all with Daniel. Introduce me."

After shaking Stavros's hand, Wren, in his Colin role, volunteered to get the drinks. Scotch for Stavros, bourbon for himself, and another club soda with a twist of lime for Daniel to make Stavros think of him as nothing more than a bodyguard.

When Stavros attempted to pay, he batted his money away. "No, put your wallet away. I invited you to my table, so I'll pay."

Wren settled back to begin a subtle interrogation. "Stavros, is one of the homes you own here in Monte Carlo?"

"No, I'm renting a villa in the hills above the city. I too am on vacation. I've always liked Monte Carlo, but this is too much of a party city for me to stay for very long, especially when the Grand Prix reaches here, and it becomes impossible to move in this city."

"How long are you staying? My vacation runs out at the end of next week. Perhaps you can show me the city's attractions."

"I'd like that very much, Colin."

Wren was aware the terrorist didn't mention how long he intended to stay in Monte Carlo, but the brochures in the hotel said the race would end in Monaco on the last Sunday of November. Stavros interrupted him before he could ask another question.

"Perhaps you and Daniel would like to join me tomorrow for lunch on my yacht?"

Colin widened his eyes to appear suitably impressed. "We'll be happy to, Stavros."

"Excellent. My yacht is moored at one of the slips in the Marina. Her name is *Kismet*." Stavros tried to say something more, but the DJ interrupted with an announcement.

"Your attention *Mesdames et Messieurs*, here's the final record for the evening, and then you can take your bump and grind to more discreet locations."

Colin surprised Elmoudowi by taking his hand and tugging until he rose from the table. "Dance with me, Stavros."

The last song of the evening turned out to be "La Mer," and he sang the French lyrics softly to Stavros as they danced. When the song ended, he kissed the man on the lips and waved goodbye after agreeing, again, to meet him for lunch.

He and Geordy didn't say much to each other as they caught a cab back to the hotel.

***

Wren remained silent as they rode the elevator up to their room, and, as soon as Geordy unlocked the door, Blade brushed past him.

"I need a shower. Good night, I'll see you in the morning."

That left him standing alone and confused before he could return his own good night.

As he hung up his clothes, Geordy realized he had something wrong with his vision. Well, not wrong, exactly, he could see quite clearly, except for the green tinge covering everything. From the moment his teammate made contact with that bastard Elmoudowi, Geordy couldn't tear his eyes away. He saw every touch, every caress the terrorist gave him.

Capping his evening with the vision of Wren kissing the man guaranteed he wouldn't drop peacefully to sleep, despite it being three o'clock in the morning.

A small part of his brain said he had no right to be jealous, and so he counseled himself. C'mon, Campbell, man up. It isn't fair to go all jealous lover on Wren because he's doing what the Agency sent him here to do. And besides, you can't start acting like you and he are romantic partners. Not if both of you intend to stay in the Marines.

Geordy dropped off to sleep at last when logic overcame jealousy, only to be awakened a scant fifteen minutes later when the object of his angst crawled into bed with him.

He rolled over and switched the bedside light, and Wren winced at the sudden brightness. "What's the matter?"

"I can't sleep, I keep seeing and feeling Elmoudowi all over me, and asking myself why I didn't tell Jack Adams to go fuck Elmoudowi himself if he wanted to find out when he intended to kill Marines. I'm sorry I got you involved, Geordy. This whole situation sucks, and now that we've made contact with the man, I want no part of it, but I'd feel like the biggest coward in the world if I backed out before completing this mission."

Blade's confession of his feelings on having to wine and dine the terrorist mollified him enough to ask "Is there anything I can do to help?" He certainly didn't object when Blade demonstrated his anxiety by rolling into his arms and shivering like he had the flu.

"Hold me until I fall asleep. I can't play nice with Stavros if I'm sleep deprived, yacht or no yacht."

Geordy stroked Wren's back until he felt him relax in sleep. The guilt engendered by his pettiness assailed him. He never considered the personal angst Wren would suffer to complete this assignment.

He could do better, he would do better and support Blade with whatever he needed. Resolution made, Geordy switched off the light, spooned Wren, and fell quickly asleep.

Chapter Twenty-Three

Since they would be on the water this afternoon, Wren, once again fully in the persona of Colin, chose to wear his recent purchase of a green cashmere V-neck sweater with gray dress slacks. But when he studied himself in the mirror, he didn't like what he saw. No, the boxer briefs would have to go—they were showing a definite line beneath the slim-fitting slacks.

He stepped out of the trousers, shucked the briefs then zipped the pants over his bare assets. The small flat jar on the top of his dresser caught his eye, and he froze. Should he take the beetle cream along, just in case? Duh, yachts had staterooms, and Stavros's reluctance to part with him last night made him certain the stateroom would be included as the last item on the tour.

Colin slipped his thin wallet into his back pocket, and concealed the special jar in the anachronistic small waist pocket that was still tailored into men's dress slacks. At least its tell-tale bulge was covered by his sweater.

With a deep sigh, he jammed his feet into deck shoes and went in search of Geordy. This was going to be a very long, nerve-racking day.

***

Jabir mopped up the condensation from the champagne bucket and twisted the neck of the champagne bottle between his hands. He wanted the champagne chilled just right. He also made sure there was a fresh bottle of carbonated water chilling in a bucket of ice beside one of the easy chairs across from the sofa. He then fiddled with the placement of sliced lemons and limes on a gold-rimmed porcelain plate on a nearby table for Daniel's use.

When one of his crew members placed an arrangement of fresh flowers on the dining table, he tsked his disapproval. He wanted it in the exact center of the table. He caught the crewman's slight frown and knew his entire crew would be glad when his guests arrived. His demands for the last hour were driving them crazy, but he wanted everything to be perfect. He only had a week to convince Colin to quit his boring job and travel the world with him as his lover, his permanent lover, and one who'd have no further need of a bodyguard.

He rushed toward the gangplank when Colin's voice drifted through the open window, requesting permission to come aboard.

He stood beside Captain Heinrich as he granted permission, and then ushered Colin and Daniel to the combined dining and living area. He waved off the crewman and took over the task of opening the champagne, after gesturing for his guests to seat themselves in the living room adjacent to the dining room.

"You have a beautiful yacht, Stavros. This is my first time on a yacht. Would you show me around?"

"Of course, Colin, but my chef would be most upset if I do so before lunch. He's created a wonderful culinary experience for us, but we do have enough time to enjoy our champagne and chat for a bit."

"Stavros, would you mind if I talk to Captain Heinrich while you and Colin tour the boat? I'm curious as to what it takes to run a yacht, and I want to catch a view of the harbor from the bridge."

Elmoudowi readily agreed to Daniel's request and motioned for him to seat himself on one of the taupe-colored, raw silk easy chairs as he joined Colin on the sofa.

"Before I forget, I wanted to invite you to go swimming tomorrow."

He smiled at Colin's exaggerated display of craning his neck to see out of the sliding glass door off the living room, and give an exaggerated shiver.

"But, Stavros, darling, it's October. Don't you think the water might be too cold?"

Stavros laughed and cupped Colin's chin. "The Mediterranean is still warm enough to swim, if you are from northern climes, but I have to admit my blood is too thin to find swimming in the sea comfortable at this time of year. I meant come to the villa I'm renting. One of the reasons I rented it was for the glassed-in, heated pool."

He couldn't restrain himself when Colin moved thigh-to-thigh with him. He gave the inside of his thigh a surreptitious squeeze.

"Sounds like fun. But you must come with Daniel and me after lunch. I love antique or unusual cars, and I understand that Prince Rainier has quite a collection of them open to the public. We could while away the afternoon and have dinner afterward."

When Daniel turned away to pour himself a glass of carbonated water and add a twist of lime, Jabir, emboldened by Colin's lack of objection to his first touch, ran his hand slowly along the inside of Colin's thigh. His heart leapt when Colin widened his legs a fraction, and so he continued, but stopped before the gesture became lewd. He gave another gentle squeeze as Daniel began to turn around, and casually picked up his own champagne glass before responding to Colin's offer.

"It pains me to say this, Colin, but I'll have to decline. A major annoyance of an import-export business is you receive calls at odd hours. One of my clients will be calling around three o'clock, and I'll need to be near my computer to solve his problem."

Before he could say more, a crewmember announced lunch was served.

He made sure to include Daniel in the conversation but struggled to appear interested in the man's responses. He couldn't tear his eyes away from Colin. The man had exquisite manners, but watching his lips close over the tines of his fork did something very wicked below his belt. Too much time had passed since the last time he and Dawud made love.

His steward's question befuddled him when he asked if he and his guests would care for brandy. His empty dessert plate gave him a clue, but he couldn't remember what had been served.

"Would anyone care for brandy to aid digestion?"

He got an affirmative from Colin, and the expected request from Daniel, as they followed him back to the couches."

"Stavros, may I be excused to speak with Captain Heinrich on the bridge while you and Colin enjoy your brandies."

"Of course, Daniel, but be aware Captain Heinrich will fill your ears with yacht minutia. He's very proud of his baby."

As Daniel climbed the stairs to the bridge, Jabir waited impatiently for the steward to pour the brandy and leave. He restrained his eagerness until Colin took a small sip, and as soon as he did so, claimed Colin's lips.

"I couldn't wait a moment longer to return the kiss you gave me last night when you said goodbye at Bacchanal."

He didn't let Colin answer, just cupped his face and moved in for another kiss, which Colin returned with equal fervor.

Breathing rapidly, he asked, "Would you like to go below to the master suite?"

His accursed cell phone chose that moment to ring. Unless it was a dire emergency, no one used that particular number, so he accepted the call.

He withdrew a little distance from Colin and barked, "Yes? One moment."

Stavros turned to Colin and apologized. "I'm sorry, Colin, but I must take this. Please excuse me."

***

Colin nodded and pulled his sweater back down from where Stavros had hiked it up to caress his chest as they kissed.

He pretended disinterest when Stavros, aka the fucking terrorist, stepped out of the sliding glass door to the deck and slid it closed behind himself, but relief left him giddy when he discovered the window in the dining room was still open. His ears pricked up at the fact Stavros was speaking in Arabic.

He poured himself another smidgen of brandy and then sat facing away from the balcony, the better to eavesdrop without giving away the fact he was doings so. He pictured engraving Elmoudowi's words in stone to memorize them as he listened.

"This had better be important, and whatever your reason, you better not be calling to explain why you're not boarding that freighter in Marseilles tomorrow."

Through the corner of his eye, Colin saw Elmoudowi wave his arm about in agitation.

"What do you mean one of your recruits is getting cold feet? I thought you said they were eager to martyr themselves for such a cause? No, you listen, if you can't convince him of the righteousness of the cause, you will make sure he isn't alive to leave that ship in Wilmington.

"I don't believe this. You can't be asking me how to dispatch him. Selim, I chose you for this operation because you're one of Allah's special warriors. Kill the man and send his body out of the ship's garbage chute with the rest of the slops. The sharks following the ship will take care of disposing of the body after that."

Colin sucked in his breath at that pronouncement and hoped his face didn't show any reaction in case the bomb maker glanced his way.

"Do what you have to do, Selim, but if you're not in place to begin the operation by six o'clock on the twenty-third of this month, there is no place in this world you or anyone else on the team can hide. I will find you, and your death will be...."

Fuck, Jabir had turned away, and the wind carried his words out of his hearing. He now knew the day and month of the operation, but Elmoudowi hadn't mentioned how the operation would be conducted, or which Marine installation would be hit.

Colin's hand shook slightly as he raised the brandy snifter to his lips, but not from fear, more from frustrated rage and the realization that, if Elmoudowi had inadvertently spilled the exact time and place of the attack, he would have ensured the terrorist's body followed his own words out to sea.

Colin was supremely reluctant to allow the twisted sonovabitch to paw his body without using one of his martial arts moves to kill him, or at least break every bone in the hand he used to touch him, but he turned and pasted on an affected expression of mild concern when Stavros re-entered the room.

"Was it bad news, Stavros? That phone call has obviously upset you."

Stavros sat on the couch forcefully enough to bounce, and picked up his glass of brandy and drained it before answering. "I'm fine, Colin, just a personnel problem. Sometimes you have to make allowances for someone else doing the hiring. I'm sure the situation will be resolved in a few days. I know I promised to show you around the yacht, but...."

Stavros left the rest of the sentence unspoken when Daniel descended the stairs from the bridge. "Ah, here's Daniel. Since you expressed a desire to visit Prince Rainier's automobiles, I won't feel too guilty over begging off showing you around the rest of the yacht. That phone call has led to more work, I'm afraid. Please allow me to make amends for conducting business rather than pleasure by inviting you both to my villa tomorrow?"

"Of course, Stavros. No need to apologize. We'd be delighted to visit with you again tomorrow."

Colin checked the time. "Come along, Mr. MacEwen. If we hurry, we can reach the auto gallery with plenty of time to tour the whole thing."

***

Jabir waved as Colin and Daniel departed the yacht after he gave them detailed instructions on how to find his villa. But before heading back inside, he called to the crewmember that had been with him the longest.

"Follow those two, and if they visit the royal car museum, you may return here. If they don't, you will follow them and report on where they go and who they talk to."

He hadn't lived so long by being stupid. He would take precautions against Colin not being who he claimed to be, or that he didn't speak any other languages but English and French. For Selim to call while he was entertaining was most unfortunate.

After giving the order to have Colin tailed, he couldn't settle but chose to pace around the open-air seating above the swim platform. Several of his yachting neighbors called greetings, and he returned them with a wave, only to return to worrying over whether or not Dawud's manifestation in the form of Colin MacAulay was a gift from Allah or Satan.

Damn Selim for calling at such an inauspicious time, but the man would soon martyr himself and no longer be a problem he had to deal with. Jabir found killing in person distasteful, but he'd make an exception in Selim's case, if, by a strange turn of events, he lived beyond the twenty-third of this month.

He only began to calm himself when the crewman returned within fifteen minutes and reported his guests had gone to the museum and purchased tickets to enter. Now, he must call his distant cousins and put enough fear in them so they didn't screw up their part in his plan to kill many, many Marines.

***

"Man, oh man, can you believe this car?" Colin stopped in front of a 1963, twelve-cylinder Ferrari.

"Wouldn't you like to take this baby home, Daniel?" He was still in character because both of them had noted the car following them from the docks, and weren't sure if their tail followed them inside.

"No, I wouldn't."

Colin eyed Daniel with disbelief. "Oh, come on, no one passes on a classic Ferrari."

Daniel crossed his arms over his chest as he stared at the gorgeous piece of automobile history. "Colin, even if you could afford to buy a car like this, I don't think you could afford the many speeding tickets you'd rack up exceeding the posted speed limits. This model idles faster than 55mph. According to this sign, maximum speed is around 309 km or 180 mph. You'd be committing a crime against all Ferraris if you bought one and never let the horses loose."

Colin turned toward Daniel and huffed, "Your mother should have named you Spock instead of Daniel. Sometimes your Scottish logic is a real buzz kill."

Daniel MacEwen enjoyed seeing the eclectic collection of cars Prince Rainier found collectable but refrained from mentioning what happened on the bridge of the yacht until they were back in their suite, and he used a device issued to him in London to determine if their room was free of electronic bugs. He didn't have to prod Blade to get the ball rolling, for he opened up as soon as he gave him the all clear sign.

"Elmoudowi got a call while you were upstairs discussing all things yacht with Captain Heinrich. He went out on the balcony to take the call, and although he closed the door behind himself, I was able to hear his conversation because the dining room windows were open. Whoever called him was speaking in Arabic, because that's the language Elmoudowi used to answer him."

Geordy, relieved of his bodyguard duty, retrieved a bottle of scotch from the cabinet in the living room, and after receiving a nod from Wren poured two glasses of scotch. "And what did you learn from the one-sided conversation?"

"Well, someone named Selim is supposed to board a freighter in Marseilles tomorrow and he has a team with him, one of whom seems to be reconsidering his plan to martyr himself. Jabir told Selim to off him if he couldn't be convinced of the rightness of murdering Marines. I believe his actual directions were to off him and send his body out the trash chute to let the sharks dispose of the body."

"Nice guy," was Geordy's only comment before taking a sip of scotch.

Wren agreed. "Yeah, a real sweetheart."

Geordy moved over to let Wren sit on the sofa and stretch out his legs.

"To continue, he also mentioned the ship would dock in Wilmington, but which Wilmington is the big question. If this Wilmington is in Delaware, the target could be somewhere around Virginia, which means Quantico or the Marine Barracks at 8th & I are likely targets."

Geordy added, "And if docks in Wilmington, North Carolina, that could mean Camp Lejeune or even MARSOC. What else did you overhear?"

"Our buddy Stavros told Selim he had to be in place by the twenty-second of October because the attack had to commence early in the morning of the twenty-third. And that was when the fucking wind shifted and carried his voice out of range."

"Well, you didn't catch the rest, but I did. I was trying to give the impression I was very interested in learning the correct mixture of gasoline to maintain optimum cruising speed when the sound of Elmodawi speaking Arabic caught my attention. I was already leaning up against the wall near the window, so all I had to do is paste an interested expression on my face and nod while Captain Heinrich droned on"

Wren interrupted, "I wonder if the captain is aware he works for a terrorist?"

"If he is, then Elmoudowi has to pay him a lot more than the average captain makes for his services. Elmoudowi sort of lost his temper when Selim asked him if he could trust someone, and he got hot and said of course he could trust them because they were distant cousins who ran a beach shop. He claimed their loyalty didn't need to be questioned because their shop is a front for laundering money for Hizballah. He also mentioned something about paint cans being already loaded with shrapnel, and the cousins would have the necessary documentation to back up their disguise. He hung up after that little tidbit."

Wren scrubbed his face with his hands and distractedly ran his fingers through his hair. "Paint cans? Think they might be going to pose as painters? Something about the date is bothering me. The twenty-third of October, why is that date bugging me? I can't put my finger on it."

Geordy drained his drink and put the glass on the coffee table. "Yeah, I can't place the date, either."

When Geordy took his cell phone out, Wren asked, "Are you calling who I think you're calling?"

"Yeah, I think we should contact the Agency's man and fill him in on what we have so far. Maybe they can put the pieces together. At least we've narrowed it down to a hit on the East Coast, and the day and general time of the attack."

Wren stood and pulled the green sweater off. "Come on, let's go work out. I'll drive myself crazy if I just sit around here trying to figure out the significance of that date."

The workout didn't involve much conversation because the room was crowded and noisy, and after few laps in the pool they agreed on room service for dinner. Neither one of them felt like dressing for dinner or trying to maintain interesting conversation.

Wren finally gave up and went to bed around eleven o'clock. An unheard of hour to retire in Monte Carlo.

Geordy gave up at midnight after he read the same page twice. He must've fallen asleep at some point, for he was startled awake by having the covers dragged off him.

"Damn, this is getting to be a habit, Wren. A habit, I might add, that needs to be broken, or I'm going to break you."

"Anybody ever tell you, you're not a cheerful riser, Geordy?"

"Nobody who still draws breath. What's the deal? Why are you in my room?"

"I remembered the significance of the date, and when you hear what occurred on that date, you're going to smack yourself upside your head."

Geordy grabbed the covers out of his teammate's hand and covered himself before sitting up and turning on the light. "I doubt very much I'll be smacking myself, but go ahead, enlighten me."

Wren sat at the foot of the bed and put himself into the lotus position with a flexibility Geordy admired. He also admired his lack of a robe or pajamas. He had to force himself to concentrate on his teammate's words.

"October 23, 1983. That's the date of the bombing of the Marine barracks in Beirut. Two hundred Marines from Camp Lejeune lost their lives that day due to a truck bomb. The attack occurred around six-thirty in the morning."

Geordy fulfilled Wren's prediction by smacking himself on the forehead with the heel of his hand. "How could we have forgotten that? We attend the memorial service in Jacksonville every year. Do you think Elmoudowi plans to reprise that by a hit on Camp Lejeune? Hey, don't painters carry their stuff in some kind of panel van? With today's Semtex and C-4 loaded into one of those, he could get an even bigger bang than the one in Beirut."

Wren unwound himself from the lotus position and started to pace the bedroom. "Yeah, he could, but even if we took that dirt bag out today, we couldn't stop the hit because we don't know the name of the freighter the team is supposed to go out on. And there's the small detail that Camp Lejeune is huge, and we don't know which unit or building he's targeted."

Geordy watched Blade pace for a moment and then stopped him by giving a disgusted grunt. "The truth of the matter is we're not sure he plans on hitting Lejeune. MARSOC is near enough to Lejeune to be a target, and I think Elmoudowi is well aware the drone that took out his lover in Afghanistan came from MARSOC's 2nd Battalion Area of Responsibility.

Blade stood stock still as he considered Geordy's point. "Damn, we seem to be broadening the target area instead of narrowing it."

Geordy hopped out of bed to wrap his teammate in a headlock and rub his scalp with his knuckles. "Well broadening or narrowing the field, we will contact the Agency man again and tell him the significance of the date. Maybe this puzzle will be solved one piece at a time."

"I hope the Agency man paid attention in the CIA's puzzle solving class."

"Me, too, but I'm not about to solve anything on a growling stomach. I'm hungry. Let's throw some clothes on and find a restaurant open for breakfast. Walking might even clear away some of the cobwebs. But one thing is very clear, we're both going to need to stay sharp when we visit Jabir aka Stavros this afternoon. You need to keep his attention focused on you at the pool while I search the house."

Blade jerked back in surprise. "Aw, shit, I forgot about the swim date. Damn, you just killed my appetite. Thanks a heap."

***

The small jar, once again hidden in a pocket of his brown dress slacks dug into his hip, and Colin tugged his camel-colored sweater down to hide the bulge. With his red-blond hair, brown slacks, and camel sweater, he had the ridiculous thought he could pass as a walking fashion ad for fall attire.

He didn't attempt conversation with Geordy as he drove the Mercedes to Stavros's villa. He was too busy constructing, and then rejecting, scenarios on how he could avoid having to use the sexual stimulant. He wished he knew a magic word to make all the planets come into alignment and smite Stavros with a migraine, or something more painful, to discourage him from playing satyr to his water nymph in the heated pool.

A deep sigh stated his mood as Geordy pulled the car into the villa's circular drive, but he had no time to wallow in self-pity for Stavos answered the door wearing a large smile and nothing but a bathrobe, and Colin forced himself to smile and hug the man as he stepped back and gestured for them to enter.

"Come in, come in. I'm so glad you could come."

Colin studied the beautiful entranceway and ornate wooden

staircase and asked, "Would you mind showing us around, Stavros? Of course, we don't want to interfere with the duties of your staff."

"Delighted to, Colin. As to the staff, I don't keep one. I have a housecleaning service that comes in on Mondays and the pool cleaner comes early Friday mornings. I cook for myself or eat out, so I'm the only one rattling around in the villa. My work is stressful most times, so I enjoy playing hermit while I'm on vacation. Oh, and let me apologize again for conducting business while you were aboard the yacht. I have no control over that now the entire world is connected via cell phone. Hopefully, we will not be interrupted today, but I'm sorry to say, I can't guarantee the day will pass without an interruption or two."

Stavros took them room-by-room through the villa, and whoever the decorator was knew what they were doing. The décor was lavish but not gaudy, and the antiques were gorgeous but functional.

The last area they were conducted to was a glassed-in pool large enough to do laps, and surrounded by palms and lemons trees in large terra-cotta pots. There was a cabana at the end opposite the diving board, and the lounges were padded in blue-and-white striped canvas and wide enough to hold two adults quite nicely.

When Daniel began to make his apologies, he gave a convincing performance of a straight man wanting to vacate the area because he knew how his gay host intended to while away the afternoon by the pool.

"Stavros, would you mind if I use your library? I don't plan to swim, and I'm sure you and Colin do. I'll just find a book and read until Colin's ready to leave for the day."

Colin kept the distaste from his face when Stavros didn't bother disguising his delight at having him all to himself.

"But of course, Daniel. I'm sure there are one or two English novels to be found in the library."

From where he stood on the pool deck, Stavros pointed to the last window on the left on the second floor. "That's the library. Go through the French doors behind you and take the stairway to your immediate left, and you'll be right outside the library door."

Colin didn't say a word as Jabir aka Stavros seated himself on one of the lounges and patted the space next to him after Daniel left.

"Why don't you change. There are robes in the cabana for your use."

Colin held up the small bag he'd brought with him. "I have my suit with me. I'll just be a moment."

He stopped, rooted to the spot, when his host laughed.

"Come, come, Colin. A suit won't be necessary. I never use one. I don't like tan lines."

Colin had the sudden, wry thought Stavros might be related to the American actor who played in the camp film, *Zorro the Gay Blade*. He didn't like tan lines, either.

But Stavros's big reveal showed, while not as ripped as himself, he was in decent shape, and as he hoped, the bomber did indulge in manscaping. Thank God. He didn't think he could keep the disgust from his face if the man had been hairy, or so fat he had to lift his distended belly to find his dick.

"Ah, I'll just be a moment. I need to get out of these clothes."

Was that a giggle? Hard to credit Uncle Sam's most wanted terrorist bomber giggled.

Walking to the cabana without dragging his feet took effort. He used more effort to convince himself to shuck his clothes. His flaccid dick told him the expended effort was all for nil.

Sighing, he dug the little jar out of his pants pocket and scooped a small portion out. With a "beetles don't fail me now," he massaged the ointment into his member and donned one of the terrycloth bathrobes.

He returned to find Elmoudowi wearing nothing but sunglasses.

Colin dropped his robe and moved swiftly to the chaise lounge to stretch out on his stomach. He didn't want the fact he was currently sporting an erection to encourage Stavros to jump him. If he was going to do this, then by God he would insist on foreplay.

He forced himself not to recoil at the sensation of the bomb maker's hand cupping his ass.

"You are so beautiful, Colin. But you are also so fair. I'm afraid you will burn. Let me put some of my special suntan oil on your skin."

When he murmured his agreement, Stavros straddled him and began rubbing an oil that smelled mostly like coconut into his skin. He lay quietly as his host started at his back and moved steadily downward. He awarded the terrorist a brownie point for some control when he skipped his ass and continued the massage at his thighs and down his calves.

The man was thorough, and despite his personal qualms, the repetitive motion was relaxing him, until he felt a finger at the crack of his ass. He used considerable willpower not to flinch or shove the terrorist into the deep end of the pool with one of the heavy chaises tied to him to serve as an anchor.

"I want you, Colin. Let me prepare you."

The word "prepare" made him flash back to a pool somewhere in Saudi Arabia, and the master ordering, "Prepare me, Wren." And suddenly he was no longer a Marine but a lost teenager. He froze, and Elmoudowi had to repeat himself.

"Let me please you, Colin. I'm very good."

He used more than his stomach muscles to force his upper body off the chaise and look over his shoulder at Stavros. He swallowed back the bile climbing his throat as he said, "Yes, I would like that, but not without a condom. We are unaware of each other's sexual history, so using a condom is non-negotiable. No condom, no sex, Stavros.

"Of course, of course, my delight. I have come prepared."

Colin bit his lip to keep the goggle off his face. Stavros held a string of condoms and waved it in front of him. He did the only thing left to him, and put his head back down on the chaise.

The slow, in and out insertion of Stavros's oiled finger was not making his artificial erection any less painful. The man had very thick, blunt fingers was his last insane thought before he felt Stavros's hands tighten on his hips, urging him to come to his knees.

He began to comply when Stavros's cell phone rang, instantly accompanied by two groans: one of relief, in his case, and one of frustration in Stavros's.

He pretended to drowse as Elmoudowi wiped the lotion from his hands and answered the phone.

"Yes? Ah, Hanzel, how are you? You did? That's excellent my friend. Where and when would you like to meet to discuss your requirements?"

"I do remember that restaurant, it's the one on *Denkmalstrasse* that serves the best *raclette* in Lucerne. You want to meet on the twenty-fourth of this month at eight o'clock? That would be perfect. I'll...."

As he feigned disinterest in Elmoudowi's business transaction, and baked in the bright sun like a seasoned shrimp on charcoal, an evil bit of payback sprang into his head. Yes, he knew the prank verged on childishness, but it suited his mood.

Waiting until Elmoudowi turned his way, he rolled to his back and picked up the bottle of suntan lotion to squirt a line of it down his chest, ending just above his pubic hair. His hand followed the path of it, and he began to caress his painful erection. He smiled to himself when Stavros stuttered into the phone.

"Ah, sorry, Hansel, could you repeat that? Yes, fine, I'll meet you in Lucerne on the 24th. *Auf Wiedersehen*."

The bomb maker's self-control surprised him when, instead of tossing the phone back on the table, he began to dial.

"*Guten Tag*, Herr Dortmund. Yes, this is he. I just learned funds have been transferred into my temporary account, and I want them transferred to my savings. Yes, I can verify the account number."

He listened as Elmoudowi recited a string of numbers, but he didn't worry that he was being obvious because the man had eyes only for what his hand was doing to his balls. He made sure to groan and pump his hips, and increase his breathing to simulate an approaching climax.

"Yes, yes, that's fine, Herr Dortmund. Yes, transfer the whole amount. Goodbye."

Karma was its usual bitchy self, as he discovered when Elmoudowi tossed the phone away without a care as to the landing, and pounced on him. Before he could even protest, the man ripped open a condom package, flipped him like a flapjack, and rammed himself home.

If he lived long enough to be entered into the *Guinness Book of World Records*, he would still regret lifting his eyes to the library window. Geordy had seen Elmoudowi mount him.

He closed his eyes and endured in shame until the man gasped, "Dawud," and rolled off him.

No one had made him feel like nothing more than a sex toy in quite some time, but to be used by another man in front of Geordy, and called another man's name as Elmoudowi climaxed, recalled his brutal childhood in vivid detail.

In one lithe motion, he rose from the chaise and dove into the pool. Maybe, if he was lucky, his head would hit the bottom and put an end to him.

***

Geordy now knew why Peeping Toms were recidivists. He couldn't tear his eyes away from the scene by the pool. He wanted to run down there and rip Elmoudowi away from Wren and then stomp him into formless goo. The realization he also wanted to mount Wren in the same way as soon as he dispatched the terrorist made his stomach cramp, and he began to back away from the window, but not fast enough. Wren chose that exact moment to look up and caught him staring.

He jerked away from the window and right into a pole lamp with a hand-blown, glass shade. He managed to catch it before he turned the library into an accident scene. Too upset to feel foolish about standing with his arms wrapped around the antique, Geordy took deep breaths to calm himself before moving a safe distance away from the lamp.

Cursing his clumsiness, he returned to his task of searching every shelf in the library. The dust he found on the books told him Elmoudowi was not a reader, and none of them had been used to hide something inside.

The Italianate desk presented itself as his next search area, but he made the mistake of going to the window to gauge whether or not he had time to rifle through the individual drawers. Having just witnessed what he hoped to one day scour from his memory, he doubted Elmoudowi would have the strength to climb the stairs for at least another ten minutes. His assessment was based on experience. Wren had left him spent and gasping more than once.

Why did you always find something in the last place you searched, he groused to himself, as he discovered the object of his search in a bottom drawer? He studied his discovery, and wanted to pull the gun nestled at the small of his back, and put enough lead into Elmoudowi's body his death photo would rival that of Che Guevara, another well-known terrorist tracked down by American Special Forces in conjunction with the Bolivian Army.

***

Jabir lay back on the chaise and couldn't quite catch his breath. Even though he whispered Dawud's name at the moment of his climax, he knew he hadn't made love to Dawud. Dawud had never moved like that. The thought Dawud had been robbed of the time to learn such moves started a sharp pain in his chest.

His heartbeat was taking much longer than usual to return to normal, and he began to worry he might be confusing *le petit mort* with a heart attack. Jabir chuckled softly at such a cynical thought. He needed a drink, but he liked his wine chilled, and the bottle, even though sitting in a bath of what had started out as ice, was too warm for his enjoyment.

He groaned under his breath as he levered himself off the chaise and put his robe on.

"I'll be right back, Colin. This bottle of wine has grown warm. I'll just fetch another."

He stayed a moment to admire Colin as he swam effortlessly through the water. He envied the younger man's stamina.

As he opened the French doors to step inside, the thought struck him he'd let a total stranger have free run of his house. Berating himself for being a love-struck fool, Jabir opened the drawer of the small chest just to the side of the door and withdrew a 9mm pistol. He always kept a weapon by every door, especially when staying in a foreign country, because one never knew who might come knocking on your door with malicious intent.

His bare feet made no sound as he ascended the stairs. Jabir didn't alert Daniel to his presence until the man moved to refold the map of North Carolina.

"Most unfortunate you found that, Daniel, if Daniel is your real name. Would you be so good as to step away from the desk and put your hands up?"

***

A movement at the library window caught his attention as he climbed out of the pool, and he lifted his eyes before he could tell himself not to.

What the hell? Geordy stood framed in the window with his hands raised like someone was pointing a gun at him.

In that instant Wren realized Elmoudowi had been gone longer than necessary to retrieve a bottle of wine.

He crossed the pool deck and ran into the house in a flash, but slowed down to tread lightly as he climbed the tiled steps to the library. As he neared the top, Elmoudowi's voice carried quite clearly.

"I detest handling wet work in person. And you, Daniel, will not be easy to dispose of. Tell me, is Colin involved in this?"

Wren didn't wait for Geordy to give his presence away by removing his attention from Elmoudowi. He gave a loud cry of "*Allahu Akbar.*" The unexpected Arabic phrase startled Elmoudowi enough to make him turn around, and Wren used a pressure point strike to stun Jabir's arm. He ignored the falling gun and followed up with a spinning kick that sent Elmoudowi staggering from the room.

The terrorist tried to catch his balance on the top step, but the small puddle of water Wren's wet feet left on the slick tile did him in. The terrorist cried out in fear as he fell backward down the steps. Wren stepped aside as Geordy rushed by him with his gun drawn.

He couldn't determine Elmoudowi's condition because Geordy's body hid the bomb maker from his view, so he called down, "Please tell me I didn't kill him. Uncle Sam will be pissed if he's dead before we find out what his plans were."

Geordy stood and called back, "You didn't kill him, the fall did. His neck is broken. What in the hell made you yell '*Allahu Akbar*'?"

Wren gave Geordy a sheepish grin. "I wanted to startle and confuse him. I'd say it worked, wouldn't you?"

"Yeah, you get points for thinking outside the box. I'll bet Elmoudowi is already in hell trying to fight off seventy-two virgins."

Wren sat down on the top step and quickly jumped back up again. The cold tile delivered a real zing to his bare ass. "Damn, what should we do? Were you able to find anything when you searched the house?"

Geordy removed his hand from the side of Jabir's neck. He found no pulse, so he left him just as he landed and climbed back up the steps.

"Yeah, I did. You need to see the map spread out on the desk in the library."

One glance and Wren broke out in goosebumps. "Shit, this is a map of Sneads Ferry, North Carolina."

He ran his finger along the yellow magic marker line that ran from Highway 210 down to a circled spot with the annotation "Last hotel before causeway," and a larger circle at the junction of Old Folkstone Road and Highway 210, marking the location as a beach shop with the grim words "staging area." A red marker had also been used to trace the route from the beach shop to the front gate of MARSOC.

When Geordy entered the library to stand next to him at the desk, he gestured at the map and said, "I can't believe he was stupid enough to risk the operation by leaving a map here."

Geordy shook his head. "I don't think it was a case of stupidity, I think he simply forgot it was here. I didn't discover this map until I tried to pull the desk drawer open and something prevented me. And that's when I found part of the map sticking out. The rest had fallen behind the drawer and gotten wedged in there. Speaking of stupid, I should never have let Elmoudowi sneak up on me. In my eagerness to study the map, I forgot to keep one ear cocked for company. Thanks for saving my life, by the way."

Wren flapped his hand in dismissal and asked, "What do we do now? I never had to hide a body before."

Geordy reached into his coat and took out his cell phone. "I'm going to call our contact and tell him we need a cleanup on Aisle 7, and you're going to go put your clothes back on."

He re-entered the house after taking a quick shower in the pool cabana to wash every trace of suntan lotion from his body, and found Geordy talking to, he correctly assumed, the Agency's man in Monte Carlo.

From his observation, the man was perfect for the job. One glance and you forgot him, completely. He was dressed decently, but unremarkably. Only when you were close enough to see his eyes did you realize they didn't miss a hell of a lot.

Wren accepted the offered hand as the man introduced himself as Monsieur Jean Dupont, and despite the serious situation, he couldn't contain the instantaneous chortle at meeting the French version of John Doe. A knock on the door inhibited his internal imp from breaking free.

"Ah, that is my cleaning team. Would you please move into the living room and wait for me to give them their instructions? One quick question, did all the action occur in the house, or shall I tell the cleaners to inspect the outside as well?"

His instantaneous blush stung his cheeks as he admitted, "You'll need to tell them to cover the pool area. I believe his cell phone is still on a table out there. He and I were, uh, swimming before he came back into the house for a bottle of wine. Oh, and I used the shower in the cabana before I got dressed."

He bit his lip and forced himself to stop babbling, and followed Geordy's broad back into the villa's living room, and sat on the opposite end of the couch from his teammate to wait for the agent to finish directing his team.

Geordy quirked an eyebrow at him when he muttered, "Let the grilling begin," as Jean Dupont sat himself in the armchair facing their sofa.

"Let's start at the beginning, shall we?"

He and Geordy were expertly grilled for a very long half hour before one of the cleaners walked into the room and gave them some respite. At least he thought so, until the man held up two evidence bags and then he wished he could simply disappear.

The technician held up the bags as he said, "I found these by the pool." One bag held Elmoudowi's cell phone, and the other a string of condoms. He couldn't bring himself to look closer to determine if there was a used one included in the bag.

Jean Dupont held out his hand, "I'll take the phone. You may dispose of the rest."

Wren almost jumped out of his skin when Geordy slid closer and gave him a quick fist bump on the arm. He was sure Geordy did so as encouragement, or a sign of solidarity, but all he wanted to do was crawl in a hole and not come out until Toto woke him up back on the little farm in Kansas.

But as the agent turned the bag with the phone around in his hands, he remembered the two phone conversations Elmoudowi had conducted by the pool.

"Monsieur Dupont, while we were poolside, Elmoudowi received a call from someone he called Hansel. He agreed to meet the man on the 24th of October to, and I'm quoting here, 'to discuss his requirements.' They were to meet at a particular restaurant in Lucerne, Switzerland on *Denkmalstrasse*. He didn't mention the restaurant's name, only its reputation for serving the best *raclette*. Oh, and the meeting time was eight o'clock.

"Elmoudowi then made a phone call right after he ended Hansel's call. He spoke to a Herr Dortmund. He acknowledged that a deposit had been made into his temporary account and ordered the money transferred to his savings account. He verified the number as," and Wren recited the string of numbers Elmoudowi gave to Herr Dortmund.

"Oh excellent work, Monsieur MacAulay. Please repeat those numbers so I can write them down."

He waited until the man withdrew a small tablet then repeated them before asking a question of his own. "Is that the number for a Swiss bank account?"

"We'll let our forensic accountants determine that. You might just have made our mutual Uncle Samuel a lot wealthier. Do either of you have anything else to add to what occurred here this afternoon?"

Geordy spoke up. "Only that Elmoudowi has a cleaning team that comes in on Mondays and a pool service that cleans the pool on Friday mornings. He said he either cooks for himself or eats out, so there are no other staff members in the villa."

"Wonderful, Mr. MacEwen. That gives us a timeline as to when people might start noticing his absence.

"All right, here is what you will do. You will return to your hotel, pack your clothes, and you will arrange your checkout for six o'clock tomorrow morning. You will then drive back to Calais and spend the night at the same place you stayed when you arrived from England. The car provided to you will be collected at the hotel. Leave the key with the concierge, and have him arrange for a taxi to take you to the dock to catch the ferry back to England, where you will drop off the equipment you received for this mission. Your flight arrangements back to the States will be ready by the time you reach London. Upon arrival, stateside, someone from the Agency will meet your flight and you will be debriefed at Langley."

Wren turned his head in Geordy's direction, and Geordy merely shrugged his shoulders to say he had no problem with the exfil plan.

"Any questions? No? Well then, let me say you both did a good job, and with impressive speed. We now have the exact location and time Elmoudowi intended to strike. We have the location of the hit team's hotel, and where they will find the equipment and false identification they need to get through security at the gate. I assure you, they will be stopped before they ever get near enough to MARSOC to even see the gate."

Jean Dupont extended his hand and shook both Wren's and Geordy's hand. "You both performed a great service to the nation and to your fellow Marines. Well done. Now, please leave so we can secure the site."

Wren relaxed a little to find the body gone from the bottom of the steps when he and Geordy made their way to the front door, but he still shivered as he walked past the spot where the terrorist had lain.

Chapter Twenty-Four

Wren was acting strange on the way back to the hotel. He was uncharacteristically quiet, for one thing, and he wouldn't meet his eye when he tried to draw him into conversation. Geordy bided his time to find out what was bugging him until they were back in the hotel room.

Having a direct Scot's nature, he got directly up in Blade's face and asked, "What the hell is bugging you? You heard Dupont. We completed the mission with time to spare." For a moment he didn't think Blade would answer since he sidestepped him to wrench open his closet door and pull out his suitcase. "C'mon, talk to me. Why are you so pissed off?" Geordy backed off quickly when Blade tossed his suitcase on the bed and crossed the room to stand nose to nose with him.

"Pissed off? Yeah, I guess you could say I'm pissed off, monumentally pissed off. After I left Saudi Arabia, I swore no one would put me in such a situation again, and, no, I'm not going to tell you what happened there, but here I am in some sort of déjà vu time warp, as I was when I was eighteen, only, lucky me, this one is worse because you saw me play bitch to that terrorist, and I can't make you unsee it. But I want you to know, if Adams had used any other argument but for the security of American lives, I would've told him to shove it up his ass." He stopped speaking, and he turned away to start pulling his clothing out of the dresser.

Geordy left Wren alone to regain his composure, and only returned when he had the shower running. He came up behind him as he was trying to fold a dress shirt, and reached around from behind to slide his sweater up and off. When he made no move to step out of his reach, he moved on to his belt and zipper.

"What in the hell are you doing, Geordy?" Wren asked in a hoarse voice.

"I'm undressing you for your shower."

"I took a shower at Elmoudowi's villa."

"Not like this one you didn't. One of the most religious and logical Marines I met in Force Recon was a crusty Gunnery Sergeant, and he told me he goes through a purification ritual every time he leaves combat. He makes sure he takes a shower in country before he gets on the plane to return home. He says the water washes away the stain of combat, the recriminations, the guilt, the anger, and even some of the grief of losing friends in combat. He says that's the only way he can greet his family and friends with a clear mind when he gets off the plane. I started doing the same, and it works." He saw the surprise in Blade's eyes to find him equally nude when he turned around.

His battle buddy didn't resist when he took his hand to lead him into the bathroom, but he did flinch a little when he climbed in behind him to begin soaping his back. Blade braced his arms on the front of the shower wall, and remained still as he worked steadily downward to his feet.

"Turn around." When Blade complied, Geordy gave him direct eye contact from his kneeling position and said, "Now, as I wash the front of you, I want you to say to yourself, I'm leaving the dirt of combat behind. I'm washing away the negativity, the bad feelings, the guilt, the sorrow. What I did, I did for my country. I obeyed my orders to the best of my ability." He waited until Blade's lips begin to move before continuing, and he had enough experience with this type of emotion to understand the tears weren't from soap in his eyes. He handed the soap to Blade and asked, "Would you do the same for me?"

Shower over, Geordy handed him a towel and waited until he finished drying himself, and, once again, took his hand, this time to lead him to the bed.

"Now this is me paying it forward. You once told me, when I was distraught over the loss of my mother, I wasn't as alone as I thought I was. And now I'm telling you, and showing you as you did me, you aren't as alone or as damaged as you think you are."

***

Geordy's lovemaking was exquisitely tender, and he didn't even try to resist surrendering to him. But afterward, as he lay there being cuddled and petted by his very generous lover, he was certain this operation had broken something inside him, maybe irreversibly.

While Geordy didn't reject him, as he feared he might be after seeing him play man-whore by the pool, he understood with every fiber in his body he couldn't go back to business as usual. He couldn't climb back into his box when they got back to MARSOC, because this little stunt had nuked the damned thing, and he had no energy left to build another, not even for Geordy.

Geordy's hand on his chest twitched, and his breathing deepened in sleep, and he decided to stop picking the scab off his most recent psychic wound, and shut his eyes to join Geordy in dreamland. His last cynical thought before sleep claimed him was, too bad they only awarded Purple Hearts for wounds you could see.

***

"This is weird, don't you think?"

Wren turned to face Geordy where he'd dropped his suitcase on the floor and sat on his bed in their dorm room. "Weird how?"

"Weird that after landing, and being hustled to Langley to be turned inside out by Jack Adams and crew for our debriefings, we're now back at MARSOC waiting for something to happen. Something, I might add, we will never hear about, unless Elmoudowi's team eludes the FBI, or whatever other agencies they activate to round them up, and several MARSOC dorms, maybe including the one we're presently sitting in, get vaporized. And if they do find the team before they make anything go bang, I doubt anyone will read headlines saying Islamic terrorists were captured as they tried to blow up a Marine installation in Sneads Ferry, North Carolina."

Wren appeared to consider Geordy's point, but his own experiences with *outré* situations demanded a more extreme level of strange and unusual than what Geordy described.

"Yeah, I'm not a fan of that kind of suspense. Speaking of weird, the dorm is too quiet with the team gone. I wonder how they're liking Africa."

Geordy began unpacking his suitcase. "Yeah, and I wonder what scut work Master Sergeant McClean and Captain Schuyler will find for us to do while we wait for the team to return from the land of the tsetse fly."

He returned his attention to his own suitcase and, after lifting out the green cashmere sweater, had to chuckle. "First time someone ever paid me in clothes. At least we got some decent threads to show for our effort."

"Uh-huh, we just can't explain why or where we got them," was Geordy's quick retort. "Or where we might ever wear them. I don't think Jacksonville is up for me in a Saville Row suit. Hey, I just remembered Jack Adams's face when you pulled that wad of euros you won in the casino out of your wallet. That was priceless."

Wren snickered. "Yeah, and probably the first time in history the man was speechless."

"Well, I'll bet the second time was when he told you, you could keep it, and you said you wanted him to use the money for the next Toys for Tots campaign as an anonymous contribution from MARSOC."

"Just call me Santa Clause. Um, Geordy, I'm hungry. I'll wait for you to shave and then we can go to the chow hall."

"Shave? Why do...? Oh, man I forgot about the beard."

"Yeah, the beard. It defies the Marine Corps regs. I'll wait until you're finished with your molting process."

He sprang off his bunk fifteen minutes later when Geordy stood above him to ask, "Did I miss any spots?"

He started to caress Geordy's smooth skin but stopped himself. He wasn't going there, ever again. He just couldn't.

"Nope, it's good. I don't know about you, but being back in cammies and boots makes the last month seem like a bad dream."

Geordy nodded, "The fancy clothes were nice, but cammies and boots are a lot more me than silk shirts and Italian shoes. C'mon, let's go eat."

Although they made small talk in the chow hall, Wren dreaded leaving the facility to go back to their room, but Geordy made no comment on his slow pace on the way back. But things changed when he closed the door to their room and he had to evade Geordy's hug.

"No, Geordy. I-I can't. We can't. I don't think you've changed your mind about staying in the Corps, and while I can't honestly say I still want to stay in, I'm not going to do anything that would make either one of us need to leave if we don't want to." His heart sank as Geordy's face closed down and he backed away.

"I understand, Wren. My blowing hot and cold must be confusing for you, but you, and only you, shake my resolve to make a career out of the Corps. I'll respect your wishes, but can we still be, uh, friends?"

Wren accepted the hand Geordy extended and shook it. "Yeah, friends, teammates, roomies." He left the "just no longer lovers" part unsaid.

Smacking his alarm clock back into silent mode the next morning was a big relief. The long night of torturing himself with what ifs was over. He must've fallen asleep at some point for he never heard Geordy leave his bed, but the sound of the shower running told him he had.

He dragged himself to the sink and began to shave. Gah, doing the right thing shouldn't make you feel this lousy. He added extra toothpaste to his brush to remove the taste of bitter rue from his mouth.

***

They reported in to the team room, and Master Sergeant Woodrow McClean called over to Captain Schuyler, "What do you know, Pacer, Fox Company's two MIAs are reporting for duty."

Captain Schuyler turned his chair away from his computer and grinned at them. "Well, Woody, they don't appear any the worse for wear, wherever the hell they've been. There are no gaping wounds, so they must be fit for duty."

Geordy answered, "Yes, sir, we are. What would you like us to do?"

Captain Schuyler asked, "Woody, did you reply to the school request I told you to cancel?

"No, sir, I was just going to do so. You still want me to cancel?"

"No, belay that. Since Mountain has returned, he can fill the slot." Pacer turned to Geordy and enlightened him.

"There's an opening for a Farsi language slot at the Defense Language Institute in Monterey, California, and you're going to fill it. Hope you didn't bother unpacking from your mystery assignment."

Pacer turned to Master Sergeant McClean. "Woody, start on Mountain's travel orders. If I read the request correctly, he'll be finished with the language training about the time the rest of the team comes back from Africa. Don't you just love it when loose ends come together?"

Pacer got a raised finger from Woody by way of answer.

Wren spoke up. "Uh, Captain, what about me?"

"Ah, Blade, you are the lucky recipient of the short end of the stick. Since Woody and I so selflessly jumped into the breach in the team's absence, there isn't much left to do, which means you can catch up on your medical and dental requirements. You can start with the flu shot you missed. I don't want you back here until your shot record is up to date, and the dentist has counted all your pearly whites to ensure you still possess enough remaining teeth to properly chew your food.

"You're both dismissed. Mountain to pack, and Blade to get shot by a corpsman."

***

Wren didn't cross paths with Geordy again until he returned to the dorm at the end of the day. The pain in both of his arms bore testimony to his visit to the medical center. That was the trouble with deploying to areas of the world topping the Center for Disease Control's list of places to visit at your own risk. Pulling his T-shirt over his head tomorrow morning would be interesting without the use of his arms.

He noted the packed suitcase by the door. "When do you leave?"

Geordy put his finger in the book he was reading. "First thing tomorrow morning. The class starts the day after that. Woody said if you drop me off at the airport tomorrow, he wouldn't kick if you reported late for duty."

"Sure, no problem." He started to lift his hand to scratch his face, but winced and let it fall back down. "Uh, I had the misfortune to hit a slow day at the med center, and the corpsmen took great delight in using me to relieve their boredom. I'm not sure, but I think I got a few more shots than I needed, and I swear to God the needle for the last shot went in sideways."

Geordy got up and stretched. "Well, come on then, let's go grab dinner before I need to spoon feed you like a baby."

"That's just cold, Mountain. Empathy much?" Wren groused as he followed Geordy out the door.

But he did need Geordy's help the following morning when he tried to pull his T-shirt over his head. His arms were just too sore to lift that high.

Geordy laughed at him and offered, "Do you need help tucking it in, too?"

"No, fuck you very much, I can manage."

They didn't speak much on the ride to Jacksonville, but the lack of conversation wasn't uncomfortable. He nodded as Geordy enthused on learning Farsi to add to his Pashtu and Urdu. And he agreed with his roommate that speaking three of the local languages made him a real asset if he ever got sent back to Afghanistan.

Wren pulled up in front of Jacksonville's small airport, and was surprised when Geordy didn't hop right out, just turned in his seat to face him.

"I'm thinking this trip has come at a very good time. Although both of us are working hard not to be uncomfortable in each other's presence, it's obvious we are."

He had no intention of lying to Mountain. "Yeah, maybe if we had different jobs or were in different units, this would be easier. I'm not going to lie and say I'm able to put aside my feelings at the snap of a finger, and I don't think you can either, so maybe this separation will give us the breathing room we need."

"I think so, too. I, uh, I just want you to know, Wren de Lassy, you'll still be my friend, and I'll still watch your six, when I return."

"Same here, Geordy Campbell." Wren waited long enough for Geordy to enter the terminal, and then drove back to MARSOC. Unlike the Bard, he didn't think parting was such sweet sorrow, parting sucked. And most especially when you returned from saying goodbye to a former lover only to be confronted by a pissed off master sergeant and captain.

"What the fuck is this about, de Lassy?" Master Sergeant McClean flapped a piece of paper in front of his nose.

"I haven't a clue, Master Sergeant."

Captain Schuyler chose to enlighten him. "Those are orders, Blade. Orders for your transfer to JSOC."

"JSOC? Why would I be transferred to JSOC? That's a Tier One organization."

"Yeah, and you, so these orders say, have skills they need. Congratulations, Blade. It's an honor to be asked."

At Woody's snide, "honor my ass," Captain Schuyler added, "Don't let Woody's anger dissuade you from accepting. The master sergeant hates to see his chicks leave the nest."

"Uh, when am I supposed to report, Captain?"

Woody shook the official document again and answered in a calmer, but still disgusted, voice. "Says here, at the losing unit's earliest convenience."

Captain Schuyler threw his arm over his master sergeant's shoulders and said, "There, there, Woody. You must let the chicks go when they are ready to fly."

He turned and grinned at Wren, "If you start your out-processing today, you can probably report for duty up at Fort Bragg on Monday. There's really not much else for you to do while the rest of the team is away, so you can devote all your attention to out-processing."

"Yes, sir, that sounds good."

"And now that you are all caught up on your medical and dental requirements, there's no reason for them not to release you. Just make sure you return your library books. I'd hate for MARSOC to snatch you back from JSOC just so you can pay the overdue fines."

Wren curled his lips to stifle the laugh at Woody's profane description of what he thought of JSOC's robbing Fox Company of a team member.

"I'm sorry the team isn't here to give you a proper sendoff, Blade, but Woody, when he finishes venting, and I will bid you fair winds and following seas. You do the Raiders proud while you're at JSOC, you hear, Staff Sergeant? You're a Marine Raider, de Lassy, don't forget it. You show those Green Beanies, SEALs, and Air Force weenies how to do things the right way, the Marine way."

"Aye aye, Captain. I'll do my best. It's been an honor serving in Fox Company and on your team."

Out-processing was a royal pain in the ass. Running to various places all over MARSOC to put the right signature in the right block, turn in issued equipment, and stand there while someone verified he had the right pieces, and that no pieces were missing or broken, and then run to another place and do it all again was a humbling lesson in patience.

Turning in his personal weapon was the last hurdle, and he was at the armory as soon as the doors opened on Friday morning. Like all Marine Raiders, he kept his weapon in pristine shape, so he doubted the armorer would find anything to complain about.

He had to admit, his heart gave a thump when the armorer signed off on his checkout form and carried his weapon away. No, the M16A4 was no longer *his* weapon. That somehow made his leaving MARSOC all the more final.

After calling Sensei Dai to tell him he was being transferred and wouldn't be able to continue attending his class, the only thing left to do was swing by the dorm and pick up his duffel, climb into his truck, and put Sneads Ferry, North Carolina on the list of places he'd been.

Maybe if the team had thrown him an actual farewell party, he wouldn't have the feeling he was slinking out of town. Maybe if Geordy had called just once from Monterey, he wouldn't still think he made the wrong decision to ask for space. Maybe, maybe, maybe.

Maybe he should just walk his ass to the dorm, pick up his duffel, and put MARSOC in his rearview mirror.

Wren gave Room 304 a last check. Nope, nothing left behind. But, as he lifted his duffel from his bed and crossed the room on his way out, Geordy's book case drew his attention.

Not being able to resist the impulse, he drew his fingers over the titles of the history books, language books, and came to rest on Omar Khayyam's book of poetry, *The Rubaiyat*, and reconsidered his resolve to leave without a trace.

While he packed his gear, he wrestled with the idea of leaving a farewell letter and decided not to. One, he didn't want to risk having anyone other than Geordy finding it, and, two, he didn't think he could write what he really felt. Perhaps this was the way to go.

He opened Geordy's desk drawer and grabbed a pad of yellow-lined legal paper, and sat at his desk chair to write:

Geordy:

My transfer came up unexpectedly. A JSOC unit needs my edged weapons skills. While I would've liked to say goodbye face to face, maybe this is better. Check out verses LXXXVII and XXV. Perhaps we just needed to meet in a different place and time....

Rather than the standard "fair winds and following seas," I'll leave you with the wish that you someday find a Druid bird who will make its nest in your house and protect it with lightning.

Semper Fi,

Wren de Lassy

He finished signing his name, stuck the sheet of paper in the book of poetry, and put the book under Geordy's pillow. He hesitated at the door but didn't turn around. Next stop, Fort Bragg.

***

Random Farsi phrases continued to swim through his head, and he couldn't make them leave. Damn Pacer and Woody for not telling him the class was an accelerated one, and three weeks later he was brain fried, but he could at least make himself understood, if he ever ran into a native Farsi speaker.

As he climbed the stairs to his room, he felt a little guilty for not calling Blade once while he was in California. But, hey, he'd expressed the need for some time, and he gave it to him.

Yeah, he gave him space, but that didn't change a fucking thing, as far as he was concerned. He still wanted him. He wanted him so badly here he stood all alone in the stairwell suffering heart palpitations at the thought Wren might have managed to eradicate all feelings for him while he spouted Farsi in California. He should have called him.

His overworked brain accompanied the sound of his steps as he continued to climb to the third floor. Woulda, coulda, shoulda. Woulda, coulda, shoulda. What a relief to unlock the door and step inside. It would be good to hang out with Vlad and Blade again. He wouldn't even mind if Vlad dropped a few of his wry Russian proverbs on him.

Well, shit, no one home, but something about the room didn't look right. When he figured it out, his stomach hit the floor. There was nothing on Blade's bed but a bare mattress. He spun around and took in the bare bookcase and, suddenly, he needed to lie down before he fell down.

Vlad's stuff was still in the room, why not Blade's? He found the answer when his head hit his pillow and he pulled out the book of poetry someone put there.

The *Rubaiyat* was a very long poem, so he needed to turn to the pages to read the verses Wren chose to impart his message. He started with the first one he'd written down, verse eighty-seven:

Geordy began rocking back and forth. The verse spoke of lovers remolding life nearer to their hearts desire, and while he didn't think he had the fortitude to read the second verse in the letter, he pressed on because he wanted to understand what Wren had been thinking as he made the selection. Geordy turned back the pages until he got to verse twenty-five.

The prophetic words made him clutch the slim volume to his heart and chant, "Oh God, oh God, oh God." When he finally found the strength to stop, he curled into a fetal position on his bunk. His roommate had used the words of a Persian poet to warn him life was too short to live without love.

Wren had left to make the most of his life, and nevermore would he be with him, and, as Khayyam prophesied, he remained behind without song, and without singer, and without the end he hoped one day to realize because he let the one man who had music and poetry in his soul slip away.

Chapter Twenty-Five

Troll hung up the phone after speaking with his counterpart at MARSOC. Shit! His two-week hunting leave would be delayed a couple of hours while he drove from Fort Bragg to Sneads Ferry to attend a teleconference. A MARSOC unit had tangled with Amin Alizai near the Afghanistan-Pakistan border. Alizai, the slippery bastard, topped JSOC's High Value Target List, and Troll wanted to sit in on the teleconference debrief of the team that sent the man scurrying back across the Pakistan border.

Since Wren was included on this hunting trip, he needed to find him to explain the delay in departure time. As he suspected, he was with the rest of his team cleaning weapons after an hour on the firing range.

Troll still felt guilty about blabbing Wren's whereabouts to Jack Adams. One solid year had passed since his transfer from MARSOC, and the Wren he first met in Saudi Arabia still remained buttoned up from whatever occurred after Jack sank his hooks into him. Oh, he joked around with his team, but despite winning their loyalty, they knew him to be something of a recluse. He rarely deviated from his studio apartment above Otter's garage and the JSOC compound. He didn't even go into Fayetteville, except to attend instruction at the dojo for another martial art to add to his resume, Muay Thai.

As Troll observed him reassembling his cleaned rifle, it struck him this was a mature and sleeked out Wren who manifested what his JSOC training made him, a very, very lethal killer.

Troll sent a curse winging Jack Adams's way for his part in killing whatever gentleness de Lassy had inside him. He didn't think the early promotion to gunnery sergeant the Agency had probably dangled as bait had been worth the personal cost.

Troll knew better than to clap him on the back and surprise him. He didn't want to feel his ass hit the floor when Wren decked him in reflex. Instead, he loudly announced his presence.

"I hope you fuckers were able to hit the broad side of a barn this morning."

As expected, he got nothing but rude responses. De Lassy's team was one of the best.

Troll continued, "Say goodbye to your playmates, Gunny. We need to hit the road now."

At the questioning look, Troll explained. "Plans have changed. I need to go to MARSOC before we head north. I figure I'll do what I need to do there, and you can visit with your Raider buddies while I'm in the G-3's office. We can change into civvies at MARSOC when we're ready to leave.

"We'll be a couple of hours late getting to Ross's place, but we'll still be able to leave for Pennsylvania tomorrow morning. I already spoke to Nels, so he knows we'll be late getting in."

"Sure, Colonel, no problem."

Troll didn't miss the minute flinch when he suggested visiting his MARSOC buddies, and it reminded him that the few leave slips he signed for him never listed going to Sneads Ferry to visit them. Wren's closed face made him doubt he would ever tell him why he cut his ties with his Raider buddies.

***

The closer they got to Sneads Ferry, the tighter his stomach got. When he left MARSOC, he'd vowed he wouldn't come back, and he'd kept that vow until today. What a kick in the nuts to know, if he had politely declined Troll's offer to go hunting with him and Ross, he wouldn't currently be driving to the one place guaranteed to make his heart beat irregularly.

It would be good to see his old team again, with the major exception of Geordy. He didn't think he was a good enough actor to carry off coming face-to-face with the man he'd thought about every night for a solid, fucking year. And that thought thoroughly pissed him off. True, he made no move to contact Geordy, but Geordy, likewise, made no effort to call him. You would think the distance between their two locations was separated by a couple of continents, instead of a two-hour drive.

All too soon for his liking, Troll turned into the headquarters parking lot and turned the engine off.

"It's nine o'clock, so meet me back in the G-3's office at noon. I should be ready to go by then."

Wren nodded and watched as Troll hit the long sidewalk to enter the headquarters main entrance. Both of them left their cell phones in the truck, as no electronic devices were permitted in any of the buildings.

He started to walk to Fox Company but broke into a trot. Fuck dawdling like a cringing pussy. This was going to be painful, but he had the feeling it would be just as painful for Geordy to see him walk into the team room. He caught his old team finishing up a meeting. Pacer was the first to spot him.

"Well, well, Woody, the Good Book repeats itself. The Prodigal Son returns."

Wren found himself being thumped on the back and generally mauled by his former teammates, who were quick to both congratulate and ridicule his promotion to gunnery sergeant.

To his relief, Pacer was one of those Marine officers who knew the good stuff wouldn't be talked about until the brass left, so he quickly withdrew to his office.

"Come on, Master Sergeant, let's let these youngsters catch up on old times. Glad to see you again, Blade. People down there at Bragg tell me you're doing a good job of upholding the Raider name."

"Thank you, sir. I haven't forgotten for one second I'm a Raider."

Byte pulled out a chair for him and Wren joined the rest of the team around the table.

"So, you're planning for another trip to the Philippines? Hope this one goes better than the one I was on."

Mercury answered his jibe. "Hey, we can do no wrong there. The Philippine Army spun that little snafu to favor the Philippine Special Forces, who came in for the mop-up operation, but they know who saved their bacon."

He smiled and opened his arms to encompass the table. "Catch me up on what's been happening to you since I left."

Byte took the bait and pointed at Vlad. "Would you believe the Russian bull here got a ring put through his nose? The girl who was supposed to teach him how to ride horses turned the bull into a lap dog. The wedding is next summer."

Wren turned to Vlad, and the blush on the man's cheeks confirmed Byte's announcement. "Congratulations, Vlad. You can start your own family now."

"Thank you, but the proverb is true. Adam ate the apple, and we men still have toothache from it. Winning her mother over to having a Russian son-in-law hasn't been easy."

Tecate jabbed Vlad's shoulder, "At least you won't have a Mexican mother-in-law. My brother has one, and she's very hard to please. According to her, the only thing he did right was give her a grandson."

Wren joined in on the ribald suggestions for how Vlad could please his future mother-in-law, and when the group settled down, he asked the question he most wanted answered.

"Hey, guys, where's Mountain? Don't tell me he's gone back to language school. How many languages does one man need to speak?"

His pulse began to pound when the room became quiet.

Byte shook his head slowly and spoke for the team. "I guess the news wouldn't make it into that heavily fortified compound at Bragg, but Geordy's gone, Blade."

It was a damn good thing his ass was in a chair, because he would've hit the floor. The blood drained from his head, and he went momentarily blind and deaf. He came to when Vlad squeezed his shoulder as he castigated Byte.

"*Bozhe Moy*, Byte. You could have phrased that better. You've given Blade a fright.

Shortly after you left, Mountain asked for a transfer to 2nd Battalion. He felt, with his language capability, he could be more useful in Afghanistan."

Wren spoke over the loud beating of his heart. "So Geordy's in Afghanistan?" Once again, the table got quiet, and once again, cold sweat dampened his T-shirt.

Mercury glared at Byte, and cut him off before he could scare Blade again. "Uh, no, Geordy, um, a sniper got him and...."

A loud string of Russian stopped Mercury mid-sentence. Vlad

313

stood and announced, "*I'll* tell him what happened. You fuckers are scaring the shit out of him. Listen, Blade, Mountain did go to Afghanistan. One of the vehicles in his convoy was hit by an IED, and it threw the driver completely out of the vehicle. The man was still alive, but unable to move because a sniper thought he would be cute and shoot near him every time someone tried to get to him.

"This particular sniper was an Iranian working with the Taliban, and playing cat and mouse was his signature. He always killed the mouse when he got tired of playing.

"Well, Mountain got so pissed off, he charged in and got all the way to the wounded Marine, but when he tried to carry him back to safety, the sniper included him in the game. One of the shots he meant to put near him ricocheted off a piece of the damaged Humvee, and it shattered Mountain's knee."

A sudden, awful thought made Wren blurt, "He didn't lose his leg, did he?"

Vlad pumped his hands up and down in a calm down gesture. "No, he didn't, but he didn't let a shattered knee stop him. You know Mountain, when he made up his mind to do something it was hard to make him change it, but the fucking sniper sure tried.

"As Mountain low-crawled back to safety dragging the concussed Marine, another ricochet hit him in the hip. Now both of them were stuck on open ground, and everyone thought they were goners."

Tecate spoke up, "That's because they didn't know Mountain as well as we do. Mountain doesn't quit."

The rest of the team laughed and Vlad continued. "One of the guys in 2nd Battalion told me Mountain yelled for the bullhorn they carried for crowd control. When it was tossed to him, he called back to his men huddled behind their vehicles and asked if they'd forgotten which end of their rifles the bullets came out of."

Vlad snickered with macabre, special operations humor. "Some wise ass actually had nerve enough to say, 'We've got to see him to shoot him, Gunny.'

"That's when Mountain picked up the bullhorn and started speaking in Farsi. This may or may not be exactly what Mountain said because I think it lost quite a bit in translation, but Mountain called out that the sniper was a coward and not a real man, because he hid behind whatever he could find. Indeed, he could only acquit himself as a man when he lay between his mother's legs."

Vlad waited until the rest of the team stopped chuckling. "Even the Afghan translator the team had with them gave Mountain props for the unique way of calling that Iranian sniper a motherfucker."

Mercury spoke up over the general snickering. "Well, it worked. The sniper reared up to take a killing shot and one of the team scout snipers nailed him. The sniper did a real job on Mountain, though, they had to airlift him back to Bagram and then to the States. He had some heavy-duty rehab time in front of him with a shattered knee and a bullet imbedded in his hip, but when the docs told him, even with a new knee and a healed hip fracture, he couldn't swing the loads necessary to remain in the Raiders, Geordy opted to take a medical discharge. Mountain was awarded the Silver Star for saving the wounded Raider, and for putting his own life in jeopardy to take out the sniper. Blade, Mountain went back to his home in Tennessee."

Wren wanted to say something, anything, but the solid lump in his throat wouldn't let words past. Master Sergeant McClean saved him.

"All right, guys, break up the gabfest. You're due at the shoot house in fifteen. Let's get a move on."

He endured the back slaps, the handshaking, and the fist bumps, and smiled and waved as he left the team room. Thank God he remembered where the head was in the building because he managed to reach a stall before losing his breakfast, and the previous evening's dinner.

As he rinsed his mouth out, the mirror above the sink reflected the shock in his eyes. Geordy almost died in Afghanistan. Geordy was home in Beltrees learning how to use his new knee and mended hip. But as he dried his hands and face on the paper towel, he was struck by the thought Geordy never called him to tell him he was out of the Marines, and didn't that make his heart writhe in pain.

He headed back to MARSOC HQ on shaky legs. Geordy never picked up the phone to call him. Did that mean he should stop hoping for some sort of miraculous, divine intervention so he and Geordy could hook up and live the happily-ever-after part of the fairy tale? He thought it did.

Thank God, and his archangels, too, Troll enthused about deer stalking, deer killing, deer dressing, deer meat, and oh yeah, let's not forget deer racks. He didn't have to do much more than nod or make the appropriate exclamation of approval on the long ride to Ross's house.

Chapter Twenty-Six

Nels didn't say anything as Wren begged off accompanying Ross and Troll to the Irish pub after dinner. Something was gnawing at Wren. He barely ate the lasagna Ross made for dinner, even though it was one of his favorites. Although, Nels noted, he tried subterfuge by shoving the pasta around his plate to make it seem like he relished it, the amount remaining belied his enjoyment of it.

Thus, it didn't surprise him when the man climbed the stairs to his third-floor studio under the pretext of watching him work on a very large canvas. His subject was a lighthouse as seen through a curtain of fog, and his visitor remained silent as he layered different shades of white on the canvas to give the fog depth.

"That's going to be an awesome painting, Nels." Wren stretched out on the leather chaise to watch Ross's partner perform magic with a paintbrush.

"It must be hard to part with something you spend so much time on, especially something so beautiful."

Nels turned at the wistful note in Wren's voice and began to clean his brush. He didn't intend to paint until he got to the bottom of whatever was causing the malaise. Even though the man stretched out on the chaise wore the same face as Wren, he was an imposter. Indeed, this manifestation had been around for over a year, since the CIA tapped him for a hush-hush mission last year. Ross and he had never been told the details, and, as Ross explained, they never would be. However, the man who returned from that operation was not Wren. The old Wren was quixotic, full of laughter, irreverent, interesting, and a joy to be around. The phantom presently taking up space in his studio possessed none of those attributes.

Nels had a theory to explain part of his change of character, but verification would require digging, so dig he would. He and Wren had a special bond born of suffering. If anyone could make him spill the cause of his depression, Nels could, and so he attacked the problem head on.

Nels turned away from his workbench. "Does your current sadness stem from the man Ross told me about last year? He said you told him you loved someone who was even more conflicted than you. And don't bother denying something is bothering you. I can read you as well as you read me."

At Wren's unexpected groan of pain, Nels joined him on the chaise and wrapped him into his arms. "Talk to me. I'll help you any way I can."

At first, he didn't think Wren would say anything at all, but he waited him out. He silently rejoiced when he relaxed in his arms and started to speak.

"His name is Geordy Campbell. He was my teammate in the Raiders, and my roommate, and sometimes my lover before I went to JSOC."

Nels listened as he spilled his love for the man, and cursed his inability to speak the words in his heart. The anguish in Wren's voice when he told him about having to learn of Geordy's wounding from his former teammates and not from Geordy himself came across loud and clear.

Wren ended his narrative on a deep sigh, and Nels gave him a brief squeeze and then offered his insight.

"Well, as the holder of a PhD in history, I can tell you history frequently repeats itself. It is most prone to do so when people don't learn the lesson the first time around. And you, Wren de Lassy, failed to learn it."

"Come on, Nels, I'm too tired to play guessing games. Tell me where I failed."

"Have you forgotten what kept Ross and I apart? Neither one of us told the other one what we were feeling. Indeed, neither one of us told the other we were even gay. You dared me to tell Ross what I truly felt for him, and I'm so glad you did, because I doubt Ross and I would now be together. Ross loves me, but I don't think it occurred to him to tell me so."

"Yeah, A clam babbles more than Ross." Wren snickered.

"It sounds to me like your Geordy Campbell is an amalgamation of Ross and me. He needs to, as in Ross's case, be hit over the head with the actual truth, and, as in my case, he probably didn't call you because he didn't think you wanted to be burdened with someone who was less than perfect."

Wren shook his head, "Geordy could never be less than perfect to me. Whole or in pieces wouldn't change what I feel for him."

"Then you need to do exactly what you told me to do. You need to seize the brass ring of happiness. You need to tell Geordy Campbell the depth of your feelings for him. In modern vernacular, you need to say the L word. If Geordy is even close to feeling for you what Ross felt for me, he's at this very moment pining for what he didn't ask for. Unless you screw your courage to the sticking place and tell him the truth, you'll both remain two ships passing in the night."

Wren hugged his stomach like a cramp had hit him. "And the truth shall set you free...*not*. What if he picks me up and tosses me ass over head out his front door when I tell him every sordid detail about

Colin MacAulay aka Wren de Lassy?"

Nels kissed Wren's temple. "Then you pick yourself up and come back here to lick your wounds, secure in the knowledge Geordy Campbell isn't worth your love, but at least you tried. Grab some sleep. Tennessee isn't that far a drive from here. I'll make your excuses to Ross and Troll when they get back from the pub. If you leave at a reasonable hour tomorrow morning, you can be at Geordy's house for dinner. Oh, and you can take Ross's SUV. He won't need it because he's driving up to Pennsylvania with Troll."

***

As Ross's SUV ate up the miles between Virginia and Tennessee, he went over multiple courses of action for how he could spill his guts, and not have Geordy pity him before showing him to the door.

He gave up when he realized the last half hour sped by with him trying to come up with ways to wriggle his way into Geordy's decision matrix before he could say something irrevocable like "Get the hell out of my house, you sick son of a bitch."

The hollow sound the tires made as he crossed the bridge over the stream running alongside Geordy's property, echoed the feeling in the pit of his stomach. However, as he parked the car and stared out the windshield, the sight of Geordy's beautiful cabin strengthened his resolve. This could be home, his home, and by God he was going to fight for it.

The sudden, loud bugle of a very large hound made him jump, and he laughed at his display of nerves. He opened the car door and had to fight his way out because Crockett was as determined to enter the vehicle as he was to leave it.

"Down boy, let me out and I'll pet you. Yes, that's a good boy. Man, you turned into a huge dog. Geordy's taken good care of you. You still friends with Rob Roy?"

Wren continued talking nonsense and wrestling with the frisky animal until the coon hound broke away and ran toward the cabin, where Geordy stood on the porch.

Taking the silence as better than an order to vacate the area, he straightened and walked slowly toward the man who held his future in his hands.

Geordy's failure to greet him was not auspicious, but since he didn't break his silence with a threat to call the police, Wren stood his ground.

"What are you doing here?"

Wren had to tilt his head back to see Geordy's face clearly. He swallowed hard at the sight. Geordy wore a kilt, the same modern kilt in dark blue his cousins wore to work in the pub. Indeed, Geordy's white T-shirt had the pub's logo emblazoned on the front. Gray knee socks and dark-brown hiking boots completed the picture of a modern Scot. A very handsome, and outwardly healthy Scot with dark hair gleaming in the late afternoon sunlight. He noted Geordy currently wore it long enough to cover his ears and the nape of his neck. It made his fingers itch to run themselves through the thickness of it.

He realized he should say something when Geordy cocked his head at him.

"I just heard from our old team that you were wounded, and I needed.... Um, I thought I'd pay a visit to make sure you were healing well. Is everything going okay for you, Mountain?"

Rather than answer the question, Geordy turned back toward the front door, and Wren forgot to breathe.

As he headed inside, Geordy called over his shoulder, "I was just about to feed the animals and watch the sunset on the back porch. Care to join me for a drink?"

He had to draw air back into his lungs before he could answer. "Sure, that sounds great."

His knees wobbled like jelly as he climbed the steps and followed the ramrod straight back of Geordy Campbell into the house.

***

Crockett's bugle drew him to the window to find out what the racket was about. The sight of a black SUV with tinted windows and Virginia license plates put a gripe in his belly. If this was one of Jack Adams's minions, it would only take a minute to snatch up the 12-gauge from his bedroom. He wanted no part of anything the CIA had to offer.

The breath whooshed out of him when the car door opened and the sunlight created a nimbus around Wren's head.

Geordy touched his left shoulder, and his thumb stroked over the talisman high on his left pec. Could he be so lucky? He didn't dare to hope, but he couldn't help not. One thing was certain, he needed to slap a guard on his tongue. It would be mortifying to assume and be wrong.

He winced inwardly at his less than friendly invitation as he led the way inside. Dissembling was not something that came easy for him.

Geordy hoped Wren missed the shaking of his hands as he poured the bourbon into two glasses and handed them over.

"Here, take these outside. I'll be along as soon as I measure out dinner for the animals."

It was one of his strays that broke the awkward silence between them. As he lifted his glass of bourbon to his lips to stall for time to construct an opening sentence, Wren leaned forward in his chair and pointed.

"What the hell is that? Is it a lynx?"

Geordy bit down on his lip to keep from laughing. "Nay, just a cat."

"Really? It sure as fuck is big enough to be a lynx, and its ears are tufted like a lynx."

Geordy laughed at Blade's consternation. "Aye, there are similarities between Charlie and a lynx. He eats meat like one, and in large enough amounts to keep a lynx healthy. He's also an excellent hunter. He's a Maine Coon cat, and they are noted for liking dogs and people, and not being averse to water."

"He showed up, unannounced, one morning. I think someone, a breeder perhaps, abandoned him because of his odd eyes, one bright blue, and one yellow as a gold coin, a defect as far as breeders are concerned.

"I couldn't turn him away, mainly because of my soft heart where abandoned animals are concerned, and because His Royal Highness, Bonnie Prince Charlie, earns his room and board by keeping my barn rodent free. His Highness taught me to be careful where I put my feet when I step out the front door in the mornings. The Bonnie Prince likes to line up his trophies just past the doorstep."

"Please tell me the Bonnie Prince is not a lap cat."

With understated Scots' humor, Geordy responded, "Only when he wants to be. Don't worry, he tolerates brushing, so you'll only have to remove enough cat hair from your shirt to make a small sweater if he cuddles with you. That's the main reason why I gave Charlie his own insulated castle in the barn, not the house. Ah, he's decided to check you out."

Wren listened to the cat's loud rumbles and couldn't help asking, "Is he growling at me? If he is, there's a throwing knife in my boot, and he'll find himself tacked to your barn wall like a coyote hide if he decides to attack."

"He's no' growling; that's his purr." Before Geordy could elaborate, Charlie made a chirping, trilling sound, and leapt into Wren's lap.

"Oof. He's no light weight." He had to crane his head around the very broad cat to see Geordy."

Geordy winked at him. "You are now part of His Majesty's retinue."

"He was relieved when Charlie jumped down to explore his food bowl, and it struck him there were three bowls.

"Hey, is one of those bowls for Rob Roy? Is he still around?"

"Aye, but with the Bonnie Prince now in residence, Rob Roy prefers to dine at a later hour."

Shit, leave off with the animal kingdom dialogue, you twit. Say something, say the fucking words, you coward.

Geordy took a sip of Campbell Dhu for courage, and waited until the bourbon warmed a path to his belly, but when he opened his mouth, Wren interrupted.

"Geordy, I honestly did come to check on how you were doing after being wounded, but I also came to tell you something."

Geordy put his glass back on the table. He didn't trust himself not to spill it after he started shaking like a palsy victim. Had Blade traveled all this distance to tell him he finally found someone who would love him as he so rightly deserved?

A gust of wind reminded him it was the tail end of November, and he shivered. Noting Wren did so as well, Geordy stood.

"Let's go inside. I'll light a fire, and you can tell me what you came here to tell me."

Seeing the hard resolve on the man's face, he suddenly needed another glass of bourbon. Geordy didn't think his tale would be the one he would've chosen. He picked up the glasses and let Wren hold the door open for him as they headed for the living room.

Wren poured generous tots into both glasses as Geordy put a match to the already laid fire. After his tell-all confession, both of them would need the strong drinks. He settled back on the sofa and winced just a little as Geordy chose to sit in the leather recliner across from him, not next to him. Maybe it was better, he might lose his resolve if Geordy touched him before he started.

He wondered if Geordy might also have been wounded in the left shoulder, because he kept touching it, and rubbing it with his thumb. Knowing his mind was wandering to avoid opening his mouth, Wren focused his attention on the burning logs and began.

"I came here to come clean about certain things, but I need to ask you a question, first." Wren leaned forward and transferred his attention from the fire to Geordy. "Are you seeing anyone?" The question made Geordy sit farther back in his chair.

"Why?" Geordy rasped.

"Because, if you are, then I'll say thank you for your hospitality, I'm very glad your wounds have healed, and I'll take my leave now."

"I'm not seeing anyone."

His blood pressure began to return to normal, until his internal imp made him blurt, "Not even the man you met up with in Myrtle Beach? What was his name, again?"

"Stefan, his name was Stefan. No, Stefan and I are not dating each other. In fact, that time I went to Myrtle Beach I broke up with him. I'll be honest and say the breakup was by mutual accord. Dating civilians is tough when you have to answer most of their questions as to time and place for leaving and returning with 'I'm sorry, that's classified.' I spent the week at the beach all by my lonesome. As for the present, The VA rehab center isn't an ideal hook-up spot. And now I'll ask the same question of you. Are you seeing anyone?

Wren's green eyes never wavered from Geordy's face as he said, "No. No one. Not since I left MARSOC." He didn't wait for Geordy to respond, but asked, "Do you still have the watercolor Nels did? Yes? May I bring it out here?" He went to fetch the drawing at Geordy's nod.

He propped the framed drawing on his knees and pointed to it. "You were right, Geordy, the person drawn by Nels is a man. In fact, I was the model. This was done in Saudi Arabia when I was eighteen."

Geordy sat up in his chair and blurted, "Nels, your brother's husband, was the lover you spoke of?"

Aaaand here was the hard part. No more pussyfooting around and sewing lace doilies on the beast in an attempt to hide its ugliness.

Wren averted his eyes from Geordy's confused face as he said, "The only way I can answer that is to start at the beginning. My answer won't make much sense, if I don't."

Geordy crossed his arms over his chest and nodded.

He smiled at the steadiness of his hands as he set Nels's

watercolor aside, and leaned over to switch on the lamp next to the sofa. He didn't want the dimness of firelight to hide the truth of his words.

"The name I was born with was Colin Daniel MacAulay, that's why Jack Adams used it for my cover on the Elmoudowi op. My parents were kids who never really grew up. My mother got pregnant and didn't finish high school, and neither did my dad because his parents kicked him out of the house for getting a girl pregnant."

Geordy hissed, "I can relate to getting kicked out of the house."

"My folks told me they lived in a commune for a while but decided to rent a house in Denver after I was born. With neither one of them having a high school diploma, or the intention of ever getting one, the jobs they got didn't pay much, and we lived in a rough neighborhood. My dad came up with the brilliant idea of growing his own weed and selling the surplus. He soon learned the electricity it took to keep the grow lights working in the garage was more than he could afford on his salary as a grocery shelf stocker, so he decided to steal it from his neighbors. Our garage soon resembled one of those Rube Goldberg designs. My old man understood fuck all about electricity and wiring, and that's why our house burned down one day while I was at school. I think the whole neighborhood got high on the fumes, and were bummed when the firemen put it out. Sad to say, my dad didn't survive the fire."

"Oh, Wren, I'm sorry."

He waived Geordy's condolences away as he continued, "My mom had gone to the drugstore to buy cigarettes right before the house caught fire, so we at least had a car to live in after that." He stared down at his hand as it made a circular pattern on the sofa cushion. "My mother had never lived on her own before. My dad may not have been a stellar pillar of strength, but she did rely on him to make decisions. The fire left her as rudderless as it did homeless, and she began using more than weed to calm her anxieties."

"Ah, that explains your aversion to taking unnecessary medication."

Wren nodded. "Yes, and that's why you will never find me selling, using, or giving anyone anything that a doctor hasn't prescribed for them. Once my mother switched from weed to crack, it was a greased slope to the bottom. The welfare checks got eaten up by her habit, and the more she used, the more she wanted. She started turning tricks, and I had to threaten to turn her ass in to Child Welfare when she suggested I should get friendly with some of her clients as well."

"Jesus, didn't you have any other relatives to go to? I understand why you wouldn't want to go to your grandparents, but didn't you have any aunts or uncles?"

He shook his head. "If there were, my parents never mentioned them, and, to be honest, I was too ashamed of our situation to want to search for them. The bottom came when both of us were huddled up in the car freezing our asses off, because a Colorado winter is cruel when you don't have heat. The last of our money went up her nose rather than into the gas tank so we could run the car for heat. I was cold, hungry, and angry at her that night, and I spoke my mind very strongly for an eleven-year-old, and my mother lost it. She dragged me out of the car and we started walking to where she said I could find the hot meal I was whining for, and there'd be something for her to blot out my sniveling."

Geordy deliberately gave Wren a brief respite by standing to throw another log on the fire, and then returned to his chair, and leaned forward to encourage him to continue.

"As we walked, I couldn't help but notice we were headed into a neighborhood even rougher and seedier than ours, and I began to doubt my mother's promise of a hot meal, but, for once, she didn't lie. The man who owned the house did serve me that meal, and it was quite tasty until I threw it up after my mother told me what she'd done. She sold me to that man, a sex trafficker, for a shot of heroine. When I started to cry, she let it all out. She told me she never wanted a kid. Hell, she didn't even want to marry my dad. She called him a loser who didn't have balls enough to provide better for his family, and she was tired of having the weight of me around her neck."

"Fuck, your mother sounds crueler than my dad."

Wren's voice went soft as he said, "She never hugged me or kissed me, just turned around and walked out of that house. It was my first rejection by someone I thought loved me, and, as rejections go, it was a whopper. Later, I overhead the man she sold me to laugh over the phone to someone that the bitch who sold her son to him was most likely dead under an overpass somewhere because he gave her the pure stuff. It was ironic, but the sex trafficker took better care of me than my parents did, until he sold me to a Saudi Arabian pedophile."

He reached for his bourbon but reared back when Geordy stopped his hand.

"Enough of that, you're white as a sheet. Come, I'll make dinner."

"But I'm not finished."

"You're finished for now. There will be plenty of time after dinner to pick it up again."

He was both relieved to be given time to slow his galloping heart down, and saddened when Geordy pulled back his hand from where it stopped just inches from caressing his cheek.

"If you would excuse me, Geordy, I'll, uh, I'll just go wash up. I remember where your guest bathroom is."

By the time he shored up his crumbling resolve to finish what he started and headed to the dining nook, Geordy had the table set and a picnic of his aunt's fried chicken, potato salad, and baked beans waiting for him. He smiled his relief when Geordy sat down and asked, "So tell me about our old team."

Wren regaled him with the news of Vlad's impending marriage, and how Geordy had become a legend at MARSOC for his unique use of Farsi to call out the sniper, but dinner was over all too soon.

"I'll help you with the dishes."

"No, you won't. You'll go fetch your suitcase. You'll stay here. There will be black ice on the mountain roads this time of night."

While Geordy failed to offer undying love, his offer of a bed gave him hope. Crockett accompanied him back the car to grab his bag.

Geordy handed him a mug of coffee after he finished stowing his gear in the guest room and sat himself back on the sofa.

"It's obvious you drove all the way out here to say your piece, so I'll do you the honor of listening."

He took heart when Geordy chose to sit on the couch next to him, rather than across from him.

"I was eleven when the Saudi, who ordered me to call him Master, bought me. I was eleven, and he was thirty, and very good at switching between the carrot and the stick. I was eleven but, thanks to my mother prostituting herself for drug money, I understood what he wanted, because a few of my mom's tricks offered for me, but I became good at making myself scarce when she had company.

"As awful as this might sound, I'm glad that sex trafficker gave your mother a lethal dose."

Wren squeezed Geordy's hand and continued, "I was not the first boy the master purchased, but thanks to Ross de Lassy, I was the last. At first, he was patient with me, gave me whatever I wanted, and I gradually got used to his touch. His innocent touch. But as I continued to resist more sexual advances, the punishment became harsher." He studied the flames in the fireplace for a moment and turned to face Geordy. "The one I hated the most was having my bare feet beaten with a thin rod. It left me unable to walk for days. The master was always careful to leave my face and body unmarked. But I was only eleven and it didn't really take much force to break an eleven-year old. The master forced himself on me then complained about it. He said I needed better instruction on what pleased him, and if I learned well, he would be much gentler with me.

"Wren, I'm—" He stopped Geordy with a finger over his lips.

"The master was an inventive lover, and I learned all the techniques to please him. He was also quite generous in his perversity. All I had to do was ask, and he made sure it was provided, as long as I didn't ask for freedom, clothes, or outside contact with anyone but himself and his mute servants. Although my resume says I graduated from high school, I didn't. I am self-taught. I was not permitted a computer, telephone, or television, but I was allowed to ask for any kind of book I wanted. I had nothing to do but read when the master didn't want my skills as a catamite.

Geordy swallowed back his rising dinner. Wren's tale was making his stomach spasm.

"Like one of the Arabian fairy tales, I was kept nude in a tower, and slept on a large round bed. The master loved my hair, and wouldn't let his servants do anything more than remove the dead ends. By the time I was rescued, my hair had reached the top of my ass. You can clearly see the length in Nels's drawing. I slept with it braided every night to make it wavy."

Wren scrubbed his face in embarrassment. "Why I felt the need to tell you that is beyond me. Moving on, the master excelled at keeping me off balance. If I pouted, I got the rod, but then he'd lavish his attention on me. If I didn't please him to his satisfaction, the sex would be rough and I'd be left alone to heal and reflect on the error of my ways."

Geordy burst out, "For the love of God, tell me the fucker died a painful death."

Wren shook his head and continued. "For me, the real torture was the solitude. I had no one to talk to, and spent many hours and days alone when the master returned to his normal family of a wife and kids. I later learned he was the son-in-law of a man related to the Saudi royal family. I didn't know the servants had had their tongues cut out, I just thought they'd been ordered not to speak to me. When I learned they couldn't speak, I felt awful for all the rude things I'd said to them over the years.

Geordy tapped Wren on the knee. "How did you ever manage to survive this cruel mental and physical torture?"

Wren covered Geordy's hand with his own, but didn't resist when Geordy withdrew. "I didn't mean to give the impression I was subjected to a continuous horror show, because, at one point, things appeared to be improving. Another boy, younger than me, joined me in the tower room. But the poor kid never stopped crying, and one day he wasn't returned to the tower. I never learned his name, and, likewise, he was never told mine. The master named me Wren because he said I amused him like the tame little birds he saw for sale in the bazaar, but sometimes I wonder if karma will catch up to me for not trying to do something to help that kid. Even at twelve, I knew the master didn't send him home, but I didn't speak up, and I didn't want to know where they buried his body, but I'm still plagued by guilt for the sorrow his family must feel to never learn what became of him."

Geordy's voice carried a hint of anger as he said, "I hope the psychologist you went to afterward told you the only one who should be blamed for the boy's disappearance was your so-called master."

"He did. But to continue, I soon had other worries. I started growing hair in places the master did not like. My balls dropped and grew hair, and I became very afraid I would follow that unknown boy into the shifting sands of Saudi Arabia, for the master loved boys not men, and he had money enough to replace me. Indeed, that became a new psychological game to be played when I displeased him. He frequently threatened to replace me with someone younger, and sell me to a brothel to service anyone with enough money to buy my skills, or, worse yet, his personal bodyguard, Abdullah, could have me."

Geordy hissed, "What more could Abdullah do to you than what had already been done? You were beaten, raped, left in solitude, and confined to one room."

"Abdullah was a very real threat, Geordy. The man was hung like a stallion, and way too much dick for someone young and delicate. I can still picture the evil grin on the man's face when the master ordered him to show me what sort of pain I could expect if he gave me to Abdullah. Let's just say, after that demonstration I worked extra hard to be the best sex toy I could be, and I endured having my entire body waxed regularly so the master would not be offended by body hair. Imagine my surprise and worry when one night a bearded blond

Viking was tossed into bed with me. The master was smitten with the silver-blond hair and the arctic-blue eyes of Nels Kirkegaard, and purchased him via computer when the sex trafficking ring that snatched Nels off the streets of Alexandria, Virginia, offered him for sale. The master demanded I teach Nels, now named Templar, how to please him."

Geordy surged forward and wrapped Wren in his arms, but Wren broke the hold.

"Please, Geordy, don't touch me or I won't be able to continue. If, after I spill the entire, sordid story you still want to touch me, I'll welcome it, but I need to purge myself of this so I can finally stop thinking my entire adult life was constructed atop a sand dune of lies.

"Where did I leave off? Oh, yes, Nels was to be my pupil. I would teach him every trick I used to please the master. That was quite a clever move on the master's part. He was adept at breaking boys, but a full-grown man would take some strength."

"I've never met Nels, but I hope he handed the master his teeth when they met face-to-face."

"Oh, he tried, but the master was never without his guards. I think the master should have been an interrogator rather than a pedophile. He would have been a good one because he was able to size up a person's weakness, seemingly, just by looking at them. In my case it was the fear of being rejected. My mother did a real tap dance on my psyche by the manner in which she left me, and the master somehow intuited it. He would reject me from time to time just to keep me off balance and scared, and when that didn't work, he'd let Abdullah play show and tell. As much as I hate to give the master a compliment for anything, I have to say the way he broke Nels was, er, masterful. He immediately sized the Dane up for an honorable man, and an honorable man would not let a delicate boy on the verge of manhood be abused as punishment for his resistance."

It took Geordy a moment to stop swearing. "Are you saying Nels submitted to the perv to save you?"

Wren chuckled softly., "Neither the master nor I realized Nels was gay. Nels actually preferred men, but he was so far into the closet I don't think he admitted it to himself until his kidnapping and subsequent rescue by Ross forced him to come to terms with his sexual preference. However, when the master threatened to have me seriously hurt, if Nels continued to resist my instruction, Nels caved. Well I say 'caved,' but Nels turned the tables. He made his surrender to me one of love and not sex, and it was the first time I'd ever experienced the difference. I soon found myself in love with the man, even though, when he climaxed, he called a woman's name...or so I thought, until I saw Ross's first name on his genealogy chart. Nels called for Roslin not Rosalyn as I'd thought."

Geordy interrupted to ask, "Weren't you afraid Nels might switch the master's affections from you to him, and he'd rid himself of you?"

"He might have, eventually, but things happened very quickly after that. The master became jealous of my infatuation with his new toy, and despite promising not to punish me if I taught Nels to please him, he gave me to Abdullah while he took what he wanted from the Templar."

The awfulness of that statement made Geordy grab another log for the fire and use the poker with more force than necessary to stir the flames. Wren continued when he resumed his seat.

"Like you, Nels discovered how well the beetle cream works. Otherwise, I doubt he would ever have been erect enough to satisfy the master, even as much as he wanted to protect me from the master's threats."

"I'm assuming this Abdullah bastard is dead because after what he did to you, I don't think you would've let him live, once you let Ross teach you how to handle a knife."

"He is, but I didn't do it, one of Ross's team took him out. After Abdullah raped me, my spirit was crushed. The master allowing Abdullah do what he wanted with me was my second rejection, and I retreated inside myself. The master gave me to Abdullah like I was nothing more than a toy to be passed around. Afterward, Nels fought hard to keep me from slipping away. Abdullah hurt me badly because I fought him, and because he got off on hurting me. As I lay in Nels's arms and tried to decide if living was worth the effort, he told me about Ross. About how good Ross was at finding things, and I remember saying, that was a nice story but his happy ending didn't include taking me along. I was nothing to Ross. Even though Nels assured me I would leave with him, I was too jaded. I believed, if Ross ever found the Templar, he wouldn't bother saving someone he didn't know, and there would be no one to stop the master from discarding me once and for all."

Geordy held up his hand to stop him with another question.

"How did Ross and Nels meet? You really didn't go into detail when you told me they were married."

"Ah, I guess I left that part out. Ross first saw Nels when he went to a client's house to deliver his report and saw Nels playing tennis with the client's son. Nels had been hired to be the son's tutor. He ran into him again when he joined his former team at an Irish pub for drinks, but the team was called away unexpectedly, and Ross decided to eat dinner at the bar, and discovered Nels occupied the stool next to his. They got to talking, and Nels volunteered to help Ross restore the two town homes he purchased. When Ross found out Nels had been taught woodworking by a master carpenter, his grandfather, and his tutoring job was up, he hired him."

"Wow, talk about a serendipitous meeting. If Ross didn't have special operations training, Nels and you might still be in Saudi Arabia."

"Or dead. Thank God Ross had a talent for finding people. When Nels was taken, he tracked him down to Saudi Arabia, and learned the name of the man who purchased him. While surveilling the master's compound, Ross discovered the master, in league with one of his father-in-law's own sons, was in the process of setting up a hit on his father-in-law. That gave Ross leverage to make Jack Adams, who was the CIA's man in Riyadh, call in his former team to take out the bomb maker Ross witnessed the master hiring. And, since the father-in-law was a highly placed OPEC official, the mission was blessed by Washington."

"*The* Jack Adams who sent us after Elmoudowi?"

"The very same. Since I didn't enter Saudi Arabia with a passport, Jack Adams pulled some diplomatic strings, and I was given one with the surname de Lassy to leave Saudi Arabia without creating embarrassment for the royal family. Ross became my legal guardian, and he twisted the CIA's arm to get the necessary legal papers to backstop my new identity. The man who commanded Ross's former team was then captain, now Colonel Trollinger, the G-3 at JSOC. Jack Adams remembered Troll was friends with Ross, and played him for my location when he saw a picture of Elmoudowi's lover. When Troll found out the real reason for Jack's call, he was livid. I suspect that's why I'm now at JSOC, although Troll never said so."

Geordy scrubbed his cheeks and then shook his head. "Amazing, just amazing how a chance meeting can have such strange consequences. Kind of like someone volunteering to room with a gay Marine."

Wren turned on the couch until his knee almost touched Geordy. "Now I'm going to ask you a question, but I don't want your answer until tomorrow morning. I want you to sleep on it and give me a solidly thought out answer before breakfast." At Geordy's slow nod, he spoke. "Since you were my third and fourth rejections this will be a very hard question for me to ask. No surprise, but I don't take rejection well. My shrink says that's a characteristic of a throwaway kid, but each time you put me back in the 'I don't date fellow Marines' box, I wanted to just give up and walk away from you. I guess the fact I'm here on your couch says I'm a stubborn bastard, or maybe one too stupid to read the handwriting on the wall, but now that you know where I came from, what I did to survive, and the fact that I suffer from a self-directed anger management problem, will you marry me, Geordy Campbell?"

Geordy's sudden, indrawn breath made him back away and hold up his finger in a "wait one" gesture.

"In my defense, let me add, I love you, Geordy Campbell. I will never love anyone as much or in the same way as I love you. I have no words to describe this love I have for you, and it's not fair to ask you to marry me while I'm still serving, but I can promise you I won't re-up when that time comes around in a year and a half." He stopped himself from touching Geordy. "Now I'll say good night."

He didn't hesitate but headed directly to the guest room. No need to display the excess moisture leaking from his eyes, because he refused to influence Geordy in any way, but it had hurt when he stayed seated rather than rush into his arms. Damn, this was going to be a hellaciously long night.

**

Although not the slightest bit sleepy, Geordy banked the fire and headed for his bedroom. He needed to separate himself from the heavy emotions still hanging around the living room.

He replayed Wren's request in his mind, and wanted to hit himself in the head when the niggling doubt surfaced. Geordy began to question whether or not he actually asked what he asked, or did he just imagine him uttering the words he longed to hear from the first moment he agreed to be his roommate.

Geordy stripped down, but sat at the edge of his bed rather than crawl beneath the covers. He started to reach for the lamp to turn it off, but a flashback to the day he was wounded, checked his action.

His ears once again rang with sound of the team medic giving a status report on his patients as he called for the evac helicopter. "Right, two wounded, one severely concussed with a TBI from an IED with pupils still reactive. The other with a kneecap shot to hell, and an entry wound without an exit in the hip region. Yeah, you copy, fucking in, but not fucking out. I need that chopper fast as you can fucking make it, the gunny's spurting blood like Old Faithful."

When the medic tossed the phone down and began to attack his blood loss, Geordy had tried to convey what he thought might be his last message. "Doc, tell my bonnie de Lassy I'm sorry I never...."

The medic interrupted him.

"You can tell Bonnie you're sorry for whatever you did in person, Gunny. I'm sure she'll forgive a big bad-ass warrior like you. You're about a quart low, but, hey, you're a Raider, which means you're too mean to die."

The chopper arrived, and the shot of morphine kicked in before Geordy could correct the medic. The person he wanted to bid farewell was Wren.

His awareness of Blade sleeping in his guest room made him rub the talisman he had tattooed on his shoulder after he got out of the Raiders. He always hoped the inked charm would bring him luck, but he never thought it would possess the power to deposit the object of his desire on his doorstep.

Geordy switched off the lamp and rolled into bed. He wouldn't approach Blade until morning, but he would use the long night to pray for the courage to be as honest as Wren had been, and that his once-upon-a-time lover didn't spent the night regretting his proposal.

Geordy punched his pillow, but he really wanted to punch himself. He knew he was guilty of playing fast and loose with Blade. He was selfish to take what he so freely gave, and not reciprocate. He never considered his feelings over his own when he shut him down each time they returned to MARSOC. He never considered how cheap he made him feel about sneaking around when they were away from the flag pole. Never until now, and lying awake throughout this long night was not going to be recompense enough for hurting the man he loved and never saying I'm sorry or, more importantly, I love you.

Geordy lay in bed until released by the first droning note of his cousin Aengus's bagpipe. About fucking time was his thought as he jumped from bed and headed into the bathroom.

After showering, shaving, and throwing on jeans, T-shirt, and heavy wool socks, Geordy went in search of his unexpected guest. After the painful confession the man made last night, he didn't think his former teammate slept much.

Geordy found him sitting at the kitchen island, staring into his coffee cup.

"Good morning. By those dark circles under your eyes, you must've slept about as well as I did."

Wren gave Geordy a lopsided smile and pointed to the coffee pot. "Coffee just finished perking." He couldn't meet Geordy's eyes, and played with the sugar spoon as he said, "You were right, I almost squashed two dead mice when I stepped out on the porch to find out what the weather was like. The Bonnie Prince left two 'Welcome to Beltrees' presents. I lobbed the frozen carcasses into the woods. I also came face-to-face with a four-point buck nibbling on your shrubbery. We had quite a conversation. I told him he was very lucky to be a Tennessee deer rather than a Pennsylvania one, because his northern cousins were being stalked by two excellent shooters intent on turning them into deer burgers and hat racks. I was supposed to be the third in that party. Ross and Troll are at his folks' cabin for two weeks."

Wren was babbling like he expected to hear bad news and wanted to delay it as long as he could, and it made his heart ache, so he walked up behind his stool, and put his arms around him, and whispered into his ear. "Yes, I'll marry you, Wren de Lassy. Yes, I love you as much as you love me. What Colin MacAulay did or didn't do in no way affects my love for the man I met at MARSOC." He felt Wren's body sag, and he hugged him tighter before adding, "I don't want to wait until you get out to marry you."

Geordy released him when he struggled to turn around.

"But I only have two weeks' leave. That's not enough time for the license and blood tests...do they still do blood tests here? Do they even allow gays to marry here? Um, speaking of blood tests, I had myself tested when I got to JSOC, and on my honor as a Marine, I never hooked up with or had sex with another man or woman since then. I'm clean and healthy, Geordy."

Geordy stared into Wren's concerned green eyes, and then kissed his mouth shut. He was through denying himself. Wren opened for him, and he savored the taste of coffee, toothpaste, and just plain Wren, until both of them were breathing like war horses.

Geordy broke the kiss and stepped back before he threw Blade over his shoulder and went all caveman on him. "I had myself tested as well before I got out. Ditto on the clean-and-healthy part, and ditto on remaining celibate, but fuck that, I want you now. We can discuss marriage plans later, much, much later."

Geordy threw his head back and roared when Wren deliberately considered the counter top and shook his head like it didn't meet his requirements, and opined, "We could do it here on the island, but the drop to the floor might cause some damage, should one of us roll off."

He didn't have to ask twice for him to follow him into the bedroom, and batted his hands away when he started to undress. "Stop. I want to do that. I've dreamed of undressing you every night for a year now, and I won't be denied this morning."

Geordy reached under Wren's T-shirt and slowly ran his hands up his washboard abs until he got to his neck. "Put your arms up." He pulled the shirt off and dropped it to the easy chair next to him then reached out to touch Wren's nipples. He played with them until he groaned, and then he knelt on one knee, and slowly unzipped Wren's fly. He went still when Wren stopped his hands. "Something wrong?"

"Er, not wrong, Geordy, just something new." Wren blushed furiously and laughed. "Um, something new and blue. I had it done as soon as I got to Bragg." He didn't resist when Geordy parted his jeans and shoved them, and his briefs, to the floor. He stood perfectly still as Geordy examined his body art.

"It's a thistle, a beautifully detailed one at that. Why did you choose this particular tattoo, Wren?"

"Because a Scottish man once kissed me on that very spot, and I was marked forever as his. After we went our separate ways, I got the tattoo to serve as a reminder of that kiss, and no one but you will ever put their lips there, Geordy Campbell."

Geordy flashed back to the first time he kissed Wren on the spot below his navel. He smiled at the memory of him turning to putty in his hands, and he bent to do so again.

"No, no, no, Geordy. Not yet. My turn to undress you," Wren gasped as he shucked his socks. "Stand, please."

Geordy stopped Blade's hands right before he started to lift his shirt. "Wait. You're not the only one with secrets to be revealed."

Wren stepped into Geordy and murmured, "I want to see the scars. You needn't worry I'll find your body any less beautiful. Scars are only on the surface, but your beauty goes all the way to the bone, Geordy."

Geordy kissed Wren's cheek, and then stood back to let him remove his shirt and examine the stylized Celtic wren tattooed on his left pectoral.

"Aengus drew the design, and I had the tattoo done in Nashville after I came back here for rehab. I wanted it to serve as a sort of talisman."

Geordy dropped his head and a faint blush stained his cheeks." I rub it every time I think of you. I hoped, someday, my wren would forgive me my transgressions and come to make his nest in my house." Geordy broke the serious mood by assuming a cheery voice.

343

"Now, if you want to see scars, feast your eyes on these." Geordy stepped back and dropped his jeans and kicked them away."

He shivered as Blade ran his finger over the long scar of the knee surgery, and didn't protest when he turned him to study the scar on his hip where they cut him open to retrieve the bullet. He groaned in need when his tongue traced the path.

"Ah, love, it's been so long I'm about to go off just from the heat of your eyes on me. Come to bed, please." Wren chuckled and followed him down to the mattress, but when he rolled over and covered his body, he grew serious.

"What would you like, Geordy? Tell me, and I'll do my best to make our first loving as an engaged couple as memorable as I can."

He knew exactly what he wanted, but first things first. Geordy moved down Wren's body until he got to the thistle. As he knew he would, he began to writhe as he sucked on the lavender blue flower. He finished by lapping up the pearl of dew from the head of Wren's dick.

"Do you remember what we did when we were lying in bed in the loft, listening to the rain on the tin roof?" He waited while Wren closed his eyes to search his memory. Green eyes flew open and sparkled in remembrance.

"I introduced you to the mythical ouroboros. The dragon who swallows his own tail."

"Aye, you did, and I very much want to meet him again." Geordy turned to position himself, and Wren helped him form the circle with his body. Given their long periods of celibacy, the second meeting with the dragon was all too brief, but the cuddling and petting afterward made up for it.

They woke mid-afternoon, ravenously hungry, but took a few

moments to watch snowflakes falling outside the French doors leading to the deck.

Geordy slapped Wren on his bare ass and softened the sting with a caress. "JSOC must not be feeding you enough. You're solid everywhere, and the depth of your inguinal creases tells me you're down to only five present body fat." Geordy tried, and failed, to gather a pinch of skin at Blade's waist. "Not to worry, Aunt Euna's cooking will put a little softness back in you, but, for now, you'll have to make do with mine. Go start a fire in the living room while I rustle up lunch."

They ate the homemade cream of potato soup and grilled cheese sandwiches in companionable silence, or at least he thought it was companionable until Wren pushed his half-eaten lunch away and asked a very pointed question.

"Why? Why didn't you call me after you got out, Geordy? I'm having a hard time reconciling your acceptance of my proposal with the fact that, if Troll hadn't made me tag along with him to MARSOC, I would never know you were wounded and out of the Corps, and I wouldn't be here today, and we wouldn't be planning on spending the rest of our lives together."

The hurt in his partner's voice added one more item to his list of damage he'd inflicted on the man he loved. It really was a miracle Wren, despite his ill treatment of him, still wanted to be part of his life.

Geordy wiped his mouth and turned to face him as he gave him the answer to his question.

"I didn't call because I wanted to wait until I had my life in order. I wanted to be able to offer you a secure future. There's a lot of pride in me, Wren. Maybe it's misplaced, but I didn't want to show up at

Fort Bragg or Alexandria with just my discharge papers, a gimpy body, and no job as inducements to marry me. And if you think I didn't worry every minute of that time someone would come along to give you want you wanted, then think again. Waiting until my situation was secure enough was a gamble, but I worried every single day, and lay sleepless at night thinking all my efforts would be worthless if I lost you because I waited too long to get my ducks lined up." Geordy left his stool and rummaged around in one of the kitchen drawers. "Here, I got this in the mail the day before you showed up."

Wren took the paper and glanced at it. "These are loan papers. You took out a loan? I thought the cabin was paid for."

"Aye, a loan, but not for the cabin. I took a loan out to begin building a brewstillery."

Wren scratched the side of his ear, "A what? What's a brewstillery?"

"A brewstillery brews beer and distills whiskey. My Uncle Aillig and my cousins and I are in this together. They will sell the beer and whiskey I distill, in their pub, and they put up money toward building the brewstillery. The loan was to purchase a defunct grain-and-feed store in Beltrees, and reengineer the building to produce beer and bourbon." Geordy crossed the kitchen to the hat rack by the door and tossed a baseball cap at Wren. "Read the logo."

He studied the design and grinned as he read, "Moonshine U? Are you serious?"

"As a heart attack. I enrolled in Moonshine U when I could walk without limping. I'm a proud graduate of the basic and intermediate courses of Moonshine U in Kentucky. I need more experience under my belt before I can go for the advance degree. Once the grain store is re-modeled to contain my distilling equipment, I plan to produce

Campbell Dhu, and this time I won't run afoul of the revenue man, because I jumped through all the bureaucratic hoops to get the zoning permits and liquor licenses." Geordy fished around in the same drawer and held a piece of paper out to Wren. "Here's the design for the brewstillery's logo."

He studied the drawing of a coon hound, a very large cat, and a raccoon, and grinned up at Geordy. "The Strays Brewstillery. I can see Aengus's hand in this. Do you have room in your brewstillery for another stray?"

"Another one? I don't think my budget can handle feeding another stray animal, especially one who eats like the Bonnie Prince."

"Well what about one who would buy into your brewstillery? I want to contribute to your endeavor. I managed to amass a respectable nest egg from living on a fraction of my salary and letting Ross invest the rest." When Geordy started to speak, he held up his hand. "I'm not asking for an instant decision. Discuss my offer with your uncle and cousins, first. They may not want to open the business to another investor, and if they don't, don't worry, my feelings won't be hurt."

Geordy tried to answer him but Crockett came roaring out of the living room from where he last saw him drowsing by the fire, and skidded across the kitchen floor to the door, barking and wriggling to be let out.

Geordy shook his head in feigned disgust. "I think I need to redesign the logo. Instead of a coon hound and a cat, it'll be just a raccoon."

"What has Crockett's tail in a twist?" Blade asked, as the hound almost knocked him off his stool.

"Let him out, and you'll find out."

Wren did exactly that, and Crockett shot off the porch and tumbled head over heels with the Bonnie Prince wrapped around him. Geordy came up behind him and wrapped his arms around his waist.

"I guess Charlie got bored with hunting mice in the barn, so he came up to the house so Crockett can amuse him. They play quite well together. They'll cover most of this mountain playing grab ass. At least the ground is frozen, so I won't have to worry about them coming back covered in mud."

Wren's eyes twinkled as he watched the cat and dog dart around the yard in an impromptu game of tag. "Hmm, playing grab ass sounds like a wonderful idea. Wanna come out and play, Geordy Campbell?"

"Hmm, we Scots are a hardy lot, so playing nude grab ass outside in November, and having my balls turn blue wouldn't slow me down, much. But with you having only enough meat on you to cover your bones, and liking the delicate shade of pink of your balls, I think we should play the game in the bedroom." Geordy slapped Wren on the shoulder. "Tag, you're it."

Geordy managed to evade the laughing Marine all the way back to the bedroom, where he let himself be caught. Wren used one of his martial arts moves to roll him over and pin him, face down, on the mattress, and didn't let him up until he pounded out the wrestler's "you win" sign. He rolled over to find a no longer smiling, serious Wren.

"Make love to me, Geordy. I want it slow, and deep, and hard. I want the scratch of your beard on my cheek, I want you to make love to me the same way you did the first time you ever took me. You made me yours then, and I thought you would keep me, but I was wrong.

Show me you're going to keep me, Geordy."

"Aye, this time I won't be such a craven coward. You're mine, and I'm not giving you up for anyone or anything. It will take death to separate us after today."

When he opened his nightstand and fished out a condom, Wren stopped him.

"No, let's begin as we mean to continue, in love and in trust."

The first skin-to-skin sensation had him gritting his teeth to keep it slow. He could tell by Wren's growl of pleasure he, too, felt the difference, and so continued the in and out dance of love until his partner became more vocal.

"Yes, yes, yes, *yesssssss*, there, right there. Ungh, Geordy, please, please, *please*."

Geordy thought Blade might say he cheated when he sent him over the top by pinching his nipples hard, but he wanted them to climax together, and that meant right now.

Geordy pumped into Wren and saw electric blue and other amazing colors not found in nature behind his closed eyelids. His tight grip on his lover's hips ensured he stayed on the bed after he collapsed. Wren surprised him by rolling to face him, rather than be spooned.

"Geordy, I need ask you something."

"What? If your questions is whether I love you, then I didn't do a good enough job of showing you just now."

"Oh there are no worries in that department. My question is, since you didn't use protection, will you'll still marry me if I become pregnant?"

It took a moment for the ridiculousness of Wren's question to make sense, and then he started to snicker, and then guffaw, and then laugh until he choked. When he could speak again, Geordy stared into green eyes alight with mischief, and answered, "I'll marry you, even if you are as fat as a tick full of blood by the time we find a minister willing to perform the ceremony." Wren grinned and rolled back over to let him spoon him, but Geordy had a question of his own. "Would you handfast with me?"

Wren rolled back to face Geordy. "Handfast? I'm not sure what that is."

Geordy unscrunched Wren's eyebrows with the tip of his finger as he explained. "In the Scottish Highlands, it could be months or even years before an ordained man of the church made it to their village, so people would speak their vows in front of witnesses, and they would be contracted to each other, to live as man and wife, or in our case, man and husband, for one year. If, at the end of the year, the couple decided they didn't suit as mates, they could dissolve the contract, no recriminations or repercussions. Oh, there was one caveat. If the year they spent together produced a child, then the handfast contract became permanent. So, see, if you are pregnant de Lassy, you're stuck with me."

"Oh you're stuck with me, Geordy Campbell, knocked up or not. Yes, I'll handfast with you, but when I finish my hitch, we're making our union legal by civil law, even if the year isn't up."

Geordy held his lover, and they drowsed until the light in the bedroom began to dim, and he reluctantly shook his soon-to-be contracted husband awake. "Sorry, but we can't spend all day in bed. I promised to help Conall muck out the wee beasties' stalls this evening. Oh, and since I was invited to dinner after, I can ask Uncle Aillig if he would, as head of Clan Campbell in Beltrees, officiate at the handfasting ceremony, and you can let Aunt Euna stuff you with her excellent cooking." When Wren offered, "I'll race you to the shower," Geordy demurred.

"That'll be separate showers. We don't have time to do what I know we'll do if we shower together. Come on, if we hurry, we'll have time for a drink while we feed the stray menagerie."

***

Wren sat huddled in his parka and watched Geordy place the feed bowls on the porch. He listened to the stillness of the woods surrounding Geordy's cabin. It was snowing harder, and it dampened the normal rustling of the trees.

The sudden thought this would be an ideal place to spend Christmas both pleased and saddened him. Pleased him because there *would* be Christmases spent with Geordy and his family, and saddened him because this coming Christmas would more than likely be spent in the drab browns and grays of Afghanistan, or in some other armpit place where hostile bullets replaced presents under the tree.

He jumped in surprise when a sizeable stick poked his leg. He laughed to find himself being stabbed by the Bonnie Prince himself.

"Have you taken to collecting twigs instead of mice now, Your Highness?"

"He wants to play fetch. Toss the stick."

"You're kidding me. This cat plays fetch?" Geordy's answer was drowned out by Charlie's unique, loud chirping trill, so he tossed the stick Charlie dropped across his feet.

Ten tosses later, the Royal Prince declined to play in favor of inspecting the inside of his food dish. Wren stood when Geordy said,

"Time to feed the wee beasties."

"No, I'm not falling for that 'wee' part again. Those Percherons are the size of earth movers, but I would like to call them into the barn for feeding."

As they climbed out of Geordy's truck in front of the barn, he had a sudden thought, and he stopped Geordy before he could enter. "How do you think your family will take the news you and I plan to marry?"

Geordy pointed to something behind him and answered him, "A very good question. Why don't we tell Conall and see how he reacts?"

Wren swung around to see Geordy's cousin, Conall, standing at the barn's entrance grinning at him.

"Tell me what?"

The sight of Conall holding a pitchfork didn't ease his nervousness, but he never considered backing down. "I wanted to know how your family would react to the fact I asked Geordy to marry me, and he accepted."

Wren flinched at the sound of the pitchfork hitting the floor, but didn't have time to avoid being crushed in Conall's arms.

"Oh thank God. The family was considering an intervention with circus clowns to cheer Geordy up. We are all heartily sick of his moping and bad temper."

"Hey," Geordy protested. "I do not mope."

He laughed at the stink eye Conall gave Geordy, and followed the arguing cousins into the barn. It took the three of them a solid hour to shovel out all the stalls, and then Conall handed him the can filled with dry corn.

"Here you go, Cousin. Call the wee beasties to dinner."

Geordy laughed at his sudden blush to be called cousin, and

laughed even harder when the blush deepened when he kissed him in front of Conall.

It took only a few shakes of the can before the air was filled with the thunder of galloping hooves. Wren moved quickly to the side of the barn to avoid the stampede.

When the horses were each in their own stall, Geordy handed him an apple.

"Here, why don't you give this to Bruce?"

Wren walked to the stall with Bruce's name carved on the door, and backed up quickly when an enormous head suddenly appeared over the top of the door.

"My God, Conall, what do you feed these horses, Miracle Grow? Bruce is even bigger than the last time I saw him."

Conall snickered as he watched Bruce grab Wren's parka at the shoulder and draw him right up to the stall door. "Let Bruce have his apple, unless you want him to eat your coat, instead. Yeah, the beastie is larger than the last time you saw him. He was just a baby then, but he grew larger than I thought he would. He's a right giant now at twenty-two hands tall. But he's still quite gentle."

The sound of the dinner bell turned them in the direction of the house, and Conall clapped his cousin on the shoulder and said, "Congratulations to you, Geordy. This is going to be fun telling everyone. Tell you what, let me propose a toast to the engaged couple as a way to introduce the topic."

"Sounds as good a plan as any," Geordy agreed.

Wren followed the broad backs of Conall and Geordy into the house, and laughed when Caillin, who came to greet Geordy, jumped in surprise when he ducked under Geordy's arm. "Boo." He laughed even harder when Caillin called out, "Hey, Ma, your bonnie aspen's back."

Euna nudged Caillin aside to wrap her arms around Wren. "Oh thank God, my prayers have been answered, the golden man has returned, and now Geordy can stop moping."

Wren colored at Euna's effusive greeting, and his blush deepened when Conall stuck his face close to his and called out, "Dang, Ma, we should call you the aspen whisperer. You can make them change color almost as fast as Mother Nature."

Given the size and bulk of the Campbells, he did resemble a lone aspen in a forest of mighty oaks, a felled one at the moment. Uncle Aillig's enthusiastic clap on the shoulder almost sent him to his knees.

"Welcome, welcome, Wren. We missed you. You're looking good."

Before he could respond, Euna interrupted her husband, "He's not. He's far too thin, but I can remedy that." Euna hugged him again and kissed him on the cheek to soften her words. "I'm so glad you came back to us."

Wren thought he might, finally, have a chance to speak until Aengus picked him up and gave him a mighty bear hug. Caillin saved him.

"Put the poor man down, you daftie. He's no' one of your bagpipes to be squeezing."

Aillig's ordering everyone into the living room for a drink to honor his return, allowed him to regain the air Aengus's massive hug displaced.

He accepted a glass from Caillin, but almost spilled it when Conall nudged him and winked.

"I want to propose a toast," Conall announced. When he had everyone's attention, he raised his glass of bourbon and said, "Here's to the engaged couple, Geordy and Wren."

He began to sweat when the toast was met with silence, total and complete silence. He sent big eyes to Geordy, and found him to be as flummoxed as himself, until the room erupted in a thundering, "To the couple!" Pandemonium ensued shortly after. Both he and Geordy were hugged and thumped until Aunt Euna saved them.

"Leave off, Campbells, or there will be nothing left of either one for a wedding."

Geordy put his arm around him and addressed his family. "Uncle, Wren and I would like to ask if you would officiate a handfast ceremony for us. He's only here for two weeks and then he returns to Fort Bragg, but we want a formal contract between us until he finishes up his military duty."

Aillig set his now empty glass on the fireplace mantel and rubbed his hands together. "It's been quite a while since I performed one, but I'm happy to do so. When were you wanting it done?"

Wren turned to Geordy, and they chorused, "Tomorrow."

Aunt Euna stepped forward. "Have you written your vows, yet?"

At the bewildered face she saw on her nephew, Euna added, "I thought not. Well you'll have most of tomorrow to consider what each of you wants to say to the other."

Aillig cleared his throat and clapped a hand over Geordy's shoulder and asked another question. "Do you plan to exchange rings?" He laughed at the "Yes. No" answer he got from Geordy and Wren.

Geordy gave Wren a one-armed hug. "My mother gave me my great grandmother's wedding band, and told me I should use it if I ever found the right partner. I want you to wear it."

Silently cursing the ease with which he blushed, he at least gave

Geordy a steady response. "It will be an honor to wear your family ring, but I didn't plan on a handfast, so I don't have a ring for you. We can choose one tomorrow, if that's okay."

Before Geordy could answer, Aillig spoke up. "I have my great grandfather's Claddagh ring, the mate to the one your mother gave you, Geordy. Why don't you use it to match the one Geordy gives you, Wren?"

Aillig's offer shocked him. "Whoa, don't you want to save it for one of your sons to use?"

"Pshaw, have you seen the size of their hands? The ring wouldn't fit on one of their pinkies. Geordy's hands are the right size for the ring, and I like the idea the matching rings will be used together."

Wren saw all three of his soon-to-be cousins grinning and nodding at him. "Thank you, I accept. I also like the idea of keeping the rings in the family. Now can you tell me what a Claddagh is?"

Euna spoke before anyone else could offer an explanation. "You can tell him over dinner. Now I need to put some meat on him so Geordy has something to hug on a cold winter's night."

Chapter Twenty-Seven

Wren's groaned as he bent down to untie his hiking boots. "I can't believe I ate that much. I think your aunt's dinner put five pounds on me."

Geordy chuckled from his place on the sofa. "I think that was her intent. You lost a lot of weight, Blade."

"Well, JSOC training is a bitch, and when the choice is between eating or sleeping, I always choose sleep. The toys we play with are damned dangerous if you aren't mentally at the top of your game."

He flopped down next to Geordy and picked up his hand to place it on his knee. He asked, as he ran his thumb over the back of Geordy's hand, "Not to bring down the joy this day has brought, but I wanted to ask you if this is going to cause an even greater rift between you and your father and brothers. I don't like the idea of returning to Bragg and leaving you alone to face their public ridicule for handfasting with me."

Geordy captured his hand and turned it over to kiss the palm.

"No worries, then. It wasn't a month after I moved back to Beltrees that my father put his house up for sale and moved to the western part of the state. My brothers followed him out there.

"After the scene he caused at the wake, relations between my father and uncle were strained and neither one of them had the inclination to mend that broken fence."

Geordy tugged lightly on Wren's hand to coax him off the couch and into the bedroom, and made him groan for a second time when he ran his hand down his chest and discovered a bulge where his flat stomach had been.

"Oh my God, Geordy, I'm pregnant. You must marry me now."

"I'll marry you, but first...." Geordy made Wren squeal with laughter when he bestowed a large raspberry on his over-full stomach. The wrestling contest was on.

Wren launched from the bed with the first note of Aengus' bagpipe and discovered Geordy had done the same. "What the hell, Geordy? Did Aengus buy a loudspeaker for that thing? It sounds like he's playing right outside on your front porch."

"Nay, no loudspeaker. He *is* playing outside on the porch. You better come along with me to see what he wants. My aunt would appreciate it if you stop me from killing him."

But when Geordy swung the door open, he was forced back by a stampede of cousins.

"Damn," Caillin groused, "This morning is cold enough to freeze a man's balls."

Conall didn't comment, just marched to the fireplace and started to lay another fire, as Aengus blew the last note on the bagpipe and followed his brothers inside to ask, "What's for breakfast?"

Wren put his arms around Geordy and squeezed, not so much as a display of affection, but more to keep Geordy from throttling Aengus.

He tightened his grip when Geordy's tone of voice told him the jury was still out of Aengus's continued existence.

"What in the fucking hell do you mean by showing up at this ungodly hour? Normal people sleep until the sun rises."

Conall, satisfied that the fire had caught, wiped his hands on his jeans and fielded the question.

"We're here to do our duty as groomsmen. It's unlucky for the groom to see the, ah, groom on the wedding day. Ma says you're to wear your kilt, Geordy. It will be a true Scottish handfast."

Geordy's sigh of resignation was the clue for Wren to release his grip.

"Well then, I best start breakfast."

Wren bumped into Geordy's back when he stopped suddenly, and he peered around him to see Caillin filling the coffee pot, Aengus putting bread into the toaster, and Conall setting a dozen eggs on the island.

He snickered when Geordy grabbed him around the waist and whispered into his ear.

"Are you sure you want to marry me? My cousins are part of the whole Campbell package."

Aengus didn't give him a chance to reply, but handed Geordy a cast iron skillet and a pad of paper and pen. You can write your vows after breakfast. I like my eggs over medium. Wren, why don't you go shower up while Geordy cooks breakfast? You'll be leaving with us when we finish eating. We're going to ensure you have everything you need for the handfast."

He turned to Geordy, who just gave a shrug, and then to the cousins to ask, "What am I going to need?"

Caillin slapped Conall on the shoulder and they both chanted, "Something old, something new, something borrowed, and something blue."

"Well the something blue will be my jeans, because I didn't pack with a handfast ceremony in mind. I didn't bring any dress clothes or shoes."

Aengus removed two slices of toast and added two more to the toaster as he enlightened the anxious groom. "Not to worry, Cuz, we've got it covered."

Wren left the kitchen carrying the cup of coffee Caillin handed him. He returned to find the Campbells already seated at the table.

It was a raucous breakfast and he laughed along with his new cousins when Geordy ushered them on their way with the warning, "You'll no be getting my groom drunk today. And don't even bother trying to deny that was part of your plan. He's got to be sober enough to say his vows and the 'I dos' in the right places."

Wren tapped Aengus on the shoulder from the back seat of Aengus's truck. "Now that you kidnapped me, where are we going?"

Caillin answered before Aengus could. "We're going to the kilt shop. You'll need a true Scottish kilt for the ceremony."

"I guess I can subsist on beans and weenies for the next month. I don't know much about kilts, but I hear they're expensive."

Aengus turned his eyes away from the road in front of him to catch Wren's in the rearview mirror. "Not to worry, Cuz. This is our wedding gift to you. By the way, Geordy mentioned you were born a Scot, a MacAulay. Did you know the MacAulays, like the MacEwens, are a sept of Clan Campbell?"

"Thank you all for such a generous gift, and, no, I didn't know the MacAulays are a sept of the Campbells. But like Geordy Campbell feels about Clan MacEwen, Wren de Lassy has no love of Clan MacAulay. So, if you're thinking of dressing me in a MacAulay tartan, you can think again. It'll be the Campbell tartan or nothing."

Conall grinned and reached across to deliver a not so gentle punch to his arm. "Just as well, the MacAlay tartan is red. It will clash with your hair."

Conall's comment engendered several minutes of biting sarcasm from his brothers as to his fashion sense, until Aengus pulled into a parking slot in front of the kilt shop called The Caledonian.

It took several hours before his new cousins were satisfied he had everything he needed from the top of his head to the soles of his feet. Wren's lips twisted wryly at the thought it took about two hours too long. If his cousins could ever agree amongst themselves, dressing him in a kilt wouldn't have wasted so much time.

On his way out the door, he spotted something, and his ever-present imp surfaced. "Hey guys, give me a second. I'll meet you back in the truck."

When his cousins shrugged their shoulders and carried the shopping bags out with them, Wren called the saleslady back to the counter, and pointed to what had caught his attention.

"Could you please wrap one of those up for me? I don't want anyone seeing it until the proper time."

"Certainly, sir. Since you've chosen the Campbell colors, I'll fetch one to match. It won't take long to wrap."

As he climbed back into the truck, he asked, "Where to now?"

Caillin turned in his seat to respond, "We're headed back to the pub. Da will be busier than a one-armed paper hanger if we don't show up to help him through the lunch hour. You can sit at the family table and eat lunch and write your vows."

Lunch turned out to be a roast beef sandwich au jus, steak fries, and a mug of red ale, which Aengus removed from the massive tray he carried before heading to several tables to deliver other lunches. Conall, who'd drawn bus boy duty, dropped a yellow legal pad and ballpoint pen off on his way to bus tables to make room for other diners.

"Here, you can write your vows on this. Oh, and Caillin wants to know how to contact your family. He can set up FaceTime so they can watch the ceremony. Your family should be there, Cuz. Write down the phone number and email address and Caillin will set it up."

Wren had to bite down hard on his inner cheek to keep the sudden tears from showing. God, this family was unbelievable in their kindness and consideration. He gave Conall Nels's information, knowing Troll's remote cabin had spotty reception.

***

Wren stared at the empty page and froze. Not because he couldn't' think of anything, but because he wanted to say too much. That thought embarrassed him enough to sit back in his chair and scrub his cheeks with both hands. Although Geordy would probably not be embarrassed to compose a profound declaration of love, he couldn't say the same for himself. Despite his brashness, the core of himself was shy. He was demonstrative, physically, but verbally was an entirely different matter. What to say? What to say?

He borrowed a poet's words to say what was in his heart when he left MARSOC, but now the onus was on him to come up with what he wanted to tell his life partner. Suddenly, the KISS principle came to mind, so he kept it simple and succinct. He wrote the words to his vow in one go. Aengus's shadow darkening the table made him come back to the here and now.

"Time to go, Cuz. We need to have you dressed and ready to go before Geordy shows up. Knowing my cousin, he's probably been wearing a rut in his carpet pacing back and forth until he can show up for the handfasting. Da has already posted the closed sign in the window."

Wren allowed himself to be swept away by the preparations. He stood, alone, and fully clothed in the accoutrements of a Highland Scot, as he waited for his cousins to tell him it was time to confront his groom. His mind recalled Geordy's saying the word "accoutrement," and he had to grab his eager dick and squeeze it into submission. No way would he stand before his new family, sans underwear, and with a blatant cock stand. He won the wrestling match just in time, for Conall entered the bedroom Aunt Euna had designated as his dressing room.

"I'm here to give you the something borrowed. The old was our Great Granda's ring, the new was your kilt, and the blue was the Campbell tartan, so you need something borrowed. Here's my sgian-dubh for your sock."

Wren accepted the small knife with the cairngorm agate inset in the top and slipped it into the top of his knee sock.

"Thank you, Conall. I'm delighted to be part of this family."

Conall's reply was forestalled by his mother, who entered after one knock.

"Oh my, you make a bonnie Scot, Wren. Come now. Geordy's here and champing at the bit to see his groom."

As he walked toward the living room surrounded by his three cousins, also in full dress regalia, he couldn't help thinking they resembled a moving war council of eighteenth-century Highland Scots, very powerful Scots. The sudden, *I wouldn't want to mess with us,* thought made him smile. The smile froze when Aengus moved to the side and he came face-to-face with Geordy. This was his first glimpse of Geordy in a dress kilt, but like he said of his dress blues, Geordy Campbell rocked it. The hiss of his indrawn breath was matched by Geordy's.

He wanted to laugh when Caillin used his finger to shut Geordy's gaping jaw, until Conall performed the same service on his own. Uncle Aillig saved them from being teased by opening the handfasting ceremony.

"Geordy and Wren, today you are surrounded by your family who are gathered to witness your exchange of vows, and to share in the joy of this occasion. Let this be a statement of what you mean to each other and a pre-commitment of the marriage you will make when service obligations are satisfied."

Aillig pointed to Conall who held up a laptop with Nels grinning back at him.

"I am honored to be invited to your handfasting ceremony, Wren. I'm ecstatic you and Geordy are making such a commitment. I just wish Ross were here to witness it as well, but you know the reception is non-existent at Troll's cabin."

Wren shyly brought Geordy closer to the laptop and introduced him to Nels. "Geordy is a big fan of yours, Nels. He purchased one of your watercolors before he even met me, but I'll let him tell you why he did so when he meets you."

He and Geordy returned to their positions in front of Aillig when he gestured for the ceremony to resume.

"Geordy and Wren, since you were both trained as special operators, I will couch my advice in terms you can relate to. You were taught to identify and use many different weapons, and most of these weapons use bullets. Bullets come in many calibers, and all can cause damage to a human body from the lightest, a graze, to the most severe, a fatal wound. But I doubt the Marine Corps taught either one of you the most lethal bullet of all is the lowly word. Yes, words can be used to wound.

"There are the light calibers such as the thoughtless word, the belittling word, the snide word. Then you move up in wound capability with the angry word, the cruel word.

"All hurtful words, if not cleared from the chamber of your dwelling each night, can cause an infection that must be treated promptly or the infection will spread and kill the marriage.

"So, before you end the day, you must ponder the words you spoke to your partner and, if you injured him, cauterize the wound by saying you are sorry for the pain you caused him. Tell him what he did or didn't do to make you fire those words, and he will know, if he does that or says that again, he will be causing you harm.

"A word of caution here. There is another caliber of words that can be inadvertently lethal if you don't learn how to use them correctly. These are words of encouragement, love, or repentance, and you need to say these aloud and mean them when you do: I love you. I'm sorry. How can I help you? Please. Forgive me.

"The strongest marriages are those built on two-way communication. You must communicate your happiness, sadness, anger, fears, and hopes to your partner, and he must do the same to you. It is this sharing of information that allows you to work together to a common purpose, to operate as a team, to love each other without doubt that you love and are loved by your partner.

"The promises you make today are the words that will bind you for a year of your lives, or the rest of them if you pursue an official ceremony when the year is up. Geordy Campbell and Wren de Lassy, do you seek to enter this contract of your own free will?"

Wren turned to Geordy and felt his cheeks rise in a huge grin to mirror Geordy's, and he responded at the same time, "I do."

"Please grasp each other's right hand and respond with 'I will' in unison when I ask a question.

"Geordy and Wren, will you share each other's pain and seek to alleviate it?"

Wren echoed Geordy's, "I will."

Aengus stepped forward and tied a strip of Campbell plaid around his cousins' conjoined hands. As he stepped away, Aillig pronounced, "And the binding is made."

"Geordy and Wren, will you share in each other's laughter and seek the brightness and the positive in each other?"

Caillin tied another strip around his cousin's hands at their joint 'I will.' And once again Aillig pronounced, "And the binding is made."

"Geordy and Wren, will you take the heat of anger and use it to temper the strength of this union?"

After the "I will," Conall handed the laptop to his mother and tied the next strip of plaid around his cousins' hands. As he stepped back to reclaim the computer, so Nels could continue to witness the ceremony, Aillig continued, "And the binding is made."

"Geordy and Wren, will you honor each other as equals in this union?"

As Wren gave his response, Nels's voice made him lift his eyes from where they rested on the bindings joining him to Geordy.

"Your Aunt Euna agreed to be my surrogate for tying the binding on this last question since I can't be there in person."

Conall carried the computer closer for Nels to see as Euna tied the last of the bindings, and Aillig pronounced, "And the binding is made."

Aillig stepped forward and placed his hands over their bound ones. "May your hands be blessed this day. May they always hold each other. May they be strong enough to cling to each other through the storms and adversity life will throw your way. May they caress each other in love, gentleness, and healing. May they offer protection, solace, and guidance.

"I now will ask you to seal these vows by giving and receiving rings. Although made of gold, the real precious element in these rings is the love infused in them by the previous wearers. May these rings continue to grow in value with the addition of your love for each other.

"Geordy, as you place the ring on Wren's finger, tell him the words your heart wants him to know."

Aengus made everyone's eyes go round with anxiousness as seconds passed while he searched inside his sporran for the ring.

Aengus's "Sorry, the claddagh's a wee thing, and my sporran is deep," made Wren roll his eyes and bite his lip to keep his sarcastic quip unsaid.

But he grew serious again when Geordy slipped the claddagh on his finger and squeezed his hand until he got his full attention.

"Wren, both of us had the misfortune to have a parent abandon us, but standing here before the people who care about us the most, I make you a solemn vow I will never abandon you. Only death will part us from this day forward."

Wren saw the ring Conall handed him through a watery mist. He widened his eyes to keep the tears from falling as he placed the matching claddagh on Geordy's finger and squeezed his hand the same way Geordy had his.

"Geordy, your uncle was right about how dangerous the unspoken word can be. I never said 'I love you,' and it cost me a year of pain and anguish thinking I lost you. It was a hard lesson to learn, but learn it I did. I love you Geordy Campbell, and I'm not embarrassed to say so in front of witnesses, and I'll continue to say and mean it until I no longer have breath to do so. And when your turn comes to leave this earth, you will be able to say with absolute certainty, Wren de Lassy-Campbell loved me."

Geordy clasped their bound hands to his chest and pulled him in for a fierce kiss on the cheek. They broke apart when Conall nudged them, and held up the computer for them to see Nels raising a glass of champagne.

"Let me be the first to offer my congratulations to the newly contracted couple. May your year pass in happiness and love. I know I speak for Ross when I say we look forward to meeting you in person, Geordy."

"Thank you, Nels. I do as well."

Conall broke the connection, and Aengus picked up a tray of bourbon glasses and raised his voice, "Let the festivities begin. Caillin, untie the couple so they can use the proper hand to drink their bourbon."

The sound of Aengus filling his bagpipe with air reminded Wren of the item he purchased at the kilt shop. He drew Geordy aside to tell him what he wanted to do.

"Oh, that's bluidy brilliant. Let's do it." Geordy fetched a straight-backed chair and waited until Wren sat before clapping his hands and calling for his family's attention.

"Listen up, Campbells. My groom had his own idea as to what the something blue should be, and I think we should honor his wish to continue a wonderful tradition. So, to all my unmarried cousins, please march your large Scot's arses front and center for the garter toss."

Wren caught Euna's eye and winked at her. "I'm doing this for you, Auntie. If it works, it'll give you some space in this house and a lower food bill."

Euna laughed so hard Aillig had to give her his arm to hold her upright.

When his cousins stood in a row with sheepish and somewhat nervous expressions, Geordy knelt and began to hike Wren's kilt above his knee. He showed his concern with widened eyes when he rucked up a considerable amount of fabric and still found no garter. Leaning in, he whispered, "I better find it soon or my aunt will be able to commit another set of cock and balls, besides my uncle's, to her memory."

No sooner had he said it, his hand touched the lacy bit of fabric. He raised his head to find Wren grinning at him with a decidedly mischievous expression. "Auntie's virtue was in no danger. I knew you'd find it...sooner or later."

Geordy stood and twirled the garter around his finger. "Now tradition has it, the man who catches this will be the next to wed, so prepare yourselves, Campbells."

With that, Geordy pulled the garter back like a slingshot and shot it directly at Aengus's broad chest. The man caught it more out of reflex for being shot than because he wanted to.

Geordy delivered the *coup de grace*. "That's for waking me so damned early on my wedding day, cuz. Maybe after you find a warm body to cuddle with, ye'll want to spend longer than the crack of dawn abed."

Aengus took his brothers and cousins' ribbing with red-faced grace. His mother saved him from further verbal abuse by announcing dinner was served.

***

As soon as they returned to the cabin and Geordy turned the lights on, he leaned on the kitchen island and groaned. "I didn't think it was possible for your aunt to outdo herself, but, if I hadn't counted the wee beasties for myself earlier this afternoon, I'd swear she carved one of them up. That was the largest, thickest steak I ever ate. Damn me for a glutton, but I couldn't put my fork down. Now I feel like the lone tick in an army encampment, bloated fit to bust.

"Sounds like you need some exercise to help digest that mound of protein in your gut. Dance with me, Wren. I want to dance a slow dance with you. I want to put my arms around you and sway to the music. You know, we've never danced with each other before. The Texas two-step, Scottish reel, and a disco parody don't count. I want to hold you close enough to feel your heartbeat."

Geordy grabbed Wren by the hand and led him into the great room, and fiddled with the radio until he came to an all-night station that played nothing but romantic ballads. He opened his arms in invitation when Enrique Iglesias began to croon the lyrics to his song about being someone's hero. His husband stepped into his arms, and he wrapped his arms around him and began to sway to the music. But when the chorus about being a hero and kissing away the pain filled the silence of the room Wren stopped, and he had to move quickly or step on his partner's toes.

Geordy laughed, "Wren, dancing means moving your feet. If you just stand there, it isn't dancing." He stopped laughing when he moved in to hold him again and felt him trembling. Is something the matter? You aren't...? You aren't changing your mind about...?" Wren put his fingers over his lips to stop him.

"Shh, I'm very happy about handfasting with you, Geordy. It just hit me that I can now lay claim to a large family with a husband, cousins, aunt, and uncle. I also share a house with the man I love. There is even a dog, cat, and raccoon to go with the house. These are things I once despaired of ever having. Perhaps if we'd waited until I got out of the Marines, it wouldn't seem so jarring, because my mind would've had more time to adjust to hitting the mother lode of my desires. I'm not shaking because I'm afraid, Geordy. I'm shaking because I'm overwhelmingly happy."

Geordy cupped Wren's face in his hands and gave him a soft kiss and then resumed dancing until they entered the master bedroom. Wren stopped again.

"My turn to lead."

Geordy cocked his head at his husband and asked, "Shall I cue up another waltz?"

"Um, no, this dance will be a *pas de deux*."

Geordy knew the meaning of the ballet term and grinned back at his lover. "I guess a kilt could be substituted for a tutu in a pinch. But I'm concerned, husband mine." Geordy's eyes twinkled. "Concerned that when I do several twirls and then leap for you to catch me, you'll suffer a hernia. I'm a brawny Scot, not an anorexic ballerina."

Wren moved into Geordy's embrace and let him spoon him. He reached for Geordy's arm and held it over his waist as he responded, "I thank you for considering the safety of my internal organs, husband mine, but not to worry. My pas de deux will be an *avant garde* one.

"Avant garde? How so?"

Wren turned and began to undress Geordy. He grinned at how

fast a kilt could be shed. Geordy was standing nude and proudly erect in a trice, and he matched him a second later.

"Avant garde because there will be no tutus, tights, or trusses worn, and the entire ballet will be performed horizontally." He glided into Geordy and used a hip roll to throw him to the mattress. "I hope you possess stamina, Campbell. Ballets are rather lengthy."

"Dinna fash yoursel, husband. We Campbells are endowed with enough stamina to dance all night long, so cue the orchestra."

Chapter One

"Sorry to make you trek out to the old homestead, Mr. de Lassy, but I thought it best to discuss this out of the office. Would you like something to drink before we get into the sordid details?"

"A finger of scotch would be welcome. I prefer it neat."

Roslin de Lassy waited as J.P. Morgan, no relation to the famous financier, splashed a generous, thick finger of scotch into the rock crystal glass. A man's glass, meant to be held in a powerful hand.

As Morgan fixed his own drink, the pock of a tennis ball hit with a certainty proclaiming skill in the sport attracted Ross to the wall of windows dominating the man's study. Two men, well, upon closer inspection, one man and a teenaged boy, engaged in a ferocious volley. From what little he knew of the sport, the man, who moved with the liquid slide and swing of a pro, dominated the court and seemed to anticipate where the boy would place the ball. Whoever he was ran the youngster to the edge of his physical stamina without noticeable effort on his own part.

The volley, and the match, came to an end with the boy's vociferous curse.

"Shit! You must have eyes in the back of your head."

Ross had to agree. He'd seen the boy place the ball right on the far court line, and the man run full tilt with his back to the net to return it to the far court on the boy's off side to catch the kid wrong-footed and clumsy. The kid's desperate return slammed the ball right into the net.

Morgan pointed to the tennis court. "My son and, believe it or not, his tutor. The man can play, and he's an even better academic teacher. Thanks to him, my son received a higher score on his SATs than we'd dared to hope for and got accepted by my alma mater. At the beginning of the year, I didn't think Junior's grades would get him into a trade school. Tennis is the first sport he's shown any aptitude for, and I'm hoping he'll try out for the tennis team."

J. P. pointed to one of the leather chairs before his desk and ordered, "Now, grab a seat and tell me who's been fucking with my company's web and how much damage they've done."

Ross took a small sip of the excellent scotch and gave the bad news first. "Your hacker is a pimple-faced eighteen-year-old. The good news is, while the hacking has been inventive and annoying, we found no nefarious intent, and no company secrets broadcast to competitors. The kid's a techno-wizard bored out of his gourd working in the mail room. He spends most of his day playing high level games on your Internet and creating anonymous jabs to wound your pride."

Morgan drained his drink and slammed the glass down. "Well, I hope he has a handheld device so he can continue to play his games in the unemployment line."

Ross took a moment to peer out the window at the now empty tennis court. "Are you sure you want to fire him? Seems to me a kid with so much talent can be put to better use than distributing mail."

"Okay, I'll bite. What would you do with him? Make him a VP?"

While Morgan's suggestion smacked of sarcasm, Ross nodded. "Oh, he'll get there soon enough, but for now, I'd put him in charge of Web security. Who better than a hacker to know how to prevent hacking? Give him a small office and a title with commensurate pay increase and responsibility, and he'll work his ass off to keep your company secure because it'll be his company as well. No hacker wants another hacker pissing in his sandbox."

"I wish to God I'd hired you first, de Lassy. I spent a lot of money on another firm, and they couldn't find the source of those annoying emails to my private account. You've managed to find the little fucker in just one week, so I'll follow your advice. I'm also putting your number in my personal contacts in case anything else pops up. I'd be happy to recommend you should any of my associates need a firm that delivers discrete, on time results for a reasonable fee."

Ross laughed. "Well, I'm a firm of one at present, but new clients are always welcome. I have a certain knack for finding things.

Ross accepted the check from the man's hand, and they shook. He didn't glance at the amount; the CEO didn't strike him as a penny pincher. He hoped his prediction concerning the teenaged hacker turned out well for the company.